SHADOW OF EDEN

LOUIS KIRBY

To Nick

This is hopefully food for thought – since it involves the medical-industrial complex.

enjoy – !

Scale Publishing

Correspondence should be addressed to:

Scale Publishing, 3219 E camelback Road, Suite 809

Phoenix, Arizona, 85018

Library of Congress Control Number: 2013915468

ISBN 978-0-9894493-0-4

Cover designed by Cali MacKay

Scale Publishing

For Carol and Kira

ACKNOWLEDGEMENTS

Most humble and sincere thanks to:

Captain Philip Tucker of British Airways, who showed me around the cockpit of a 747 while in flight.

Admiral John Batzler, a Navy Top Gun pilot, a carrier fleet captain, and ultimately admiral, who gave me key information about the operations of a carrier fleet.

I have a deep debt of gratitude to John Calverley, MD, the late department of Neurology Chair of the University of Texas Medical Branch, who mentored me during the three years of a fascinating neurology residency and is an expert in all things clinical.

I need to thank my two book editors, Marlene Adelstein and Shannon Anderson, who each provided me with critical and timely feedback.

I had multiple thoughtful early readers, each of whom provided me with their wisdom and insight. These included Robert Allen, Malca Resnick, Joseph Rogers, Harvey Tilker and Guy Pilato.

And most importantly, to Carol, my wife and advisor who supported and encouraged me through multiple drafts and edits.

SHADOW OF EDEN

CHAPTER 1

The cockpit of a 747 in flight is normally a quiet place. Captain Ralph Palmer's head, however, jack-hammered with pain. As he rubbed his thumb against his throbbing temple, he decided to take more Advil, despite his inflamed stomach. Maybe it would calm the pounding long enough to land.

His right arm jerked twice and his mind flitted back to the nightmare that threatened to rush back in. His sudden jerks attracted another concerned glance from his first officer, Joseph McElroy.

"Joe, I need to make another bathroom run before initial descent. Can you mind her?"

"No problem," McElroy sighed, putting down his clipboard.

Palmer backed his seat out. "Thanks. You have the plane."

"I have the plane."

Swinging his legs past the throttle console, Palmer stood up and stretched, grimacing at the surge in pain. The space behind the pilots where Palmer stood was spacious by cockpit standards, with two additional sheepskin covered seats and a seven-foot ceiling.

Another flashback burst into his brain as his right arm twitched in concert. They had occurred intermittently during the five-hour flight from Heathrow to Dulles. He had not told McElroy about the flashbacks, but the arm jerks would not be disguised.

When he had first noticed them following take-off, McElroy had asked him to scrub, but Palmer had casually brushed them off as 'no big deal.' McElroy had reluctantly accepted his decision but from that point on had watched him carefully, refusing to engage in the usual cockpit chitchat. Despite his apparent casual attitude, Palmer would be glad to get this flight behind him. Especially since an ice storm was threatening to move into the Washington DC area.

The plane was approaching initial descent and if he was going to down any more headache meds, he had better do it now.

Palmer called the upper galley and within a moment, Enrique Oliveros, the purser, knocked on the door. Palmer pushed the release button, allowing his entry. "Enrique, can you spot me another trip to the head?"

"I sure can, Captain."

Slipping into the lavatory, Palmer downed four more Advils and chewed six Tums. Sighing, he leaned up against the door and closed his eyes. *Why is this happening?* He was proud of his health. He had passed every physical thrown at him, even after his release from the North Vietnamese prison camps.

As a young pilot, he had been shot down and captured in the last year of the Vietnam War. He had lived through nearly nine months of torture and near starvation by the North Vietnamese. Upon release, his physical health had quickly recovered. In fact, exercise had become his refuge and ultimate escape from the paralyzing flashbacks that had routinely flooded his mind. Although he had received counseling and his wife, Yvonne's, careful nurturing, Palmer attributed his recovery from the flashbacks to the rigorous training schedules he undertook for running marathons. The offer from United, soon after his release from the service, confirmed in his mind that he had achieved his full recovery. He had carefully maintained a rigorous exercise program throughout the years, at least until his knee had started bothering him last year.

Why had his old flashbacks returned? Starting only last week, but with startling realism, he had begun to re-live his Vietnam nightmare, his nighttime ejection over the jungle, his brief attempt to flee, and his inevitable capture. As strong and as tough as he had become, he could not believe they were back.

He had mentioned his flashbacks and the new headaches to Yvonne. She had begged him to see a doctor, but he had put her off. Now, he wished he hadn't.

He closed his eyes and tried to relax. The headache had gotten steadily worse the last few days, and because of it, he hadn't slept last night.

A sudden wave of nausea ejected his stomach contents in a gush, spraying the mirror with yellow liquid and pill fragments, which quickly ran down into the sink. Palmer leaned over, spitting out more of the bile and cursing the headache. No more pills. Not now. *Twenty minutes*, he thought. *I can hold out that long.*

Palmer cleaned himself up and returned to relieve Oliveros. "How's the weather?" he asked McElroy, easing back into his seat.

"It's closing in fast, but we just got initial clearance," said McElroy. "We should be down before the worst hits."

"Good, I . . ." His arm twitched and he was back in the inky Vietnam sky. *Anti-aircraft tracers streaked past the cockpit window and he heard the staccato screech of metal piercing metal. I'm hit! Fire! He twisted the fire control levers and then realized he had to punch out . . .*

"Jesus, Ralph, that's the worse one yet." McElroy's voice cut through the flashback.

Palmer's eyes cleared. His right arm had ceased shaking. "It's nothing. See?" Palmer held up his hand. "It's gone." But the terror unleashed by his vision hung on.

"Christ. Better have that checked out when we get in. No, better yet, switch with Marvin to take us down." McElroy's look at Palmer was sharpened by the instrument glow in the dark cockpit.

"Look, I'm fine."

McElroy's glare tightened. "I don't believe you. I've watched those tremor things get worse and I actually lost you on this last one." He shook his head. "No, it's way past time."

McElroy was right, of course, but Palmer wouldn't give in. "Look, I've landed at Dulles a thousand times," he proposed. "You keep the plane."

"Not good enough. We've got weather up ahead. I want Marvin up here. And you back there."

Palmer shrugged. "You're not going to get it. So, are you going to fly the plane or not? You can land in this weather."

McElroy pulled his water bottle from its holder and took a long drink. Swallowing, he fixed Palmer with narrowed, considering eyes. "OK, I'll keep the plane. Ready for initial descent," McElroy said, dialing the new heading into the computer.

Palmer looked at the readings. "I confirm." This last vision had been so real; he could still smell the burning fuel. Maybe he would go see the doctor and get a physical. It would probably not amount to much, but it would make his wife happy and he'd get something for his dammed headache.

McElroy flipped on the PA to notify the passengers of their approach.

Palmer's right arm twitched, signaling another flashback. He grabbed it with his left hand. By focusing on the instruments in front of him, he managed to suppress his visions, but the effort left him breathing hard. McElroy gave him a sidewise look and continued his public address.

Increasingly unsettled, Palmer reconsidered switching with the back-up pilot. This was not safe and he knew it. He waited until McElroy finished and turned off the intercom. "OK, you're right. I'll call Marvin."

He reached for the intercom, but his arm leapt with powerful irregular shakes. A rush of terror engulfed him as he plunged back into the dark Vietnam jungle. *He saw flashes of gunfire directly in front of him. Run! No! Not this time, dammit. Not this time, you fucking gooks!* He snapped his seatbelt off.

"Ralph!" McElroy saw Palmer's wild look. "It's OK. Settle down."

Palmer sprang out of his seat and snatched the fire extinguisher from its buckles. With a fierce look, he raised it over his head, holding it like a short baseball bat.

"Ralph! Stop!" McElroy twisted around straining to see Palmer behind him. He threw his arms up as Palmer swung down. McElroy's left wrist snapped at the impact. The next strike landed solidly on his head. He screamed.

Palmer struck again. He raised the extinguisher once more, but the copilot had slumped in his seat harness, no longer posing a threat. Palmer lowered his arms. The extinguisher slipped from his grasp and clanged to the floor.

CHAPTER 2

"Damn."

Secretary of State Linda Resnick swore at the ringing phone, more for what she feared it meant, than for the early hour. She felt for the receiver in the dark.

"Yes?" Her voice was husky with sleep. She squinted to see the green-glowing clock radio digits. It was 4:06 A.M.

"Secretary Resnick?" She identified the voice of Larry Calhoun, her director of intelligence.

"Yes," she repeated.

"You told us to call if anything breaks out in Hong Kong, you know, the Falun Gong demonstration."

It *was* Hong Kong. All sleepiness evaporated. "And?"

"They've shut down the media and the army's surrounding the park where the demonstrators are. Something big's going to pop."

Damn, damn, damn. "Okay, I'm on my way." The Secretary of State swung her legs out of bed and sat up. As her feet searched for her slippers, she tried to find some reason to think there would be a peaceful end to the massive protest, but she doubted her own hopes with a cynicism that surprised her. She walked into her closet and began looking through her dresses for something warm and comfortable. The situation would turn bloody; she just knew it, and today, of all days.

It was Thanksgiving.

CHAPTER 3

In the galley, behind the cockpit, Oliveros heard muffled shouts. He frowned and stood still for a minute, but did not hear anything more. He looked into the passenger cabin, but all was quiet. Unsettled, he picked up the intercom and buzzed the cockpit.

There was no answer.

He turned the corner and rapped hard on the cockpit door. When there was no response, he tried to open it, but it was locked. He turned the handle and pushed his shoulder into it to no effect.

Oliveros thought hard. When Captain Palmer had gone to the bathroom moments ago, nothing seemed out of the ordinary. Why, then, would they ignore his intercom? The plane was flying straight and stable and there didn't seem to be any emergency. Still, the shouts had been unmistakable.

Palmer dropped back into his seat and rubbed his eyes. It had felt so real, like he was actually back in Vietnam, back in the putrid jungle, running from the North Vietnamese. But this time, he had counter-attacked, charging the gun flashes instead of running. He had found and killed a Vietcong; he was now safe.

Palmer opened his eyes and looked over at his copilot. McElroy was slumped over in his seat. Puzzled, Palmer leaned over. "Joe? Joe, what's up?" He saw the blood oozing in rivulets down McElroy's unconscious face. "Oh my God. What have I done?" As Palmer clutched his throbbing head, he became aware of a hammering at the door.

Oliveros pounded on the reinforced door with his fist. Abruptly, the electronic door latch clicked and he pushed it open. In the dim nighttime cockpit, he saw Captain Palmer holding his head.

"Captain Palmer?"

Palmer turned and looked at him with unfocused eyes. Something was not right. Then, with a shock, Oliveros saw the bloody scalp of the slumped second officer. Running back to the hallway, he grabbed the intercom and buzzed the main cabin downstairs.

"Carol here."

"Carol, get Marvin Verness up here right now. It's an emergency."

"Good God. Okay, I'm on it."

Next, he hit the overhead intercom button. "If there are any doctors on board, please report to the second deck galley, immediately."

The announcement awoke Steve James with a start. He had just dozed off from writing down his thoughts following his private meeting in Edinburgh. Irritated, he opened his eyes and stretched. A male flight attendant stood at the front of the compartment anxiously looking around at the passengers. Gradually, Steve processed the words. *They needed a doctor*. He hoped it wasn't serious. He stiffly unfolded his lanky body and stood up. Smoothing his rumpled white dress shirt, he approached the flight attendant.

"I'm a doctor—a neurologist, if that makes a difference."

"Perfect. Follow me."

Steve followed him into the dim cockpit, ducking under the doorway. His eyes swiftly took in the condition of the two men. *Jesus.* Steve bent over the copilot. He found a strong carotid pulse and saw that the man's breathing was normal. Steve's fingers explored the bloody scalp and found two lacerations, but no skull depression.

He glanced at Oliveros. "I think he'll be okay." He then turned to the pilot. "Sir, how are you?"

The pilot looked at him through bloodshot eyes. "I thought I killed him. A goddamn flashback. Is he going to be . . ." His eyes glanced behind Steve. "Marvin. Thank God."

A medium-built man in a pilot's uniform had joined them.

"What the hell happened?"

"Captain Verness, let me—" Oliveros began.

"Never mind," Verness snapped. "Ralph, it's time to get out of here." He pushed Steve towards the copilot. "Look after him."

Palmer's right arm started shaking and his gaze turned glassy. To Steve, he looked like an actively hallucinating schizophrenic.

"I'm hit! Fire! Fire!" Palmer yelled. He reached up and yanked all four fire extinguisher levers.

"No!" Verness grabbed at Palmer's hands, but too late. The jet fuel shut off and halon fire suppressant sprayed into each engine, shutting them down. Cabin lights flickered and alarms filled the cockpit. The jet's abrupt slowing flung Verness into the center throttle console, slamming him into switches and knobs, including the overhead intercom button.

"Help me out here!" Verness shouted, as he righted himself and grabbed Palmer from behind. Oliveros sprang to help. Steve hurriedly moved out of the way and leaned over the copilot's seat waiting for an opportunity to assist.

Palmer thrashed and punched as they pulled him out of his seat. "You can't take me again, you bastards!" He kicked like a madman, striking the control yoke with his foot and shoving it forward.

The floor of the cockpit plunged like an elevator with a snapped cable. Everyone flew upwards. Palmer, Oliveros, and Verness slammed their heads against the ceiling. Steve, still hunched over McElroy, smashed his back into the knob-laden ceiling; the metal switches puncturing and lacerating Steve's back.

Gasping with the sudden pain, Steve twisted to dislodge the metal from his back but the centrifugal forces of the diving jetliner still held him against the ceiling. And despite his pain, a single thought pierced through Steve's mind. *There was no one flying the plane!*

Below, he saw the empty pilot's seat and, right underneath him, the still unconscious co-pilot. His gaze swept out the windshield and down past a break in the clouds. The distant lights were drawing closer with each moment. They needed a pilot to pull them out of the dive. The three other men floated in a tangle against the ceiling next to him.

"Hey!" He grabbed the arm of the nearest man, the new pilot called Verness, and shook him. The arm was limp. As he looked closer, Steve realized the pilot was out cold. He looked at the others. They were all unconscious—or dead.

CHAPTER 4

Steve's heart raced as he glanced out at the approaching ground lights. They would all die in seconds. *It was up to him.*

He had taken glider lessons in the Arizona desert years back and knew the basic controls. As the instructor had put it, pull the stick back, the ground gets farther away, push it forward, it gets closer. What Steve had now, was one big, fucking glider. He just had to get to the pilot's seat.

Following the downward acceleration, they were in free fall, making Steve weightless. He pushed off the ceiling towards the pilot's seat, and moved far enough to grasp the pilot's control yoke. With the yoke in hand, he curled up his legs and braced them on the floor and immediately pulled back on the yoke. Unexpectedly, the control resisted his initial tug. He pulled again, harder. It moved, but only slightly.

He repositioned his hands and pulled as hard as he could. The yoke shifted slightly towards him and he felt the nose ease upwards. Straining, he continued pulling and ever so slowly it slid towards him. Gravity returned, pulling him into the seat.

Why was it so hard?

A shrill vibration began to shake the jet.

Steve adjusted his feet for better leverage and pulled more effectively, his eyes fixed on the few lights flickering through the intervening haze.

Gradually, so gradually, they moved lower as the jet's nose fractionally rose.

As gravity returned, he heard a muffled sound behind him. The floating knot of men had landed on the floor. Looking for assistance, he twisted his head around, but saw no movement from them. They lay in a strewn heap of legs, torsos, and arms. Beyond, through the still open cockpit door, he glimpsed rows of frightened faces and locked eyes for a moment with the terrified face of a man in the first row before he turned back to his battle with the control yoke.

Gravity came on in earnest, now. His increased weight pressed him deep into the seat.

"What's . . . going on?" rasped a voice behind him. It was the new pilot's voice.

"I'm pulling . . . on the yoke." Gravity stuffed Steve's words back into his throat.

The man grunted with strain. "Keep pulling . . . hard."

A mechanical voice cut through the din: "Terrain, pull up. Terrain, pull up."

"What else?" Steve croaked.

Gravity distorted Steve's vision and his shaking arms felt like he was holding up the entire plane.

The vibration worsened as if the plane were shaking apart.

They were below the clouds now. He could see lights and even some cars on the streets below. *Jesus, they were close!*

"Keep . . . pulling." The voice from behind sounded tremulous from the vibration, like he was talking into a fan.

The gravity fought to drag Steve's arms off the yoke but the sight of streets, cars, and buildings rushing by underneath kept his hands locked in place.

A deafening bang rattled the plane. "What?" Steve exclaimed. The vibration ceased, but the massive jet swayed sickeningly like a car on ice.

"Coming . . . apart," Steve heard Verness's barely audible voice.

Steve glimpsed some buildings up ahead, through . . . *trees?*

Tree tops slapped at the nose of the plane. Dead ahead, three office buildings, modern and well lit, loomed directly in his path. The buildings rushed towards him at a breath-taking rate.

Shit! We're not high enough to clear!

With a massive effort, he yanked hard at the yoke and it pivoted back even more. The jetliner's nose moved higher and the buildings vanished under the jet.

CHAPTER 5

Lieutenant Scott Kuss slid his F-16 just outboard of the left side of the 747. The two jets skimmed at 120 feet of altitude and cruising at 622 knots. He had just watched the jetliner flatten out after diving from altitude.

What in the hell was going on? It sure looked like a terrorist act.

Phillip Piper, his wingman, trailed the jetliner in a position to fire if necessary.

Pulling even with the cockpit, he looked over. In the dim light of the 747 cockpit, Kuss saw . . . *Jesus!* A pilot that looked like a civilian.

The control tower had been unable to raise the United flight. Either the damn civilian couldn't operate the radio or he didn't want to.

He keyed his own mike to see what would happen. "United 1733, this is the F-16 off your port side. Please respond. You are in restricted airspace."

No answer. And no apparent response from the man in the cockpit that Kuss could see.

His wingman spoke. "Kisser, I can't get heat lock. I think the engines are cold."

"Cold? How?"

"No shit. I'm backing off for a radar shot."

"Roger." *What in holy hell was going on?* The engines were out, a near supersonic dive to an altitude below radar coverage, radio silence—and a civilian pilot. If there were an explanation not connected to a terrorist attack he could not think of it. Worse, the Pentagon was directly ahead; he had to assume the worst.

He changed radio frequencies. "SF thirty-one to Base. Requesting authorization to terminate United flight 1733."

Inside the 747, the gravity eased as they leveled out. "Can you get up here?" Steve yelled.

"I think I can. Wait." In a moment, Steve saw the arm of the pilot reach around his left side and grab the yoke. "Okay . . . got it." That left the right side open for Steve to slither out. Verness jumped in and rapidly flipped switches. Quickly surveying his instruments, he commanded to Steve, "Wake up the copilot."

Suddenly, bright lines streaked in front of the cockpit window. "Shit! Tracers!" Verness flipped a switch and a voice filled the cockpit.

"I order you to deviate this flight thirty degrees starboard or you will be shot down. This is my final warning."

Picking up his headset, Verness responded. "This is United 1733. We are in flame-out status. I am Captain Marvin Verness now in control. We are not . . ."

"Deviate now. This is my final warning."

Verness examined the instruments and made a quick calculation. "Listen, ace, I have no engines. If I turn, I lose airspeed and without power, we will stall."

Lieutenant Kuss had watched the change of pilots in the dim cockpit light. The new guy appeared to be in uniform. Who was the other guy?

"You must deviate your course now," Kuss repeated.

"Negative. I cannot turn until I have an engine and power," the voice reported, "It takes two minutes to spool our engines up."

Damn! The 747 pilot had put him in a quandary. The new pilot was right. The glide ratio of the unpowered 747 jet was roughly similar to a lawn dart. Kuss's stomach knotted in indecision. He had precious little time to make up his mind—with the Pentagon dead ahead.

"Kisser," his wingman's tense voice spoke. "Locked on and ready for your order."

"Wake up, wake up!" Steve shook the unconscious copilot by the shoulders. The co-pilot's body was limp and unresponsive. Steve read his name tag. "McElroy, wake up!" He shook him again.

A half-filled plastic water bottle sat in a cup holder right under Steve's elbow. Snatching it up, he unscrewed the cap, and dumped it over the man's head. McElroy's eyes flickered open momentarily and he inhaled deeply, followed by a groan.

Steve shook the copilot again. "McElroy, wake up!"

McElroy's eyes opened slightly and stared ahead blankly. "Leave me alone." He batted at Steve's hands. "Ohhh . . . my head." He raised his hand to his scalp and touched it gingerly.

"You've got to help us."

He turned to Steve with a glazed look, "Huh?"

Verness bellowed up. "We're on dead stick. We need your help."

"What?" McElroy sat up, more alert, and quickly glanced around trying to absorb what was every pilot's worst nightmare. "Holy shit."

"Number two's gone somehow," Verness announced. "Starting number three. Take over."

"Roger." Reaching with his left hand, McElroy yelped and grabbed his wrist. "Is this right? he asked incredulously, "six hundred feet and five-thirty knots?"

"Speed's dropping fast." Verness added acerbically, "Not to mention getting shot."

Verness twisted a dial on the radio transmitter and spoke. "Washington tower, this is United 1733."

The reply was immediate. "United 1733, this is Washington Approach."

"Tower, we've flamed out," Verness's controlled voice reported. "Request emergency landing priority."

"Roger, United 1733. Head for runway one-eight, heading one-seven-zero. Priority approach. You've got two F-16s escorting you. Good luck."

"Call off the dogs if you can. I plan to walk away from this, God willing."

"Washington National?" McElroy protested. "They're not rated for wide bodies."

Verness made another course adjustment before replying, "I know."

Oliveros, now awake and mobile, enlisted Steve to wrestle the still unconscious Captain Palmer into the passenger cabin. Oliveros motioned the two passengers on the left side of the aisle to stand up and Steve and Oliveros slid Palmer into one. After buckling Palmer in, Oliveros motioned Steve to take the aisle seat.

"Stay here and keep an eye on him," Oliveros instructed. He then hustled the two displaced passengers farther back in the cabin. Steve plopped into the aisle seat beside Palmer, but sudden bolts of pain from his back made him quickly lean forward.

Only then did Steve notice the groans and cries for help. He realized with a shock there had to be lots of injuries back there, there might even be some deaths. Remembering Oliveros' command, he examined the slumped Captain and found him breathing easily and with a normal, steady pulse. Steve next checked the captain's scalp and saw some sluggish oozing from a laceration, but it did not appear to be serious.

Satisfied with Palmer's condition, Steve tried to relax, but his back hurt too much. Shifting his position back and forth, he soon realized that he could lean far enough into the aisle to see McElroy through the still opened cockpit door. He leaned over even more for a better view and almost bumped heads with a white-haired man with nearly black eyebrows wearing a grey suit, sitting across the aisle from him, doing exactly the same thing. It was the man he had seen earlier from the pilot's seat, the terrified face in the first row. They traded glances, and then turned their attention back to the activity in the cockpit. Steve soon realized he could hear the cockpit conversation through the overhead intercom.

"United 1733, you must deviate twenty degrees to the west."

"Negative. We'll stall."

"United 1733, deviate now, or I will shoot."

"I've almost got my engine. Hold your horses."

"You've got fifteen seconds. No more."

CHAPTER 6

"Number three turning," McElroy reported. "Ignition in one."

"Make it quick," growled Verness, sweat rolling down his forehead. They were lower now, less than 300 feet. He traded a little more altitude for speed. He had to maintain their velocity over 240 knots, the airspeed that would spin the engine fast enough to start.

Verness examined the horizon ahead for buildings in their path. Something massive and dark lay in front of them, but he couldn't quite make it out. He knew he should recognize it, but . . .

"Fuel pressure's up," reported McElroy. He leaned over awkwardly to use his right hand, the left one being useless. Absently wiping some coagulated blood off his forehead, he stared at his instruments.

"I'm giving more altitude," Verness said as he tilted the control yoke forward. "Down to one-twenty."

The vast, nearly-black mass loomed up in front of them.

"What's that?" McElroy asked.

Verness just then identified it, "Shit. The Pentagon. Cripes, no wonder that stick jockey is so touchy. Gimme that engine now or we'll get a sidewinder up our ass."

He eyed the altimeter—one hundred feet and dropping.

"Seven seconds. Turn now!" Kuss could see the headlines if he failed to protect the Pentagon. He knew it would take at least two of their radar-guided Phoenix missiles to stop the jetliner. The air-to-air missiles were designed for much smaller fighter aircraft; their explosive payload would not easily take down a huge 747.

The reply actually sounded irritated. "Look, ace, the captain twisted all four fire extinguishers and it takes time to spool up again. I grew up in Norfolk, Virginia, the son of a Navy Captain and became a navy flier, flying F-4s. I'm not a friggin' terrorist."

"Who was the civilian in the seat before you?"

"A doctor who pulled us out of a dive while I was KO'ed on the floor."

Time had run out. Kuss had to make a choice.

"Kisser?" Piper's tone demanded a response.

"Fuck, I know."

"All I know is he's aiming right for the Pentagon."

Kuss shook his head trying to decide. The picture of his wife and daughter taped to the left of his instrument cluster caught his eye. There were wives and daughters on that United flight. He recalled the US Airways flight 1549 that ditched in the Hudson River and how the passengers were so grateful to be alive. He absently shook his head. He had to give the United flight passengers the same chance.

Kuss keyed his mike. "Captain Verness, good luck. Make my decision the right one."

"Roger, buddy."

The lieutenant pulled back his stick, increasing his altitude to a high vantage point from where he would watch the consequence of his decision.

"Ignition on." McElroy tried not to show his nerves, but his shaking hands belied his tension.

They had sunk so low, Verness could no longer see the roof of the Pentagon. If they didn't get that engine soon . . . the Pentagon loomed larger. It's now or never, thought Verness.

"We're hot," McElroy shouted. "Go, go, go!"

Verness shoved the throttle to the stops, but felt a pitiful thrust. It was like accelerating a barge. Verness had never flown with one engine, even in the simulators. Was one engine enough? He was breaking entirely new ground here.

"What a fucking pig." Verness's eyes were glued to the altimeter as he wondered how high the Pentagon was. The altimeter digits crept north at a snail's pace. He risked a gentle turn.

"It's going to be close." McElroy's voice betrayed his tension. "I don't know . . ."

The enormous mass of the building slowly moved to the left as Verness banked right.

"Nice . . . nice." McElroy marveled, in a breath of relief, even as the curt 'Stall, stall' warning announced their critically low airspeed.

Verness, despite himself, smiled with a touch of satisfaction. It had been close. He straightened the bank and gained more speed silencing the warning. They were now cruising at a mere 75 feet; he scanned the ground carefully for tall power poles and broadcast towers.

The F-16 pilot spoke again. "United 1733, continue on your expected landing approach and do not threaten any more buildings."

Verness keyed his mike. "Roger and thanks. Washington tower, United 1733, ready for final approach."

"United 1733, turn right to heading one-seven-zero," a crisp female voice directed. "You are too low for standard approach."

"Roger."

"Number one fuel on," said McElroy. The two-minute engine start cycle began again. "I think we'll be on the ground before this one heats up."

"I'll need it for the reversers. Hurry it up," Verness commanded. He had accumulated enough speed now for another slow turn and banked right to line up with the runway.

"Tell the attendants to prepare for landing," Verness instructed.

McElroy reached for the intercom switch and gasped. "Oh, shit."

"What?" Verness snapped.

"The intercom. It's been on this entire time."

Verness lips turned up slightly. "Won't they have stories?"

A brief smile broke through McElroy's frown. "Flight attendants, prepare the cabin for landing. Emergency positions. Landing in one minute."

Verness radioed, "Tower, I'm underpowered for full flaps. I'll be a little hot coming in." To McElroy he said, "Gimme that engine."

"Fuel pressure's up," the copilot reported. "Thirty seconds, tops."

Verness carefully orchestrated the landing sequence in his head. He knew full well that the physics of landing the massive, underpowered aircraft on a wet runway in a brisk crosswind were not in his favor. On approach, there wasn't enough power to counter the drag of the wing flaps, which would require their landing at a higher than normal speed. Worse, the landing strip was wet and possibly frozen. He noted the critical lack of a second operating engine on the opposite wing. If he applied reverse thrust from the unopposed engine, it would almost certainly rotate the plane off the runway. His tactical plan had to be timed just right and executed in near perfect order if they were to have any chance at all. If they landed safely, it would go down in the books. If they didn't, well, he probably wouldn't much care. The runway was fast approaching. It was time.

"Drop the gear on my signal."

"Roger."

"Ready . . . Now!"

McElroy twisted the lever and dropped the landing gear into the air stream, instantly decelerating the plane. The jetliner stalled and slammed onto the leading edge of the runway. With squealing tires, the crabbing 747 suddenly rotated into alignment with the runway. The torque pitched Verness hard in his harness, but he managed to drop the flaps and apply his air brakes. With both feet, he stood hard on the landing gear brake pedal. The runway flashed by at an alarming rate.

"Give me that Goddamn engine."

The jolt snapped Captain Palmer awake. His head hurt. Wait. He felt a new and different pain. He rubbed his scalp and fingered a tender lump. *How?*

As he rubbed his scalp, he looked around, puzzled. He realized his cockpit lay directly in front of him. *Why am I not in it?* He tried to remember the sequence of events. He had been flying his plane and then a bunch of people had started wrestling with him, pulling him out of his seat. In a flash of anger, he realized someone was flying his plane. His tremors hit again, although briefly, but they again disoriented him. *I've got to fly my plane.* Unbuckling his seat belt, he staggered towards the cockpit.

"Hey . . ." Steve had been intently watching McElroy in the cockpit and Palmer's move surprised him. He tried to stand up, but was jerked back by his seat belt. Steve popped the latch and sprang down the short corridor to throw his arms around Palmer's chest. The burly captain easily shrugged him off and kept walking. Thinking quickly, Steve grabbed Palmer's belt and fell backwards pulling Palmer down on top of him.

"Give me that engine," Verness ordered.

"Three seconds."

The rain-slicked runway rushed underneath them, as the anti-lock brakes pulsated. Verness struggled to steer the huge jet straight on the slick runway. The black Potomac River waiting at the end of the runway was coming at them alarmingly fast. *Too fast.* They would go in. He made a fateful decision.

"Engaging reversers." Deftly, he lifted numbers one and three thrust-levers, pulling them back to full reverse. Straight away, he felt the increased deceleration. Would it be enough?

Engine number one, just coming up, and without full operating thrust, did not completely counteract the rotational torque from number three. The tires could not resist the torque of the unbalanced reversed engines and the 747 edged towards the side of the runway.

CHAPTER 7

Verness swore as the right main gear slipped off the runway, twisting the plane even more to the right. The front landing gear next skidded off the pavement and the weight of the jetliner drove it into the soft earth. The stress exceeded its design limits and snapped the locking pin. The massive nose of the widebody jet dropped to the ground spewing standing rainwater skyward in forty-foot sheets.

The impact suddenly decelerated the plane, hurling Steve and Captain Palmer through the cockpit door and onto the console between Verness and McElroy. The two pilots barely glanced at them as they focused on their controls. Verness applied hard left rudder and modulated his reversers, but the plane twisted fully sideways on the grass next to the runway. The landing gear collapsed and pitched the massive belly of the plane onto the soggy ground. The left wing, now leading, plowed the soft earth, progressively buckling and folding as the plane slid, but it slashed the speed.

McElroy and Verness watched the cold waters of the Potomac draw close.

"We're going to get fucking wet," Verness muttered helplessly, having lost all control of his aircraft. "Cut the engines."

McElroy quickly shut down the now useless engines.

The remaining stub of the leading wing slowly ground across the gravel riverbank just dipping into the dark, murky river and then the massive jetliner shuddered to rest.

Verness rapidly flipped switches. The plane shook as the emergency slides deployed. Looking over the instrument panel, he shook his head. "That was ugly as hell."

McElroy blew out a huge breath. "It sure was, but at least we're here to bitch about it."

Verness slid his seat back and unbuckled his harness. He stood up and steadied himself on the seat back, just then really noticing Palmer and Steve.

Steve, white with pain, had pushed Palmer off and rolled onto his side to get off his back. He gritted his teeth waiting for the waves of agony to subside. Palmer held up his hand for help and Verness hauled him to his feet.

"What in the hell happened, Ralph?" Verness demanded.

Palmer collapsed into the jump seat behind McElroy and rubbed his temples. "I don't know. Jesus. Flashbacks, like I was—" He looked around as if seeing everything for the first time. "Did I . . . ?" Seeing Verness's expression, he murmured, "Lord save me."

Steve pulled himself up from the floor and took two unsteady steps. Dropping into the second jump seat, he breathed deeply.

Verness smiled at him. "Thanks for saving our asses up there, doc. We're here because of you."

"No problem," Steve shrugged. "I'm pretty happy to be here, too."

Verness put his hand reassuringly on Steve's shoulder. "You did good up there. Thanks." He then turned towards the door. "I'm going to go help the passengers. McElroy, you stay on the com with the tower."

"Roger, Marvin."

Lieutenant Kuss, trailed by his wingman, circled over Washington National airport one last time, feeling a wash of emotions as he saw the passengers climbing out of the emergency exits and walking away from the plane. There would be lots of injuries and maybe some dead, but most were alive and safe.

"That was one hell of a bad landing," Piper said.

"Roger that."

"National's not rated for wide bodies," he added. "It wasn't going to look pretty no matter what."

Kuss knew his wingman was trying to distract him, but still, what he might have ordered rested heavily with him. He felt sure he would catch hell for ignoring protocol, but he also knew that his decision had been the right one. He turned the fighter's nose east and skyward, back towards Washington and their usual patrol route.

"Kisser?" His wingman said, turning along with him.

"Yeah?"

"Good call."

Lieutenant Kuss gazed at the panoramic view of Washington DC spread before him. The massive Capital building and the Washington Monument lined up below. The stately Jefferson and Lincoln Memorials each gleamed in their grandeur while the White House, small by comparison, sat off to the side, a bright splash of light in the darkness. He never tired of the sight.

"Yeah."

CHAPTER 8

STATE DEPARTMENT, WASHINGTON, D.C.

Linda Resnick marched into the State situation room wearing a charcoal wool wrap-around dress, her unwashed chestnut hair pulled up into a loose bun. Her face, once too beautiful to be taken seriously, now had the ageless look of a Mother Superior. Dropping into the dark leather chair at the head of the conference table, Linda looked around at the busy staff. Larry Calhoun, her Chief of State intelligence and Research, known as the INR, had a phone stuck to his ear, but glanced up to nod at her arrival.

An aide walked over with a fresh pot of coffee and an empty mug and poured a cup. He dropped two yellow packages of Splenda and a red plastic stirrer next to the cup.

"What's new, Larry?" Resnick inquired after he had hung up. She hoisted her hot mug of coffee and held its warmth in her chilled hands.

"Look here," he replied, pointing at the wall-mounted plasma monitor. A fresh satellite image scrolled down the display. "This is Kowloon Park." He drew a red circle with his laser pointer.

She put on her glasses, as he pointed to a large area filled with people. "There are about thirty thousand Falun Gong demonstrators in this area. Now, over here," he indicated several other areas with his pointer, "you can see about two thousand army troops forming a perimeter around the Park. We can also see that more soldiers are disembarking from this train here, as we speak." His pointer moved to a dark line at the confluence of several train tracks.

He continued. "About five hundred or so have fanned out across the city and are occupying intersections, guarding the China News Agency and other key places. More, say two hundred, are even on Hong Kong Island."

Resnick frowned. "How old is this image?"

"Uhh," he squinted at the time stamp at the bottom of the image. "Six minutes. Oh, and they've also brought in APCs."

"Armor?" Linda asked, surprised.

"Yeah. My China desk-lead tells me that was the pattern before the break-up of the Tiananmen demonstration. The spooks say the same thing. I think we're going to see some nastiness before the night is over."

"Anything from the demonstrators?"

"Peaceful as a church full of church ladies."

"What time is it there?"

Calhoun glanced at the row of clocks above the bank of TVs. "About six forty-five P.M. It's pretty dark there now. We expect they'll move in anytime. Here's the kicker. They've shut down every major independent news outlet, except for sporadic field reports from CNN."

Resnick considered this information. "That's bad."

Larry looked over at a slight man with a vanishing hairline. "Harry, can you update us?"

Harold Wright, Calhoun's technical analyst, looked up from his laptop. "OK, sure. Well, my information shows that the news agencies' satellite uplinks are all cut off. Some reporters have apparently been detained. They've also shut off all landline and most cellular phone communication into and out of Hong Kong, virtually cutting off the area to outside communication. We have no pictures or eyewitness reports coming from the demonstration, except the CNN reports. Their main station's off line, but they're getting field reports relayed from, we believe, a hidden satellite truck the Chinese haven't located yet."

Resnick finished the thought. "They don't want anyone to watch. So how come CNN is still on the air?"

Calhoun answered. "My friend, Ernie Whiteside, who's stationed here at CNN Washington, clued me into their secret. Apparently, their HK station chief used to be assigned to South Korea and had to find work-arounds from periodic government interference. Guessing there might be a media crackdown, he hid the satellite truck well in advance. Pretty clever. But," he added, "they're the only on-site source of information we have."

"Your estimate of the possibility of significant violence?"

"High. How much? I don't know, but one earlier CNN report said the army had their assault rifles out."

Linda chewed her lip while she digested the information. "Get Ambassador Gung on the line for me. Let's let them know we're watching." She took a long drink from her coffee, feeling the heat burn its way down her throat. It would aggravate her reflux, but right now she didn't care.

"Ambassador Gung," an aide announced presently and handed the phone to Resnick.

Linda cleared her throat and put the handset to her ear. "Mr. Ambassador?"

A sleepy, heavily accented voice came over the line. "Yes, Madam Secretary. What can I do for you?"

"Can you tell me what the PLA's intentions are with respect to the Falun Gong demonstration in Kowloon?"

"Nothing. I understand there is to be no interference."

"Are you aware that several thousand troops have surrounded Kowloon Park and have brought in APCs?"

"I'm sorry, Madam Secretary, I do not know what you are talking about." Gung's voice sounded more alert.

Could he not know? Resnick wondered. "Mr. Ambassador, I have satellite pictures in front of me of your troop mobilization. We see about three thousand armed PLA troops dispersed throughout Kowloon and Hong Kong, and currently amassing around Kowloon Park. I pray they are there to observe and not intervene. Most worrisome is that all independent broadcast media have been essentially shut down."

She kept her voice level and controlled, a technique learned from years of high stakes negotiations, honed while she was ambassador to Saudi Arabia and Pakistan. "I am extremely concerned about this."

"Linda, I am unaware of any of this, I assure you."

"Turn on CNN." Linda's words were like ice. "I think you will find it interesting. Check with your government. And please express the extreme concern of the United States. We will look with tremendous disfavor at any action that harms peaceful demonstrators."

Resnick listened to a short silence before Gung replied. "I will communicate that to my government. I'm sure I will call back to assure you that your concerns are unfounded."

"I sincerely hope so." Linda hung up the phone, her lips drawn into a thin line, considering.

"The President needs to see this."

CHAPTER 9

Steve sat on the side of a stretcher in his curtained-off Emergency Department cubicle, listening to the controlled bedlam of doctors and nurses managing the large volume of injured passengers. Many of the injured from his flight had descended upon George Washington University Hospital.

Several hours had passed since the 747 landed. Steve had stayed with Captain Palmer until they arrived at the hospital after which Palmer had been taken right back. Only later did they have room for Steve. Finally, an emergency room doctor had performed a quick evaluation in the hallway and later, after they had opened up a cubicle, a harried medical student had sutured his back. At least the lidocaine and some ibuprofen had eased the pain somewhat.

A huge, red-haired Celt stuck his head around Steve's curtain. "Dr. James? I'm Dr. Martin Walker." When Steve waved him in, he thrust out his beefy hand and they shook. Dr. Walker's ruddy face, shrouded by a bushy red beard, wrinkled up in a friendly smile. The white coat did nothing to hide his massive size. Steve could easily imagine him swinging a mace or battering down castle walls. Outside the hospital, one would not mistake him for a physician.

"A pleasure to meet you. It's Steve, by the way."

"Okay, Steve. I'm Marty. I understand you were the man who had the presence of mind not to panic." Steve had to smile at his comment.

"And best of all, you're a neurologist. Welcome to GW. I trust the service wasn't too plebian?"

"Not bad if you like being a patient."

"Ouch. As bad as that?" Walker grinned, then turned serious. "Some case you drug in, Steve. I've sent the captain off to MRI on the way to his room. What do you think's up?"

Steve thought a minute before answering. "He's got moments of altered awareness with directed violence during what he calls flashbacks, complaints of severe headaches, and myoclonic twitches that are intermittent. They seemed to be connected to his hallucinations."

Marty nodded as Steve continued.

"Except for the myoclonus, I'd bet on a pretty normal exam. I spoke with him a little afterwards and he seemed reasonably intact, but I felt like he had lost his edge."

Marty nodded again. "Quite on the mark. I found the same thing, including some cognitive impairment, possibly from his concussion. We'll see about that. Plus," Marty raised a finger, "he's anosmic."

That surprised Steve. "Why did you test that?"

"I'd like to say it was me being my compulsive self, but the fact of the matter is, he complained of a loss of interest in food; it didn't taste right. So I checked and sure enough, he couldn't smell."

"No kidding. Of course, you know all the reasons."

"And I'll eliminate most of them on the MRI. He'll get thin cuts through the nose."

"Anything else?"

"That's about it. Denies any meds and his drug and alcohol screen were negative. The routine lab was fine, also."

"Hmm." Steve chewed his lip. "Confirms my first axiom of neurological diagnosis: 'Nothing's ever easy'."

Marty chuckled. "Are you through here? You weren't hurt too badly?"

Steve thought a moment. The medicine had done its job. "Nah. I just need my final paperwork and then I'm through. I'd like to look at Captain Palmer's scan."

"Right. I'll go dictate and then we'll go see the films." He shoved the curtains aside and walked out. Just outside the curtain stood a man in a gray suit, flanked by two blue-suited aides, apparently waiting to speak with Steve. His black eyebrows contrasted greatly with his silver hair, an appearance made more striking by his exceptionally pale face. Steve recognized him as the passenger he had seen from the cockpit during the dive and with whom he later had nearly bumped heads.

"Jacob Castell, Secretary, HHS," the man introduced himself and extended his hand.

"Steve James." He took Castell's proffered hand.

"Good to meet you, Dr. James," Castell nodded. "I saw what you did in the airplane cockpit. You did a heroic job rescuing us from certain death."

Steve shrugged. "Just lucky, sir."

"No, Dr. James, more than luck. I was there. You acted when you had to. A moment's hesitation and neither of us would be standing here talking."

Steve's mind flashed back to the cockpit and its now jumbled montage of sounds and lights. "Well, you're welcome. You might say I had a dog in that hunt as well."

Castell smiled. "So, I just wanted to thank you in person since we didn't have time to meet properly before." He chuckled. "You're a hero, Dr. James. Have you dealt much with the media?"

"A bit. A few interviews here and there."

Castell leaned forward and lowered his voice. "Some advice. They love you today, hate you tomorrow. Don't let the adoration you're about to receive go to your head. Believe me. Keep them at arm's length."

"Good advice. Thanks." Steve liked his privacy and did not care much for that kind of attention, but he recognized the wisdom in Castell's words. There was liability in fame.

CHAPTER 10

PHOENIX, ARIZONA

Edith Rosenwell sighed as she walked into her kitchen from the dark carport, carrying a handful of plastic grocery bags. She had stopped on the way home at an all night Safeway, and after a double shift at work, was exhausted. She was looking forward to a quick shower and crawling into bed.

As she set the bags down on the tile countertop, she heard a loud scream from down the hall. *Shirley!*

Edith ran down the hall and into Shirley's bedroom. A bedside light cast pale yellow daggers onto her twenty-four year old daughter, cowering in a corner.

"Help!" Shirley shrieked, clutching her cotton blanket to her chest. "They're coming at me!" Her arms and face twitched in that strange way again, her eyes wild and frantic.

"Honey, it's okay. Stop yelling now." Edith knelt and put her arms around her daughter. "It's okay. It's just another dream."

"You're scaring me!" Wild-eyed, Shirley pulled the blanket over her head and kicked at her mother. "Get out! Get out!"

Edith pulled back from her daughter's thrashing. Why had the childhood nightmares returned with such an evil vengeance? This was by far the worst episode, and those twitches! They had never been this bad.

As a little girl, Shirley had often crawled, trembling with fright, into her mother's bed, fearful of the monsters that came at her in her dreams. These night terrors, as the doctors called them, had persisted until Shirley was twelve years old, when finally they faded into a bad memory. Edith had attributed their slow disappearance to the lack of a reassuring masculine presence in the house. Shirley's father had died before her first birthday.

This nightmare— No! This was far worse than a nightmare. It was an evil that possessed her. These things, these awful, malevolent things had steadily destroyed her personality and devastated her life.

Shirley's jerking gradually diminished and then stopped. Edith gently pulled the blanket down. Shirley looked up, her eyes searching Edith's face. Recognition slowly crossed her features. "Mother?"

As Edith put her arms tightly around her daughter, she decided, gripped now by guilt that she had waited too long. She had abided by Shirley's fearful avoidance long enough. It was time.

Edith wrapped the blanket securely around Shirley and tenderly tucked it in around her neck. "I'll be right back, Honey." She ran into her small kitchen and dialed the telephone.

"Nine-one-one emergency."

"My daughter is very ill." Edith choked up. It was several moments before she could speak again. "Please send an ambulance."

She hung up and went back to her daughter's room to wait for the paramedics. Shirley sobbed quietly, hugging herself as she rocked back and forth. She let her mother sit next to her and after a little coaxing, she laid her head in her mother's lap.

Edith wept, gripped by the helpless frustration of a parent with a sick child. What was happening? As she tenderly stroked Shirley's wet face, she prayed that the doctors would know how to make her daughter well.

CHAPTER 11

"What in the hell is that?" Steve's finger touched the large MRI display screen.

Dr. Walker pulled up a rolling chair next to Steve and filled it with his considerable bulk. "I don't know," he said after a minute.

Steve and Dr. Walker stared at a pair of 30-inch computer screens, their faces bathed by the cool bluish light, and examined Captain Palmer's brain images, arrayed like rows and columns of thinly sliced walnuts.

"It's like a bulldozer, no, a pair, plowed right through his brain," muttered Dr. Walker. He hunched closer to the screen and frowned at the pair of parallel white bands that cut through the brain images. "M.S.?"

"Can't be," Steve replied, pointing. "Look. It involves the gray matter, too." He sat back as a strange déjà vu feeling came over him. He had seen a scan like this before . . . but where?

"Herpes encephalitis?" Marty speculated, interrupting Steve's thoughts. "But it doesn't really fit that either."

Steve turned back to the scan and mentally reconstructed the series of two dimensional brain slices into a 3-D image. "It looks like it starts here." He pointed with his finger. "See, the orbital-frontal area is brighter than the rest. From there, it tracks to the midbrain, then the temporal lobes, and to the cingulate gyrus, here." He straightened up. Yes, this was a pattern he had seen before.

"You're right, it's following the olfactory radiations," said Dr. Walker. "It must have wiped out his smell, then spread to his memory and emotional centers."

Steve's face knotted in thought, "Let's put this together. We've got an airline pilot who has a disease affecting his frontal lobes, with a loss of judgment. His temporal lobes are affected, and somehow are recreating his Vietnam experiences."

"Right," Marty added, "memory's stored there, triggered by this thing somehow. That would explain his flashbacks."

"And," Steve continued, "his limbic centers are involved, either increasing the intensity of his flashbacks or maybe making them seem credible. Otherwise, he would have felt like he was just dreaming or remembering things. Instead, he acted as if it were really happening."

"I see what you're driving at. He found himself in the middle of his memory, having to act it out all over again." Marty scratched his head. "Interesting. And frightening. I wouldn't want to go through that."

"But what is it?" Steve stared at the picture as if it would talk. "A virus? A toxin? Fungal? And why did it start here?" He pointed to the frontal area. "Nasal entry of a toxin that spread back through the axons?"

"Good question."

As they talked, Steve stared at the brain images, mentally picturing a pathogen entering the nose, tracking into the brain through the fine olfactory nerves, and then progressively spreading along nerve axons through the brain pathways into the most secret and prized parts of Captain Palmer's brain. He imagined it seeping from the affected nerves into the adjacent brain tissue, extending the damage and eventually becoming confluent, wiping out brain tissue until there was nothing left. He shivered.

Where had he seen this pattern before? Steve tried to round up the scraps of that memory. Bits of the image floated just outside his grasp, like a partially remembered dream. He had been in a dark X-ray reading room much like this one and he had been standing next to another doctor, also male, but he could not remember who. The scan had not been one of his patients, but whose?

"Steve?" Marty broke his thoughts.

"I've got a bad feeling about this," Steve remarked, turning to look at Marty. "Let's stay in touch."

CHAPTER 12

Secretary Resnick finished crunching a Rolaids as she walked into the Oval Office. Jeff Bell, President Dixon's Chief of Staff followed her in and closed the door. Dixon and Bell had worked together as far back as Dixon's first run for the Senate and they both had deep Virginia roots. "I've called in the team," Bell announced. "They'll be here soon."

President Robert Dixon rose from a fireplace chair to greet her. He had dressed in a pair of Levi's and a worn Yosemite sweatshirt. "Hello, Linda. Sit, sit. Coffee? Wesley's making some."

"No thanks, I've had plenty already." She sat down in the chair in front of the fireplace opposite Dixon. "I am very sorry to wake you up," she began, "but . . ."

"Nonsense. So what's going on? China?"

"China has several thousand troops in Hong Kong surrounding the Falun Gong worshippers in Kowloon Park demonstrating for religious freedom."

The President frowned. "The Falun Gong . . . ?"

Resnick knotted her brow. "Yes sir," she said deliberately. "We spoke about it in yesterday's meeting. I said it was a potential target for the Chinese government to break up."

Dixon's face registered recognition. "Oh, yeah. I guess I need the caffeine pretty quick. So the PLA's got them surrounded. So . . . ?"

"We're expecting some violence. How much I can't say."

The phone rang and Bell picked it up. After a moment, he hung up. "That was Larry Calhoun, Linda. He says to turn on CNN." He opened the curved wall panel hiding the TV and hit some buttons on the remote. The CNN picture was dark and grainy and at first Resnick couldn't make out what she was seeing. Titling at the bottom of the screen told them this was live from Kowloon Park.

"It's dark," a woman's voice shouted. "All the lights have gone out." Her words could barely be heard over nearby cries and yells. "People are frightened and— Oww! Pushing . . . hard to breathe . . ."

The camera image streaked with movement. They could make out a few words from the newscaster. "Can't keep people off . . ." They heard some staccato pops that made Linda jump. Gunshots? The camera image blurred again before it settled on white smoky streaks against the lit night sky. "Tear gas . . . crowd is panicking."

Resnick heard several sharp reports and the camera swung again, stabilizing on a podium in time to see several man-sized silhouettes crumple and fall, with others quickly following. In just a few heartbeats, all the men at the podium had ceased standing, apparently shot.

"Jesus Christ!" The sudden outburst from Dixon startled her. His face was red and his hands were balled into fists as he stared at the TV. "I need to talk to the Chinese leader!" He looked at Resnick. "He's got to stop this crap!" Dixon rubbed his temples, looking suddenly very tired. "Can someone get him on the phone?" Looking around he shouted. "Where's that coffee? Wesley!"

"I'll get on it," Resnick said, also shaken. She walked out to the reception area where Joan Pascal, Dixon's personal secretary hurried in, looking as hastily put together as Resnick felt.

"Hello, Madam Secretary," Joan said, managing a weak smile as she dropped her purse into a drawer of her desk.

"Hello Joan. I'm glad to see you. Can you get Chinese Premier Chow on the phone and patch in our translator from State's situation room?"

Joan stuck out her bottom lip in thought. "I can do that," she said slowly. Give me about five minutes to get someone on the line."

"Right. Thanks, Joan."

Back inside, Dixon and Bell still stared at the CNN broadcast. It now showed the darkened silhouette of the woman reporter facing the camera, backlit by the dim city glow. Behind her, scores of dark shapes ran or quickly walked by. "Okay, Okay, I'm Amy Chan in Kowloon Park, surrounded by panicked demonstrators." She coughed several times and quickly wiped her eyes with her sleeve. "We've been hit with tear gas. People are panicking, not knowing what to do or where to go. This is the sorry state of the largest demonstration of the Falun Gong ever. It was peaceful and organized until literally moments ago when all the speakers on the podium were shot, cut down apparently by snipers as they stood before the demonstrators, calling for peace and non-violent resistance. About thirty died right before our eyes." She stopped in a fit of coughing.

The camera moved in closer, jerkily, and the features of the reporter became somewhat sharper. Chan was a young oriental woman, disheveled, her black hair in disarray. Composed again, she resumed speaking loudly to be heard over the din. "And—wait . . ." she looked over her shoulder. "Just now, I hear bangs, gunshots, I believe, fired from," she turned her head and listened, "Yes, different directions, lots of shots, probably hundreds, hundreds of shots." Faint pops, like strings of firecrackers firing all at once, came through the TV speakers.

"The crowd is in a frenzy." Chan was shouting again. She moved still closer to the camera. "Shots continue even as we speak. One man I spoke to just half an hour ago said all he wanted was to go home to his family; he expressed no political interest, just a desire for religious freedom. He had no idea the army would—"

A group of demonstrators collided with Chan, knocking her to the ground. Resnick saw a tangle of bodies, punching and kicking to get free. Then the screen went blank.

"Jesus!" Dixon exclaimed, pacing back and forth in front of the TV. "Where's the goddamn Premier? Get him on the line, now!"

Resnick stared at the President in surprise. Dixon rarely swore.

The scene cut to anchorman Frank Robinson who looked up from his monitor and into the camera. His expression betrayed his alarm. "We will resume the live broadcast from Kowloon Park when it becomes possible. We now have a live voice report from George Liu in Hong Kong who is calling us from a satellite phone. He is outside Kowloon Park and has been giving us reports of the actions of the Chinese Army. Here is George Liu."

"Herb," shouted a man's voice, identified on the screen as George Liu. "They're shooting! They're shooting into the Park!"

"Are you sure it's live ammo?" Another man's voice, clearer than the first, answered George. Titling on the screen identified the second voice as Herb Wong, CNN's Hong Kong station chief.

"I'm close. I'm just outside Kowloon Park," Liu continued, "behind a car and I can see the crowd. Oh! Oh! They're . . . they're stampeding between two buildings. They're running down the stairs between the buildings and . . . and the Army is . . ." His words took on a hysterical note. "I can't believe what I'm seeing! They're shooting, Herb! Point blank, with machine guns and, and assault rifles. People are being stampeded from behind and pushed right into the shooting range of the Army."

His voice rose in anguish. "It's point blank range. This is awful! People are dying by the hundreds. There's a pile of bodies in front of the Army and still they are being pushed over . . . and . . ." He stopped talking and Resnick wondered if they had lost the signal.

"George?" Wong shouted.

"I'm here." Liu continued in a much more subdued voice, almost whispering, and Resnick found herself leaning towards the TV. "There is no telling how many have been killed or trampled already. It's horrible, horrible. I've never . . ."

"George, are you okay?"

"I don't know. I'd better get out of here. I'm leaving."

Resnick's stomach roiled. This was as raw as it got.

"Are you safe?" Wong demanded.

"I'm walking away, now, away from the Park. I only hope the Army's not— Wait! Wait! Oh, no! The Army's going in. I repeat, the Army's moving into Kowloon Park."

"Where's the goddamn Premier?" Dixon shouted again. "Joan!"

She yelled back. "Working on it."

"This has got to goddamn stop!"

CHAPTER 13

Joan walked in, a frustrated look on her face. "Boss, no go. Premier Chow is indisposed and cannot take your call."

Dixon looked at his secretary, unbelieving. "What in the hell does indisposed mean? Is he sitting on the crapper?"

Resnick voiced her first thought. "Perhaps he is no longer Premier."

Dixon laughed without humor. "So maybe he got flushed down the can. Dammit, what the fuck can we do about this thing?" He pointed his coffee mug at the TV, his glare challenging Bell and Resnick. "What?"

Resnick, frustrated at the killing she knew was going on at this very moment, heard herself speak calmly. "At this time, sir, nothing. At least to stop the killing."

Dixon shifted his glare onto Resnick. "I gathered that. What else?"

Tyrone Grune, President Dixon's Press Secretary, walked into the Oval Office followed by August Crusoe, the National Security Advisor. Dixon pointed at the TV. "You guys up on this?"

"Been getting reports from my staff," Crusoe said, his pipe already lit and filling the Oval Office with its pungent smell. "Terrible. Tiananmen all over again, worse."

"Ty," Dixon said to his press secretary. "I want something by ten-thirty, ten would be better."

"Right. I'll get you on for a five minute statement." Grune, a tall, gangling, word genius with a red pencil perpetually stuck behind his ear, vanished down the hall.

"Camera's on," a male voice announced from the TV, drawing their attention back to the events in Kowloon Park. The story was impossible to resist, reality TV at its voyeuristic worst.

Chan was leaning against a palm tree, breathing hard. Her image was ghost-like, silhouetted against the faint light behind her. "Okay," she said, "I'm Amy Chan with cameraman Rudy Winchong. We have just escaped a group of Peoples Liberation Army troops who entered the Park and are apparently shooting at anybody in their path. We have seen many victims of the shooting, both wounded and dead. I got spattered with blood, I was so close."

She held up her hand showing the blood on it. As Ms. Chan looked at it, Resnick could see a puzzled look cross her face.

"Oh, no, it's my blood! I've been shot in my hand! Funny, it doesn't hurt." Her laugh was tinged with hysteria. Resnick's insides filled with bitter dread, like the horror movies where the woman turns around to look at her pursuer and trips and falls and cannot get up.

"Rudy, are you hurt?" Ms. Chan asked, looking past the camera.

"No, I'm okay," an off-camera voice said.

"Good." She looked back at the camera. "We've been through some scary moments this last bit and I don't know if we will get out alive. It seems the Chinese Army is slaughtering every one in the Park. As far as we can guess, they've covered all the exits. We hear gunshots from all directions. They are apparently killing the demonstrators just because, because, I guess, the Falun Gong want the freedom to worship like they want."

As Ms. Chan's words poured forth, Resnick sat down hugging herself, leaning forward in her chair, her eyes fixed on the dim TV picture.

Chan's eyes sharpened with a fresh poise and calm to her voice. "We have an English legacy here in Hong Kong and while we never reached full independence, we enjoyed many freedoms: freedom of expression and peaceful assembly, freedom of the press and freedom of religion. All of these were brutally slaughtered today in Kowloon Park by the callous, calculating powers in Beijing. There is no love for the individual in Beijing, only love for the money Hong Kong brings to China. That and the power they cling to with their threats and—Ohh!"

Chan's neck erupted, spewing blood and tissue. She jerked like a marionette as more projectiles ripped through her body.

The camera spun toward the source of the shots and showed the brutally impassive face of the army private who had just ended Amy's life.

They heard a man's cry of pain and the camera image streaked. The picture stabilized with a disorienting sideways image of grass. Just at the edge of the screen, they saw the still jerking leg of a man on the ground.

CNN cut back to the ashen face of anchorman, Frank Robinson. He stared a long moment at the camera. "We've . . ." Robinson stopped. He took a deep breath. "It appears reporter Amy Chan and her cameraman, Rudy Winchong, have been shot, apparently by members of the People's Liberation Army, the Chinese regular army. I—I don't know what to say." He paused, took off his glasses and rubbed his eyes. When he replaced them a few moments later, he appeared more composed.

"Our heartfelt condolences go to their families and the families of all those demonstrators slain in the Kowloon Park Massacre." Then, in a steadier voice, he turned to a map displayed on a monitor next to him, showing Kowloon Park. "As best we can tell—"

Dixon muted the sound. "Good God." His voice had a changed timbre, making Resnick tear her eyes from the TV to look at him. "This will not fucking stand." Dixon stared at the silent image and then slid to his knees, grasping the arm of the chair and bowed his head in prayer.

Resnick exchanged a surprised glance with Crusoe at this new and unfamiliar act.

"Ambassador Gung's calling, Madam Secretary," Joan Pascal said over the intercom. "Line three."

With a deep sense of disquietude, Resnick walked over to the President's desk and, picking up the handset, punched the line. "Secretary Resnick." Her voice was husky and dry.

"Madam Secretary," Gung said. "You were right. My country has assembled the military around Kowloon Park, but . . ." he spoke as if he were reading, ". . . its intentions were humanitarian. I was initially unaware of the buildup, but it was done under an emergency situation."

Linda detected strain in his voice.

"It was an attempt to prevent the Falun Gong from committing mass suicide."

CHAPTER 14

"Larry, I need State to help us with our Hong Kong staff." Ernie Whiteside, CNN's senior Washington producer, stood in front of Larry Calhoun's desk. Balding and gray at the temples, Whiteside nevertheless had the square, handsome face of an ex-news anchor. "Our coverage has jeopardized the safety of our remaining staff. They are all in hiding asking us what to do next."

Whiteside had called Calhoun to request an ASAP meeting after the China massacre. They had known each other for several years and had developed a good working relationship that verged on friendship.

"I'm pretty sure we can help," Calhoun replied. He voiced the question he had been thinking about all morning. "Ernie, was this all to eliminate the Falun Gong? Maybe you can provide some insight here. I've been scratching my head over this whole massacre thing."

"You can't stamp out a religion. It's been tried." Whiteside sat down heavily in one of the tufted leather chairs, worn from serving three administrations. He looked as tired as Calhoun felt. "With that in mind, and I assume the Chinese know it as well, I can't figure it out either. I still can't believe their fucking balls for trying to pull that mass suicide bullshit."

He continued. "Obviously, they learned from the damage the media caused over Tiananmen. With us out of the way, and they goddamn nearly succeeded, they can pretty well say and do what they want, including lying about what they really did."

"Larry," Whiteside returned to his earlier request. "Can you help us? We're hurting bad. We lost two people and one is unaccounted for. Herb Wong and three more are in hiding. Worse, one of our engineers got shot in the knee for resisting the order to shut down the station's transmitters and is now in a hospital. We hope. Larry, we want you to assist Herb Wong and his staff, five in all, get out of Hong Kong, preferably to the States. We also want you to provide political cover for our other people spread throughout China. I have a list here." Whiteside slid an envelope across Calhoun's desk.

Calhoun opened the envelope and glanced over the list. "We would be happy to grant asylum and give them Visas."

"I'm afraid I'm asking for more." Whiteside paused. "They may need some more direct help."

"Like what?"

"The Army's presence throughout Hong Kong has pretty well stranded them. They're already in hiding. We need to get them out ASAP before the PLA locates them. Anybody you have there to help make that happen would be greatly appreciated."

It took a while for Whiteside's meaning to penetrate. Calhoun had thought he could shield them in the consulate or grant them diplomatic immunity, but, no, Whiteside was asking for more. "You want an agent to extract them."

"Yes."

"You're asking a lot."

"I know."

Calhoun pondered the possibilities. There were State ramifications for that direct an involvement, although at that precise moment, he really didn't give a damn. He knew that all ground assets would be critically busy in their assigned roles—far too busy to assist CNN, but as he rolled it over in his mind, an idea struck him that involved an old ally. The more he thought about it, the better it looked. He would have to get the Secretary's sign-off, but judging by her initial reaction towards the massacre, he figured that would not be difficult.

"I'll call you in a few hours; maybe we can do something for your people."

CHAPTER 15

The events in China had preceded the regular morning National Security Council meeting. While it was ten o'clock at night in Hong Kong—an hour and a half after Amy Chan's death—it was nine in the morning Washington time.

The morning crew, as Linda called them, assembled on time and took seats around the mahogany table in the Roosevelt room, temporary quarters while the Oval office was set up for the presidential address. Seated around the table were Vice President John Sullivan; National Security Advisor August Crusoe; CIA Director George Bingham; Secretary of Defense Mark Painter, and Resnick. The last official member of the council, Secretary of the Treasury, Helen Norris, was in Brussels. Chief of Staff, Jeff Bell, rounded out the group.

"Let's get started," Dixon said curtly. "I'm really angry about this—George?"

"Here's the latest," the CIA Director began in his southern drawl. "The Chinese-controlled media sources continue to claim the Falun Gong demonstrators committed mass suicide."

"What?" Dixon exclaimed. "What the hell did you say?"

Resnick frowned. She had told President Dixon about that right after her call from Ambassador Gung. Had he forgotten?

"They're printing it and broadcasting it all over China," Bingham continued, using his fingers to form quotation marks in the air, "'Falun Gong demonstrators mysteriously commit mass suicide.' Realize, Mr.

President, this is all the Chinese people have to go on since there are now no international news sources to provide a counter to the government. The only external news sources are the Internet, which China has mostly closed down, some satellite TVs and satellite phones. They've pretty much locked down most everything else.

"According to the Chinese version," Bingham continued, "the People's Liberation Army had been tipped off about the intended mass suicide and tried to muster a force to prevent the slaughter, most regrettably too late." Bingham rendered "most regrettably" in a sarcastic tone. "They are blaming the thousands of innocent deaths on their deranged leaders, who had them all under mass hypnotism—their terminology."

The President stood up and walked over to the fireplace and watched the burning wood crackle. "Jesus! Who ordered this?"

Bingham thought about the answer a moment before replying. "I don't really know, but we suspect a junta of hardliners led by General Yao Wenfu. He has gone on record repeatedly about the FG and his objection to its foul infestation of China." Bingham shifted in his chair. "He's the likely candidate here, but realize, this is only conjecture."

Dixon rubbed his eyes. "Linda, what have you got for me?"

Linda cleared her throat. "Ambassador Justice has hit a wall. Nobody's talking. So, except for Ambassador Gung, there is no word directly from the Chinese leadership. Apparently they are letting the media talk for them right now."

"That's alarming by itself, Mr. President," National Security Advisor Crusoe interjected, waving his pipe for emphasis. "This likely indicates serious instability at the top. Our intercept of their internal communications is confused and contradictory. I haven't seen this kind of pattern since Tiananmen."

"Explain," the President demanded.

"I don't think the government is united on the massacre decision. There have been long nights at Zhongnanhai for four nights in a row, which is part of what tipped us off on their operation in Hong Kong. It's not the usual hand-it-off-to-the-military either. This has the full attention of the politburo subcommittee."

"So it's political," Vice President John Sullivan summarized.

"And controversial. We believe there are serious divisions at the top. I'm afraid, and George agrees, that the leadership situation could be in flux."

Dixon turned to his Defense Secretary. "Mark?"

Mark Painter leaned forward in his chair. "We're watching for any signs that this Hong Kong action is a cover for a military venture, and our Pacific units are under increased alert. So far, we haven't seen anything unusual. Otherwise, there isn't much for Defense."

"Okay," Dixon snapped, "Now I want options. Good ones. Linda?"

"Mr. President, you know our options are few, limited to booting their top level diplomats, technology transfers, scholarships, trade—"

"I don't want to hear about trade embargoes or tariffs."

"Our repertoire's pretty thin, sir."

"Apparently," Dixon responded acerbically. "And our allies?"

"Publicly and personally outraged, but in talking with them, I don't get the feeling that they want an all out confrontation over it." Linda had been surprised and considerably dismayed at the tepid official responses coming from Europe and Asia.

"They don't huh? I suppose they're all too friggin' tied up economically," the President said bitterly. "If you're rich, you can get away with murder."

"We can get a UN resolution," Linda said weakly.

"Great, a goddamn UN resolution." The President walked back to his seat and picked up his water glass. Sipping at it, he stared at the ceiling. Unexpectedly he slammed the glass back on the table, making everybody jump.

"Dammit. We've got to do something." He pointed at the group. "Find me a way to make those bastards wish they'd never done this."

Press secretary Tyrone Grune stuck his head in. "It's time for your address, sir."

"Excellent, Ty. Let's go." Dixon strode quickly out of the room.

CHAPTER 16

Steve's plane pulled up to the gate at Phoenix Sky Harbor International Airport. Standing up, he stretched and yawned. Last night had become a blur. He had spent over two hours at the hospital in taped debriefings with the FAA. Upon leaving, he had faced a barrage of reporters and television cameras. Hospital security helped elbow him through the throng shouting questions at him and into a waiting taxi. By the time he had reached his DC hotel room, it was five o'clock in the morning, with only enough time to call his wife, shower, and get back into his old clothes before heading back to the airport.

While he had called Anne right after getting to the hospital, it was brief; just an "I'm okay and I love you." He did not mention his cockpit experience, but by the time he had reached her from the hotel phone, she had heard the story from the TV news. She pressed him for details, which by then, with time and fatigue, had become indistinct.

Heading home to Phoenix on the first flight out, he had longed to hold Anne and Johnnie again. Little John was seven and would absolutely wiggle with embarrassment. Steve couldn't wait.

Leaving the gate area, he walked past security and into the terminal where a wall of blinding halogen video lights greeted him, behind which were a crowd of reporters yelling questions. Blinking in the harsh light, he looked around. Where were Anne and Johnnie? Pushing past the cameras and reporters, he heard his shouted name in a voice he instantly recognized.

"Steve!"

It was Anne. *Anne*! He looked over the crowd and spotted her, smiling and tear-streaked, standing on a chair and waving. Next to her stood his son, Johnnie, jumping up and down in his excitement. Steve rushed up and wrapped his arms around her slender body in a tight bear hug, picking her up and swinging her around like any returning sailor. The cameras followed, sucking up every move. He buried his nose in her long black hair and breathed in her familiar fragrance.

"I'm back, honey," he whispered in her ear.

Anne didn't talk but held him close. Johnnie pulled at his belt. "Daddy, Daddy!"

Steve, smiling broadly, picked up his son and held him up over his head. "Little John, good to see you, sprout."

"Daddy, you're a hero!"

"Miss me?"

"Yeah. Did you bring me a present?"

CHAPTER 17

The television camera framed a very presidential-looking Dixon sitting at his desk in the Oval Office. Pictures of Elise, his wife, and their two grown sons sat on the credenza behind him.

"Ready in ten seconds," a technician said.

Dixon cleared his throat and looked at the teleprompter just above the camera lens. Already "Good Morning." was showing, dark blue on a neutral background. The flow of words would start as he began to speak. The technician, sweating in his unaccustomed suit and tie, used his hands for the final three seconds, and then the red broadcast light came on over the camera.

"Good morning," Dixon began. "Last night in Hong Kong, a large group of religious worshippers gathered to hear from their leaders. It was a peaceful collection of ordinary Chinese citizens, all law abiding except for one thing. They desired to worship in a religion that has been outlawed by the Chinese Government . . ."

Resnick leaned against the back wall of the Oval office and watched him on one of the TV monitors the technicians had set up. Press Secretary Tyrone Grune, standing next to her, read his copy of the speech along with Dixon. The President looked solid, his voice firm and tone right. Robert Dixon was very good on TV.

". . .This religion, called the Falun Gong, is viewed as a threat by the Chinese Government despite no declared political agenda. Suddenly and without warning, the leaders of the gathering were slain by Chinese army sharpshooters, the lights went out, plunging the park into darkness and tear gas canisters were fired into the crowd. The demonstrators did what you and I would do. They panicked and ran. And as they tried to escape the park, the Chinese army waited for them with machine guns and assault rifles and cut down the peaceful, unarmed Chinese people, murdering them in cold blood." Dixon paused for effect.

Was he overdoing it a bit? Resnick wondered. His even tones had given way to a rise of emotion she knew was boiling right under the surface.

Grune heard it too. "Easy, easy," he muttered.

"That's not all. As many of you know, the government shut down nearly all international and independent news media before their premeditated massacre of the peaceful worshippers. The freedom of the press that we take for granted in our country is not known nor recognized by the Chinese leaders."

"What?" Grune grunted. "That's not in there."

"What's more, they shot and killed members of the international corps of reporters. In addition, the army under orders, shot and killed . . ."

Grune flipped through the three pages of his large-type speech. "He's off script." Grune whispered shaking his head. "He's off script!"

Linda, having read and approved the speech, listened more carefully.

" . . . Today on Thanksgiving day, a day we all set aside to thank the Lord for the blessings we enjoy here . . ."

"He's back on, thank God."

" . . . Remember that the Chinese citizens do not have so many things to be thankful for. Our disagreement is not with the Chinese people, for you have seen that the Chinese Government is against its own citizens. And since the government's massacre of its people, thirty thousand fewer Chinese are home with their families and loved ones to share dinner."

Dixon's tone sharpened. "I, and all the free people from around the world, condemn the actions of the Chinese government in the strongest terms and . . ."

"He's off again." Grune whispered, helplessly waving the script in frustration. "I have no idea where he's going."

" . . . I call on the Chinese government to stop lying to its people and apologize to the victim's families at the very least . . ."

Jesus, thought Resnick. *Stop—now.*

" . . . and better yet, embrace the freedoms that are fundamental to a moral government—freedom of the press, freedom of religion, freedom of peaceful assembly and freedom of petition."

Dixon stared into the camera a long moment. "God bless America and the freedoms we all enjoy. Never, ever should we take that for granted. Thank you for listening."

CHAPTER 18

Standing in front of her bathroom mirror wearing a simple white chemise, Anne pulled her hairbrush through her straight hair, mentally reviewing the day's events. The press had been relentless, chasing after the hero *du jour*. Steve had given countless interviews to the local TV stations, several newspapers, and radio stations. The national news outlets interviewed him at their local affiliates for broadcast during their evening segments. The day had dissolved into a sea of faces and microphones. She and Johnnie had also gotten their fair share of attention and even some of the neighbors were interviewed.

Steve, Anne knew, disliked the attention and hubbub, consenting only because he viewed it as a way to get them off his back as soon as possible. "This'll kill me if it goes on more than a day," he had told her as they were driven to ABC's local affiliate, Channel 10, in a network chartered limousine. Johnnie, however, loved every minute. The thought made her smile. He couldn't wait to get back to school to brag about his dad.

When she walked in to the bedroom she found Steve lying on his side, covers down to his waist. Anne stood at the side of the bed for a while and watched him breathe in the dim moonlight that slipped in from the window. The sight eased her anxiety. She examined the sutures and bruises all over his back. He had made her pull off his bandages as soon as he had gotten home.

His body looked so peaceful as it lay there, lean and angular from regular mountain biking in the desert hills. She smiled at his shaggy auburn hair. He never seemed to have time for a haircut. She would call Monday to make him an appointment.

She slid into bed next to him and gently touched his shoulder. "Are you asleep?" she whispered.

"Nope." He sounded fully awake.

"You must be exhausted."

Steve rolled onto his back and stretched, grimacing at what must have been the pressure on his injuries. "A little wound up."

"Can't blame you. Did you take anything for the pain?"

"Tylenol."

"Terrific," she said sarcastically. "That'll knock it right out. Come here, let me rub your neck."

Steve rolled over onto his side facing her and laid his head on her chest sliding his legs alongside hers. She loved his touch and his closeness aroused her. She kissed the top of his head, smelling his freshly washed hair. She had anticipated his return for a week, but with all that had happened, she knew he must be too tired to make love to her.

"The best place in the world," he said snuggling in. His left hand sought out hers and the wedding bands clinked softly as they touched. Steve pressed his ring against hers and she returned the pressure in a custom they had been doing for years. Steve once explained that it came from the Green Lantern cartoon hero, who had to recharge his power ring every twenty-four hours. He was such a weird romantic, she had thought, but immediately adopted the gesture.

Steve's hand then found its usual place on her right breast, cupping it. Anne treasured the secure feeling of his hands and never slept well when he was gone. She craved the physical touch of his body during the night and would move towards him until she felt his warm skin. "Bed Buffalo," he teased her from the way she gradually bulldozed her way onto his side of the bed.

She stroked the back of his neck and hair softly. "It must feel good to have saved all those people."

Steve did not answer immediately. "I'm glad I'm here with you and Johnnie." A moment later he added, "Yeah."

"Were you scared?" She had wanted to ask that ever since he had landed. She was afraid of what he must have endured.

"Not really. Too busy to be scared, I guess."

"Later? After it was all over?"

"A little but I was still pretty busy up until I called you."

Anne cradled his head, thankful he was safe and afraid to imagine what might have happened.

"Funny thing," Steve continued. "I thought about this during one of the interviews today. You know how neurology is full of grey areas and choices? Like when to take someone off an anti-seizure med knowing if you do they may have another seizure. Or when to take a driver's license away from someone who has early dementia. The sort of things I do all day."

Anne just listened, happy to hear him talk. "Mmm, yes."

"Well on the jet, it was clear. No choice. I knew what I had to do."

"I see what you're driving at. It was you and no one else."

"That's true, but I was actually driving at something different." He leaned up on an elbow and looked at her. "We rarely have that kind of clarity in our lives. We have so much choice. Like, what am I going to do in life, what am I going to wear, what color am I going to paint my house, you know? We are always faced with choices. But on the plane, there was no choice."

He lay back down and snuggled closer to her. "We rarely have that level of clarity or that level of consequence. I can't remember ever having that feeling before. Mostly, we go through our lives wondering if we are making the best choices but we can't tell, not really. It is a strange place to be . . . And in all reality, I'll never be there again."

"Well," she said knuckling his hair. "I'm glad you had your big insight. And I hope you never have an opportunity to be that clear again."

"Yeah, yeah. Now, lift up your legs." Steve pulled her closer to him, wrapping his legs up under hers.

He softly stroked her stomach as she lay on her back. "You feel wonderful." His hands were strong and confident, triggering a flow of desire. His fingers found her navel and teased her with light circles before sliding down and between her opening thighs. She realized how much she needed to connect with him. Today had been unsatisfying. He had been close, touching her often, but not really with her, not in a way that she needed. Now she finally had him to herself.

His erection pressed against her thigh. Anne pulled Steve's face up to hers and kissed him deeply. He smiled at her between kisses. "I want you."

Yes. She had almost lost him and now he was back and safe with her. She reached down and held him in her hand. *Welcome home, hero.*

CHAPTER 19

Linda Resnick hung up her phone and pushed back from her desk. Walking to the window, she gazed out over the morning's mist-en-shrouded trees that lined the Potomac, dark gray from the reflected over-cast sky. She watched a couple of outboard fishing boats make their way down river, the anglers tossing their lines with practiced snaps of their rods.

The call had been from the US ambassador to China, Pierre Justice. When the boats finally slipped from view, she turned her thoughts back to the call.

"Things here are in flux, Linda," he had said. "It's four days since the massacre and they are all afraid to say anything—even my highest placed and usually most candid contacts. Everybody is diving for cover. Something big is going on, bigger than I have so far seen, and I can't get a hold of it."

The conclusion she had to make was that someone was pulling the strings behind the scenes, but not yet secure enough to go public. Was Chow still in power, or was there a running succession struggle going on even now? Clearly, the signals indicated great instability at the top, but without knowing any details, she was left in the insecure position of having to make unilateral national policy. It was tough to dance without a partner.

Justice's call capped a long, rough weekend of trying to orchestrate international condemnation of China's actions with little success.

Her frustrations had been nicely summed up in today's *Washington Post*. Following the slaughter, it had reported, the China News Agency translated its mass suicide story into all the major languages and distributed the fiction widely to the foreign media, complete with video of army troops walking at dawn among the dead demonstrators in apparent shock at the mayhem. China's account invoked the mass insanity surrounding religious cults and specifically cited the Jonestown slaughter. The *Post's* analysis suggested the account had had the intended effect of providing a semi-plausible explanation for the deaths and thereby blunting overt international criticism of China's actions.

CNN, too, had actively distributed their shocking images—the pictures of Amy Chan and the nameless, impassive face of the army private who had killed her. With those images splashed on the covers of nearly every non-Chinese news publication, the world knew the truth. But, as the *Post* had written, even though everyone knew what had really happened, China's story and its economic power, had effectively swayed official positions to its side and after the first twenty-four hours, few governments had publicly condemned the slaughter. The story so closely mirrored the State Department's internal findings that Resnick wondered if the *Post* had gotten its information from an internal source.

Not reported were the CNN staff's efforts to escape China. After hearing Larry Calhoun's idea on how to help Ernie Whiteside, she had readily agreed and requested aid through MI6 for a British agent to assist with the CNN news crew's extraction. Calhoun had been correct that England maintained a considerable undercover presence in its former colony, and MI6 had agreed to release an agent to extricate Herb Wong, George Liu, and the others.

As currently formulated, their plan was to make their way north, overland through China until they were opposite Taiwan. From there they would attempt to charter an aircraft or boat to cross the Taiwan Straits into Taiwan. A complication was the need to rescue the injured technician from the hospital. If they could not accomplish that objective, they would be forced to leave him in Hong Kong.

Resnick would welcome the news that they were safe, but in view of the muted international response to China's massacre, she also wanted the PR that would come from their successful emergence from China.

Glancing at her clock, she saw it was almost nine o'clock and nearly time for the morning National Security Council meeting. Resnick had spent her morning preparing her policy recommendations for the briefing, anemic in light of the international recalcitrance. President Dixon wanted meaty response options, but her dilemma—and the President's—was that any unilateral US moves that would hurt the Chinese, would also hurt American interests. Dixon was unwilling to do that. The other options were strictly symbolic—for public consumption—and everyone knew it.

The phone rang, her official phone, not the outdated AT&T Merlin system that provided standard State communications. This was the direct access line from heads of state and their ambassadors. She looked at her watch, seven minutes to the meeting. If she answered the phone she would be late . . .

She picked it up.

CHAPTER 20

PHOENIX, ARIZONA

The hallways of Banner Samaritan Hospital had been freshly wallpapered in a bright yellow pattern, but the pictures had not yet been hung, giving the place a hollow, institutional appearance. Steve walked into the 4B nurses station and up to the white Formica secretary's counter. Spinning the lazy Susan chart rack to the right slot, he pulled out the plastic loose-leaf chart with 'Rosenwell' written in block letters on its spine, his first consultation following the Thanksgiving weekend.

Still on London time, he was up and in the hospital by five-thirty. He hadn't been able to sleep since his return anyway, his nights filled with visions of plummeting out of the sky while helplessly pulling on unresponsive controls as the ground raced up towards him. Getting back to the hospital actually felt good; something to occupy his mind.

Lying on the counter, he saw a two day-old newspaper that had his face plastered on the front page. The lead story shouted "Phoenix Neurosurgeon Saves Diving Jet," in huge letters across the top. He rolled it up and slid it into the trash. The headline still irked him.

After reviewing the chart, he stepped into the darkened hospital room to observe the recumbent figure on the bed. A young woman in her mid-twenties lay still as if she were sleeping, then abruptly, her eyes flew open and she screamed in terror, flailing her arms like she was trying to fight off an attacker. It was right out of a horror movie. The attending nurse quickly closed the door. An older woman, her mother, Steve surmised, bent over the patient stroking her forehead and speaking soft words.

Then he saw the irregular muscular twitches in the young woman's face, neck, and shoulders. He walked to her bedside and touched her right shoulder, evaluating the movements. *It couldn't be.* But, he cautioned himself, there were entire books written on diseases that cause delusions and myoclonus, the medical term for the irregular jerks. Hers could be any one of them.

She stopped screaming and sank back into the bed with heavy lids half-closed.

"Hello," he said to the woman standing next to the bed. "I'm Dr. James."

"I'm Edith, her mother. Dr. Reese said you'd be coming." She looked down at her daughter. "This is Shirley." Edith's worry lines around her eyes and her thinning, gray-streaked hair pulled back in a clip betrayed a hard fifty or so years. She was dressed in a pair of sweat pants and a large American Eagle t-shirt with faded gold lettering across the front.

He leaned towards Shirley and asked softly, "Can you hear me?"

Her eyes opened and she looked at him with scant expression. "Yeah. You going to give me another shot?" Her voice was groggy, either from the disease or sedation. Her chart indicated she had been getting injections of Haldol, a powerful tranquilizer.

He smiled. "Not me. I can't stand needles. I'm Dr. James and I want to talk to you for a little bit." She had a pleasant, surprisingly familiar face with fine, straight brown hair that cascaded across the pillow. A light blue hospital gown draped her slender body.

"I'm so scared," she wept, her eyes wide and teary. "It feels like they're coming to get me. They're so real."

"It'll be okay, Shirley. Tell me what you see when you get your nightmares." He pulled up a chair and sat down.

She got a frightened look in her eyes. "Men . . . bad men, and monsters, like when I was little—but worse, you know, and really scary, like it's really going on. Can you make them go away?"

"I'm going to find out what's causing your visions and try to stop them, but I'll need you and your mother to help me."

"Okay. I'll try."

"Can you tell me what happened to her?" Steve asked Edith. "I'm sorry. I know you've already told it lots of times."

Edith nodded faintly and thought a minute before speaking. "I guess it began around the time when she started complaining about headaches. They weren't too bad at first, but more than normal, you know?"

"When was this?"

"About three months ago. Back then she lived with her boyfriend, so I didn't see her too often and couldn't tell much."

"But they got worse?"

"Yeah. Then about a couple of months ago her boyfriend left her and she had to give up her apartment. After two years! I'd expected more from that boy. She moved back in with me, not that I could really tell. She would go into her room and not come out for hours. I figured it was depression or something, so I got her in to see Dr. Reese who put her on Prozac, I think. That seemed to help her some and she slept better at night, but it didn't do anything for her headaches at all. After a while, she stopped the Prozac and began taking my Darvocet until they ran out. That was about three weeks ago."

"And then?"

"Her depression seemed to just get worse. She would lie in bed most of the day and wouldn't go outside. She wouldn't go see Dr. Reese again. I don't know why."

"When did she develop those twitches?"

"Just recently." Edith paused. "Maybe a week ago. Maybe ten days. I can't really say." She played with a lock of Shirley's hair.

"And her nightmares?"

"Oh, my God, those nightmares." She sighed. "When my Shirley was a little girl, she had the worst nightmares. Night terrors, her pediatrician said. All the way through sixth grade, she would come into my bedroom trying to hide from the monsters that were trying to get her. It was terrible. She finally got over them, but now they're much worse than ever."

"More when the shaking is worse?"

"They do seem to happen at the same time, but I never really put them together before."

"What made you bring her in?"

Edith's lower lip trembled and eyes welled up. "I was late getting home from work and—" She pulled a wadded up Kleenex from her blouse pocket and carefully wiped the corners of her eyes, each time wrapping her finger with a dry part of the tissue. "I heard her screaming and she, she didn't recognize me."

"A nightmare?"

Edith nodded. "It was just awful. My baby, my little baby. I . . . I just couldn't help her."

"And the nightmares? Getting worse?"

"Oh yes. Much."

"Did she use any street drugs?"

"No, never. I think she smoked some pot in college." She smiled faintly, "But none recently."

"What about medications?"

"Well, quite a bit, I'm afraid. She has bad allergies and takes Claritin. She took lots of Advil and Tylenol for her headaches, also Eden for her weight. She took bus—or butt—something or other for her nerves."

"Buspar?" Steve suggested, scribbling everything down.

"That's it."

"Anything else?"

"Vitamins, lots of them. Bee pollen, Q ten or something, multivitamins and St. John's wort, and some energy formula. I forget what it was called."

"Can you bring them in for the nurse to write them all down?"

"Okay, if you think it will help. Oh, yeah, she took an asthma inhaler, but I have no idea what the name is, and some nasal spray for her allergies, some cortisone or something."

Steve looked at the list. "That is quite a lot." He capped his pen and put it back into his pocket. "I'm worried about her, Edith, and I don't know what's causing this yet."

"She's only twenty-four. She shouldn't be sick. It should be me." She held her daughter's hand.

Steve nodded. "I know. Our children should never get sick." Opening his black bag, he laid out his equipment for his exam. He checked her eyes, facial muscles, sensation, and hearing. Her twitching caused some problems with muscle testing, but she had no clear-cut weakness or reflex abnormalities. As he put his instruments back into his bag, his fingers touched his thimble-sized jar of camphor, making him recall Dr. Walker's comment about Captain Palmer's loss of smell.

"Shirley, can you smell things?"

"I think so."

"How do things taste?"

"Awful. I can't taste anything."

Holding his open jar of camphor under her nose, he said, "What do you smell?"

She sniffed, gingerly at first, and then inhaled more deeply. "Am I supposed to smell something?"

Steve sniffed himself just to make sure. Yes, still strong, like Mentholatum.

Shirley had twitches, delusions, and headaches, but nothing on exam except myoclonus. She also had no readily identifiable cause of her illness and, like Captain Palmer, Shirley had lost her sense of smell.

Outside, at the nurse's station, he wrote an order to move her to the Intensive Care Unit and, after double-checking the chart, he ordered a brain MRI.

He figured he already knew what it would show.

CHAPTER 21

Secretary Resnick arrived ten minutes late to the White House National Security Briefing to find CIA Director George Bingham already in the process of updating the President on the China situation. Quickly taking a seat, she saw with some surprise that Dixon looked unusually tired. His hair, normally combed with that Dab-O'-Brylcream look, appeared like he had just rolled out of bed.

"All independence groups," Bingham continued after acknowledging her arrival, "and all non-sanctioned religions, democratic movements and otherwise have disappeared from sight. Field assessments say most have stopped all activity, presumably for fear of being killed. Nothing like a good purge to quiet dissent," he added dryly.

"But, we have lost contact with so many—even their Internet communications have stopped—that we are wondering if many of them really were deep sixed by the PRC. In particular, we have found no public sign of any recognized Falun Gong leader and there have been no reports of members practicing their signature exercises in public. They are literally scared for their lives and, to that extent; the massacre has apparently had its intended effect. China's walking the tight wire of telling its people the FG killed its own, yet relying on the key leaders of the movement to know what really happened. Quite remarkable if they pull it off. Plausible deniability on a national scale."

Bingham glanced down at his notes. "Analysis of the government situation indicates that top level discussions continue at the Zhongnanhai compound. This mirrors activities seen every time there has been a major policy change or internal crisis, including Tiananmen, the death of Mao and Deng, and the dumping of Zhao. Either they're consolidating their initiative begun in Hong Kong or there's an internal power struggle. Since the massacre was such an irrational and aggressive action, I must conclude that there is an irrational and aggressive element at the top and that the late nights in Zhongnanhai indicate significant dissent or factionalism."

"Mr. President," Bingham swept his gaze around the room. "I am worried the Chinese government is not currently in control of itself. This instability has enormous risk for us, just as Russia's did during their early transition of power to democratic rule. Mr. President, I do not know who is currently in charge of the government, nor do I know who is in charge of the nuclear trigger. I recommend, and Mark and August agree, that we go to DEFCON three as a precaution."

Vice-President Sullivan leaned forward. "DEFCON three? Why?"

DEFCON stood for Defensive Condition and described the five levels of military alertness with particular relevance to a nuclear confrontation. Level 5 indicated normal peacetime activity; each lower number indicated increased military alertness, leading up to war at DEFCON one.

President Dixon did not react overtly, leading Linda to surmise that Bingham had already briefed him. This had enormous State ramifications. Why had she not been consulted ahead of time?

Defense Secretary Mark Painter answered the Vice-President. "We've conferred, George, Augie, and I, and it is definitely the best move at this time. We're seeing some pockets of military activity in China that corroborates what George is saying. I can go into more detail if you want, but we may be overdue for a raised DEFCON stance. While I don't think there is any overt threat to the United States; if you recall, when Russia shot down the Korean Airliner, we had strong indications that Russia was trying to provoke us into launching a limited pre-emptive strike. We got up to DEFCON two before the situation was diffused."

"Why not DEFCON four? Why skip to three?" Vice-President Sullivan inquired.

"Much stronger message to the Chinese, reflecting our uncertainty and unease about China's leadership," Painter said.

"Okay, but—"

"At DEFCON three," Painter said, "we put them on notice that they need to carefully consider their next move."

"Well, I agree with your concern," Sullivan said after a pause, "but I'd like to know more detail, especially what the fallout could be."

From a security standpoint, Resnick knew the DEFCON move made some sense, but on the other hand, an elevated DEFCON status, even at a low level, would feed the PRC's legendary communist paranoia. Not to mention squawking NATO members, who hadn't been notified ahead of time, as well as Russia and China's other neighbors. No doubt raising the DEFCON status would cause a ripple of international concern; if only she had been consulted before the meeting.

Sullivan turned to her. "Linda, what do you think?"

Before she could answer, Dixon spoke up. "As God is my witness, I authorize DEFCON three."

Resnick blinked in surprise as the President cut off discussion. It seemed obvious that he had been briefed ahead of time This smelled like an organized *fait accompli.*

"Linda," The President said, apparently moving on, "how can we hurt those bastards? I don't want any panty-waisted embargoes or UN shoe pounding; give me something painful. Short of dropping the big one, of course."

Linda dropped her eyes to her papers, inwardly fuming from the DEFCON decision. She had nothing that would fit the President's request, except . . . "I got a call just before I came," she began. "That's why I was late. It was from Zhou Lishin, Taiwan's US ambassador. He wants to set up an urgent summit between you and President Quin Shi Lai."

"The China thing, I suppose."

"Yes, sir." She paused, choosing her words. "I think they are going to declare independence."

The room froze at her words.

The President recovered first. "About fucking time."

"Sir?" Linda was shocked President Dixon would even contemplate such a move. "There's no way we can support it. It would irreparably damage relations with—"

"Oh, come on now, don't spoil my fun. That's the best idea I've heard all day. Does China think they can just murder thousands and skate? Is that the sort of friend we want to play with? I'd just as soon throw them out of the sandbox."

"Administrations come and go," Linda countered. "The Chinese people hate the government for what they did. This is an opportunity for us to exploit and enlarge. But if we recognize Taiwan and support their bid for independence, that will unify the Chinese people and the dissenting factions within the Chinese government against us, and stifle any reform movement."

"And let the world know that any important country can just slaughter its own and we will continue the status quo? That's the O.J. fucking Simpson bullshit. 'I'm rich and I can get away with murder'."

Linda carefully composed her response. "Remember what George said about the probable turmoil at the top levels of Chinese governance. I have looked over his reports and agree. There's foment there and we can help it along in ways favorable to our interests, if we stay out of it."

The President stuck out his bottom lip in thought. "I get your point, dammit, and I have to agree with you, although acting like the goddamn French in public policy really pisses me off."

Linda had not remembered the President swearing so much since he lost the Iowa primary.

"In the meantime," Dixon continued, "please make arrangements for the visit as soon as possible. If you want to cancel my trip to Utah and Oregon next week, whatever it was for, that's okay with me."

"Just having their President here will create a firestorm with China," Linda warned.

"China cannot dictate the guest list of the President of the United States." Dixon was animated now. "If the Taiwanese President wants to come, then make it a very public state affair. I want it known to God and all the world that Taiwan is our friend."

CHAPTER 22

Steve plopped his feet up on his office credenza and leaned back in his chair, his morning energy having worn off. As he had expected, Shirley's MRI scan looked identical to Captain Palmer's. While examining the images, that same déjà vu feeling had come back. After a long period of thought, he still had failed to identify when and where he had seen that MRI pattern before. Perhaps it was a false recollection. Or maybe not; he couldn't be sure.

The pile of open textbooks on his desk, the result of his research into Shirley's illness, stared back at him. He called a halt to his reading as the jet lag finally slammed him into a wall. Maybe a call to Walker would wake him up. He punched Marty's number up on his cell.

"How's Captain Palmer?" he asked, after exchanging the usual pleasantries.

"About the same, still no diagnosis. Spinal fluid showed a slight white count, six, all lymphocytes. Everything else was normal. Still waiting on the MS panel and some esoteric stuff."

"I've got a little surprise for you," Steve announced.

"What's that?"

"I found another case."

"Another what?"

"Just like Captain Palmer's. A young female—"

"The same MRI pattern?" Marty's booming Welsh voice deafened Steve.

"Identical."

"Clinical presentation?" Marty demanded. "What about that?"

"The same, right down to the delusions and twitches," Steve said.

"Anosmia?"

"Couldn't smell camphor and complained about taste. And so far, my work-up is negative."

"Well, blow me down. What the hell's causing this? So far the Captain's stumped our infectious disease guy and our neuro-toxicologist, but I got one hell of a differential. Until I get an answer, I'm going to get every one of my NIH colleagues to come have a look and we're going to drain this poor chap of every drop of body fluid."

"Marty, can you send me your complete records on Captain Palmer? I want to compare them."

"Right-o. And get me yours, but for the life of me, I can't think of anything that would connect them. He's a healthy fifty-four old male living on the east coast and she's a young woman in Phoenix." Dr. Walker sighed, "How in the hell do you put them together?"

The next afternoon, Shirley's screams met Steve as he entered the ICU. Fortunately, the closed sliding-glass ICU doors muffled much of the sound. Jeanne, Shirley's nurse, and Edith stood by her bed, trying to calm her. The Ativan IV, twice increased overnight, clearly wasn't working any better than the Haldol.

He sat down heavily at the counter and pulled Shirley's chart out of the rack. The lab results so far were mostly normal, which didn't surprise him. The FedEx package of Captain Palmer's records had arrived that morning and after reviewing them, he found, true to Marty's predictions, the two patients had little in common. And so far, her work up—and lack of positive findings—paralleled Captain Palmer's. How then, were they related?

He pulled out the sheet of yellow legal paper on which he had written the major categories of neurologic disease: infectious, immunologic, demyelinative, degenerative, vascular, traumatic, neoplastic, and toxic. Under each he had listed every possible diagnosis for Shirley, which by now had grown to about forty diseases in all. After reviewing the lab tests, he crossed out the incompatible ones. He looked at the remainder of the list. It still had entries under toxins, immune diseases, demyelinating diseases, and diseases related to cancers or infections.

Last night, after initially falling asleep, he had awakened in a sweat. He had again dreamed of being crushed against the ceiling of the 747, with the streets below rushing up at him. Only this time he was paralyzed, unable to move, and awoke just as they slammed into the ground.

His movements must have disturbed Anne, for she had moved over to hold him and rock him gently. But, like the previous three nights, he had waited until she fell back asleep before gently extricating himself; lying in bed fully awake, until finally dozing off around four in the morning.

Staring at the paper, he tried to muster the energy to analyze the remaining possibilities, but the words became just so many letters dancing on the paper. He folded the paper and shoved it into his black bag. He just had to get more sleep tonight.

He went into Shirley's room. She was lying on her back with her eyes closed. Beads of perspiration dampened her forehead and she moaned slightly. There was a slight acid smell that Steve recognized as ketones. He made a mental note to ask about her food intake.

Steve leaned over the bed. "Shirley?"

"Yeah?" Her voice was slurred.

To Jeanne, he remarked, "She's too sedated. Let's hold the Ativan unless we really need it." Turning back to Shirley he asked, "How's the headache?"

"Terrible." Shirley's face began twitching with irregular, tic-like movements that jerked her mouth repeatedly to one side in an irregular grimace. Steve completed his examination and then motioned Edith outside the room.

"Edith, I'm going to start a new medicine to try and control her nightmares. The ones we've tried so far obviously have not worked. Hopefully, we can find something that is more effective. Her tests haven't shown anything yet, but the key tests won't be back for several days." He pursed his lips. "Right now, I am not sure of the cause of her problem, but I expect we'll know soon."

"But you can treat her?" Her question was more of a statement.

Steve shrugged, feeling uncomfortable. "If it's a virus, I'm already giving her the best medicine we have, but it won't help if the problem is from something else. My only other course would be high doses of cortisone. I may do that soon, but I'd like to have a better idea about what's going on first."

"But she's going to be okay?" Edith clutched his shirtsleeve.

Steve shook his head. "I don't know."

CHAPTER 23

Even though he was expecting it, the sharp rap on the door made Dr. Green jump. He looked up from the chart he was reviewing. "Come in."

A blue-suited man entered and, folding up his dark glasses, looked around like an interior decorator appraising a house. He walked over to Green and stuck out his hand.

"Rhodes. Secret Service. We met yesterday. He'll be here in just a minute." Rhodes moved about, re-familiarizing himself with the room. It was a typical physician's office, dominated on one side by a coffee-stained wooden desk piled with medical journals, and on the other by dark wooden bookcases laden with heavy texts and more piles of journals. A wood and vinyl examination table covered by thin white paper stood against a wall with a blood pressure cuff mounted above. Dr. Green watched Rhodes make his systematic scrutiny of the office for the second time in two days.

Thomas Green was used to the routine. A sturdy black man with salt and pepper hair and a trim, nearly white beard, he had been President Dixon's personal physician for the three years of his presidency. Green and Dixon had met in undergraduate chemistry at the College of William and Mary where Dixon had registered pre-med to follow in his grandfather's footsteps. The class had been difficult for the gregarious Dixon, but with Green tutoring him, Dixon had passed and the two had formed an unlikely, but lasting friendship. Dixon later switched to political science and then finished a Masters in economics before he entered politics. Once he got to Washington, it was only natural for Green, now a physician and on the faculty at Bethesda, to take over his care.

Rhodes stared out the windows for several minutes before whispering into his hand. After a moment he announced, "He's coming down the hall now." Moments later, Robert Dixon walked in.

"Hello, Tom." President Dixon's personality filled the room as it had even back in college. Dixon shook his old friend's hand warmly, but Dr. Green saw an uncharacteristic edge in Dixon's tired expression. Rhodes retreated following a final look around and closed the door. Dixon was dressed in a navy suit, but in a departure from the standard white shirt and tie, he wore a golf shirt underneath, a subdued dusky orange. His straight dark hair had a distinctive gray splash on his right temple. "So, Tom," he said, "Have you been following the news?"

"Hong Kong?"

"Yeah."

"Terrible—"

"The worst sort, the bastards."

The outburst surprised Green. They never talked politics, particularly during his annual physicals. He pointed for Dixon to sit on the exam table. "What are we going to do about it?"

Dixon slid onto the table and took off his jacket. "Crap, that's what. Nothing."

Green cleared his throat. "Well, let's talk about something good. Your tests are back."

Dixon brightened. "OK, what've you got?"

Dr. Green pursed his lips as he scanned the paper. "Well, they're good. Normal. Your cholesterol and triglycerides are back to normal, even your glucose."

The President's face relaxed for the first time since he had come in. "How about that?" He did not look in the least surprised.

"Robert," Dr. Green continued looking at the chart, "You've dropped almost thirty pounds since the last visit. How did you do that? I thought any diet or exercise changes were reported in the Post."

"Thirty? I didn't think I'd lost that much. Been feeling great, though." Dixon's lips lifted in a faint smile. "I stopped the Prilosec you put me on. I didn't need it anymore. Never felt better."

Dr. Green cocked his head. "So what's your secret? I'd like to pass it on."

Dixon leaned over and whispered conspiratorially, "I'm a first termer, remember old chap?"

Green's eyebrows shot up. "Of course, I should have realized."

Dixon winked and flashed a grin, a semblance of the old Dixon Green knew, the Dixon from college, full of mischief and passion. "Gotta look good for the cameras."

CHAPTER 24

"How do you spend your free time?" People Magazine reporter Sherry Fontaine asked. She sat in a sumptuous suede leather chair in Vicktor Morloch's office, high above the streets of Philadelphia, enjoying a spectacular view of the Delaware River. She was in the midst of a daylong interview with the CEO of Trident Pharmaceuticals, which included tailing him at work and then following along as he went out on the town that evening.

Marcus Hinojosa, her photographer, snapped off several pictures while Morloch sat at his desk, answering her questions.

"I play competitive tennis and polo," Morloch said, pushing back his chair and standing up. "But you probably already know that."

"No, tell me." She played innocent, hoping for some new information not printed in any of his previous interviews she had read.

He walked over to inspect several pictures on the wall. One showed him astride a tall roan horse. "I played polo as soon as my dad would let me ride by myself."

Morloch smiled and, on cue, Hinojosa snapped off a few more candids. "I wish I could spend more time playing, but," he spread his hands, "I love my job here at Trident. My apartment is on the penthouse floor here, so I'm never far from my work." Sherry knew he was reciting. They were crafted phrases, but for some reason, he could pull it off. His lean, sinuous movements actually resembled the horses he rode.

Vicktor Morloch was very rich and very eligible, and People Magazine had assigned her to interview him for their World's Richest Bachelors feature. Initially, she had wished her editor had assigned her to one of the younger, hunkier men, but while researching this fifty-something captain of industry, her opinion evolved. He was a legendary ladies' man and after meeting him in person, she felt drawn in by his monied allure.

"I understand you had some controversy at a championship polo match." Morloch had allegedly swung his mallet at the hind leg of the rival team's horse during a sprint for the ball. The impact broke the horse's leg and it fell, injuring its rider. Morloch's team won the match after a bitter dispute over the incident.

Morloch turned back with the faintest irritation in his voice. "An accident, as it was finally adjudicated. I was trying for the ball and hit Sloan Thompson's horse by mistake. It's all in the record."

"They had to put the horse down," Fontaine probed.

"Of course." He shrugged indifferently, "It was unfortunate all the way around, but it's part of the danger and risk that I love about the game."

"But now that your drug's such a phenomenal success," she asked, "why don't you take more time for your polo?"

Morloch's answer was smooth and rehearsed. "Sir Winston Churchill said, 'The price of greatness is responsibility' and I take the responsibility for our shareholders and patients very seriously."

"But then, how do you find time for your women?" People's readership was sixty-eight percent women and this was an important topic.

"Ahh, but women are a priority." He flashed a quick, boyish smile. "And there is always time for a priority. Women are truly a gift from heaven and should be treated as such."

She knew that he had dated many women, including some celebrities, but none of the ones she had contacted would say a bad word about him. His reputation for treating women very well was apparently true—or he had blackmailed every one of them. Fontaine smiled at that last thought, although it had just popped into her head. But, with his kind of money, anything was possible. Actually, surrounded by the luxury of his office and knowing how much money he made, Fontaine found herself understanding the seductive power of great wealth. She shivered.

Hinojosa aimed his camera at a plaque on Morloch's desk and shot a quick series of exposures. Fontaine glanced over and saw that it was a quote: *All great things must first wear horrifying and monstrous masks, in order to inscribe themselves on the hearts of humanity* – F. Nietzsche. She mentally shrugged, not sure of its meaning, but made a note to ask back at the office.

"With the millions of women who can't live without your drug," Fontaine continued, "I'd say it is a gift from heaven."

Morloch nodded graciously. "That's why we call it Eden."

CHAPTER 25

The intercom buzzed in Secretary Resnick's office. "The Vice-President's here to see you."

"Show him in, please." Linda took off her reading glasses and slipped her Rolaids back into her lap drawer.

"Linda," John Sullivan greeted her as he walked in. "Thanks for seeing me on such short notice. I know how busy you must be."

She smiled, coming around her desk to shake his hand, "Not at all, Mr. Vice-President. Have a seat." She motioned to the small conference table. "Something to drink?"

"No, thank you," he said, sitting down. Linda brought her glass of water to the table and joined him.

The Vice-President cleared his throat. "I won't keep you long, but you didn't have a chance to comment on yesterday's DEFCON decision. I wanted to hear your thoughts about it."

She looked at Sullivan's strong features, just starting to lose their edge with his sixty-odd years. His graying temples gave him the appearance of a statesman and he had the credentials to back that up, having served as ambassador to Sweden and Japan, following his eighteen years in the House.

"These things never occur in isolation, as you know," she began. "Especially strategic moves like this. The NATO members are angry with us; more so, it seems, than with Beijing." Fatigue crept into her voice. "I've been telling everyone that it's purely a defensive move—with a mixed response."

"Best crystal ball opinion?"

"We play word games for awhile and then it thaws. That's the rational outcome. For the irrational, you'd better call Vegas."

"But you have to plan for the irrational. Especially since the massacre was irrational."

"Was it?" Linda rejoined. "From our perspective, it was murder at its government- sponsored worst; but to the Chinese, it might be a logical reaction to a threatening populist movement. Plus, my analysts think that it's an internal show of strength for the hard liners."

Sullivan spoke carefully. "What I know about the evolving Chinese government mentality is more rather than less sensitivity to Chinese popular opinion."

"Yes. That's why this massacre was such a surprise, but there's probably a thread of reasoning underneath the surface that makes sense to China's rulers that isn't apparent to us."

"What George said about a divided government bothers me. It's dangerous. What do we know about this new Premier Chow. He's a little . . . umm . . . green. Your call?"

"That's our take. A populist who appeals to the public."

"A compromise candidate?" Sullivan asked.

"At least. I was very surprised when they picked him. He might be a straw man."

"Isn't that a little harsh? In theory, there are always puppet masters behind the scenes, but since Deng, there has been no faction strong enough to put up someone simply as their order-taker."

"Chow's weak, John. He doesn't look, from what we know, like he can stand up to the entrenched powers. My China desk thinks his base is too narrow and doesn't include the military. His populism may actually be a liability."

Sullivan nodded. "I've heard that, too."

"We've analyzed every identified faction in the Government, but the situation is fluid enough that we don't know who is really in charge and with whom we should negotiate. Now, China's charting new political territory, which must make them nervous. That said, my estimates agree with George's, that General Yao is behind much of the recent mischief."

"And your conclusion about the DEFCON move?"

Linda sighed. "I still have reservations and the jump to level three was more than we needed. It serves the hardliner's agenda and polarizes the government and people against us."

"Official China response?" Sullivan asked. "Since it was directed at them."

"Nothing yet. It usually takes them a day to respond. There was a surprising lack of initial posturing from Ambassador Gung, almost to the point of his expecting it. Perhaps that was part of the hard liners' plans."

Sullivan looked at the Secretary of State for a long moment before standing up. "Thank you, Linda, for helping me understand these issues. I'll get out of your hair and let you get on with your day."

"John?"

"Yes?"

"Taiwan. What's your take on the President's intentions?"

Sullivan thought for a moment. "It is the stated policy of the U.S. Government to support Taiwan, without recognizing it as an independent nation, but of course, you know that. I don't think that has changed. Why?"

"I wonder if the President is considering recognizing it."

"Hmm." Sullivan pursed his lips. "I expect not."

CHAPTER 26

"Steve, can you make me some coffee?" Anne called from her desk in their home office.

"Sure, honey." Steve and Johnnie were huddled over a paper airplane they were constructing together. Johnnie drew 'USAF' on each wing with a dark blue marker pen. "You've got it just about perfect, Sport," Steve said, getting up from the kitchen floor where they had spread out their project.

"Can I have some too?" Johnnie asked. "Please, please, please?"

"Sure, Son." Within a few minutes, the fragrant smell of hot decaf coffee filled the kitchen. Lining up three cups, Steve poured the dark brown liquid into each, only spilling a little. He had never mastered the knack of dripless pouring. Anne, of course, was a pro.

"Sugar." Johnnie called out without looking up, intent on his airplane decorations. The plane actually flew pretty well and after Steve had shown him some paperclip weighting techniques, it flew even farther.

Steve spooned a generous helping of sugar into Johnnie and Anne's cups. Picking up the gallon jug of milk, he poured enough in his and Anne's cup to color the coffee a light brown and started to add milk to Johnnie's, remembering too late that his son didn't like creamer. Oh, well, Steve thought looking at the color; it was only slightly lightened. He slid it in front of his son. Taking a testing sip from his wife's mug, he carefully walked back to the study.

"Hi, Stevie," Anne flipped her black hair behind her shoulders and smiled at him. "Thanks for cleaning up and letting me work."

"You're welcome, Baby." Steve bent over and kissed the top of her head.

"You didn't eat anything at supper." Her eyes looked concerned.

"I nibbled while I put the dinner together," Steve lied. "You didn't see everything."

"Yeah, sure," Anne snorted. "Ever since you got back, you haven't eaten or slept properly. Let's get you to bed early tonight."

"Hanky-panky?" Steve's hand slipped down her tee shirt, cupping her right breast. She didn't have a bra on and her nipple stiffened under his touch.

She held his hand tightly to her chest. "Sure, Studly Do-Right, but afterwards, you have to get some sleep."

"Remember, I'm on call tonight."

Anne made a face. "I'll shut off that lousy beeper."

Kerry, their mostly golden retriever, rescued years ago from the pound, pushed his head between them and whined for attention. Steve's hand reluctantly left Anne's breast. He knelt to rub Kerry on his favorite spot behind his ears and Kerry, attention hound that he was, looked at him with a most satisfied expression. Steve leaned over for a lick, which Kerry readily supplied. It was therapeutic. Maybe he would sleep tonight.

"Daddee!" Johnnie's shouted complaint filtered in from the kitchen.

Steve stood up. "Right back."

Johnnie yelled again just as Steve was entering the kitchen, slightly irritated by Johnnie's demanding tone. "Yes, what is it?"

"Daddy," Johnnie complained. "You got milk in my coffee."

"Just a little bit. It tastes the same."

"No, it doesn't; it's spoiled."

"Just taste it," Steve requested, with a little more irritation than he intended.

Johnnie made an exasperated face. "Daddy, no."

"Why?" Steve knew it was a lost cause and turned towards the cabinet to get a fresh cup. Once Johnnie made up his mind, the argument was not only useless; it was over before it started.

Johnnie's explanation was actually logical for a change. "Even a tiny bit spoils the whole thing." Johnnie held the cup up to his dad. "Please?"

Steve poured a fresh cup and slid it in front of Johnnie with the sugar and a spoon. "I'm way ahead of you."

"Not a chance, Daddy," Johnnie replied, in one of his new stock phrases brought home from school. "You're way behind the eight ball."

That brought a rueful smile as a mental image of Shirley came to mind. Indeed he was.

CHAPTER 27

The phone rang somewhere on Dr. Paul Tobias' desk. Covered as it was with papers and photocopied articles, it took four rings for him to locate it and another two to retrieve it without wrecking his improvised filing system. "Tobias."

"Paul, it's Ari. How's the weather there in Philly?"

"Hey, Ari." Paul's face broke into a smile. "Overcast and cold. How are you?" Tobias was Trident Pharmaceutical's Chief Medical Officer and he had been collating material for an article he was writing.

"Puzzled, that's what. I have a strange case and I wondered if you had some insight for me."

Paul propped the phone against his shoulder while trying to remember upon which pile the papers still in his hand were supposed to go. "I'll try, he replied."

"It's about a really nice lady that I've known for several years, a mom with two kids in school. She has been exceptionally healthy, but recently, she came down with an aggressive encephalitis that I can't figure out. I've done the full court work-up, but—nothing."

"How serious?"

"Very. I don't think she's going to make it."

"That's too bad, Ari."

"That's why I called. She was on Eden for weight loss. She's been on it for almost two years, and I was wondering if you guys have had any reports similar to hers. I know it's a long shot."

"What's it like?" Paul asked, dropping the articles askew on the desk.

As his old medical school friend described the patient's medical history and clinical features, Paul's face lost its color.

"So, Paul what do you think?"

"Well, we don't have any cases of anything like this linked to Eden. It would be a completely isolated case."

Ari sighed. "I didn't think so, but I thought since you were working there at Trident, I figured I'd ask anyway."

Minutes later Tobias had run up two flights of stairs and into Oscar Perera's office.

"Hi, Paul," Oscar said, from behind his dark wood desk. Perera was Trident Pharmaceutical's Chief Safety Officer and like Paul, was an endocrinologist. The two of them had worked closely together on Eden's development since Trident's early days.

With an ominous look, Paul closed the door and walked over to the desk. "Oscar," he said, "have you gotten any reports of encephalitis?"

As the safety officer, Oscar Perera collected and evaluated all reports and queries from physicians and patients regarding Trident's only marketed drug, Eden. He pursed his lips and thought a moment. "No, I haven't. Of course, you would be one of the first to know."

"I'm glad to hear that." Visibly relieved, Paul sat down in a tall-backed armchair.

Perera leaned back in his chair. "Why do you ask?"

"I got a call from an old medical school buddy who has a female patient with symptoms identical to what we've been watching for. His patient had delusions and myoclonus with no apparent cause that he can find." He paused dramatically. "She was on Eden."

Perera shrugged. "Well, if it were one of ours, it would be a chorus of one. It's been on the market for over two years; I hardly think we'd be just starting to hear about it now."

Paul took a deep breath, and let it out slowly. "I guess you're right. We are pretty well out of the danger zone, aren't we?"

"I think we are. It's all going according to our predictions. Your worry is misplaced, Paul. I'm sure your friend's patient must have something else."

"Okay, good." He stood up to leave.

"Oh, Paul," Perera said, stopping his colleague. "Did you give your friend any idea that we might be responsible?"

Paul shook his head emphatically. "Are you nuts?"

"Good. By the way, who is he?"

"Ari Brown. Lucky guy, living the California life in San Fran."

"Sounds like you two stay in touch."

"Not much, really," Paul replied. "Mostly on the holidays."

CHAPTER 28

Steve sat in the Intensive Care Unit nursing a dour mood and a Styrofoam cup of bitter coffee, heavily doused with dry creamer. He dictated his admission note on Mrs. Snyder and then sat back sipping his coffee. It was just after six in the morning and he had been in the ER since three, stabilizing her fresh stroke. True to his prediction earlier in the evening, his beeper had gone off, and with Anne still grumbling, he had kissed her and driven in to the hospital. Without time to drive back home, he would have to catch a shower and shave in the on-call room and wear ill-fitting hospital scrubs the rest of the day.

Sliding Mrs. Snyder's CT scan off the counter, he walked over to the X-ray rack to file it. As he pushed the heavy jackets back to make room, Shirley's MRI caught his eye. He glanced over at her room, and realized that Nancy Snyder had been put in the room next to Shirley's.

Steve compulsively pulled Shirley's large X-ray jacket from the file rack and slid the films out. He positioned the first sheet on the X-ray view box and snapped on the light. He sat back down and propped his feet on the counter and stared at the images trying to remember where and when he had first seen the pattern.

Since he reviewed MRI films daily, isolating that one episode would be difficult. Maybe if he associated the event with other things that were going on at the same time, he might be able to get a fix on it. Memory worked best like that, by associations and relationships, not in isolation. While it was cliché to ask what someone was doing when John F.

Kennedy was assassinated, few could recall what they were doing the day before. Without the paired event or a distinct emotion, events in isolation simply did not stick.

He let his mind drift back to try and remember what he had been doing before or near to the time of the MRI. That didn't work; so he changed tactics and thought about his emotional state at the time. His mind floated back and then settled on something. Anticipation. What for? Then he remembered—a trip. He had been looking forward to a trip somewhere.

Then it hit him. He and Anne had been about to leave for India on vacation. Years before, they had honeymooned in India and had vowed to return. They had seen the Taj Majhal, tracked free-roaming tigers in Ranthambhore National Park, and chased monkeys in Jaipur. Then, during Johnnie's last Spring Break, they went back this time taking their son. With that establishing a time reference, he replayed the days just before leaving. Within a few moments, he had it. He had been with Dr. Goldstein.

Jeanne, Shirley's nurse walked up and pointed at the MRI scan. "Can you show me what's going on up there?"

"Sure." Steve stood up pleased that he had figured out the mystery doctor's identity. If only Dr. Goldstein could remember the patient.

Jeanne wrinkled her nose at the series of twenty miniature pictures laid out in sequence on the sheet of X-ray film. Jeanne and Shirley were close in age. Steve knew such patients were more emotionally draining for their nurses, especially since it was possible Shirley would not recover.

Like any long-term unit patient, the nurses had adopted Shirley, bringing her treats and gifts, including a stuffed otter that Shirley kept tucked under her arm. Jeanne's interest, therefore, was not idle.

Pointing to the scan, she asked, "Okay, what's this white stuff? It doesn't look normal."

"That's right. It's probably inflammation or edema. Look." He pointed to a spot on the scan. "This is the nose. The white tracks start in the brain just above the nose, like something got into her brain through the nose and spread from there."

"Like sniffing glue?"

"That's right, but it doesn't have the right pattern for glue."

"Well, what else could it be?"

"Maybe a pesticide or a solvent, but it's not right for them either—I can't figure what."

"Well," Jeanne remarked, crossing her arms, "Shirley was on Eden. It's sprayed into the nose."

"Right," Steve agreed. "But there have been no reported cases. So, that's not likely it."

Jeanne shrugged, unconvinced. "How can you be so sure? I mean, it goes up her nose every day."

Steve rolled the thought over in his mind. *Eden?* Patients administered Eden by a nasal spray so it would be absorbed across the nasal membranes. Theoretically, Steve knew, it could work its way into the brain through the olfactory nerves.

"You have a good point, but Captain Palmer wasn't on it, so it couldn't be Eden. I need to find something common to both."

"Who's Captain Palmer?"

Steve yawned. "Oh, right. He was the captain who was flying the airplane I was on."

"He's got this too?"

"Yeah."

Jeanne looked disappointed. "Well, then it couldn't be Eden."

"I just can't see how. But it was a good thought."

"Funny we should be talking about Eden. Just yesterday I caught my daughter—Whoops, she's getting up. I better go check on her." She hustled into Shirley's room, closing the door behind her.

Steve stared at the scan, thinking about what Jeanne had said about Eden. Was that the key to Shirley's illness? If so, then how? Jeanne's suggestion had caught him off guard. In fact, it was an excellent suggestion, but he had been too tired to spot it. Still, he had combed through Captain Palmer's records and there was no mention of the drug Eden. He clearly remembered when he was in the ER, Marty Walker telling him that the Captain had not been on any meds.

He sipped his lukewarm coffee and looked at Shirley through the sliding glass wall. Edith awoke with a start and climbed out of the reclining chair she had been sleeping in. Shirley began her myoclonic twitches, and was screaming with fright, although Steve could barely hear her through the closed glass doors. This was a bad spell. Edith, still in her nightgown, held Shirley's hand, patting and stroking it, trying to calm her daughter, while Jeanne mopped her forehead with a face cloth.

A change in Shirley's jerking caught Steve's attention. Her twitches had turned rhythmic and violent—a convulsion!

As he raced into the room, he heard Jeanne yell for help. A flood of nurses poured in behind him, one pulling the crash cart into the room. A male nurse ushered a terrified-looking Edith out of the room.

Shirley's body bucked and jerked with powerful muscular convulsions that prevented her from breathing. The heart monitor skewed wildly with each movement, obscuring the cardiac activity. Jeanne struggled vainly to hold down Shirley's arms.

"Valium, ten milligrams I.V.," Steve barked standing at the bed and taking control of the code.

"I.V. Valium, ten milligram syringe,' the male nurse manning the crash cart repeated. He produced a pre-filled syringe from the crash cart and slapped it into Steve's outstretched hand.

"I.V.'s out. No access!" Jeanne yelled. Steve saw blood oozing from the intravenous site in Shirley's left arm where the catheter had pulled out.

"Why isn't there a central line?" the charge nurse complained to no one in particular.

Two nurses pushed the bed away from the wall so that they could get to Shirley's face and put a plastic airway in her mouth. Oxygen would follow.

Shirley's seizure showed no signs of slowing down. If she did not stop soon, she would get extensive brain damage from the lack of oxygen. Valium had to be given intravenously and there was no time to start an I.V.

"I'll inject it," Steve growled. "Let's get going. Time since seizure started?"

"One minute forty seconds," responded the chart nurse.

Steve capped the Valium and slid the syringe into his shirt pocket. "Tourniquet, please." He held out his hand and a flat rubber strap appeared in it.

He sat on the bed and tightly wrapped the tourniquet around Shirley's right arm. He felt for a vein in the slender white shallow of the elbow region and found nothing except for a delicate blue streak, under the skin. It was a small, pitiful excuse for a vein, but it would have to do.

"Alcohol, please." Another nurse, anticipating his request, swiped an alcohol pad over Shirley's arm.

"Countdown by fifteen second intervals to four minutes since she started," Steve instructed. Shirley's lips and fingertips were turning blue, a sign of low oxygen.

"One minute and thirty seconds remaining."

"Prepare to intubate her at my order," Steve directed. The senior anesthesia resident slid into place at the head of the bed with his tackle box of equipment and began setting up.

Steve pulled the Valium out of his pocket and yanked the rubber cap off with his teeth.

"Okay," he muttered, "hold her still."

Jeanne held Shirley's arm as tightly as possible but still the arm danced around. He held the needle over the vein, trying to move in concert with her writhing, and plunged it through her skin. Shirley's arm unexpectedly twisted, dislodging the needle.

"One minute and thirty seconds."

A nurse had connected a pulse oximeter to Shirley's other hand. The red LED readout flashed a warning and beeped its alarm. "Pulse ox, sixty-two," the nurse reported. Normal was one hundred. Shirley was fast running out of oxygen.

Steve held his breath and with the needle's point, followed the vein still dancing before his eyes. With a smooth movement, he expertly slid the needle in. A telltale flashback of blood in the syringe hub told him he was in.

Jeanne snapped off the tourniquet, and he began pushing the Valium. Shirley bucked, but Steve, gingerly holding the syringe, moved with her, keeping the needle in place. While injecting ten milligrams of Valium should take at least a minute, Steve did not have that long; he pushed it in faster than recommended. "Two milligrams in," he called out.

"One minute."

"Pulse ox, fifty-five."

By now, the crowded room had become stuffy and sweat dripped off Steve as he concentrated on holding the needle in place. Shirley continued jerking as Steve pushed more Valium in. "Six milligrams," he reported.

"Six milligrams at oh-five-sixteen," the chart nurse chanted in response. Shirley made a vigorous jerk. "Easy now," Steve pushed in another half milligram and saw the telltale bulge of extravasated medicine under the skin. The needle had slipped out of the vein after the last jerk. *Damn.* "Lost the vein."

"Total six milligrams in?" The chart nurse queried.

"Yes. Get a line in her other arm." He jabbed the exposed Valium needle into the mattress in frustration and watched the still convulsing Shirley. Fearing the Valium on board was insufficient to stop her seizures, he called for the second line drug.

"Ativan, please." Ativan given intramuscularly would control seizures, but it worked slower than the intravenous Valium. He swabbed alcohol on her thigh for the injection.

"Thirty seconds."

"Pulse ox forty-eight."

"Intubate, please," Steve ordered and watched as the resident fitted the clear plastic tube smeared with KY jelly into Shirley's left nostril.

"Ativan, two milligram syringe," the male nurse reported, handing Steve the syringe. Steve pulled the cap off with his teeth and bent over Shirley's thigh to inject it.

She stopped jerking.

Everyone held their breath and watched. She jerked once again and then stopped. Shuddering, Shirley took a deep breath.

Steve watched her closely as her breathing resumed, deep and rapid.

"Pulse ox, seventy eight."

The color began returning to Shirley's face and fingers.

"Do you still want me to intubate?" the resident asked Steve, who was still holding the glass Ativan syringe. The resident had stopped inserting the tube when she started breathing on her own.

"Wait a minute."

"Left peripheral I.V. in." The nurse working on the other arm announced as she plugged the tube from the old intravenous bag into the hub of the catheter.

"Hang seven hundred milligrams of Cerebryx to run in over ten minutes," Steve ordered. "And monitor her blood pressure as it's going in."

He capped the Ativan needle and leaned over to check Shirley's pupils. They both constricted to light as he opened and closed her lids. *Good.*

He pinched her right thumbnail and the arm pulled away. He looked up at the resident. "Don't intubate now, but stay close." Steve watched the EKG monitor and her vital signs until he was satisfied.

"Thanks, everybody." He stood up to leave.

Turning, he saw Edith's tear-streaked face pressed against the glass window.

CHAPTER 29

The stairs seemed longer and steeper than normal to Dixon as he walked up to the residential floor of the White House. His head ached and his arms and legs felt unusually heavy. It was almost like being back on the campaign trail. He was thankful he had cancelled tonight's dinner with the Daughters of the American Revolution, excusing himself because of the Chinese massacre. There was nothing, really, for him to do, but his heart wasn't into the political chitchat, not while the China thing hung over him.

He found Elise in the bedroom curled up in an overstuffed chair reading a book. He smiled. It was the most relaxing thing he had seen in a day filled with meetings, briefings, and reports delivered by overly attentive bureaucrats and staffers. She looked soft and feminine, dressed in a beige cashmere turtleneck sweater and taupe woolen skirt, colors that set off her short ginger hair. In contrast to so many presidents and their wives who had slept in separate beds, Dixon and Elise refused to part. They were still young in their mid-fifties and their passion for each other was still strong—a frequent topic of the tabloids. Elsie did keep the First Lady's bedroom for her clothes, as the closet in the master suite was too small for both of their wardrobes.

"What are you reading?" he asked.

Elise looked up, smiling. "Something mindless."

Dixon fell into the chair next to hers. Side by side, the chairs faced opposite directions so he and Elise could talk to each other while they relaxed. Elise slid her slender hand over to hold his wrist as it lay on the cushioned arm. "Long day?"

She unerringly sensed his moods, he mused, although today he had probably telegraphed it to the entire White House.

"Yeah." He slid deeper into the overstuffed chair to rest his head.

"China?"

"Yeah."

"Feel like talking about it?" Her voice was gentle, supporting. He found that he did want to talk to her about his mounting anger and frustration. While he eagerly anticipated the Taiwan President's visit—whatever his name—he knew the visit alone wouldn't really satisfy his desire to punish the bastards ruling China. His profound frustration would remain.

"Guess so." As he answered, the soft supper-bell chime came from the next room.

"Why don't we talk over dinner?"

"Sure. Know what's on tonight?"

"I ordered your favorite. Red bell pepper soup. Come on."

Inside the private dining room and comfortably seated at the dinner table, Dixon picked up his spoon as he eyed the hot soup with a tendril of steam curling up. Suddenly, he realized he wanted to say grace. "Let's pray," he said.

Elise glanced at him curiously, but bowed her head. Dixon prayed silently, sensing how much the weight of his job had pushed him closer to God. "Amen," he said and dipped his spoon into the soup.

"It's good." Elise pronounced.

Dixon cocked his head as he tasted. "Not really much flavor."

CHAPTER 30

"Paul came by my office yesterday and asked if we had had any human encephalitis cases," Oscar Perera reported. Trident's Chief Safety officer sat in a heavy leather chair in front of Victor Morloch's massive desk. "He got a call from a doctor friend of his, a Dr. Ari Brown, who has a case that sounds like ours. Apparently Brown had suspicions linking Eden with his patient and called Paul directly. Paul seemed pretty bothered by it."

Morloch frowned at the news. Paul Tobias, a longtime member of Morloch's inner circle, had been kept in the dark about the human encephalitis cases already reported to Perera over the last year—a mandate to Perera from Morloch. "What do you think?"

Perera considered a long moment. "I think he's getting cold feet. His daughter, you know."

Morloch had already decided that, but needed to feel Perera out since Paul was his colleague. "I agree," he said slowly. "What would you do?"

Perera took a long moment to reply. Morloch could guess what was running through his Safety Officer's head. After all, he and Paul had worked very closely together to make Eden possible, and true to Morloch's promise, they had been hugely rewarded for their efforts as well as their discretion. It would be hard on Perera, Morloch knew, but there could only be one answer.

"Keep an eye on Paul."

"You sure?"

Perera nodded, looking unhappy.

"Tell me about Dr. Brown."

"Neurology faculty at UCSF."

"And the particulars?"

Perera slid a CD across the desk to Morloch. "Right here."

Morloch rested his elbows on the desk, tenting his fingers. "Okay. Thanks, Oscar."

Perera nodded and walked out, closing the door behind him.

Morloch pushed his chair back and swung around to face the Delaware River, easily seen from their high-rise office building. This Dr. Brown was the latest doctor questioning a connection between their drug and a patient with encephalitis—the second in the last thirty days. It was all still containable—but for how long? The FDA had Trident's new weight loss medicine, Paradise—without Eden's encephalitis risk—under review, but it could still take months before they approved it for marketing. Only then could they replace Eden and stop more deaths caused by Eden.

Only Paul and Oscar knew of the encephalitis risk and fortunately Perera had proven his discretion. Tobias still might be salvaged, but that remained to be seen. Morloch had Mallis and Associates monitor virtually everybody in the company to prevent loss of sensitive materials and this included Paul and Oscar. He would convey his new concern about Paul to Kirk Mallis and he needed Mallis's risk assessment of Dr. Brown. Reaching back to his desk, he picked up his cell phone and punched in a number he had by now memorized. It rang twice before it was answered. The scrambler clicks preceded the muscular voice. "Mallis."

"Kirk? Morloch. I have another project for you."

CHAPTER 31

D r. Harold Goldstein walked into the ICU and sat down in the chair next to Steve. "Hi," he said. "Welcome back." Dr. Goldstein was a slight man who always wore his Yarmulke. He had on a brown tweed jacket with leather elbow patches over a white shirt and his signature floral bow tie. A neurologist in solo practice, he shared weekend call with Steve and Steve's partner, making each of their lives a little saner.

"Hi, Harry. Thanks for coming."

"Sure, no problem." Peering at Steve over his horn-rimmed glasses, he smiled. "I see you've become famous. And to think I knew you when."

"That and two bills get me a Starbucks."

"Indeed. I can't imagine being famous. I treasure my privacy. Must have been terrifying, though."

"Harry," Steve asked, "can you look at a scan with me? It's on a young woman with myoclonus and severe delusions. I could use your help."

"Of course. I'll try."

Steve put up Shirley's MRI scans and stood back. Dr. Goldstein bent forward to get a closer look. He carefully looked at every image while Steve chewed the inside of his lip. After evaluating the last image he straightened up with a sad look on his face. "I'd say it looks just like one I had last spring."

The Medical Records Department resided deep in the bowels of Good Samaritan Hospital, stale and musty and filled with row upon row of metal shelves crammed with patient charts. At the counter, Steve turned in his requisition form. As he waited for the attendant to find the chart, he recalled Dr. Goldstein's story of his patient, a young woman named Rhonda Fowler. In the recounting, Dr. Goldstein had become more animated than Steve had ever seen him, almost agitated, the story laced with his professional angst and regret.

Ms. Fowler had been an eighteen-year-old who presented to the emergency room with bizarre delusions of bees or wasps attacking her. Brought in by her boyfriend, she was actively hallucinating with dreadful shrieking and sobbing apparently reliving a longstanding childhood phobia of stinging insects.

Leading up to the emergency room appearance, Dr. Goldstein related that Rhonda had become hypersexual, actively soliciting intercourse from all her male friends and even strangers from the street. After awhile, her headaches had curbed her predatory sexual desires and she later began twitching in her arms, face and trunk. Soon afterwards, the fears of bees and wasps had exploded into delusionary terrors. "And," Dr. Goldstein had concluded, "her MRI was almost identical to this one."

"What happened to her? Steve had asked.

"She died and not a damn thing I did helped."

"Did you ever find out what caused it?"

"No." Frustration, even now, had colored his answer.

"No post?"

Dr. Goldstein had raised his arms in a gesture of defeat. "No. Nothing."

The young medical records assistant plopped a thick manila hospital chart on the counter. "Here it is, Dr. James."

Steve picked it up, seeing the 'deceased' scrawled in thick black magic marker across the front. Sitting down at the Formica table, he opened the chart and started reading. After an hour, he rubbed his eyes and stretched. He now felt as if he knew Rhonda personally and her MRI was as exactly as recalled by Dr. Goldstein. Reading through the notes, he could sense Dr. Goldstein's distress as Rhonda failed to respond to his treatments, which were virtually the same as Steve's own efforts with Shirley. In fact, the chart was eerily like Shirley's in virtually every detail.

Dr. Goldstein even mentioned consulting with colleagues about her clinical course.

Steve now recalled the conversation with him in that dark X-ray room two seasons ago. He had asked Steve to review an unusual MRI on a young woman with a strange illness. Steve had listened carefully and suggested the same list of diagnoses he was now considering for Shirley. He remembered a disappointed colleague thanking him as he pulled the films off the view box. Steve had been of no help.

With a sick feeling in his stomach, Steve read the last days of Rhonda's hospitalization in the steady hand of Dr. Goldstein, and of her death, still screaming in terror of her bees to the last. It was as if he were gazing into a crystal ball showing Shirley's fate, or stepping into the future and reading her chart after her life had played out. And as Rhonda had slipped away, Steve saw the path Shirley was to take, frustrated that there was not a damn thing so far he could do about it. He closed the massive volume at last and left it on the counter to be filed away in the dusty chart mausoleum.

During his chart review, Steve learned something else about Rhonda. She had been on Eden.

CHAPTER 32

"Etta," Steve said walking into his office the next morning, "Does this name mean anything to you?" He handed his nurse an index card stamped with the hospital plate bearing Shirley's name and date of birth.

Etta had been Steve's office nurse for the last six years and knew his patients as well or better than he did. Not uncommonly patients would just drop by to chat with her and bring her a box of Arizona citrus or a pie and it was usually pecan since Etta was not shy about dropping hints. In her early sixties, she had been an office nurse forever, changing doctors as they retired before moving on to the next.

She fixed Steve with her motherly frown. "You look like you've been out all night."

That triggered a yawn. "On call," he lied. The beeper had been quiet last night, but he had spent much of it in front of his computer doing research.

"You'd better take better care of yourself if you expect to see that son of yours grow up." Etta took the card and looked at it for a minute. "Maybe. Let me check."

She walked over to her counter and sat down at the keyboard. A moment later she looked up, "Okay, I thought so. Rosenwell. She was in the Trident 108 protocol. Four years ago."

Steve smacked his fist into his palm. "That's it."

"What are you looking for?"

"Just a long shot," he said, walking into his office. He shut the door behind him.

Inside, he collapsed into his chair to think. He had enrolled her in one of their clinical trials for obesity, which was studying Eden before it had been approved. He had been the first to give Eden to her and she had probably been on it ever since. He had lost track of her at the end of the trial, but she probably had gotten a prescription as soon as it was FDA cleared.

Did that actually mean anything? Eden had been on the market for two years. If there were a time delay from exposure to onset, it would more likely develop in patients who had been in clinical trials, getting the drug several years before everyone else did. Was he, then, responsible for Shirley's illness?

But it still didn't add up. Drug companies were obligated to report any problems with their drug following its FDA approval. If there were a rash of cases, it would have shown up and the news would be out.

Besides, Captain Palmer wasn't on Eden.

CHAPTER 33

Paul Tobias told Ronnie and Samuel their bedtime story, kissed their cheeks as he tucked them in and turned out the lights. Ronnie, younger than Sam by a year, was four and by habit, went to sleep in Sam's bed. Mary, their mother, would later carry him to his room. She rocked in a chair where she had listened to Paul's story, stroking their cat curled up in her lap. He leaned over to kiss her, too. The trauma of their daughter's recent death constantly colored each moment with their two boys—now all the more treasured and precious.

"I'll be in the study."

"Don't be too long."

He kissed the top of her head on the way out. In the study, Paul took the unusual step of closing his door and then dialed Ari Brown. "Listen," he began after the pleasantries, "I wanted to ask you more about your encephalitis case. How's she doing?"

"She's probably going to pass tonight. What do you want to know?"

"I'm really sorry. I just wanted to see if I could help you in any way although I've gotten rusty since I joined industry."

"You mean the dark side?" Brown's tone was only half joking.

Paul forced a laugh even though it was a common term for those who left academic medicine and entered the pharmaceutical business. Before joining Trident, Paul had been a faculty endocrinologist at the University of Florida. "So, tell me what all you did to diagnose her."

Ari described the testing, consultations and Medline research he had done—all to no avail. The thing that stood out in Ari's mind, however, was an unusual MRI scan unlike any he had seen before. He described a pair of bright white streaks or bands that began in the frontal area extending into other brain areas. Paul already knew what it showed even before his friend's depiction.

It was the same pattern he had seen in Trident's lab animals during Eden's testing phase. Paul knew that Ari's patient almost certainly had the brain disease that his company had hoped to avoid. "Why did you call and ask about Eden?"

"Just a long shot. I heard about another very similar case here about four or five months ago and I compared their MRIs. They were almost identical. Since that guy had also been on Eden—I don't know. I was just fishing for something. It really hit the family pretty hard. She's a mom and everything."

"I'm sorry, Ari." Paul said distantly. "I'm sorry for your patient. You did a really complete work-up. I don't think I can offer anything you haven't already done." Before his friend could reply, he hung up.

Paul, sick at heart, slid down in his chair, his hands shaking. What had they done? Up until now it had all been abstract, almost a game of handicapping the chance of a human developing the disease all in exchange for the coveted wealth Morloch had promised. While they had discussed the theoretical risk of a human case, to actually hear about a real one brought home the reality in a way Paul had never anticipated. Although he had steeled himself for some acceptable losses in exchange for the great benefits Eden brought, when confronted by the actuality, he found he had no stomach for it. Sara's death had completely reversed the equation.

He clearly remembered that day when the report of the mouse study had come back from their contract lab showing serious brain abnormalities. He and Oscar Perera had read and re-read the report that indicated almost twelve percent of the animals had developed the abnormality. That finding would kill the drug Morloch had personally recruited them to develop. They confronted the unexpected prospect that their hopes and dreams of making a difference would vanish and all their rich stock options would become worthless. What would he tell Mary, then pregnant with Samuel and living in a ratty apartment? That he had left a promising academic career and joined a company with its only drug a bust?

They had met with Morloch to tell him about the report. He absolutely refused to believe the results. "Repeat them and if they're still positive, find out why. And if you find out why, find a reason to keep moving forward. We're going to make this the miracle drug we know it to be."

Paul remembered that speech as if it were a movie playing in front of him. Seeing the conviction burn in Morloch's eyes gave him hope that this was only a setback and not the end.

"Remember when you first came here?" Morloch had asked. "We were going to change the world. We were going to make an impact on people's lives rarely seen in the last thirty years—remember? Have you forgotten that Eden is nothing short of a miracle? We will, together, keep Eden moving forward."

Morloch's unyielding and indomitable will carried the moment. "I have invested millions in this company and I will not give it up. I picked you both because you were the best in your field and if anybody can find a way for us to keep going it will be because of your skill and ability—or we will have wasted years of our lives chasing a fucking dream. If you are as stubborn and bullheaded as I am, and I think you are, you'll find a way to pull us through this. Are you with me?"

Paul had looked at Oscar. His face showed he had hope again, too.

"Are you with me?" Morloch then fixed both his scientists with his gaze in turn until they nodded. Morloch never mentioned the money, but he didn't have to. Everything they did—everything—was tinged by the allure of the great wealth that was to reward their success. Morloch had just given them back their worth and hope of more riches to come.

At the time when he nodded, Paul never considered where things would go and—as he now knew—how badly he had erred. The money had seriously compromised his judgment—he knew that now especially with a mother's illness and death on his conscience.

He walked back into Sam's room and found his wife asleep in the rocking chair and Ronnie still in Sam's bed, all oblivious to the world. He looked at his family, thinking how fragile life was and how precious. He let his thoughts morbidly turn to the suffering the sick woman's family must be going through, sitting by the bedside waiting for their mother and wife to die knowing there was nothing they could do. Paul found his cheeks wet. Sara's death was so fresh, barely six months behind them. She had been so innocent and full of joy before she got the neuroblastoma. It was all over in four months and his life—their lives—had changed forever.

Paul had to do something. Just what, he was not sure, but he had to stop the poison. He went back into the study to think.

CHAPTER 34

Steve finished his afternoon rounds where he had started them, back in the ICU looking over Shirley's latest lab tests. Jeanne plopped down beside him in a chipper mood. "Three more hours and I'm off for four days."

"Sounds great," Steve said, not looking up.

"So, anything new?" Jeanne asked.

"Not much."

"You didn't like my Eden suggestion?"

Steve shrugged and glanced over at her. "It was a good suggestion. I just can't make it fit if for no other reason than the Captain isn't taking it."

A flash of recollection crossed Jeanne's face. "Oh, that's what I was going to tell you yesterday. I just remembered."

"What?"

"I caught my sixteen year old daughter using a friend's Eden inhaler the other day. Now I know it's safe and all, especially since you tell me it is, but I got into it with her about using someone else's medicine. She got all mad at me and everything and told me she'd been doing it for several months now and that was the only way she could lose weight—"

Steve stared at her. "Maybe that's it!"

Jeannie looked puzzled. "What's it?"

"I'm not sure yet. Excuse me." Steve pulled out his cell phone and looked up Dr. Walker's number.

"Marty," Steve said when Dr. Walker answered, "Was the Captain taking Eden?"

"Eden? No. Why?"

"I've got another case."

Marty exploded. "What?"

"Rhonda Fowler, eighteen years old. Came in six months ago. A colleague took care of her. Same story right down to the MRI. And she died." Steve finished with a heavy, futile feeling, in his chest.

"Well, shit. This thing's just popping up everywhere. Why Eden?"

"Well, they both took Eden."

"And?"

"It's administered through the nose."

"That's it?"

"That's the only one I can think of."

"Tenuous."

Steve began to pace in the corridor. "Marty, we did clinical studies on Eden for years. Shirley was on one of our studies and could have been on it for up to four years. Perhaps that might have something to do with this disease."

"Well, if there's a long latency period . . ." Marty mused, "but how does that explain the Captain?"

"Something a nurse just said. Maybe he was taking someone else's prescription, you know, so the airline couldn't find out about it and all."

"That's a thought," Marty admitted.

"Airline pilots aren't allowed to take prescription medications without prior authorization. I doubt United would allow its pilots to take Eden."

"So, maybe he got it on the sly."

"That'd make the case stronger."

"But, Steve," Marty logically pointed out, "It's the biggest selling prescription medicine in the world. This is likely just a statistical probability, you know, two young females. It's the demographic most likely to take it."

Steve sighed, "You're right, of course. I can think of a million objections, but I'm at a diagnostic impasse. If our Captain didn't take Eden, then, obviously, that's not it."

"Well, I'll check with his wife and see what she says."

Steve's thoughts returned to the days when he and his partner, Julia Weisgaard, first started working with Eden, then known as TP-1023. Trident Pharmaceuticals had been an infant start-up company, but its scientists were confident they had a blockbuster weight-reducing drug on their hands. It incorporated a novel mechanism that proved amazingly effective in causing genetically obese mice and rats to achieve a normal body weight without caloric restriction or special diets.

He had become enamored with the concept of a hormone acting in the brain that taught the body to shed weight. Although the initial research patients had to inject the drug like an insulin shot, it worked amazingly well. Patients who weighed up to three hundred fifty pounds slimmed down to a lean figure without any detectable risk to their health. In fact, their blood pressure and cholesterol frequently normalized even without medication.

And as long as they took TP-1023, the weight stayed off. They also felt better, healthier and happier than they ever had in their lives. Word got out about this miraculous drug, swamping Trident with publicity. Its Chairman, Vicktor Morloch, became a media darling, appearing on the morning television talk shows and on countless covers of news and lifestyle magazines.

Interest soared for the new miracle drug still in clinical testing. With each succeeding research trial, patients flooded their office desperate to get into the study. After an attempted break in, Steve and Julia had to hire a security guard to patrol the office at night. The public's craving for a truly effortless weight loss drug was far deeper than Steve ever imagined.

As the trial results began coming in, Trident's confidence proved justified. The drug, now formulated as a nasal spray and branded 'Eden,' was approved by the FDA in a remarkably short time under its fast track status program.

Initial demand proved insatiable. At first, supply was limited, making the street price skyrocket. Patients sold the inhalers on eBay at ten times the pharmacy price. Someone even hijacked a truck carrying Eden, fatally shooting the driver. In a slick public relations move, Vicktor Morloch paid a million dollars to the driver's widow and posted a million dollar reward for the arrest and conviction of the killer. It was never claimed.

Supply eventually caught up with demand and Eden broke all previous records for a drug launch, higher even than Viagra and Prozac. Within a year it had surpassed sales for any drug in history.

Even with—or despite—all the hype, Eden fully lived up to its reputation as a miracle drug. Massively obese people gradually lost their weight and looked perfectly normal. Eden's early ads had an endless array of slender people standing in their old pants and recounting their amazing size improvements and life changes. The cosmetic surgery crowd, of course, had immediately picked it up. Many others, only slightly overweight, and those just paranoid about their weight also used it. In a real sense, fat had been conquered by the daily use of the nasal spray.

The medical journals quickly filled with the health benefits of reducing obesity with Eden. Attendant ills related to increased weight all showed improvements or disappeared entirely. Scientific articles quantified reduction in diabetes, cholesterol, and hypertension in patients slimmed down on Eden. Stroke and heart attack rates had dropped and colon cancer showed its first ever decline, all ascribed to Eden. Trident had quickly begun testing Eden for these other health benefits and the FDA, based on those trial results, had subsequently approved several new indications. It all served to drive more even sales. Steve still had several trials involving Eden and its apparent successor—a new drug called Paradise—ongoing at his office.

After all his experience, Steve could not fathom how Eden could cause a major fault in the brain. Was that a blind spot that explained why it had taken him so long to implicate Eden? He had seen so much good from it and he knew it so intimately, yet, one of his early patients was dying, possibly from the Eden he had originally given her.

CHAPTER 35

Closing his black bag after another long day of office patients, Steve readied himself to go home. His cell phone rang and he slipped it out of his back pocket. "Dr. James."

Dr. Walker's voice greeted him. "Steve, are you sitting down?"

"Yeah," Steve answered even though he was walking out his private entrance on the way to the elevator.

"I spoke to Captain Palmer's wife and she said he never took Eden."

Steve sighed. As much as he wanted to find the cause, he also wanted it to be something isolated, restricted in its potential for harm. "So it can't be Eden."

"I thought so, too, but she happened to mention it to their daughter. Get this. His daughter's been giving part of her prescription to her dad for some eighteen months, now."

Steve punched the elevator button. "So it might be Eden after all."

"Apparently he wanted to take it for his flight physical and liked it so much he kept on taking it. His wife never knew, although I'm told she appreciated her trimmer, more energetic husband."

"And my guess is," Steve said, "the pilots' board or whoever does not allow Eden."

"Correct. I checked to make sure. Since it's a short protein chain, they have no easy way to test for it. Captain Palmer apparently knew that, too, and probably figured he could take it without getting busted."

Steve voiced his nagging thought. "But if everybody takes Eden, how come there aren't more cases?"

"Right." They fell silent.

Marty spoke first. "I wonder if there aren't more, but since they've not been aiming large jets at the ground they didn't get the same attention. Also with isolated cases, it is very hard to detect a trend."

"And with a long latency period, cases might just now start cropping up," Steve added. "Shirley first took the drug four or five years ago."

"But the Captain took his only eighteen months ago, which tells me there may be different susceptibilities to this, Lord knows why. But if it is Eden, there's got to be others. I bet if we look under the surface we'd find more."

"Okay. How? Call the CDC?"

"I don't think that would help. Isolating our specific parameters would entail a record-by-record search. But . . ." he paused, "I might be able to do something from here."

CHAPTER 36

It was a beautiful November night at Lake Tahoe as Ari Brown stood on the balcony of his vacation home. He turned up his coat collar against the chill as he gazed at the moonlit pine trees; their spiked tops a jagged outline against the blue-black sky. Brown, a young looking forty-seven, had a medium build with a slight paunch that weekend workouts didn't remedy. His trim goatee suited his slightly graying temples and hazel eyes. He leaned on the banister and breathed the fresh air that sifted through the rough Sierra mountain peaks.

Tall, rough-hewn wooden posts supported the rear and balcony of his house as it jutted out from the hillside, allowing a commanding view of the lake. On quiet nights, the trickle of water in a brook below filtered up through the trees. The front of the two-story house opened onto a circular gravel driveway that threaded through the dense forest down to the access road.

Kirk Mallis, clad in a black Nomex body suit, sat in a mountaineering sling strung up high in a tree with a clear view of the balcony and into the windowed back of the house. Through his powerful night vision binoculars, he watched Janice Brown open and then close the balcony arcadia door and join her husband. She handed him a cup of coffee in a large mug and slipped an arm around his waist snuggling against him. Brown smiled at his wife and pulled her in close.

Mallis spoke softly into his collar microphone. "Family scene on the balcony."

His earpiece whispered Doug's reply. "I have visual." Per plan, Doug watched the side and front of the cabin while Joe watched the dirt road approach. No fuck-ups, Mallis thought as he mentally reviewed his plan. He shifted in his sling as he fought his innate restlessness.

The couple went back inside and, as Mallis watched, they re-joined their daughter, Samantha in front of the TV. Sam, at ten, had light blonde hair and her dad's hazel, nearly green eyes. They sat together on the couch as they watched a movie. Afterwards, Sam kissed her mom and dad before walking upstairs to her room. She looked cute in her flannel nightgown and bunny slippers.

Ari and Janice lay on the couch in front of a dying fire, holding each other and talking. If you only hadn't inquired into things you shouldn't have, thought Mallis, then we wouldn't be here.

After the call from Morloch, Mallis and his team had investigated Dr. Brown, bugging his office and searching his records and hospital progress notes. From their findings, it was apparent the recent call from Dr. Tobias hadn't completely assuaged Brown's suspicions and he had continued to pursue his investigations into Eden. Mallis concluded they had to intervene.

Discovering Dr. Brown's plans for the weekend, Mallis had dispatched Doug and Joe to prepare the cabin for tonight's operation. After Dr. Brown and his family had left San Francisco, Mallis had removed all the incriminating documents and computer data from Brown's office, hospital, and house. This clean up would be quick and neat with the loose ends tied up after tonight.

The living room illumination gradually faded as the fire burned to embers. Brown pulled his wife to her feet and they, too, climbed the stairs. Mallis's watch-hands glowed twelve thirty-three. He had another hour to wait, maybe more.

At one-thirty, Mallis seeing no lights or movement from the house decided to move. "Descending. Three minutes to rendezvous."

"Roger."

Mallis traded his binoculars for his night vision goggles and methodically lowered himself to the ground. There, his rope and sling-seat slid easily into his black backpack. He walked towards the front door of the cabin where he met Doug. They each had the same brand and model of hiking boots that Dr. Brown wore, so the dirt impressions would match.

Mallis carefully pulled on a pair of latex gloves and then from his backpack slid out a Ziploc bag containing a 9 mm Ruger. It was Brown's and until last night, it had been carefully locked in the top drawer of his home bureau along with the ammo. Mallis pulled the pistol out of the bag. "It's time," he said, his Prussian blue eyes narrowing. "No fuck-ups."

Doug pulled out a key, copied from a spare kept inside the cabin, slid it into the recently lubricated cabin door lock and silently turned it. They entered, locking the door behind. They pulled off their boots and placed them into their packs, walking in their Thorlo socks. Earplugs came out next and slung around their necks by their string. Doug silently slipped up the stairs using a laser pointer to identify the previously mapped squeaky boards for Mallis to avoid.

On the landing, Mallis looked into the open door to his right and saw Samantha sleeping on her left side, flannel covers pulled up to her neck. He nodded to Doug who slowly pulled the door closed and held it.

Mallis walked into the master bedroom and saw Ari with Janice curled up around him. He padded up to Janice and watched her slowly breathe as he inserted his earplugs. Mallis placed the gun against her forehead and pulled the trigger.

Ari screamed as he jerked awake.

Mallis watched him strain to see in the darkness. "Janice!" Ari shouted. Struggling to get up, he flopped comically off the bed and onto the floor. Ari found the bedside light and turned it on. Mallis pulled his goggles off.

Ari recoiled in terror as he stared into the barrel of the pistol. He then looked at his wife. "Janice!" Ari leaped onto the bed and held his wife's head tenderly. Looking up at Mallis, he yelled, "You killed my wife!" Ari's fear turned into anger.

Anger was dangerous. Mallis would have to change that. Mallis pulled his earplugs out. "And you will die, too, Dr. Brown," Mallis said steadily, locking his eyes onto Ari's.

"But . . ." he held up his finger to silence Dr. Brown, "I will spare the life of your daughter if you cooperate." He could hear the muffled shouts from Samantha's room.

"Samantha!" Ari yelled jumping off the bed.

"Stop." Mallis said loudly and authoritatively. "Don't move."

Don't move or you'll spoil everything. Mallis leveled the gun at Ari who got the message. He stopped short, standing naked except for his briefs, confused, scared and angry. Mallis knew the look. *How could my life that was so perfect moments ago turn into this nightmare?*

"But why?"

"You made some very powerful people afraid. Now, you want to save Samantha's life? Then cooperate with me." Mallis's voice was low, sounding calm and detached without any hint how much he enjoyed this.

"You won't kill her?"

"She has not seen us and doesn't know what we look like." Mallis said. "There's no reason to kill her."

Ari looked at his wife and began to shake. "Please, why?" he whispered.

Mallis motioned with his gun. "Get on the bed."

Ari slowly climbed into the bed. "Why?" he repeated.

"This is where you earn your daughter's life."

Ari looked at his wife and began to weep. "Why her, why her?" He picked up Janice's hand and kissed it; and then looked at Mallis.

"Can I hold my daughter before . . .?" Ari choked.

"Nope. Spoils everything." Mallis walked around the bed to Ari's right side. Ari was right-handed. Everything had to fit. *No fuck-ups.* Mallis placed Ari's gun against his temple, angling up ever so slightly. His hand was rock steady.

"Who?" Ari's eyes narrowed in desperate thought. Mallis's finger tightened on the trigger. Ari's eyes suddenly lit up with recognition, "Tride—" The gun fired, stopping the word, the most dangerous word. Samantha screamed again.

Mallis turned around and walked to the master bedroom doorway. He nodded to Doug who opened Samantha's door. Samantha ran into her parent's bedroom, but stopped short by the sight of the blood and death. Her scream was cut off by another gunshot.

Walking back to the bed, Mallis placed the grip of the gun into Brown's hand, aimed it at Janice's head and pulled the trigger one last time. Mallis left the gun in Dr. Brown's hand and looked at his results. *Good.* Looking around one last time he and Doug walked back down the stairs. Brown had guessed Mallis's client. *Smart doc,* Mallis thought. *Too bad.*

As he put on his boots at the bottom of the stairs, he felt the euphoric rush he always did after an operation. He walked out the front door followed by Doug.

Mallis radioed Joe. "Coming home."

CHAPTER 37

"Mary," Paul Tobias said quietly, "I want to tell you something." Paul sat on the side of their built-in bathtub watching his wife get ready for bed. He had been dreading this conversation ever since he had made up his mind about Eden. She would find out soon enough, far better for it to come from him.

Mary stopped brushing her hair and looked at him in the mirror. Seeing his serious expression, she turned around to fully face him. "About what?"

"Eden may have been responsible for someone dying."

"Really?" She looked puzzled. "Are you sure?"

"No, I'm not, but we know that Eden causes a serious brain disease in test animals. I now believe it can do the same in people."

"A brain disease?" She shook her head, unbelieving. "How? You told me it was perfectly safe."

"I did tell you that." He bit his lower lip, "and I thought it at the time. We all did. Trident hid the animal information from the FDA because if they had known what we knew, Eden would probably never have been approved."

"But—" She sagged against the marble countertop.

"Let me explain." As he spoke, Paul felt a lifting of the enormous burden he had carried for so long. "At first, when we were just getting started in animal testing, we got some abnormal mouse brain results, just a few. We repeated the studies and then lots of other studies like it.

We found that, in certain circumstances, Eden caused an incurable brain illness. We thought that was the end of Eden, but Morloch had us do more experiments."

"While we were pursuing the additional studies," Paul continued, "Morloch said we had to support the stock price by keeping the analysts happy. He assured us we would stop development if we got to a point where we thought it would pose a threat to people. Because of his personal assurance and without us maintaining the stock price Trident would fold, we agreed. Remember how we took a big gamble to join Trident? I was looking at unemployment and a trashed career. I couldn't face that, not after all we went through deciding to take the job, moving, and everything. I just couldn't."

Mary's face showed no sign of what she was thinking. Certainly no sympathy for him.

"So we sent diluted samples to different contract laboratories for more animal tests. That way, we had clean reports to show investors. The doctored studies made it look as though we were progressing according to plan and everybody was happy.

"With the time that bought, Oscar and I did several other studies in secret. We determined that only a very rare patient would be at any risk and even that risk was only theoretical. Based on these estimates, we started human trials."

Mary shook her head in disbelief. "How could you have possibly thought it was safe?" She sank down onto her bathroom chair.

"Fair question and one we thought about a long time. Keep in mind that animal studies are only a so-so predictor of human results," Paul said. "Here's how the data came out. In the repeated mouse studies, we saw that a fraction, about seven to twelve percent, would get the brain changes. We then gave it to gerbils. Only about a four to seven percent got the brain changes. Marmots did not get it at all. In dogs, we only got one case and that only after a year and at much higher doses than people would take. It seemed that the more complex the animal, the longer it took for any brain changes to occur and fewer animals experienced this, most not at all.

"We next put Eden in human brain tissue cultures and a few developed the changes, but only rarely and then only at the highest concentrations. So, we reasoned that the possibility of a human experiencing encephalitis was very remote. Based on that analysis, we started human trials."

"And what happened?" Mary asked sharply.

"And nothing. It worked as well as we had hoped—better, really—and no one got even a whisper of a problem with the encephalitis during all our clinical trials."

"How did you know what to look for?"

Paul shrugged. "If the conditions were at all like our animals, it would not be hard to spot. Based on what we saw, we had a pretty good idea of what we would see in humans. We did MRI scans, EEGs, and memory testing in all our early subjects and found nothing unusual. We even used a number of neurologists as our investigators for their expertise in those assessments. And," Paul sighed, "after all our worries, the entire research program was clean."

"Then, isn't that good?"

"Well, yes and no. It comes back to something called latency. It took longer to get the disease in the larger animals—the maximum duration of exposure was for a year during our long-term human clinical trials. If they got it after that, we wouldn't likely hear about it. That's why Morloch set up Oscar as the safety officer. He would be the first to know if any doctor called in with the symptoms we were looking for."

"And—?"

"He says he has never heard of any. So, since we hadn't heard of anything, now, after almost three years, we felt like we had made it."

"But now you think differently."

Paul nodded yes. "Ari Brown called a few days ago and told me about one of his patients that had been on Eden. I think it's probably one of ours. I can't be sure, you know, but it fits the pattern."

"But this is the only one. Right?"

"I don't know. And after all we've been through—I can't believe I'm saying this—I don't know if Oscar's really telling me the truth. In his position, he would get all the calls like Ari's. It just happened that Ari knew me and called me first." Paul shrugged, "I just don't know." He looked at his wife in anguish. "Ari's patient was your age and . . . I just can't live with that." He desperately wanted Mary's absolution.

His wife's eyes had hardened as Paul told his story. "Paul, I thought I knew you, but . . ." She shook her head disapprovingly. "You're telling me you rolled the dice with the life of every person who has ever taken Eden. How did you justify that all these years—how? How could you sleep at night? After Sara?" She choked.

"I didn't—" Paul ached, seeing the tears running down Mary's face.

Mary regained her voice. "How could you bear it when you knew that people could possibly die from a drug you personally knew might not be safe?" She brushed her hair in quick angry strokes.

"I have a plan," Paul said quietly.

She didn't hear him. "You'd better do everything you can right now to stop this thing—you have to." She pointed her brush at him. "I only hope it isn't too late to keep anybody else from dying. You have to do something tomorrow."

"I already have a plan."

She knitted her brow as his words registered. "You do? What?"

He had decided what to do after his second conversation with Ari. "I'm going to collect everything I can about the research—the doctored reports, the hidden data—and I'm going to an attorney. I'm planning to go public with this."

CHAPTER 38

"Sit down already," Steve ordered.

Doreen, the EEG technician, was hovering over his shoulder as he prepared to read Shirley's electroencephalogram.

"Okay." She smiled self-consciously and pulled up a rolling chair.

Steve opened the first page of the z-fold EEG paper of Shirley's most recent tracing. The hospital had not yet sprung for the latest digital EEG technology, so they did EEGs the old fashioned way on paper. On the tabloid-sized sheets were twenty rows of squiggly ink lines running across the two pages, each one representing an electrode placed on the scalp to record the underlying brain activity.

He stared at the page. *Shit.* He turned another page. It was the same. He rapidly flipped through the next twenty pages before he reached something that looked close to normal. But it wasn't, not really. The background rhythm was too slow and disorganized, considerably worse than on her admission EEG, but that was not what bothered him. It was the sharp waves coming from all over her brain. Steve's heart sank. On the last page, the edge of the paper caught his index finger and sliced deeply into it. He was so upset by the tracing that he barely noticed until he started dripping blood on the EEG. He put his finger in his mouth.

"Looks bad," Doreen surmised.

"Yep." He closed the last page and sighed aloud. "PLEDs."

"I thought so." Doreen had finished her EEG training about six months ago and was still green.

Shoving the paper aside, he asked, "Did you find those tracings on Rhonda Fowler?"

"Yeah. I dug all three up. They're right here." She slid the stack over to Steve.

Looking at the dates, Steve picked the last one and flipped through it. Dr. Goldstein's patient had more disordered, incoherent background rhythms and the epileptiform discharges, called PLEDs, were lower in amplitude. Otherwise, it looked virtually the same as Shirley's EEG.

Why hadn't he seen them before? He reached up to his box and pulled down Shirley's first tracing done the morning after he transferred her to the ICU. She had had a moderately disordered background pattern, but the sharp waves were not prominent. But now that he knew how the tracing had evolved, he could identify the incipient abnormality. Shirley's disease had significantly progressed even in the last several days.

Steve leaned back in his chair. He needed a moment to integrate this new piece of information. He pulled his finger out of his mouth and looked at his paper cut. It still oozed blood. "Tell me what causes PLEDS." He liked to teach and Doreen seemed to enjoy their Q and A sessions. As Doreen pondered his question, Steve mentally sorted through his diagnostic list, checking off the causes of PLEDs. He had already eliminated nearly all before today—but there was one possibility that had not made his original list—a glaring omission.

"PLEDs stand for periodic lateralizing epileptiform discharges."

"Good." Steve mumbled with his finger back in his mouth.

"Typically," Doreen continued as if reciting from memory. "They are caused by widespread toxic or metabolic abnormalities in the brain."

"Such as . . ."

Doreen thrust out her bottom lip. "Uhh, hypoxia, encephalitis, meningitis, abscesses, tumors . . ." She trailed off and pulled a piece of paper out of the pocket of her hospital-white slacks. "I looked this up before you got here because I knew you'd ask." She smiled sheepishly. "But I couldn't remember all of them."

"You're doing well." As they talked, Steve reviewed his new diagnostic possibility.

"Vasculitis, severe MS, liver failure, kidney failure, Crutz-Jacob something or other. Did I mention tumor?

"Yes. But it's Cruetzfeld-Jacob disease or CJD for short. Good, Doreen."

"What is CJD?"

"It's like mad cow disease."

"Oh." She responded, without sounding like she had understood it at all.

"Shirley may have something like CJD. I want you to look it up and give a report on it at our next section meeting."

Doreen made a face.

"It's the best way to learn," Steve grinned with humor he didn't feel.

"You're such a slave driver."

Steve stacked the paper EEGs as his mind seized the possibility that he now, just possibly, knew the cause of Shirley's illness. *Could it be a prion disease?*

In the rare, but well-known prion disease called Cruetzfeld-Jacob disease, prions spontaneously form in the brain, but almost always in an older person. Since it was infectious, young patients who developed Cruetzfeld-Jacob got prions from infected human sources like infected corneal transplants, growth hormone collected from infected human pituitaries, or from contaminated neurosurgical instruments since prions were immune to destruction, even by the intense heat of an autoclave. It seemed to Steve unlikely that Shirley had Cruetzfeld-Jacob.

Shirley's specific symptoms were not all that similar to known prion diseases. That was why he had not seriously considered them before. On the other hand, it was progressing at a rate not unknown for other prion-based diseases. And with the PLEDS and without another more likely cause, a prion infection seemed worth exploring.

Was it a new human variant of mad cow disease? It was more likely now that it had been found in US cattle, but Shirley's symptoms were different from the cases in England. She and Captain Palmer had progressed much faster than the typical mad cow patient. Furthermore, they had earlier psychological symptoms without the prominent gait and coordination problems seen in the English disease. The MRI scans were different, too. So while it might be a new mad cow variant, it seemed unlikely. He put that thought aside for the moment.

Importantly, each prion disease has something in common. They all have a protracted latency period from the time of exposure to the time of first symptoms, typically over a year or more. Could that explain why Eden had not caused symptoms during the clinical trials? The FDA only required the drug companies to follow patients thirty days after they participated in a trial unless something made it necessary to follow them for a longer period of time. If a drug caused a side effect beginning over a year after initial exposure, it would be nearly impossible to track it down, even with the FDA mandated post-marketing surveillance program. And worse, if Eden was just now starting to cause symptoms, there could soon be a flood of new cases.

Steve scrawled "prions" on a scrap of paper with a red grease pencil and stared at it a long time. How certain was he that Shirley's illness came from prions? Reasonably certain, he thought, but without a confirmatory test, he couldn't be absolutely sure.

The problem was, there were no commercial tests for prions. The usual means to make a diagnosis was for a post-mortem examination of the brain or, in rare cases, through a brain biopsy. Because of the one-hundred percent mortality from contracting the disease, and the impossibility of sterilizing their instruments after using it on contaminated brain tissue, most pathology labs were unwilling to do an examination of the brain, if there was any suspicion of a prion disease. Steve had no illusions about Banner Samaritan's interest in doing a brain biopsy. Here, as in so many other similar cases, the diagnosis would have to be made only on clinical grounds.

Steve pondered the bigger question last. If the brain disease was caused by prions, was Eden responsible? Eden was a short chain of fifteen amino acids. How was that linked to a prion, a huge protein? He would have to work on that part, too.

He pulled out his cell phone to tell Marty about his new concerns.

CHAPTER 39

It was a dingy morning sky that greeted Mallis as he walked through the door to his high-rise Arlington condo and glanced out the plate glass windows. The unbroken gray overcast that stretched to the horizon did nothing to dampen Mallis' mood.

He was still riding high from his operation two nights before. He, Doug, and Joe had driven back to San Francisco after which Mallis had taken a walk down Turk Street in the tenderloin district. The young whore had been especially gratifying, although he doubted she would be working again for at least a week, maybe two, while she healed.

After a shower, and with his day's first cup of hot green tea, Mallis sauntered into his study and turned on his computer. In a minute, he found what he was looking for: the San Francisco Examiner's article about a tragic homicide-suicide in the Lake Tahoe area. The prominent UCSF physician apparently killed his wife and daughter before shooting himself in the head. Mallis smiled. He scanned the article for any mention of a suspicion of homicide, but there was none. Even if the police suspected foul play, Mallis knew they would never trace it to him.

He dialed his secure phone.

"Morloch." A crisp deep voice answered.

"Hello, Vicktor."

"Kirk." Morloch's voice warmed. "How are you?"

"Fine."

"And our project?"

"Complete, as promised."

"Loose ends?"

"None."

"Wonderful." Mallis could hear soft music in the background and pictured Vicktor with one of his women lounging in bed. "Good job."

"Thank you. Vicktor. You should know that your Dr. Tobias is trouble."

"How so?"

"His conscience is eating him alive." On the way back home, Mallis's technicians had alerted him about a priority event—and he had listened to the recording of Tobias's bathroom confession to his wife.

"I thought he might be. A security risk?"

"I believe so, yes."

"Then, contain it."

"Roger."

"This one is close to home, Kirk. It must be surgical and natural. No collateral damage."

"Of course."

CHAPTER 40

President Dixon hung up the phone and found himself breathing a little fast. In fact, he realized, he felt winded and took several deep breaths, but that didn't make it better. He loosened his tie and unbuttoned his top shirt button, but that didn't help either. He pushed his chair back from his desk and stood up. For some reason he felt . . . nervous?

Maybe it was the coffee. Unlikely, since he had drunk only one cup this morning, several hours ago. And his headache was back. Maybe he needed more, not less caffeine.

Dixon glanced down at his day's agenda filled with back-to-back meetings, and fought down the rising anxiety. While he sometimes felt a little claustrophobic on crowded airplanes, he had never felt it in the Oval Office. His chest began pounding with a mounting panic that fueled a powerful impulse to get away. He needed to leave and get outside where he could breathe.

He looked at his schedule again. He had a half-hour break before his next conference. It was his scheduled time for calling congressmen to lobby for his budget, but . . .

Walking out to his secretary, he announced, "Joan, I need some fresh air. Let's go for a ride in your car."

Joan, sure that he was joking, inquired, "What, you want a run through Mickey D's?"

"I'm not kidding. I'd like to leave right now."

Secret Service Agent Rhodes, standing behind him, politely coughed. "Sir, I don't think we can allow that."

Dixon swung around and looked levelly at him. "You're welcome to come along, Agent Rhodes. We'll only be about twenty minutes. Come on Joan." He started walking towards the door. Joan looked helplessly at Rhodes and stood up.

Having made his decision, Dixon felt relieved, happier, almost giddy. He stepped outside into the brisk air and realized a car ride would be just what he needed to clear his mind—and pray.

Rhodes had no option, but to tag along. "Foxhound is moving. He plans to take Mrs. Pascal's car out on a joy ride."

There was a pause on the other end. "We have no time for jokes, Mr. Rhodes." Then he heard, "Oh, shit." He visualized the controller checking the President's transponder screen to see that the President was indeed moving away from the Oval Office. Rhodes wondered what he should—or could—do when Agent D'Agostino joined him.

"Stay with him while we rustle up an escort," the controller instructed. "We'll hold him at the booth."

"Roger," Rhodes said, his face creased. This was a new side to Foxhound, an unwelcome one.

Arriving at Joan's car, parked in the underground White House garage, the President got in the front passenger's seat, leaving the two agents to scramble into the back.

Rhodes tried again. "Sir, this is not safe."

"Okay, I'll put on my seatbelt. Joan has a superb driving record. I'm sure we'll do just fine."

"I mean this is not a bulletproof car, you don't have your vest on, and our escort is just forming up."

"I hardly think the assassins of the world are waiting for the President to emerge in his secretary's car."

He's enjoying himself, thought Rhodes. It's like he's sneaking off for a cigarette and daring somebody to catch him at it. His earpiece barked at him. "Two agents in the garage now. We'll have his escort in three minutes."

"Roger. D'Agostino is with me."

"Copy. Stay sharp."

As if, snorted the agent. He exchanged a worried look with D'Agostino.

Joan pulled out of the White House underground parking lot to the control both and the steel gate it controlled. The frowning face of Bernie Whitaker leaned over and looked in.

"Hello, Mr. President. I'd like to ask you to wait for the Secret Service escort, which will be at most two minutes."

"No thanks, Bernie, I've only got twenty minutes. I'm not going to waste ten percent of it waiting. Please open the gate."

Bernie's face became concerned.

"Now, Bernie." The President asserted firmly, but without harshness.

"Okay, sir. Be careful." The gate swung open and Joan's Buick moved forward merging into traffic.

"Ahh," Dixon said, sliding back into the seat.

Rhodes put his sunglasses on now that they were outside and radioed their position back to the security office. The best-protected man in the world was now exposed to every damn crazy and crackpot in the city. *Shit!*

CHAPTER 41

After another night of hours spent in front of the computer, this time researching prions, Steve groggily rolled out of bed at the alarm and staggered half asleep into the shower. He managed to put on a smile for Johnny as he was leaving for the hospital. Anne knew he had been up late against her express wishes, and she had been a little annoyed with him. Steve promised her he would go to bed earlier tonight.

His first stop, as was now his habit, was Shirley's room. As he thumbed through her chart at the nurses' station, his phone vibrated in his pocket. Pulling it out he saw it was Marty.

"Results? Already?" Steve asked before Marty could speak.

Yesterday, when Steve had told Marty of his suspicions regarding prions, Marty had immediately jumped at the possibility. Even better, Marty knew of an experimental test for prions being developed by a Dr. Breen at the NIH laboratories. It only required a sample of spinal fluid.

After the call, Steve had collected the fluid sample through a slender needle inserted between Shirley's lumbar vertebrae into her subarachnoid space. Once packaged for shipment, he had Etta drive it to the airport for same day air delivery to Marty's lab. Marty had taken the package, along with a sample he had collected of Captain Palmer's spinal fluid, over to Dr. Breen's lab, delivering them at nearly ten-thirty in the evening.

Marty chuckled at Steve's impatience. "Normally it takes three days, but Dr. Breen had the staff up working most of the night."

"And?"

"Positive, I'm afraid." Marty reported soberly. "Both of them."

"Damn." Steve let out the breath he had been holding. It was a death sentence for Shirley and Captain Palmer.

"We also got a repeat EEG on the captain," Marty continued in somber tones, "and it shows increased disorganization of the background with a definite alternating hemispheric sharpness, like PLEDS and triphasic waves. Steve, this is an outbreak of a new variant prion disease and it scares the hell out of me."

"But for the love of Pete," Steve said, "how does Eden cause it?"

"Well, if we had a mechanism, it would make the association easier. I mean, how can something so miniscule bollix up the whole thing?"

Steve cocked his head at Marty's statement. He had heard something like that recently. "Uh huh," he mumbled. Where had he heard that phrase before? If only he weren't so tired. It was causing him trouble at work and home. *Home!* Steve remembered now—Johnnie and the coffee with a little bit of milk in it. What were his words? Steve thought a minute and then it came back to him. 'Even a tiny bit spoils the whole thing.'

"Steve?"

"Hang on."

"Hanging on."

Steve turned the phrase over in his mind. Something small screwing up the whole thing . . . then it hit him. His mouth said it, even as his brain was forming the thought. "A catalyst. Maybe Eden acts as a catalyst."

"A catalyst? For prions?" Marty responded slowly. "That's unheard of. At least, no one has ever seen it."

"But wait. I read a report describing a short-chain polypeptide reversing the prion conversion. Then, why not one that causes the opposite? You know, prion conversion?"

"I'm listening."

"And it might explain why we have a small epidemic of this thing. If Eden caused transformation into prions, it could be a new disease variant. It fits. Look at how it seems to work its way back into the brain from the nose. That would explain the MRI pattern."

"Sounds logical, even if wildly speculative. Okay, Sherlock, how do we prove it?"

"Look, I'm just thinking out loud here, but if Eden's causing this, don't you think we could reproduce it in the lab?"

"I'd certainly think so, yes."

"I could get it tested in some nerve cell cultures. A friend of mine, Amos Sheridan, has them laying around his lab."

"I know Amos," Marty said. "Sounds like it's worth a shot."

Steve looked over at Shirley's room. Edith, as ever, sat in a chair and watched her daughter. His enthusiasm for the research washed out of him, replaced with dread for what he had to do next.

"Right, I'll let you know what turns up." He hung up and trudged into Shirley's room. Edith stood up as he entered.

"Edith, Shirley, I need to tell you some things." He sat down next to Shirley's bed opposite Edith.

"What is it?" Shirley asked, her face damp with perspiration. She punched the button that raised the head of her bed and put her stuffed otter in her lap, careful to make it comfortable.

"I have a diagnosis," he began. "It's caused by something we call prions and, I'm afraid it's bad."

"How bad?" Edith's face reflected her concern. Shirley's reaction was more difficult to judge, as if she did not fully understand what he had just said.

He pursed his lips. "It's bad."

"No!" Edith's hands flew up to her mouth.

"I'm sorry." Steve shook his head wishing there was a better way to break the news. "The spinal fluid test confirmed the diagnosis."

"How did she get it?"

"Well, that's less certain. I think, and this is very preliminary, but I think Eden gave this to her. At least that's the best we have to go on."

"Eden? How?" Shirley asked, her voice small and scared.

"I don't know yet. If we're right, this is entirely new. As in never before discovered."

"Can't you cure it? I mean, can't you do surgery or medication or something?" Edith asked.

Steve shook his head. "Not with prions, there isn't. I'm really sorry."

Edith's eyes began watering. "Why would Eden do such a thing? Maybe I don't understand Eden very well. Isn't it to lose weight?"

Steve nodded. "Yes."

"If that's what it's for, then why is it causing my Shirley to get sick?"

"I don't know. I realize that's unsatisfactory, but that's all I have to go on at the moment. We'll be doing more tests to see if we can make sure."

Shirley's eyes searched his. "You gave it to me first." Her tone was not accusatory.

"I did, but I never suspected that this ever could happen. No one did."

Edith clutched Shirley's hand, rubbing it fiercely. "What should we have done differently?"

"Nothing. You did the right thing bringing her in when you did."

"But I should have brought her in when she was getting depressed or had her headaches." Tears slid down her cheeks and she hastily wiped them with her tissue.

"And you did. Anyway, how would you have known?"

"Please figure out something to do. She's my only child. She's all I have left." She pressed her daughter's hand to her cheek. "Please find something for her. Please?"

CHAPTER 42

"But Amos, it'd be easy," Steve repeated, following Amos Sheridan's skinny, white-coated figure into the laboratory area. Steve had just driven over to see his friend and founder of the prestigious Sheridan Neuroscience Laboratories, but was surprised at the reaction his suggestion had triggered.

"Sorry, Steve. I can't. I just can't."

"But think of my patient who's dying. How many more are out there? We have to know."

Sheridan stopped by some glass apparatus and absently waved a Bunsen burner under a bubbling flask. He was more agitated than Steve could recall, even though he ordinarily moved in a blur.

"I'd like to Steve, I really would, but I'm out of cash. It's those damn NIH grants. They're at least three months late renewing them and I'm flat out of money." He looked at Steve with genuine anguish. "I can't start laying off people, Steve, but I may have to. I've already stopped my own salary."

"Amos, I had no idea."

"The staff knows. They're such a great team, I'm really afraid they'll start looking for another job. We just keep hoping the mail will bring us our renewal checks."

"Can't you spare a few nerve cultures for me? I'd pay for them if you wanted."

"It's not the dishes, it's the personnel time."

"What are they doing now?" Steve asked, desperately hoping for an opening.

"Not much of anything, actually, since we can't afford materials anymore."

"Then why can't you pull someone and put them to work on this prion thing?"

Amos paced down the aisle between black slate-topped chemistry tables, spotless with everything neatly put away in its place. Amos ran a tight ship.

"But your premise is preposterous," he objected.

"You're one to talk." That got him, thought Steve with some satisfaction, seeing Sheridan stop pacing for a moment. Steve had been a sounding board for Amos for years now and it was unlike Amos to close down intellectually, which told Steve volumes about his friend's dire financial straits.

Sheridan shook his head, "I can't see it."

"Look, Amos," Steve persisted, almost pleading. The conversation with Edith was still fresh and his own guilt acute. "What if it only takes two weeks to convert? A few days? Think about the ramifications; Eden, the world's most popular prescription drug, implicated in a fatal brain-eating disease by renowned Sheridan Labs. You know, presentations, talks, TV appearances, plenary addresses at international meetings, and in the process, exposing the cause of a disease that may kill hundreds or more. Plus all the grants you'd get."

"Publication rights?" Amos got it.

"All the credit. I just want the answer ASAP and anything else you can tell me. I'm pulling my patients off all my Eden studies."

Sheridan twisted his blonde beard in thought. "Well, I could get Phyllis to set up and Dave could mix the titrations. We could have some preliminary results within days I'd say, depending on how active the agent is."

Steve had him.

CHAPTER 43

They've got to be here somewhere! Paul Tobias pawed through his locked file cabinet for the sixth time searching for his animal study files. He slammed the drawer shut and pulled open the one below it and looked through the folders that held his personal papers. He knew they weren't in there, but he had to look again. Nothing. Slamming it shut, he ran his fingers through his hair trying to think. It was late and he had waited until his family was in bed so that he could work undisturbed.

In what he knew was a futile effort, he went to the file cabinet in the garage that held only old family bills and cancelled checks. Still nothing. It was a replay of today's search at his office, except that he had found two folders which been misfiled and lots of empty spaces where they had been. That was it—just two out of dozens. *How?* Back in his study, he sat down to carefully think things through. He knew he had seen the folders only three days ago, but where had they gone? He knew neither his secretary, nor his wife would have dared moved them.

A chill ran up his spine. Somebody must have gone through his files at his house just like they had at work—somebody who was worried about the real story getting out. *Morloch!* It had to be him.

It all began to add up. Morloch had pushed them to forge the animal data, hide the incriminating study reports and sign off on the FDA filings. He had stood to gain the most, but . . . now Paul saw it all. Morloch himself had never signed any of the falsified documents. Morloch was busy covering Trident's tracks.

Who else knew this was happening? Oscar? Paul began to breathe faster. What could he do? The two studies he had were still plenty to cook Trident's goose, but he had nothing on Morloch. It would be his word against Morloch's and Morloch had a clean record. As a businessman and not a doctor, he would claim no knowledge or understanding of the doctored reports. He would say his senior staff acted on their own to make themselves rich by getting Eden on the market.

Did they know what he was planning to do or was this coincidental? Maybe Morloch was getting paranoid and just had some agent type clean up his and the others' files to eliminate all the evidence. Had they broken into his house? The thought made the hair on the back of his neck stand up. Wait. What was he thinking—people stealing stuff right out of his house? How paranoid!

He then thought about what he was doing and realized how high the stakes were. Frankly, if that was Morloch's concern, he should have done it sooner. But even if the files were just misplaced, he decided not to take chances.

He pulled the file with the mouse and gerbil reports out of his briefcase and went over to his fax machine. He pulled out his smartphone and looked up his new attorney's fax number. He would fax the report to them tonight and call them in the morning and tell them it was important evidence and to hold it until his first appointment. That would get it into a place it where couldn't be stolen.

Paul pulled the staples out of the reports and inserted the first twenty pages in the fax machine. He punched in the fax number and checked to make sure he had gotten it right and hit the send button. A scrape at the door startled him. He looked up, expecting it to be Mary. "Jesus!"

Standing in the doorway was a man with icy blue eyes dressed in a black stretch jumpsuit holding a pistol.

"Who the hell are you?" Paul's chest hammered.

"Nobody to be trifled with." A small smile played on the man's lips.

"You're the one who took all my files," Paul accused, terrified this man would hurt Mary or his sons.

The man shrugged casually as he walked in and hit the stop button on the fax machine and pulled the papers out of the machine. Tobias saw that only three pages had gone through, not nearly enough.

Picking up the folder lying next to the fax, the man said, "I couldn't locate this one so I waited for you to find it for me."

"What are you going to do with those?"

"It doesn't matter to you anymore."

Paul's stomach fell as the meaning sunk home. "My wife?"

"Is sleeping and if she stays sleeping, we'll leave her alone. Just come with us."

"Now?"

"Yes."

"Can't I leave a note?"

The man shook his head. "Sorry. And keep quiet. You don't want to wake anybody."

Paul's heart broke. He wasn't afraid to die, not now, he just couldn't stand the thought of not being able to tell Mary, Sam, and Ronnie how much he loved them. He nodded. Shoulders slumped as he wept quietly. He followed the man in black out of the study and through his garage door into the dark night, praying that his family would understand.

CHAPTER 44

Oscar Perera walked into the Trident boardroom and sat down at the polished table next to Sharod Houssan, Trident's Chief of International Operations. He looked around at the senior executives occupying the other chairs. "What's up, Sharod?" It was the first time he had been called into a meeting like this without knowing in advance what it was about.

"I don't know. I just got a call from Karen to be here by eight-ten."

Perera had gotten the same call on the way in, and had scrambled to get his cup of coffee and plug in his laptop before he had to be here. He glanced at his watch. It was exactly eight-fifteen.

Morloch, wearing a grave expression and a dark suit, walked in and stood at the head of the table. "I am saddened and grieved to announce that Paul Tobias is dead."

There was a murmur around the table before Morloch continued.

"He was found at four o'clock this morning in his car at a convenience store. It looked like he either had a heart attack or a sudden stroke. I don't know which, but if it makes any difference, it looks like it was quick and even painless." Morloch's voice was calm, reassuring like a funeral director's. "This, of course, is a terrific blow to our company, professionally and personally. Many of us worked with him for years and I attribute Eden's FDA approval and Paradise's NDA submission in large part to Paul's hard work and dedication."

He took a drink from a glass of water and cleared his throat. "On a personal note, Paul was a friend and confidant. He came to Trident in the early days and he was tireless in his enthusiasm and inspiration, earning my highest respect for his integrity, hard work, and infectious good humor. I will miss him." Pausing, he lowered his head a fraction, as if saying a small silent prayer.

"I have sent my condolences to Mary, his wife, and his two children, Ronald and Samuel. Services are not scheduled yet, but you will be informed when we know. In order to continue Paul's dreams and aspirations, I thought it only fitting that Trident establish a Paul Tobias College Scholarship Fund for the deserving underprivileged children of Philadelphia. This, of course, is pending approval from Mary, but I hope she will accede. I have pledged one hundred thousand shares of Trident stock to start it off." Morloch paused, looking around the room. "Of course, it in no way mitigates our loss and that of his family, but perhaps it will make a difference in the world somehow. This is a terrible thing and I know it is a shock to you all. It certainly was to me. That is all I wanted to say. Thank you for coming."

Perera's ears burned. *Paul dead?* How? He was so young and he had those two wonderful children. Poor Mary—first her daughter and now her husband. Why did he have to die? Perera then remembered his conversation with Morloch about Paul and Paul's doctor friend, Ari Brown. *What had really happened?*

Perera watched Morloch greeting well-wishers as though he was one of the bereaved himself and he thought of the doctors who had called him to report their suspicions about Eden and a strange brain illness. Some of them, he later discovered, had died unexpectedly. Although he had no knowledge of the cause of their deaths, he had for some time nursed a growing suspicion that Morloch had played some hand in them. Perera wondered if he somehow had been complicit by not investigating further.

After excusing himself, he hurriedly went back to his office. He typed Ari Brown, MD, UCSF into Google and punched the return button. The search page popped up and Oscar quickly scanned the headings. They were all news items about a murder suicide. Selecting one, he clicked on it and scanned the article. Ari Brown was dead.

Perera's throat constricted, as the cause of Paul's death suddenly became terrifyingly clear. He now gained an entirely new understanding for Morloch's repeated promise to always generously reward those who help him and Trident reach their goals.

The inverse had become transparently evident. Why had he not seen it before?

Perera was suddenly very afraid.

CHAPTER 45

President Dixon, flanked by Clarke Elementary School principal, Donna Reeves and Paducah Mayor, Sara Buckley, strode into the jam-packed Clarke school cafeteria. Camera strobes flashed as he entered, creating a staccato pattern of brilliant lights. The women blinked, but Dixon barely noticed, striding right through the reporters. He loved getting into community settings and seeing people where they lived and worked. And schools were among his favorite places to visit.

He smiled broadly as he stepped to the lectern, standing alone at one end of the cafeteria. Press Secretary Tyrone Grune took his place at the President's flank, ready with a spare copy of the speech and his 'first aid kit,' which consisted of a terry-cloth hand towel, a handkerchief, a throat lozenge, and a plastic water bottle.

Tapping on the microphone, Dixon heard his taps amplified. Leaning slightly forward, he began. "I am so happy to be here in the beautiful city of Paducah in the majestic State of Kentucky." He paused at the delighted cheers and clapping from all the young students and teachers crowding the lunch tables in front of him. A large number of parents had squeezed into the back and stood lining the perimeter walls.

After his spontaneous car ride with Joan, Jeff Bell had suggested his making this trip instead of Vice President Sullivan. Now, as he stood in front of the students and teachers, he knew it had been a good idea. It was the first time since his joy ride he had been able to take his mind off the Chinese massacre. While it had caused a firestorm with his wife and staff, he had loved every second. The blue skies and moving freely about had made him feel closer to God—it had been worth it.

His written comments were stacked in front of him. Each page held about six sentences in large type. Glancing down, he said, "They tell me you have a state geography bee champ here." He grinned at the crowd. "Is that right?"

More cheers and shouts. "Well, Geoff Durmond, please come up here so I can shake your hand." Hollers and cheers followed a tubby boy as he shyly stood up in the front row and walked up to the President. Dixon formally shook the young fifth grader's hand and then ruffled his brown hair. He smiled broadly. "Good job, son. I'm proud of you. I never won anything like this in school."

Geoff squirmed, but his flushed look told Dixon he appreciated the praise. "Thank you, sir," he stammered.

Holding the boy by the shoulders Dixon continued. "Geoff makes me proud, not just because he's a winner, but because winners are willing to do what it takes to become a winner. Geoff can tell you that it took long hours and hard work to learn all the facts it took to win." He looked down at Geoff. "About how much did you study?"

Geoff's face flushed again. "About two hours a night with my Pa."

"Geoff did his work, now it's up to us adults to do ours. Geoff, as long as I am in the White House, you and your Pa can come visit anytime. You can go sit down now. I'm through embarrassing you." Geoff, obviously relieved, almost ran for his seat.

"I know Clarke Elementary School has some of the finest teachers in the country." He smiled at some whoops and cheers that followed. "And you are accomplishing some amazing things in education. Your test scores are 20 points above the national average on standardized tests and you're regional Governor's Cup champs." He paused at the clapping. "Part of your achievement," he continued, "comes from the association your school district has forged with Paducah Community College."

"My administration has used your school district and others like it to fashion a national college and public school joint cooperative, what we call the APPLE program, Applied Programs for Learning Excellence." The applause once again stopped him.

Time for the punch line, he thought, turning to the next page of his speech. "This APPLE program and its tremendous benefits will be fully funded through a bill I am sending to Congress next week." The applause swelled, making Dixon smile. This was a natural marriage between the reach of the federal government and the innovation and energy of the local level. His headache strangely returned with a throbbing intensity that distracted him. He looked down at his notes and with relief realized he was on his last page.

"All you wonderful students remember that if you work hard like Geoff, and learn what your teachers and parents tell you, you can do anything you want. Even become president like me." Speaking over the applause, he said, "Now, before we eat lunch, I'd like to say a small prayer of grace."

"What?" Dixon demanded. He sat in the presidential limousine looking at a fuming Tyrone Grune. "I thought it went off pretty well."

Their official duties done, they drove through downtown Paducah back to the airport.

Grune stared back. "You don't get it."

"What?" Dixon said again. "Get what?"

"You prayed back there."

"Yeah, so what?"

Grune shook his head in disbelief. "The President of the United States doesn't say prayers in public schools. The Supreme Court, you know."

Dixon sat back in the leather seat, realization crossing his countenance. "Oh. I forgot. Habit, you know."

"Habit?" Grune said incredulously. "In front of three hundred witnesses and scores of reporters, you pray in a public school because you forgot? We're going to get roasted on national TV." Grune, a handsome, slender man in his fifties with graying temples, had been Dixon's chief legal counsel in the Virginia state house and now constituted the official White House worrywart. Anxiety lined his face, replacing his habitual scowl. "Unless you're deliberately making a policy change. If you were, I'd appreciate your telling me at some—"

"Stop, Ty. Enough." Dixon sighed. "I really did forget. It seemed so natural."

"What do I tell the press?" Grune fretted. "That the chief defender of the Constitution had a brain fart?" Grune waved his Manila folder. "We're screwed." Nothing in his first aid kit could do anything about presidential stupidity. He dropped his papers on the floor and pulled out his cell phone. "I've got to warn the staff."

CHAPTER 46

Larry Calhoun walked into Linda's office wearing a worried expression. "Bad news."

Resnick looked up from her desk. "Yeah? Take a number."

Calhoun collapsed in a chair opposite Resnick. "I just got off the phone with Colonel Jenkins, assistant to Secretary Painter."

"And?"

"The Chinese stole a new missile design from the Russians."

"Okay," she responded, putting her pen down. "Tell me about it."

"It's a baddie," Calhoun continued, "It's the latest generation air-launched ballistic type. It apparently has TV guidance with random number antimissile evasion programming. It's nuclear capable, too."

Resnick absently pulled at her lower lip as she absorbed the information. "That is bad. When did we find this out?"

"That's the thing. They tested it on Thanksgiving night in China." Calhoun let that sink in a minute.

Resnick got it. "When we were looking elsewhere."

"Exactly. We only caught a bit of it on an old bird and that's only because the Ruskies told us where to look."

"They're pissed."

"You bet. They notified us so it would counter any hope the Chinese had that the launch was undetected. It's a nasty bird, too. The Russians were particularly proud of it."

"Perhaps the massacre was partially used as a cover for the tests."

"Probably because it was a convenient distraction. Best part of it, according to the Russians, is its anti-ship cavitation capability."

"What's that?" Resnick asked.

"The missile explodes in the water under the ship, which causes a large air pocket. A ship is designed to have support from the water all along its length so when the water gets blown out from under it, it cracks in two and sinks immediately—with all hands on board. Cute, huh?"

Linda drummed her fingers on the desk. "I need to hammer home the connection between this and DEFCON to Ambassador Tupikov. The Chinese are playing high stakes."

"By the way," Calhoun waved a manila folder. "I'm delivering your requested China position paper on the massacre." He dropped it on her desk.

"The gist?"

He shrugged. "What's to lose if you've already conceded world opinion?"

"Economic. Trade losses. Loss of standing in international affairs." Linda replied.

"No one of consequence will stop trading with them because they have a new missile or because they are at loggerheads with us over this Hong Kong thing. Remember Tiananmen? The important thing to them is that the right people are in control. This massacre thing was all internal, a show of force by an ascendant hard line. General Yao Wenfu or his clone may be top dog and the rest of world opinion is pretty much irrelevant."

"How convinced are you?"

"Enough to make policy on it."

"Hmm." Linda drummed her fingers.

"FYI, the Taiwanese President will come to call on the President in four days. I just got the word."

"The Chinese are going to have a fit."

"No, it's good. We give them a punch in the nose and let them know we're able to parley with any government we want to."

"That's your position?"

"Yeah."

"What about not marginalizing the moderates in their government. This policy virtually hands the hard liners the power they seek and we'll have to deal with them for the next decade—not to mention the anti-U.S. activities they'll support. We jeopardize a renewal of their weapons technology exports and the moderating pressure they've exerted on North Korea."

Calhoun shrugged. "Those are things we care about. Taiwan is something they care about. If Beijing's already conceded world opinion, then they will take advantage of those opportunities despite our reaction. We should let them know we have options, too, and letting Taiwan's president come visit is one of our options. Let them stew about it." He dropped a folder on her desk. "The position paper. We just discussed the highlights."

The Secretary of State leaned back in her chair evaluating the merits of Calhoun's reasoning. There wasn't much choice, really, since the President had locked them into inviting President Lee.

"Okay, Larry, let's go with it. Since they started this, let's see if they can stand the heat."

CHAPTER 47

"We're screwed without getting to enjoy it." Tyrone Grune sat in Jeff Bell's office loudly and anxiously chewing his gum. "If we say he forgot," he said between chews, "the press asks us if he's that stupid and what other things does he do that are stupid."

Bell sat back in his swivel chair, fingertips together, listening carefully.

"And if we say it was deliberate, then he just flagrantly violated the Supreme Court ruling on school prayer. Why? He just did. No, it's not a policy change or a new initiative. See? Either way, we're screwed."

Bell nodded. "Let me think. Is there any way we can say he was misunderstood. Maybe he said . . . lettuce weigh?" Bell hadn't intended to say exactly that, but it brought a smile to the corners of his mouth.

Grune looked at Bell in disbelief. "Are you making a joke? If so, it's not funny."

"Okay, but the point remains. Can we say he was misunderstood?"

Grune sighed heavily. "Perhaps," he muttered. "At least he didn't say the Lords prayer or something out loud. Problem is, we can't just ask the networks for samples of their recordings, they'll want to know why and that effectively undercuts any claim we make about his not saying a 'small prayer of grace.'"

"Maybe we can say he was criticizing the cooks and he said, 'let's have a small platter of grease.'" Bell was genuinely concerned, but he couldn't resist bugging Grune.

"Are you taking any of this seriously?" He popped his gum loudly.

"What's worse," Bell replied reasonably. "The president mumbling something unintelligible or saying a prayer?"

"Prayer, of course. But do you think it'll fly? What if they pick it up clearly on the audio?"

"We just say he really didn't say that and, if he did, it was a mistake, since he didn't intend to say anything like that. By this time, the President doesn't remember his exact words since they were unscripted."

Grune looked hopeful. "It might work. Deny, deny, deny. I think it might work. I'll tell the staff." He jumped to his feet, almost smiling. "It just might work."

"There's a long tradition of that here," Bell remarked dryly. The observation was lost on Grune.

CHAPTER 48

"Dr. Perera."

"Hi, Dr. Perera," Steve said into his phone. "I'm Dr. Steve James, one of your investigators for Eden."

Steve was calling Trident in response to a suggestion Anne had made late last night. She had marched into his office while he was glued to the computer and demanded to know what was so damn important to keep him out of bed. After Steve had explained about Eden, Anne correctly pointed out that it was probably a coincidence that all three patients had been taking it. To drive home the point, she recommended he call the company and ask them directly.

"Well, hello, Dr. James. I have heard nothing but good things about your work on our clinical trials. I'm sorry we haven't met."

"Thanks. I called to ask a question about Eden."

"Okay, shoot."

"Do you have any cases of unexplained encephalitis related to Eden?"

Steve heard a rustle though the phone like Perera was holding his hand over the mouthpiece. Steve had been connected to Perera by asking Trident's operator to connect him to the Chief Safety Officer.

Perera spoke again. "Sorry Dr. James, I was distracted there for a minute. Now, what were you saying?"

"Do you have any reported cases of encephalitis associated with taking Eden?"

"That's a very unusual question. Certainly, as one of our investigators, you are familiar with Trident's confidential materials."

"Well, sure, but I wondered if there were any recent information that had not made it out yet."

"Perhaps if you tell me why you inquire, I can be more informative."

"Well, we have three cases of a progressive brain condition associated with twitches and strong delusions bordering on hallucinations."

"Yes . . ." Perera sounded like a bored butler.

"Well, they have this unique MRI signature and all were taking Eden."

"I see," said Perera, although Steve could tell he didn't get it. He may as well be reading Perera the phone book.

"Well," Steve continued, "Dr. Walker at GW has a spinal fluid test for prions and it was positive on two of the patients." Steve stopped for a moment waiting for a reaction.

"Prions, you say," Perera said, sounding as if prions were a distasteful word in his mouth.

"Right, prions." Steve repeated.

"Well, Dr. James, I'm surprised. You must certainly know Eden is a very popular drug. I would guess if you went to your hospital and asked three patients at random, it would be very likely that you would find three in a row who were taking Eden. This is like you had told me three patients taking Tylenol also had a strange brain illness. I can't see how you can possibly link the two."

Perera and Anne had nailed the obvious flaw with his theory. Steve began fiddling with a freebie Eden pen that had been dropped off by his local drug representative. "Well, I find it a little disconcerting that the MRI pattern looks like there is a nasal entry of a toxin that spreads in the olfactory pathways through the brain. That would fit with Eden's nasal administration."

"I see your point, Dr. James. Who did you say your colleague was at GW? I may want to call him and inquire about his technique. It sounds most interesting. Dr. Martin Walker, is it not? Has he published his technique yet?"

"Not yet." Steve had no interest in discussing the fact it was Dr. Breen's test and not Marty's. He just wanted to know about any prior cases.

"Hmm." Perera sounded disappointed.

"I plan to do some testing on Eden," Steve said, feeling increasingly frustrated and a little defensive. "I think it would put my concerns to rest if we had negative results with Eden in nerve cell culture."

"By all means. Where would you perform these tests?"

"Sheridan Laboratories."

"I know about Dr. Sheridan. He's got some interesting papers on MS, I believe. Well, by all means, Dr. James, go ahead and do your research, after all, they are your patients. But for your information, there are no reported cases of encephalitis related to Eden."

"None?"

"Correct, Dr. James, none. Please, do give me a call to let me know your findings," Perera said smoothly. "But I'm sure it's not related to our drug. Goodbye." Perera hung up.

"Fine, then. Thanks for listening." Steve said sarcastically into the dead line. He snapped the Eden pen in half spattering black ink over his hands.

Dr. Perera rewound the tape of his conversation with Dr. James and looked out the high-rise window of his office as he listened to the replay. Dr. James' voice was not questioning; it sounded convinced. And, Perera admitted, his arguments were logical and thorough, although they both knew he did not have anything that counted as proof. Perera stared out at the slow moving muddy-gray Delaware River, visible off to his right.

He recalled yesterday's conversation with Fran, Trident's on-site study monitor assigned to Dr. James' office. She had called during her scheduled visit at Dr. James' office concerned that he was discontinuing all his patients from the Eden and Paradise trials. The only explanation given to her was that it was the investigator's best judgment. She had never seen this happen before from an investigator, especially one as well established and successful as Dr. James.

If Dr. James thought Eden was causing problems, then he was doing the logical thing to protect his patients. Acting on his convictions, Dr. James stood to lose a substantial sum of money, including all the future Trident studies he would now forgo.

Perera reached the obvious conclusion. Dr. James was smart and persistent, and that was unfortunate for him. His colleague, what was his name? Walker was it? Perera rewound the tape again and listened. That's right, Dr. Martin Walker at GW would also be a problem and possibly Dr. Sheridan as well. *Shit!* This was another probable case, one Trident could ill afford, especially with a high profile doctor like Dr. James. His and Paul's calculations about the frequency of the encephalitis in humans were way too low—he knew that now. Perera had a sense of dread, as if their ship was taking on water and every new case ripped another hole in the hull. How long could they contain it? With Paul's death never far from his mind, Perera copied the digital recording onto two CD-ROMs and stored one in the pouch of his briefcase—part of his new insurance plan. It would join his other recordings and files in a large, newly rented safety deposit box opened in his brother-in-law's name. Morloch, as usual, would get the other one.

CHAPTER 49

"We come together in the name of God inside this brilliant Cathedral of yours to celebrate our Lord and the special relationship between our two countries," Archbishop of Canterbury, William Northbourne, said in his amplified English baritone.

President Dixon and Elise sat together next to the aisle in the second pew, holding hands as they listened. The Archbishop was here on a special tour through the United States with his first stop here in Washington. The ceremony was actually a secular celebration attended by members of Congress, administration officials, as well as anybody else who wished to attend. The church had publicized Archbishop Northbourne's visit well, as the Cathedral was full.

Dixon's eyes occasionally rose to take in the sweeping Gothic arches rising high overhead. He loved the National Cathedral in its cavernous majesty. Traveling through Europe as a student, he had seen many of the great Gothic cathedrals: York in England, Notre Dame in Paris, and the ornate Duomo of Milan. His favorite was still the Chartres Cathedral in France.

In his mind, the Washington National Cathedral was the most pure and beautiful of all Gothic churches in the United States. The huge ribbed piers swept up to the pointed roof almost a hundred feet above, its fingers spreading to support the stone roof in symmetrical rays. The innovation of the Gothic design with its flying buttresses allowed large windows to let vast amounts of light into traditionally dark and gloomy cathedrals.

The National Cathedral designers had filled the windows with beautiful stained glass, scattering and coloring the sunlight throughout the interior as if filtered through a thousand prisms. Today, with the mid-morning sun streaming through the east windows, the colors played throughout the nave.

"As you know," the Archbishop continued, "The stones of this very pulpit upon which I stand were donated to you by the Church of Canterbury. In the late eighteen-hundreds, stone was taken from the Bell Harry Tower and carved with depictions of the history of the English Bible before sending it to our good friends here in Washington."

Dixon hadn't known that and looked at the massive stone pulpit anew, seeing its ornately carved top, perched on squat stone pillars an easy ten feet above the Church floor. Carvings of men and Gothic designs in deep bas-relief covered the thick, solid balustrade. He would have to look at it more closely later, Dixon thought to himself.

"It seems only fitting, therefore," the Archbishop said smiling broadly, "That I start my journey across America from this very spot."

Dixon half listened to the remainder of the Archbishop's comments as his thoughts again drifted back to the church. These imposing, but graceful walls always gave Dixon the feeling he was in the very presence of God. Today, that feeling was stronger and more profound than ever. It gave him a deep sense of peace to be here so close to God, a peace he hadn't known since the Chinese massacre had turned and twisted his insides like never before. But here, in one of His treasured Gothic cathedrals, he found his inner agitation calmed and at rest. Dixon closed his eyes as he felt the relaxation wash over him and in moments, he fell into his first sound sleep in days.

"Wake up," Elise urgently whispered, gently shaking his arm.

"Huh?" Dixon only slowly regained awareness. He wiped some drool off his mouth.

"Honey, it's your turn."

Dixon's neck was sore where it had supported his hanging head as he had dozed off. He looked around trying to remember where he was. The massive piers and windows immediately told him he was in the National Cathedral. The place was unnaturally quiet although filled with people.

"Honey, get up and go talk." Elise whispered with unmistakable urgency in her voice. She pushed his arm toward the aisle where Tyrone

Grune waited. Dixon saw his press secretary's face pinched with strain. Dixon got to his feet, but a feeling of lightheadedness drained his vision. He sagged, grabbing the pew in front of him for support. Slowly his vision cleared, as did his thoughts. He had to go up to a lectern and make his welcoming comments to the Archbishop of Canterbury.

What had happened? Oh, yes, he had fallen asleep in the Lord's house. He almost smiled until he realized everyone was looking at him expectantly. A few hushed whispers reached his ears. Following Grune's direction, he stepped up to the tall dark wood dais set up for his comments. Apparently, the laity was not allowed to stand in the pulpit. Sheets of paper with his remarks were waiting for him on the lectern. He looked down at the unfamiliar words on the first page. Why had Ty put him up in front of all these people unprepared? Normally he would have practiced his speech several times before delivery. He cleared his throat and looked up at the audience, and noted the video cameras standing behind the assembled crowd recording everything he did.

He looked down at the words again and started speaking into the microphone, almost mechanically, obviously reading like a schoolboy giving his book report. Turning the page, he started remembering parts of the address and he began smoothing out his words and looking up at the audience. He still wondered why he hadn't practiced it before. He would speak to Tyrone later. Fortunately, his comments were brief and he quickly finished. Since they were in a Church, there was no applause as he concluded, which was an uncomfortable experience for one so used to it. With an unsettled feeling, he left the dais and walked down the steps back to his seat.

CHAPTER 50

Morloch watched Perera close the door behind him as he left. *Damn!* Another doctor—no, two this time, possibly three. And two were respected researchers and worse, one was the now famous doctor who had saved that damn jet from crashing. That Dr. James could blow this whole thing up in a hurry. Even the whisper of a problem from a hero like Dr. James would get unrelenting press scrutiny. But, he concluded after some reflection, there was a way to turn Dr. James' fame against him.

Morloch's thoughts turned to the bigger problem. These reports from observant physicians were getting too fucking frequent. Someone would catch the ear of the press or the FDA and make it stick. He couldn't allow that to happen, not before his back-up plan was operational. He needed to arrange a short cut to Paradise's introduction.

He dialed a number and Sharod Houssan, his Chief of Operations picked up the line. "Yes."

"Sharod, can you come up here?"

"Sure. I'll be right in."

As Morloch hung up, his thoughts turned to Oscar Perera. Once on the market, Eden had skyrocketed into the amazing success they had all hoped it would. Suspecting there might be some inquiries regarding encephalitis related to Eden, he installed Perera as the safety officer with instructions for him to report only to Morloch.

Perera, much to his surprise and dismay, had taken a physician call regarding encephalitis in someone who was taking Eden. After some careful inquiries, Perera determined that it was likely the same encephalitis they had seen in the animals—their first human case. With Paul Tobias suffering through the illness of his daughter, Morloch had pointedly instructed Perrera to keep Tobias out of the loop.

Morloch then had charged Mallis to investigate the inquiring physician and take appropriate action, which he did, eliminating the threat of exposure. Unfortunately, the first call was followed by a second, and now there were a total of six cases related to Eden—at least before today—and Morloch had called in Mallis on each one. While their luck so far had held and word had not gotten out, Morloch knew his time was running out—they were reaching the limit to how many more cases they could cover up. Morloch desperately needed FDA approval for Paradise so he could pull Eden off the market in time to avoid any public connection of Eden with the brain disease.

With Tobias now dead, only Oscar Perera knew of the problem with Eden and he represented the largest threat to Morloch. While Morloch's immediate concern had been Tobias—who would still have been productively toiling away in blissful ignorance had he not gotten that dammed call—Morloch was now concerned about Perera. Eliminating him would be problematic. Tobias' work on Paradise was essentially done and could easily be taken over by any of Trident's other scientists, but he needed Perera to field the encephalitis calls, at least for the next several years. Morloch, considering the options, decided to ask Mallis to keep a closer watch on his Safety Officer.

Houssan walked in.

"I want to accelerate Paradise's production by several months," Morloch said, without preamble.

Houssan, a large, square-jawed Egyptian, sat down and thought a minute before speaking. "Most of it rests on completing the new facility in Puerto Rico and getting Paradise approval from the FDA. We can distribute Paradise within two months after that, but you know them, it might take a year or more."

"Time we don't have."

"Well, pushing everyone to the max, I think I can start initial batch testing in a couple of months, and, pending certification, full production in another two. But it still depends on the FDA." Sharod shrugged his large shoulders. "That part is out of my hands."

Houssan's comment triggered a thought. Morloch had gotten Eden an expedited review through a generous bribe of Trident stock. Typically, follow-on compounds like Paradise don't get the expedited review from the FDA, that designation is reserved for important and critically needed drugs, but he might be able to repeat the persuasion for Paradise. That could shave six to eight months off the review process and get Paradise on the market much earlier.

"Sharod, I need you to be ready and fully certified for production in five months at the latest, in case the FDA approves it quickly. I don't want to be caught jerking off."

"Okay," Houssan sighed, "You always ask the impossible. I better start making some calls."

After Houssan left, Morloch buzzed his secretary. "Karen, can you extend a VIP invitation to Secretary Jacob Castell for our Stockholder's meeting?" He had to get that expedited review.

"I'll get right on it."

Morloch snapped off the intercom and punched a private number into his secure cell phone.

CHAPTER 51

Tyrone Grune took the podium in front of the White House press corps and pulled out his prepared comments. It was more crowded than usual, with a number of foreign news teams present, in addition to all the regular domestic networks. The bright video lights switched on and he cleared his throat.

"This morning, the President attended a secular service at the Washington National Cathedral to welcome Archbishop Sloan Northbourne, the Archbishop of Canterbury. He made some prepared comments and held a luncheon reception for the Archbishop afterwards at the White House, in the State Dining Room." He looked up at the press vultures and took a deep breath.

"During the Archbishop's address, President Dixon drifted off to sleep . . . probably like many of you have done in church at one time or another, I would guess." He had worked hard to make this comment seem offhand and casual. He flashed a smile. "The President woke up and then delivered his comments. Any speculation," Grune looked squarely through the lights at the press corps, "about the President's health is misdirected, I can assure you. He is back in the Oval Office and conducting business as usual. I will now take some questions."

Any mention of the President's health had been a matter of intense debate among the White House Senior staff. Jeff Bell had recommended against it, saying it would legitimize the concern. Grune had argued the opposite, that failing to mention it smacked of either ignorance or a cover-up. Besides it would come up in the questioning anyway. Arthur Slywotsky, the White House Counsel, threw the tiebreaker vote. The wording was also a compromise, but Grune was satisfied with the final version. Now to see if it had worked. He pointed at the front row. "Victoria?"

Victoria Hogue from the Washington Post rose. "Ty, we saw the President stagger when he stood up and then he fumbled his opening statement. Now, I've gone to sleep a few times in my life . . ." That drew a chuckle from the reporters. "But I've never woken up as confused as he looked. Is he on medication? Or does he have something you're not telling us?"

Grune nodded. "As you all know, and most of you reported, President's Dixon's health was perfect as determined by Dr. Thomas Green, the President's personal physician. I hardly think something has happened since then to affect it."

Hogue persisted. "Is that a definite no?"

"Yes, it's a definite no." Grune replied. "I believe that's grammatically correct. Alfred?" he said, pointing at another familiar face three rows back.

Alfred Maloney from the Daily Beast stood up. "I would like to hear you specifically deny that he is taking any drugs, like Vicky asked. But my question is whether or not the stress of the Thanksgiving Day massacre has affected him in a significant way and that his sleeping in church is a symptom of that?"

That one hit home, thought Grune. "That's easy," Grune began, "No drugs, no problems with stress. Sure, he's concerned about China, but they're not threatening the United States in any way, so stress is not an issue. And to be honest, I'm not sure why you're all talking about the President's health."

"You brought it up first," Eric Knowles, from MSNBC, called out bringing another chuckle. "But with his prayer at the school—"

"We denied that—" Grune interrupted.

"Of course you did, but we all heard the tapes. I think he said the word 'prayer.' My question is between the school incident and this confusion thing, I'm worried there's something you aren't telling us. Can we ask President Dixon personally about his health?"

Grune had expected this question and had rehearsed his answer. "First, your premise is faulty. The President remains in excellent health and spirits. There is no medical condition affecting the president's health and he is not on drugs."

Knowles was not so easily dissuaded. "Can we ask the President personally? I think our access to him has become an issue—at least it has for MSNBC. When can we talk to him directly?"

Grune held his ground. "He's busy, he's not avoiding you."

"Scouts honor?" Victoria Hague called out.

Grune smiled pleasantly, but ignored the question. "John?" he said pointing at another reporter.

"What about China's reaction to Taiwan President Quin's visit?"

Grune smiled graciously. Back on firm ground again. "No mystery about that. They're surprised and very irritated."

CHAPTER 52

Johnnie sat beside Steve in the Lexus coupe looking out the side window. "We're almost at your favorite part, Son." They approached the transition from the Loop 101 to the Red Mountain freeway with a ribbon of concrete curving up and over the freeways below. While marked for one lane, its generous shoulder was wide enough for two lanes or a disabled car. Johnnie's endless fascination with the sweeping bridge made Steve take the slight detour to drive over it.

"All right, Dad. I see it now." He hugged the windowsill and pressed his face to the glass. "Slow down, Dad." He always asked to slow down and Steve allowed him the request as long as there were no other cars behind them. A quick check in the rear view mirror revealed a UPS truck.

"We've got a tail. No-can-do today, Son." Johnnie seemed not to notice as he watched the other lanes pass far below. Johnnie's enthusiasm made Steve feel guilty that he had been neglecting his son lately. He would try and spend more time with Johnnie tonight.

"How far down?" Johnny asked for at least the tenth time.

"I'd guess about one hundred feet or so." Steve answered for at least the tenth time. He chuckled inside and wondered if he had been as inquisitive as a boy. Probably, he thought, but with both his parents dead, he would never get those questions answered, nor could he share his son with them.

Johnnie had been a relatively late decision, with both his and Anne's busy careers and frequent traveling. Anne, four years younger than Steve, came from a large family and one day at thirty-five, she decided it was now or never and within ten months they had little Johnnie. Steve had held the squirming bundle thinking there never had been anything quite so precious. He wanted a little girl next, but scarring in the fallopian tubes from a post partum infection prevented Anne from conceiving again and they had decided against the alternatives.

The beeping of his cell phone snapped him back to the present.

"Steve, I'm glad I caught you."

"Marty, how's it going?"

"We got over a hundred responses."

"What are you talking about?"

"The miracle of e-mail. I leveraged my NIH position and talked the American Radiology Academy, or whatever they call themselves, into sending a mass e-mail to all their member radiologists. We included representative pictures of Captain Palmer's scan and asked them to reply if they'd ever seen a similar case. If they had, they were asked to supply clinical information, a medication list, plus a sample of the film."

"And?" Steve asked.

"We got a pretty good response."

"So, how many matched the profile?"

Marty drew in a breath. "About ninety had matching MRI scans. About seventy or more of those were taking Eden, based on the med lists and more are trickling in."

"Seventy? My God, Marty."

"I bet," Marty continued, "that some of those without a history of Eden were taking it on the QT, like Captain Palmer. And this only reflects the radiologists who responded. The actual number is probably considerably higher."

"Oh, man," Steve responded, trying to absorb the information. "Any geographical patterns?"

"Nope. Small clusters in Los Angeles and New York, but other than that, they're all scattered across the map, the U.S., Canada, and Europe. Even some from Asia. Hard to spot a pattern."

"The beautiful people had to pick it up first," Steve surmised. He had a mental image of parties where they traded Eden inhalers and popped Viagra.

"Well, without an obvious pattern, this might have escaped anyone's notice for some time," Marty observed. "But it still seems odd that no one picked it up before. I went to our radiologists here at George Washington and they managed to find two more cases that matched. Different doctors took care of them and no one made the connection. This must be so sporadic that it hasn't caught anybody's attention."

"Including Trident's?" Steve still could not get over the enormity of the news. He had expected something, but not ninety. "This is really big."

"Bigger than the two of us, as Bogart said. Anyhow, based on these results, I'm going to request a full investigation."

Half an hour later, his last e-mail message sent, Marty ambled out of the door of the massive NIH lab building and into the nearly empty parking lot. A light snow fell, melting as it hit the pavement, but collected on the few remaining cars. Coming to an older Nissan Maxima, he fumbled with his keys for a moment and opened his door. After a few tries, the car started and he drove off, the wipers scraping off the wet snow.

On his way out of the vast parking lot, he passed a one-ton pickup truck with vapor trickling out of its tailpipe. Silently and smoothly, the truck pulled out behind Marty's car.

Traffic was light with the snowfall and the late hour. Marty looked forward to making good time on the beltway. His wife was on a business trip to Indianapolis, otherwise he couldn't work so late without making excuses.

The number of responses from his e-mail had overwhelmed him and cataloging each case would be a monumental effort, but he could divert some funding from some of his other projects while he wrote a grant to cover the costs. If Eden caused prion conversion, he had no time to waste.

As he rumbled up a curving overpass, Marty noticed a shiny green pickup pull even with his Maxima. Looking over at the large truck, he stared at a shadowy face staring back at him.

With a sudden chill, Marty slowed to allow the truck to edge ahead. Without warning, the heavy truck swerved into his lane. The truck smashed into Marty's front fender, slamming the lighter car into the guardrail of the overpass in a deafening screech of metal and concrete.

Marty wrenched the now useless steering wheel and cried aloud as his car pitched over the rail and fell down onto the freeway below, landing on its roof, crushing Marty's skull.

The first driver on the freeway saw the car plunge from the overpass and swerved in time to miss it. The second driver observed only the sudden, erratic move of the car in front of her and too late saw the inverted vehicle materialize in her headlights. Skidding on the wet road, she slammed into the overturned car deploying her airbag. She survived the impact, but a third car smashed into hers, rupturing her gas tank and spewing burning fuel across the road.

The pile up was one of the deadliest in Maryland's history. The flames engulfed seventeen cars and could not be effectively extinguished by emergency crews. They watched helplessly as the intense gasoline and oil fire burnt itself out, eventually pulling eighteen bodies from the smoking wreckage.

CHAPTER 53

"Steve!" Amos Sheridan nearly shouted. "Come, come, look what we've got." Amos led Steve to a refrigerator-sized hot box and with latex gloves on, pulled out ten covered clear rectangular plastic blocks. Looking closer, Steve saw that each held a number of shallow indentations arranged in a grid of six by ten.

"Here's the layout," Amos explained, lining up the blocks on the table. "We put four different concentrations of Eden into fifty different nerve cell lines and the suspension solution minus the Eden into the same fifty as a control." He pointed at the blocks. "The highest concentration went into these fifty wells, the next highest concentration in these and so on."

"I take it you got some prion conversion." Steve looked at the covered plates knowing he could not see anything without a microscope.

"I'll say." Pointing at a column on one of the blocks, "This one here shows devastating conversion. It's really active, Steve. If this happens in humans, well, to put it bluntly, they're screwed."

"Did they all convert?"

Sheridan's bushy eyebrows went up. "That's the interesting part. Now, look," he pointed with his pen. "In this cell line, all concentrations were effective. The highest concentration first converted within hours and within the day, the prions propagated in all the cells. It took another day for the nerve cells to die. Later, all the lower titrations converted in turn. But, Steve, it's like you turned on a switch. I've never seen anything like it."

"And the others?"

"Well, that's got me scratching my head."

"What do you mean?" Steve asked.

"Well, seeing the first results so soon, I expected them all to go within a day or so and sure enough, two days later, another cell line, at the highest concentration, began converting and now some of the intermediate plates are beginning to show signs of change."

"And the rest are still normal."

"Forty-eight lines so far, yeah. Apparently some are more susceptible than others. The controls, of course, are all normal."

"What do you mean lines?"

"A single person's brain. We get the cells from rapid autopsy specimens and grow them."

"You mean a line comes from a single person's brain." Steve questioned.

"Right. Unique genetic makeup and all."

"So, if I understand this correctly, one person's cells changed quickly, another line is converting more slowly, and the others haven't changed at all?"

"Correct."

"So far," Steve added.

"Right. So far or maybe never."

"But it proves the point," Steve said, "Eden is responsible for the prions showing up. We now have the smoking gun for this brain infection."

"It sure does. I need to do lots more studies, Stevie, my man," Amos Sheridan waved his arms like an excited kid getting a bicycle on his birthday. "This is just the beginning—"

"Amos," Steve interrupted the animated scientist, "there are millions of people taking Eden. They may all get it, or only a few. Just like the tissue cultures. What factors determine who is going to get this and how long do they have to take it before it starts?"

"Can't tell, too many factors. Not yet anyhow, maybe never. I need more tests." Sheridan shook his head. "The differences could be explained by the tissue, their age, nutrients, or like CJD, it could be their genetics. It could be a thousand things."

"Something's missing, Amos," Steve said slowly, trying to reason it out. "If we found this so easily, I'm sure Trident did the same testing. They had to know."

Amos pulled on his beard thoughtfully. "I would think so, too."

"So, what happened? Where's Trident's data?"

"Have you called them?"

"Yeah, but I got nowhere."

"Maybe they only tested it in other cell types or in lab animals."

"Unlikely," Steve said. "Amos, can you test it in rats? I mean can you spray this stuff into their noses?"

"I'm way ahead of you. I've pulled three techs off other projects and I'm writing a paper and five more grants. We're going to turn this whole thing upside down."

On the way back to his office, Steve punched up Marty's number. He was eager to share his new information. "Dr. Walker's office," a female voice answered.

That's unusual, thought Steve, usually it went right to voice mail if Marty was not in his office. "Is Dr. Walker in?"

"I'm afraid not. Can I take a message?"

"Where is he?"

"I'm just the switchboard operator, I can't tell you."

"Why are you answering his line?"

"There was a fire in his office and his line no longer works."

"A fire? What happened? Is he okay?"

"I am not permitted to say."

"Is he okay?" Steve nearly shouted into the phone.

"I am not permitted to say."

"Then who is?"

"You can call the neurology office."

Biting his tongue, Steve managed to stay civil. "Can you please connect me?"

"One moment," she said.

The line rang. Another female voice answered the phone. This time, Steve changed tactics.

"I am Dr. Walker's step-brother. Can you tell me where he is?"

The voice on the other end sighed. "I'm afraid Dr. Walker is deceased. A terrible freeway accident. I'm very sorry."

"What? How?"

"He ran off an overpass and crashed."

CHAPTER 54

Joe, a lean, black-haired athletic man in his forties sat in the driver's seat of a white van down the street from Steve James's house and watched it through military grade binoculars. He and Doug, sitting next to him, had watched Steve's Spanish contemporary house for over an hour after Dr. James, followed by his wife and kid, had driven off. Like so many homes in Scottsdale, it had a red tile roof and pale yellow stucco walls framing tall windows looking up at Camelback Mountain. It was set back on an acre lot with huge bougainvilleas and mesquite trees obscuring much of the front of the house—ideal for their needs.

"Show time."

"Let's go," Doug grinned, putting on latex gloves. He had a tanned face to match his sandy brown hair and eyebrows, giving him the appearance of a bronze statue. He had the good looks and lopsided smile of an actor, an asset he had put to use during his undercover years in the Drug Enforcement Agency.

They got out of the van, casually strapping on tool belts and donning white hard hats. Joe walked over to the green curbside telephone junction box and opened it with a Philips head screwdriver. Pulling out a Westronics series seven transceiver, he kissed it for good luck and attached it to Steve's phone line. Two more wires spliced a second phone line into the transceiver, allowing it to call another number and download the recorded phone calls from Steve's house.

Doug walked across the street to Steve's front door and rang the doorbell. Kerry barked at him through the door's sidelight window. Doug swiftly picked the lock and, through the cracked door, tossed in a piece of beef laced with three Ambien sleeping pills. Kerry gobbled up the Mickey Finn and in moments could no longer stand. Joe joined Doug and they entered, stepping over the groggy dog.

In Steve's master suite, Joe found a .38 Smith and Wesson revolver at the back of the sock drawer. He placed the gun into a Ziploc bag and stored it in the thigh pocket of his overalls. Moments later, he found the box of bullets in the back of the t-shirt drawer. He stowed them in another pocket.

He then extended a collapsible pole and used it to twist off a smoke detector on the ceiling. Inside, he placed a miniaturized Lucent MK-201 repeater with a sensitive cardoid microphone—a highly restricted listening device—after the requisite good luck kiss. He next replaced the smoke detector's nine-volt battery with a fresh one to prevent an untimely weak-battery alarm. Eight more devices and batteries later, he had completed his bugging. A quick look in the garage yielded a pair of used leather work gloves.

Doug, meanwhile, was at Steve's desk, pulling up his e-mail on the computer and scanning through it, making note of various phrases. He found one to Anne concluding, "Love always and forever." *Gotcha!* He pulled out a USB memory drive and within minutes, he had copied selected data files, including Dr. James's E-mail address book, the 'My Documents' folder, and the iPhone data file. He found Quicken and copied its data to the USB drive as well. He then flipped through iPhoto, copying several with good facial shots of Dr. James. He retrieved the USB drive and stowed it in his right thigh pocket.

Pulling out the built-in file drawers, he found the folders with paid bills, bank, investments, and credit card statements. He took a copy of each. Receipts in the trash yielded card expiration dates.

Joe went out the back door and around to the side of the house and in a utility closet, found the natural gas furnace and hot water heater. He turned off the gas valve to the water heater and unscrewed its connection. He fitted a three-way valve between the gas supply and the heater. Onto the third nipple of the valve, he twisted a one-inch diameter plastic tube and threaded it through the sheet metal into the supply air duct of the heat pump. It was ready for use at a moment's notice. By twisting the valve handle, he could redirect the flow of gas from the gas heater into the plastic pipe. From there, the heater fan would distribute large quantities of gas throughout the ductwork into the house. He then memorized every rock and bush back to the front of the house.

Inside, Doug had finished lubricating the doors and had inventoried Steve's shoes. They both walked through the house listening for squeaks in the carpeted floor. Finding none, Joe called a local weather service number from Steve's house. Doug, on a cell phone called a different number, but heard the same weather information from Dr. James's phone. Doug nodded to Joe and they both walked out without either one saying a word. In twenty-five minutes, Steve's house had been fully bugged and prepped—just as his office had been last night.

Settled back in the van, Joe pulled out, making a slow u-turn in the cul-de-sac, and headed back to their hotel. "Piece of cake."

"No kidding. No alarm, stupid dog, too easy." Doug reclined the seat and relaxed. "Just like sweet talking Dr. James's secretary out of his cell phone number."

They had already sent the dozen complaint letters. A seedy attorney would file the court papers this afternoon and the Arizona Republic newspaper would be getting a package from a courier service with camera-ready copy, just as soon as the images Doug had in his coveralls got manipulated in Photoshop later today.

". . . And in two days," Doug finished his thoughts aloud, "Dr. James will never know what hit him."

CHAPTER 55

"Meet ELLIOTT," Rachel Desmond said, standing on the carpeted staircase, gesturing to the manned rows of computer monitors in the large, modern, open space below her. Rachel was director of sales for Mallis and Associates, Kirk Mallis's security company. She was also a stunning brunette with an enhanced bust line that few men could ignore. Today she wore a snug gray pinstriped jacket over a matching skirt that showed her legs above her knees. Her lacy top was sufficiently low to make any man wonder if she had a bra on. She was easily their top sales person in the male-dominated security business.

Her potential client today was Wilson Taylor, Chief of Security from Hale Enterprises, a high tech manufacturing company with a series of patented processes for machining advanced composites. Wilson's objective was to ensure that the company's precious proprietary knowledge did not leave the premises.

Wilson had seen Mallis and Associates' advertisements for several years, placed as they were every month, prominently inside the front cover of Industrial Security Magazine. As his company grew and the need for first-rate security increased, he had finally called them. After a first-class flight—courtesy of Mallis and Associates—Wilson was there in person.

"ELLIOTT," Rachel purred, "is based on the NSA technology that enables the government to listen and analyze over twenty million international phone calls per day. ELLIOTT listens to every word from every one of your company phones, comparing them against key words and phrases programmed into it." From their vantage point overlooking the computer room, she gestured smoothly with her finely manicured hands at the glassed-in racks of servers at the other end of the room.

"Those key words are supplied by you, the client, to tell the computer what words or phrases you want searched. We can program as many as you wish."

Wilson looked impressed. "Nice."

"Come this way, Mr. Taylor," she said, holding firmly to his upper arm and guiding him down the staircase to the computer room floor. Wilson breathed in her perfume.

"Words like 'composite machining,' 'patented process,' the names of your competitors, and the like—as many as you want." She gave him her warmest smile. "You can even specify phrases or words in proximity to each other to enhance the sensitivity and specificity. Mr. Taylor, no one has better technology than Mallis and Associates."

"Isn't this illegal?" Wilson asked, salivating at both the technology and Rachel.

She ran her hands through her thick hair and smiled at him. "Fully legal as long as your employees are using your business phones. We have thirty T-3 phone cables here and can simultaneously monitor and analyze ten thousand phone lines." She led him through a row of monitors manned by an occasional technician. An alarm went off on one of the screens.

"There goes one now!" Rachel squealed, grabbing Wilson's arm and jumping. The word "prion" flashed across the screen and displayed other information that looked like gibberish to Wilson. He did pick out a couple of names: Dr. Steve James and Sheridan Labs. The technician slid a pair of headphones on and typed at the keyboard.

"The man monitoring the conversation reviews the last several minutes of the conversation and determines its relevance to your specifications. Any and all communications will be electronically forwarded to your attention for review. You are totally in control."

Rachel walked on still casually holding Wilson's arm. "We also monitor E-mail and web page usage. Some of the pornography sites are quite, well, unusual." She cocked her head at him. "You know, pre-teens doing all sorts of explicit things, large objects inserted in, umm, strange places, girl with girl, and so on. I can show them to you if you like."

Wilson's face turned deep red. Rachel had, as usual, managed to get her prospect thinking about things other than objections. "Uh, that won't be necessary. Thanks."

"Do you have any questions, Mr. Taylor?" Rachel leaned forward slightly, allowing the upper edge of her black brassiere to show.

"Uh, how much does it cost?"

She rewarded him with her warm smile again. "A pittance compared to your potential loss if General Dynamics gets ahold of your technology." She had done her homework and knew Hale Manufacturing feared that General Dynamics might get a whiff of their secret technology, which would put them out of business in a heartbeat.

"Are you the man who can decide?"

"I sure am."

"Good." She gently leaned against his arm pressing a breast against it. "Let's go to my office."

What Rachel failed to mention was the extra service available to Hale Manufacturing at a substantial additional price. While the vast majority of Mallis and Associates' business was legal monitoring for legitimate clients, the other line of business was highly illegal, but generated almost half the profits—unreported, of course. These clients, including many name-brand companies, wanted extra monitoring. This included listening in on anybody talking on their home phone, cell phone, or through listening devices. If you paid their rates, you could call your target.

And, for even more select clients, Mallis and Associates would arrange other more direct and much more expensive interventions. This was the main reason that Kirk Mallis had formed his company after getting booted from his government job. It made his killing almost legitimate.

By lunchtime, Rachel had closed her sale with Wilson Taylor for Hale Manufacturing.

CHAPTER 56

"Steve, can you get Johnnie his bath tonight?" Anne called out.

Steve sitting in his study, deep in melancholy thought did not respond. Eden caused prions in nerve cultures. Marty would have wanted to know that. *Eden caused prions.* What would Marty do? Call Trident? Not that pompous safety officer. But Marty was dead. What about all the cases Marty had found?

"Steve, did you hear me?" Anne called again.

He sat up to see Anne standing in the doorway, scowling. "Didn't you hear me?"

"Yes," Steve answered. "Sort of."

"Why didn't you answer?"

Steve shrugged. "I was thinking," he said lamely.

Anne whirled abruptly and walked off.

He followed her to the kitchen where she was putting away the last of their dinner. Steve realized with a pang that he hadn't even known they were eating. "I'm sorry, I didn't hear you at first."

Anne turned to face him. "Where have you been this past week? You've retreated into your study, ignoring your family. Johnnie just asked, 'What's wrong with Daddy?' I had to make up something so he wouldn't worry about you." She slammed a drawer shut. "What's going on, Stevie, to shut your family out like this? Is it all this Shirley-Eden thing?"

"That's not fair. This is important. It needs my full attention." Steve *had* dropped out of his family's life, which wasn't like him.

"Why is it that some sick woman in the hospital takes all of your day and your nights too? Don't we get some of your time?" She rapped her forefinger against Steve's temple. "Where are you? We, your family, want and need you."

"I'm sorry." Steve didn't feel like telling Anne everything. Not now. He didn't have the energy. He just wanted to be left alone.

"You've treated dying people before. What's so different now?" Anne efficiently rinsed Johnnie's dishes and placed them in the dishwasher. She had tears in her eyes. "You don't sleep, you don't eat, and you're chasing this thing twenty-four hours a day, locking us out." She began vigorously sponging the counter.

Steve tried to pull Anne into his arms, but she pulled away. "Not now." She pushed him towards Johnnie's room. "Go take care of your son who wants some time with his daddy before he turns eighteen and leaves us for good." She tossed the sponge into the sink and walked out.

Just like that, she was gone. She was entirely right, of course. He had been in his own world, except when he read to Johnnie at bedtime and talked to Anne as they were getting ready to turn in. She didn't understand what he was going through—but was that her fault or his?

Steve stared after Anne, trying to decide what to do next. It was like Eden; he had all the facts, but no direction on what to do.

He looked down and met Kerry's eyes, his tail wagging expectantly. Steve knelt and rubbed under his neck, fluffing his short fur. Kerry rolled over and put his paws in the air for more attention. Steve obliged for a moment by stroking along his ribs and stomach.

"Kerry, old pal, I'm in the doghouse. We boys got to stick together." Kerry licked his hand. Steve stood up and went into Johnnie's room, with Kerry trotting behind.

CHAPTER 57

Jeff Bell hunched over his computer in an office that was spacious by White House standards. It had a coveted window and, best of all, he did not have to share it with anybody. The bulk of the staff had to shoehorn several desks into offices meant for one, making the West Wing noisy and crowded. The President's Chief of Staff could close his door, which he frequently did, to make private phone calls and to think. Virtually nobody else had any privacy and that, Bell concluded, was the reason there were so many news leaks.

His phone rang. Somebody had gotten through his secretary or had his direct line. He picked it up. "Bell."

"Jeff, he's gone again." Bell recognized Aaron Davenport's voice. Davenport was the Agent in Charge of the President's security detail.

"Shit."

"This is his third time this week. Wesley's car this time."

"At least it wasn't an intern."

"Don't be flip. Can't you talk to him and get him to stop these sudden departures? We can't protect him like this."

"Well, we can't put the leader of the free world in handcuffs now, can we?" He waited for a chuckle, which did not come. "Okay," Bell sighed, "I'll talk to him, but I know what he'll say."

"Please do what you can, Jeff. We're losing sleep over here. We can accommodate nearly everything he wants if he just gives us time to prepare."

"It's his new trick and he loves it."

"Jeff," Davenport sighed, "we're all tricked out over here. He's got men who'll give their life for him, but he's playing this game nobody understands. Give me some help. And talk to Lassie. Maybe she can put some pressure on him."

"I can do that, but I don't think she knows any better than you do when he's going to bolt."

"What do you think's gotten in him? Was he like this when he was governor?"

"No," Bell said thoughtfully. "But the pressure of this China thing has him wound up tighter than I've ever seen him. That's something he never had to deal with as governor."

"Perhaps, but I've been here a dozen years and I've never seen this kind of behavior before from a president."

"I just don't know, Aaron, but I'll talk to him and let you know what he says."

"Thanks, Jeff."

Bell hung up, staring blankly at his computer as he mentally rewound the last two weeks of his interactions with his old friend. Robert Dixon *was* more withdrawn, more distant, and his mental edge had dulled. Bell had ascribed it to the China crisis, but maybe it was something more.

He had worked side by side with Robert Dixon through his administration as Governor of Virginia and the long, grueling presidential campaign. Only when Robert was near exhaustion did he ever slow down. At those times, the signals were clear: irritability, low energy, and mental dullness. Maybe it was just stress, but he didn't usually make dumb mistakes like forgetting his talk at the National Cathedral and scolding China over the massacre. And these spontaneous joy rides, he supposed, were a way for him to let off steam, but it was obviously dangerous.

He would speak to Elise; Davenport's suggestion was logical. It would make them all much happier if he stayed put. He hated making the call to her, but like so many things in his political life, they didn't go away by just wishing. He picked up the phone and dialed.

CHAPTER 58

Steve walked into his office earlier than usual and in a foul mood. Last night had gone as predicted. After he had tucked Johnnie in he had dutifully gone straight to bed. Anne had turned in already with the lights out and did not slide over to snuggle him like she usually did. After a fitful night, Steve rolled out of bed five minutes before the 6:00 alarm and got dressed.

Ann had given him a perfunctory kiss before he left and reminded him that it was his turn to pick up Johnnie from karate school this afternoon. And Marty was still dead and Shirley was still dying and Eden was still killing people.

He saw the certified letter laying on his desk as soon as he walked into his office. Steve puzzled over it a minute as he saw it was from the Arizona Board of Medical Examiners. He ripped open the envelope and read the letter in disbelief.

"Dr. James." Etta walked into Steve's office, finding him askew in his chair scowling. "There's a man in the waiting room who says he needs to see you. Something about papers you need to sign for—"

"Go away." Steve didn't want to see anybody, much less some prick who wanted to give him papers.

"Sorry, Dr. James. He said it was important."

"How important?"

"He wouldn't say. Just that it had to be you."

"What kind of bullshit is this?" Steve hauled his tired frame out of the chair.

"Another bad night?" Etta asked as he walked past.

As he entered the empty morning waiting room, a fifty-ish, tanned man, dressed casually in an open necked multicolored shirt and wrinkled Khaki pants stood up. "Dr. James?"

"Yeah," Steve muttered irritably, looking at the fat manila envelope the man clutched in his left hand.

"I have a delivery for you. Please sign here." He thrust a clipboard in front of Steve who scribbled his initials on the line next to his printed name. The man handed Steve the manila envelope. "Good luck, sir."

Steve looked at the envelope. Printed in large letters, the return address said Gauthier, Olgivey and Dwyer, LLC, Attorney's at Law. He ripped off the tamper-evident tape and opened the envelope. Inside was a set of stapled papers. Sliding them out, he read, 'Jane Doe vs. Steven Kyle James, MD and spouse . . .'

What the hell?

' . . . Dr. James having willfully, neglectfully, and deliberately . . .' Steve skimmed to the actual claim and digested its meaning. Steve reeled like he had just been punched in the gut, and sagged into a waiting room chair.

Etta peered into the waiting room. "Dr. James, you look white as a ghost. What is it?" She bustled over to sit next to him.

He examined the papers again, searching for a sign that it was a mistake, or that it was addressed to the wrong person. But, no, the name and address were correct. His eyes read the opening paragraph describing him in the most despicable terms. It was written by some dickhead lawyer, accusing him of every malfeasance of trust, dereliction of duty, and personal insult the lawyer could put in respectable English.

He was being sued for sexual abuse. *Goddamn it!*

He looked at the front of the papers again, reading 'Jane Doe.' They wouldn't even say who was suing him. How could he defend himself? The whole thing stunk. He walked back to his office struggling to control his anger. Etta trailed after him.

Nobody had ever sued him before, nor complained about his medical competency and here he was facing both the same day.

"What is it, Dr. James?" Etta asked quietly, breaking Steve's thoughts.

"I'm being sued for sexual abuse."

"You? Sexual abuse?" Etta tried to suppress a giggle. "Never in a million years. They delivered that to the wrong doctor."

"Nope." He tossed the papers onto his desk. He held out the medical board letter for her to read. She scanned it quickly, her cheerful face growing concerned. "Oh, my." She looked at Steve. "This is terrible."

His partner Julia Weisgaard walked in. "There are absolutely no secrets around here. I heard you just got served. What's it about?"

"Sexual abuse." Steve gave the Board letter to Julia. "And this."

"Oh no." Julia sat down in the padded chair in front of Steve's desk reading the letter. ". . . due to the number and seriousness of the complaints this communication was expedited . . .' Jesus, Steve. They want you to defend your license."

Steve paced. "I need an attorney."

"Call your insurance. They'll tell you what to do," Julia said.

"Is this even under my malpractice? I don't know if this suit was from a patient, an ex-employee or someone off the street who wants to make a quick buck. Damn, damn, damn." He wanted to hit something.

"Dr. James," Jennifer, his office manager walked in. "I just heard. I'm so sorry." She looked hesitant. "I'm afraid I have some more bad news. I was reading the paper this morning and I came across this. You may have seen it already." She held out a folded section of the paper to Steve.

Steve looked at the paper. He had been too tired this morning to read it. He saw several ads and some local news articles, but one leaped off the page at him. It had a picture of his face under a large caption: 'Have you had sexual assault or malpractice from Dr. Steven James?' It had a large 800 number posted at the bottom.

Steve sat down in despair as his life unraveled. He looked around at the concerned faces.

Julia grabbed the paper and looked at it shaking her head. "Someone doesn't like you. Who have you pissed off lately?"

The intercom buzzed. "Dr. James, there's a Mr. Talbot from the newspaper wanting to ask you some questions. Something about a lawsuit. I told him I'd see if you were in."

"Tell him to go to hell. And no calls today—at all." He stood up struggling to put all the events into context, as anger began replacing his sense of helplessness. "This didn't just happen by coincidence. This is a concerted effort to destroy my reputation. There's got to be someone behind all this bullshit."

"I agree," Julia said.

"And it's all for public consumption. Someone told the papers."

"But who?" Julia asked.

Steve's mind turned over the possibilities. "I have no idea."

CHAPTER 59

"Anne," Steve said over his mobile phone, "I may have some relatively good news." He had picked up Johnnie from karate class and they were driving back home, the December daylight having faded into a blue glow that hugged the western horizon, leaving the rest of the moonless sky black.

Earlier, Steve had told Anne everything about the suit, the medical board, and the newspaper advertisement. Her anger, if anything, was more strident than his, a she-wolf protecting her family. If there were anything good from this crisis, it had pulled them back together—a hell of a way to fix an argument.

"Steve . . ." Anne interrupted, her voice flat and distant, not at all like her earlier animation.

Steve didn't hear her. "I had a good meeting with the attorney today." He had canceled his office schedule to meet with Angela Burkholt, who came highly recommended by his malpractice insurance carrier. Steve was inclined to trust their choice since they had worked with her before and a lot of their money was resting on her capabilities. "She agrees that most of this seems pre-arranged and perhaps orchestrated, her words, but she says it'll take some time to get to the bottom of it, if ever. I'm not sure I like the sound of that last bit, but she said there were plenty of things we could do to sort this thing out."

"Steve," Anne repeated. "I've—I got something just now. Some pictures. They were left in the mailbox."

Steve glided past a jacked up one-ton pickup truck. "What is it, Honey?"

"The pictures . . . I don't know. They're . . ."

Steve could hear her choke up. "Sweetheart, what is it?"

"Pictures . . . Steve, it's pictures of you with another woman."

"What? Well, you can't possibly believe any of that, not after all that's happened today."

"I don't know what to believe. When you called today telling me all that stuff, I was plenty mad. But this—these pictures— Tell me you didn't do this because, right now I want to strangle you."

"Anne," he said as calmly as he could despite the racing of his heart. "I didn't do anything of the sort. Whatever they are, they're fake. Trust me on this."

Johnnie looked at his dad questioningly. "Daddy? Are you and Mommy arguing?" Steve smiled at him and winked as if everything was all right, but it wasn't, not by a long shot. Anne was crying. "The note says these were taken in Palm Beach last September at an investigator's meeting. How would anybody know that kind of detail?"

"Nothing happened. Nothing." This was worse than anything that could happen to him. He could never contemplate Anne's loss of trust.

"There's also a bunch of e-mails to a Natalie. They're love letters," she cried. "You signed them, 'love always and forever'. That's what you always write me. How can these be faked? Tell me, damn it."

"Daddy?"

Steve, sick to his stomach, waved him down. Johnnie stared at his father with round puzzled eyes. His mommy and daddy never argued. His face looked near tears.

Their car approached the high overpass Johnnie loved so much, but neither paid any attention. The one-ton pickup truck behind them sped up and closed the distance to Steve's car. The two vehicles passed a tractor-trailer rig chugging up toward the overpass with a large load of steel pipe strapped to a flatbed trailer.

"I don't know," Steve said. "Some sort of digital manipulation, I suppose. Take my head and put it on another body. They're always doing that with celebrities and stuff. Honey, please . . . All this happening today, it's planned. Somebody's trying to wreck my life—our lives."

Steve neared the wide one-lane ramp with the pickup nearly broad-side to his car. He looked over at the truck in time to see the driver staring at him with an intensity that raised the hair on the back of his neck. Was there a second man in the truck? As they entered the freeway transition, Steve noticed that the width was rapidly narrowing and soon there would barely be enough room for both of them.

Dropping the phone, he grabbed the wheel with both hands and stepped hard on his brakes just as the large truck swerved over at his car. Its tail hit the front end of the Lexus, smashing it against the concrete barrier with a shriek of metal.

Johnnie screamed and clutched at his father as they watched a section of the pre-fab concrete barrier break off and fall away into the dark night. Steve stopped the car, shaken and angry. He could hear Anne's voice shrieking over the phone.

The truck stopped in front of Steve and to his horror began backing up, aiming the massive jacked up rear end at him.

Steve slammed his car into reverse, but before he could back up, the rear of the truck rammed Steve's Lexus, setting off the air bags with a deafening explosion in his face. Steve barely heard Johnnie's cries.

The impact drove the truck's raised rear-end up and onto the hood of Steve's car causing the truck's widely spaced rear wheels to lose contact with the pavement. The truck slipped off the hood of the car as Steve accelerated backwards, slamming back to the ground.

"Help! Help! Daddy, please!"

It was now a contest of speed as Steve accelerated backwards as fast as he could with the truck in close pursuit. Steve saw an eighteen-wheeler's top cabin lights over the curved ramp barrier, but he could not see its windshield. *Shit!* He realized the big rig driver couldn't see his car back-ing towards him. They would be crushed between the two much heavier trucks. There was no way out!

"Daddy, make it stop. Please, Daddy." Johnnie pleaded, tears stream-ing down his face.

Steve heard his son's cries. *Not Johnnie.* Steve looked at the pickup truck and back at the tractor-trailer, thinking. . . It would be a huge risk.

He stabbed his brake slowing his Lexus rapidly. The truck hit his hood, once again riding over it and lifting the rear wheels off the ground. Johnnie screamed at the impact, which crumpled the hood and buckled the radiator, sending up a cloud of steam. As he had hoped, the suspended rear truck wheels spun uselessly. Steve then stood on his brakes, slowing both vehicles. His anti-lock brakes pulsated rapidly in a harsh staccato rhythm.

Anne's voice carried up from the floor where the phone lay. "Steve! Johnnie!"

Within moments Steve brought the car and truck to a stop. Hoping against hope that someone did not jump out of the truck with a gun, Steve shifted into drive and floored the gas pedal, his powerful engine straining with the added weight of the truck. They began accelerating gradually. *Would it be enough?*

The eighteen-wheeler swung into view behind them. Johnnie stared back at the looming mass hurtling right for them. "Daddy, it's going to hit us!" he shrieked.

Steve, through the rear view mirror, saw the massive cab shudder under the force of strong braking. Then, to his horror, it twisted and jack-knifed, filling the air with the terrible screech of metal scraping the sides of the freeway barriers like a million fingernails on a huge blackboard. Johnnie held his hands to his ears, screaming.

And still it bore down on them.

Steve stood on the accelerator demanding more speed from the taxed engine. They passed the gap in the freeway wall created by Steve's impact. The trailer of the big rig punched through the broken section, knocking off barrier sections like dominoes, pushing them off into space to fall onto the freeway underneath.

Suddenly, the trailer flipped over on its side dumping its load of steel pipe, scattering them like so many pick-up sticks across the overpass and down onto the freeway below. Several hit the rear of Steve's car, smashing his trunk, causing the car to shudder from the impact.

Moments later, Steve, still pushing the pick-up, exited the ramp. Slamming on his brakes, he dislodged the pickup truck off his hood. Steve then pulled around the truck and raced off down the freeway.

Good, he thought, they were rid of them. In the rear view mirror, however, he saw the pickup truck lurch forward to follow.

"Hurry, Daddy," Johnnie shouted, still watching behind him.

"You bet, Son," Steve said, wondering how far they could go before the engine seized from overheating. The radiator had no more water to spill. Stealing a glance at the gauge, he saw the needle creeping into the red zone.

Picking up the phone, he shouted, "We're fine Honey, got to go. I love you." He punched 911.

A woman's voice answered. "911, emergency."

Trying to control his voice, Steve said, "I'm being chased by a large pickup that just tried to ram me off the road. I need help immediately."

"Where are you?"

"Heading east—no, west on the 202 freeway. My car's damaged and may not go much farther."

"What part of the 202?"

"Uhh, I just passed Center Drive.

"Okay, I'll get someone right away. Please stay on the line."

"It'll be okay, Son." Steve checked the rear view mirror; the truck was gamely following. He wove through the traffic at over ninety miles per hour. He knew he could not go much farther before his engine died. Up ahead, Steve saw a break in the median cable barriers marked with plastic pylons; the scene of an earlier crash. He had an idea.

"Ready for a bat-turn? Hang on." Steve slammed on his brakes and turned sharply into the freeway median, his tires squealing. He performed a fishtailing U-turn to the other side of the freeway. As he merged with the traffic, he saw the pickup truck slowing down. The truck turned, but more slowly, giving Steve much needed headway. The engine temperature was now well into the red.

The operator's voice startled him. "Sir, I have a squad car headed your way. Where are you now?"

"I just U-turned across the median and I'm now headed east."

"East it is. Be careful, sir."

"Let's get lost, Son." Steve exited the freeway and turned left under the freeway and ran the red light at the cross street.

"Exiting the freeway," he informed the operator. "I'm now going north on Center and . . . And turning west onto . . . Sandy Lane."

"Okay, I'll send your new coordinates to the cruiser now."

Sandy Lane took them into an older, middle-class residential neighborhood. Steve hoped to lose the pickup truck on the dark, unlit street. He turned off his lights as he coasted down the street.

The engine started missing; it was only a matter of a few minutes before it would freeze up. Steve turned into a gravel driveway between two houses, pulling far enough to blend in with the oleander hedge and stopped, watching out of the rear window for any signs of pursuit.

"When is the police car going to get here?" he pleaded into his phone.

"He's on his way, sir."

The pickup truck pulled into view directly behind him.

"Shit!" Steve exclaimed, "How did he find us?" He was trapped again.

CHAPTER 60

Throwing his car into reverse, Steve floored the gas pedal. The car lurched backwards, but the engine sputtered and almost died. A shot shattered the rear window, grazing Steve on the right temple.

Johnnie screamed. Steve shoved his son down low in the seat.

The engine caught and, with wheels spinning, roared back, slamming into the side of the truck, partially turning it around. Steve shifted into drive and again floored the gas pedal. With the engine missing badly, the car chugged off, slowly picking up speed.

"Stay down, Son," Steve instructed. Halfway down the street, the engine quit.

"Come on, Johnnie." Steve grabbed his son's arm and, pulling him out of the car, fled between two houses and into the back yard of the nearest house.

The truck turned around and roared off toward Steve's car.

Steve realized their likelihood of their successfully escaping were minimal. But there was something he could do to save his son.

He knelt down and held Johnnie by the shoulders and looked at his son's tear-streaked face intently. "Son, remember when I told you, you were going to be a brave, strong man someday?" Johnnie nodded, wide-eyed.

"Well, that day is right now. I want you to run between those two houses to the next street and to the first house that has a light on. Knock on the door and get inside. Tell them to call the police. Now go and be quick." He gave his son a brief hug and shoved him off.

His son turned back around with an uncertain look as if to say something.

"Go, go, Johnnie! Be brave." Steve saw Johnnie get a determined expression and turn away in a run.

"I love you, Son," Steve whispered at the small figure as it disappeared into the darkness. He looked around for something to fight with, to delay the attackers and give his fleeing boy a chance to escape. He found a small stack of bricks piled up against the wall of the house and picked up one in each hand. Crouching down in the darkness, he heard running footsteps. Just before the edge of the house, they slowed.

A man holding a gun stepped around the corner. Steve hurled the brick at him hitting him in the chest. Steve heard a soft *sputt* of the discharging gun and saw a flash from the muzzle.

The second man ran around the corner holding his pistol in front of him. He saw Steve and turned his pistol to draw a bead. Sure he was dead, Steve heaved his second brick and ducked. He heard a dull thud. Perhaps the brick had hit the man. Jumping to his feet, he ran hunched over as fast as he could. He expected at any moment to feel a bullet piercing his back.

Steve vaulted a low chain-link fence into an adjacent backyard, rolling as he hit the ground. A bullet hurtled by overhead, making a popping sound as it passed. Steve, back on his feet kept running, trying to pull the men as far away from Johnnie's direction as possible. *Were they following him?* Looking back over his shoulder, Steve did not see the clothesline, nearly invisible in the dark. He ran headlong into it, nearly garroting himself. He fell heavily to the ground, clutching his neck trying to breathe. He rolled over with a profound sense of failure. Would Johnnie get away?

Several backyard lights flicked on, with male voices yelling from inside. He heard a door slam. Then there was a growing wail of a police siren approaching.

Steve tried to stand, but the world spun around and he fell back to his knees. He crawled on his hands and knees looking for someplace to hide. He hoped he had given Johnnie enough of a head start to get away. And

Anne. He prayed she believed he had never cheated or played around on her. He loved her so much.

Strangely, the men from the truck never materialized.

Then, he heard an angry voice yell at him from the next yard, the one from which he had run. A voice he had never heard before, harsh and hard with venom.

"Goddamn you, James. I'll kill you!"

CHAPTER 61

Elise Dixon, dressed in her nightgown and bathrobe, walked into the dressing room to see her husband staring at himself in the mirror. He saw her reflection and turned around. She wrapped her arms around him in an affectionate hug.

"How are you, Robbie?"

His arms returned the embrace. "I'm fine, Sweetie." His tone sounded falsely hearty.

"You don't look it." She lifted her head from his shoulder to look at him. "What's going on with you? I'm worried about you." His face masked over, but she pressed on. "Is it stress? Are you feeling okay?"

"I'm just fine—really."

"You've got to tell someone. What is it?"

He shrugged, but still held her. "I'm not entirely sure—"

Elise waited for him to continue.

"I've put my faith in God." He almost whispered. "It took the trip to the Cathedral to realize what was missing."

"You always pray," she said. "What's different?"

"I don't know, I just need Him more and I've been feeling Him inside me more. He gives me strength."

"You are one of the strongest men I know. Why now?"

Dixon released her. "I don't know. This China thing, I suppose. I never had to face that as governor. Now it's different. Back then, it was all budgets and taxes. I shared the responsibility then. Now I'm it. It's my responsibility."

"You are not responsible for the massacre." Elise spoke sharply, surprised at his words. "How can you feel that way?" She reached out to hold his hands. He averted his eyes. "Robbie?"

"I know. It just feels like I could have done something."

"How? Send in the Marines? Recapture Hong Kong?" She couldn't believe what he was saying. "How?"

"I just do. No explanations. I just feel that way."

Elise's heart went out to her husband while at the same time she felt confused. This was not her pragmatic, level-headed husband. "Honey, there is no reason for you to feel that way. It doesn't make any sense."

"I need you of all people to understand."

Elise pulled back and studied him intently. "What I don't understand are your unscheduled rides outside the White House—another one today—Jeff phoned me. Don't you know how much I worry about you?"

Dixon stared back at her, crestfallen, embarrassed like a scolded child. "It's just that I feel . . ." He hesitated, searching. "So . . . compressed inside. I need to be outside. I need the fresh air."

Elise's tone was firm. "Then go outside in the yard or schedule a trip with the Service. Five minutes is all it would take." She hugged him again and spoke with her head lying against his chest. "Please. For me?"

She felt her husband's arms slide around her. "Okay, Sweetie. I can try."

"Promise?" She pulled back to search his face. "It can only do us harm."

Dixon hesitated. "Okay, I promise. For you."

CHAPTER 62

His temple stitched and dressed, and fresh from an interview with Scottsdale Police Detective Harmon, Steve walked into the emergency department waiting room. Rounding the corner, he saw a sight he thought he would never see again—Anne and Johnnie waiting for him.

Anne jumped up to embrace him, squeezing him tightly for a long time. Finally, relinquishing her hug, she looked him over. "My God, Steve." Anne inspected his red-raw neck and his head gash, now covered with gauze. "I can't believe this. And Johnnie. If you two would have . . ." She hugged Steve again laying her head against his chest. He knew she was listening to his heartbeat as her arms squeezed him close.

"I was very brave, wasn't I, Daddy?" Johnnie tugged at his father's belt.

"Of course you were, Little John." Steve scooped him up and held him closely feeling the innocent warmth of his son's skin. Johnnie finally squirmed and Steve put him down. He couldn't resist ruffling his son's coarse dark hair. "I'm so proud of you." Johnnie beamed and then put his arm around his dad's waist possessively.

"Steve, what's happening? What are you not telling me? Whatever's going on has put your life and Johnnie's in danger."

"Anne—" He thought of the words shouted at him while he was crawling on the ground. *Goddamn you, James. I'll kill you!* "I . . . don't know." He shook his head. He looked at Anne helplessly. He didn't know why this had happened. The detective thought it was a disgruntled patient. Steve was not so sure.

Anne started crying, clutching Steve's arm. "I don't understand. I almost lost you two. Who's doing this to us?" People were watching them now.

Steve tugged Anne towards him. She initially resisted, but then let go, collapsing into his chest. Steve wrapped his arms around her.

"I don't know, but I'm going to find out." Steve tilted her head up and kissed her wet eyes.

Goddamn you, James. I'll kill you!

"You need to get out of town," Steve decided.

"What?" Anne looked puzzled.

"It's too dangerous here. Take Johnnie; go to your parents' house far away from this. That way I know you'll be safe."

Anne looked surprised, but shook her head. "No. I'm not going. I'm not going to be run out of my house by this—this thing or anybody. Besides, you need someone to take care of you. You can't do this by yourself. You said just today that we were in this together."

"Not fair. That was before I got shot at. Think of Johnnie."

"*That's* not fair—"

"Did you forget I was a bachelor before you moved in? I can take care of myself."

"Right. Boxed macaroni and cheese, polyester ties, utilities cut off because you didn't pay the bills. Steve, honestly. You're a mess without me."

"A terrible mess," Steve smiled. "But there's no way you can stay. And I can't go. You and Johnnie have to leave. Tonight."

Anne got that stubborn look he knew all too well. "No, Steve. I won't."

Steve pointed to his scalp wound and blood-matted hair. "Anne, look, I didn't know if I'd ever see Johnnie again when I sent him off. I don't want to have to worry about losing you or Johnnie. You have to. For his sake."

Anne forced a smile. "I'm not splitting up our family for anything. Whatever we face, we do it together. Besides, you're no James Bond."

"Don't worry, Mom," Johnnie piped up. "Daddy's gonna kick butt."

"Johnnie!" Anne frowned at him.

"It's on TV, Mommy," Johnnie said in his logical voice.

Steve ruffled Johnnie's hair again. "Thanks for the plug, Son." Then he leaned over and whispered to Anne, "The detective said there was a good chance whoever it was would try again."

Anne's eyes told Steve her mind was made up. "Well, he's finished for tonight. I'm sleeping in my own bed. We'll talk about it tomorrow."

The TV news in the waiting room caught their attention.

". . . The terrible freeway crash we showed you earlier this evening . . ." The screen showed a helicopter view of the freeway pile up. ". . . was allegedly caused by Dr. Steven James. Dr. James, the hero doctor that saved the falling 747 was today rocked by scandal with multiple malpractice allegations and a sexual abuse suit. This evening, our sources tell us, he attempted suicide that resulted in the multiple vehicle pile-up, with serious injuries to eight persons. And, we understand, Dr. James had his seven year-old son in the car with him at the time. Scottsdale Police are holding him for questioning."

Steve stared in disbelief at the TV. "That's bullshit, you bastards!"

Everybody in the waiting room stared at him. A huge tattooed man spat at him. "Fucking hero—look at you now, scumbag. Your son, for Chrissakes."

Steve shook again, this time with frustrated anger. Anne touched his chest.

"Okay, Stevie." Anne was just as angry with new tears rolling down her face. Her eyes searched his face. "This is getting nasty. But we'll fight it together." Her voice broke. "Let's go home."

CHAPTER 63

Kerry whined.

Steve, lying awake in bed, sat up. "What is it, boy?" he whispered.

Kerry scratched at the sliding glass door to the back yard.

"Okay, I'm sorry, boy. I'll let you out." He had forgotten to take Kerry for his nightly walk. His poor bladder must be bursting! Glancing at the bedside clock, he saw it was two minutes after two. Kerry looked back at him and scratched at the door again.

Trying not to wake Anne, he quietly sat up in bed, which made his head and neck renew their aching. He pulled on his jeans and painfully stood up.

"I know, I know." Kerry whined again, eagerly, like he did when he had a rabbit in sight. Steve slid open the arcadia door, feeling the cool night air against his bare chest. Kerry bolted out, barking loudly, and ran around the corner to the side of the house. Seconds later, Steve heard a male voice curse.

What? In alarm, Steve leaned out to see, but the origin of the voice was out of his sight, near the side utility room. He heard a sudden but subdued pop followed by yelping from Kerry. Steve recoiled—he had heard that same sound just hours before. He fought the impulse to run out after Kerry, but instead, he slid the door shut and locked it.

"Anne," he shouted. "Get up! Someone's just shot Kerry!"

Anne rolled over onto her back, her voice thick with sleep. "What? Shot Kerry?"

Steve threw her bathrobe at her. "Come on. Get up." Reaching under the bed, he grabbed his heavy aluminum flashlight and then ran into the closet for his gun.

"What happened? Where's Kerry?" Anne, tying the cloth bathrobe belt came up to his side.

"Shit, my gun. It's gone!" Steve pawed at the back of his sock drawer. "We've got to get Johnnie." He unplugged his cell phone and handed it to Anne. "Call 911."

Crouching down, he led Anne to their bedroom door. To his left was the large entryway with its wide glass sidelights. He paused half expecting to see the shadow of a man at the front door. How many were out there? He grasped Anne's hand and they dashed past, sprinting into Johnnie's room.

Anne spoke into the phone quietly. "We've got an armed man outside our house who just shot our dog. We need someone here now, please."

Steve knelt over Johnnie, sprawled out on his stomach in his pajamas. "Johnnie, wake up. Come on, boy." He scooped up the moaning half-asleep boy and carried him into the adjacent bathroom. Anne followed, whispering information to the operator in a grim replay of Steve's conversation with the emergency center earlier that evening.

The bathroom had no windows and only one entrance. Steve hoped the men would not do a room-to-room search, but he knew that was exactly what they were here to do. Someone wanted him dead and they didn't care if they took his family with him.

Steve laid Johnnie in the bathtub and pushed Anne on top of the sleeping boy, while he crouched by the door listening, holding the heavy four-battery flashlight in his hand. *What else can I do?*

For the second time that night he was trapped. He had no other place to take his family. The entire back of his house had huge picture windows looking out onto the backyard and the mountains beyond. He could easily be seen moving around the house. Conversely, he could not risk trying to make a dash outside for fear of running into the hands of the man or men outside. And he couldn't find his fucking gun!

Anne had finished talking, but was still holding the phone to her ear.

"What?" Steve whispered.

"They're sending someone now. It'll be five minutes—"

"We don't have five minutes." He had to find a way out. But how? How? "Give me the phone."

She objected as he took it from her. "Don't hang up."

He did and then punched in his next-door neighbor's number.

"I'm sorry, that number's been disconnected or is no—"

"Shit. What's Rich's number?"

"I don't know. I never—"

"Hey, what's going on?" Johnnie mumbled, beginning to wake up.

"Shhh." Anne said.

The crash of shattering glass broke the superficial calm. It came from the kitchen. Anne leaned over Johnnie and whispered to him to be quiet.

Steve fumbled at the phone buttons again trying to make sure he dialed Rich's number correctly. The phone rang as Steve strained his ears for sounds of approaching footsteps.

"Hello?" A sleepy voice answered.

"Rich!" Steve whispered into the phone through cupped hands. "We've got an armed man in our house. Make some noise or something to distract them. Hurry."

"Got it. On my way." Steve heard a click as Rich hung up. The sound of approaching footsteps made Steve crouch even lower. Carefully putting the phone down, he grasped the heavy metal flashlight as his only weapon.

"I know you are hiding in here, Dr. James." *It was that voice!* "I have a score to settle with you." Steve's body chilled at the sound of it.

The footsteps came closer. He saw the reflection of a flashlight sweeping around outside the bathroom.

Then Steve heard loud gunshots and shouts outside. Rich! An avid hunter, he must have fired a rifle or shotgun to cause a commotion. Steve heard more gunshots.

The footsteps outside the door retreated. "Pleasant dreams, Dr. James," the voice called out. Steve heard more shouts outside and the roar of a vehicle leaving very quickly. With profound relief Steve slumped to the floor. What did he mean about pleasant dreams?

"Anne, I think it's over." Steve said with heartfelt relief. "Rich saved us." Steve then identified an unfamiliar odor, something vaguely unpleasant, like garlic.

"Thank God for him," Anne said. "That was—"

Steve suddenly identified the smell. *Gas!* It was everywhere, filling the house. "Anne, get out of here. Now!" Steve bent over to grab Anne when a tremendous force slammed him against the tiled bathroom wall. He fell unconscious on top of Anne and Johnnie.

"Steve!" Anne shrieked.

Johnnie, pinned beneath both his parents, screamed. Anne twisted around so she could look at Steve. His glazed, unfocused eyes frightened her. How was it she could see in the pitch-blackness of the bathroom? The room was lit by a flickering light. How . . .?

She looked through the shattered bathroom wall saw that the house was on fire!

"Steve!" Anne screamed, struggling to keep her and Steve's weight off Johnnie. The screech of many smoke alarms pierced the air.

Steve moaned and looked around with heavy lidded eyes. "Anne?" His speech was slurred.

"Steve, get up! The house is on fire!" Smoke began filling the small bathroom causing Anne to gasp and cough.

"What?" Steve said in a stronger voice, looking around. "Oh shit!" He rolled off Anne onto the tile floor. It was still cool, but the air was heating up quickly. He heard Anne coughing. His dazed mind struggled to form a plan.

Anne tugged Johnnie's shoulders forward urging him to sit up. Johnnie, wide-eyed and in shock from the explosion, was too terrified to move. "Come on, Sweetie," Anne encouraged, "We've got to get out of here."

Steve snatched three towels from under the sink and shoved one under the faucet to wet it. He coughed from the harsh smoke stinging his nose and trachea. He threw the first one at Anne. "Wrap this around your nose and mouth."

Anne pulled the coolness of the towel around her nose and mouth wrapping it around her neck. She caught the second one for Johnnie and covered his face too.

"Keep low," Steve shouted through his own towel. His head pounded, but he was thinking clearly. The options were not good. The fire began to consume the doorframe and through the shattered wall he could see only a sheet of fire. It was becoming a struggle to breathe.

There were no windows in the bathroom. The only way out was through the fire in the doorway. And Steve only had his jeans on.

"Let's go." Steve shouted. "Into Johnnie's room." He scooped up Johnnie and stooping over, ran through the doorway, half expecting to run into a wall of fire. Anne grabbed the cell phone from the floor and followed.

What was left of Johnnie's room was filling with heavy smoke, but Johnnie's bed by the window was not burning. The window had shattered, leaving shards protruding from the frame. Anne jumped onto the bed to open the window when suddenly a shadowy figure of man carrying a rifle appeared just outside. Anne screamed, jumping back. Steve instinctively fell to the floor over Johnnie.

"Steve!" Rich's voice called out. "Anne!"

"Rich!" Anne yelled. "We're in here!"

The rifle butt cleared the remaining window shards. "Come on, Anne." Rich's powerful hands gripped Anne under her shoulders and pulled her through to safety.

Rich appeared back at the window and Steve thrust Johnnie through to his waiting arms.

Coughing from the thickening smoke, Steve looked around at his son's room and thought of the wonderful times they had all had playing together, right on this bed. All the bedtime stories he had told his son and all the laughing and tickles they had shared. It would be gone forever. A burning chunk of ceiling material fell next to Steve.

"Come on, now," Rich commanded.

Steve tumbled out head first, landing on the bougainvillea, which tore at his bare chest and stomach. Rich pulled him to his feet and helped him walk away from the house.

"Thanks," Steve said in gasping breaths, triggering a coughing spell.

Rich asked, "Who were those guys?"

Steve ignored the question and hugged Anne and Johnnie tightly. "Are you okay?" He walked them even further away from the burning house.

"We're fine." Anne held Johnnie's trembling body in both arms. "Scared, that's all."

"Kerry!" Steve exclaimed, remembering. He ran, ignoring the sharp rocks on his feet and the spiny bougainvillea that clawed his bare chest. There was no structure left on this side, the yard covered with chunks of debris, many of which were still burning briskly. He stepped carefully in his unshod feet. Kerry must be buried underneath.

Rich joined him to kick away hot, smoking chunks of drywall and framing with his shoes. Moments later, Steve found his dog. He knelt down beside the motionless form. "Kerry! C'mon, boy, it's me," he said. His heart sank. Kerry's warm neck was limp as he lay on the blood-soaked ground.

Anne and Johnnie knelt next to Steve, who cradled the lifeless dog that had died protecting his house and family.

Anne clutched Johnnie and began to cry as the shock wore off.

Steve put Kerry down and held Anne and Johnnie tightly. He had been lucky tonight—twice. He had been granted a miraculous third chance to protect his family. A swell of anger rose in his chest, deep and ugly as it was naked and unforgiving. He vowed his family would never be put in harm's way again. And the bastards who did this would pay—somehow.

CHAPTER 64

The gate attendant looked at her watch as Steve held Anne in a long embrace.

"Call me everyday. Promise?" she said as she tore herself away from his embrace.

"Promise."

"I'm going to worry horribly about you."

"I'll be fine."

"Promise?" She searched his face with her eyes, as if she would never see him again.

"I promise." He embraced her again, and then kissed each of her wet eyes in turn. Johnnie had been hugging his leg as if he would never let go. Steve stooped down to hold his little boy again, the last time, he knew, for a long while. He recalled embracing him in that backyard only hours ago thinking he would never see him again. Now, he craved the touch and presence of his family with a new urgency knowing how much he would miss them. Still, it was the right decision and he steeled himself for their absence.

"Last call, folks." The gate attendant announced, eyeing the police officer that had accompanied Steve and his family to the gate. Reluctantly, Anne and Johnnie, in donated clothes from the police station, walked hand in hand into the Jetway door. They both turned and waved until the door closed, hiding them from view. Steve stayed and watched Southwest's earliest flight to Las Vegas push back. There, they would change planes and fly to Portland. He waited until it took off and disappeared from sight before reluctantly turning away from the window. He thanked the policeman and trudged back to the main terminal.

He wanted to call Anne already, hold her and snuggle with Johnnie, the three of them together lying on Johnnie's bed, the bed that was now a smoking carcass.

Rich had pulled his SUV around to Baggage Claim where he waited for Steve.

"Where to, Steve?" Rich asked.

That question caught Steve by surprise. He had not thought that far ahead having been intent on getting Anne and Johnnie safely out of town.

Steve looked at his neighbor, his bodyguard since the fire, his escort to the airport, the provider of his shoes and shirt, and his anchor when everything had suddenly turned upside down.

The house was a total loss. Anne's car was burned and buried under rubble in their garage. All their pictures, their keepsakes, baseball caps and tee shirts from their travels, Anne's jewelry, purse, and clothes, not to mention Johnnie's school art work were all burned or destroyed in the explosion and fire. At least Steve's wallet had been in his jeans so he could buy the tickets for Anne and Johnnie to leave town.

"Good Sam," Steve finally answered, using the old term for his hospital. "There's an on-call room I can shower in and catch some sleep."

"Sure you don't want a hotel? You'd be more comfortable."

"Nah, I'm used to the hospital." Steve hoped he was making the right decision; he needed time to think and plan. The hospital was familiar and he had resources there he wouldn't have in a hotel.

"Okay, your call."

They reached the large hospital complex in fifteen minutes, maneuvering through the early morning streets. Rich pulled into the second-story emergency room entrance. "Okay, Steve, here you go. Sure you don't want a piece?"

Steve shook his head wondering where his own pistol had been when he needed it. "I don't think packing is allowed in the hospital. They have their own armed guards."

"Ok," Rich sighed. "Hell of a night. You get some rest, Okay?"

"Thank you, Rich, for everything."

"Yeah, yeah. Just call if you need anything."

"Thanks. You've done enough already."

Steve pushed the car door shut and watched Rich drive off. He looked down at himself wearing Rich's ill-fitting clothes, a plaid flannel shirt and a pair of sneakers, which were respectively too big and too tight, but would have to do. He would change into some surgical scrubs and find something to eat.

The coming Arizona dawn painted a clutch of high cirrus clouds, red, pink, and orange, striking against the deep azure sky. Ordinarily he would watch for a while, and take in the spectacle until the rising sun washed it out. Instead, he turned and walked into the hospital.

A grumbling stomach led him straight to the cafeteria where he ate alone, avoiding the doctor's lounge and ignoring the stares of the cafeteria staff.

His mind replayed last night's events. *Goddamn you, James. I'll kill you.* Someone wanted him dead, but what for? That same voice called him by name in his house. *Pleasant dreams, Dr. James.* It was cold; like a killer's. No, Rich told him he had seen three men get into a car before they drove off. Three killers. Why were they after him?

He had discussed it at his house with the Scottsdale police detective, Gershon Harmon—the same one from the hospital just that previous evening—at some length. Harmon's original take after the car chase was an angry patient. But after the fire, the detective concluded it was far more serious than he first thought.

"Dr. James," he had said, "your scalp has some determined men after it. Here." He had written a name and number on the back of his card and had given it to Steve. "Call this man. He can help you."

Steve reached into the right front pocket of his jeans, the pocket where he usually kept his keys, only there were none and no use for them. He pulled out the card Harmon had given him and flipped it over. Anthony Valenti, P.I., it read.

Magnum, P.I. Steve thought. Only rich people and beautiful widows needed private investigators. He was neither, which would, he was sure, sorely disappoint this Mister Valenti, P.I.

"Ex-FBI," Harmon had said. "Solid."

Steve needed something solid right now.

CHAPTER 65

After his solitary breakfast, Steve walked through the Emergency Room looking for some ibuprofen. His throat, injured by the clothesline, seemed to be the chief source of his misery. It pounded in symphony with the bruise on his head where it had hit the bathroom wall. That, plus his scalp wound, all throbbed in concert. The ibuprofen he had taken before going to bed, only seven hours ago, had completely worn off.

It was a particularly slow morning for the Emergency Department, unusual for a mid-city hospital. The brightly lit rooms and hallways increased Steve's head pain. He got four ibuprofen tablets from a sympathetic nurse and swallowed them at a water fountain.

Exhausted, but his thoughts in turmoil, he wandered through the hospital, an oddly dressed, restless spirit passing through nursing stations and down corridors, which gradually filled with people as the hospital woke up. He drifted through the hallways, his churning thoughts pushing him along as he tried to make sense of the events of yesterday and last night. The men after him must have orchestrated the lawsuit, the newspaper ad, the medical board complaints, and the pictures delivered to his wife. But why? And who would want to go to all the trouble?

Eventually, he found himself in the intensive care unit and collapsed into a chair near Shirley's room. The lights were still turned low and the dimness suited Steve. It was, he thought, almost inevitable that he ended up here. Shirley drew him in as surely as a flame draws a moth.

He swung his feet onto the counter and slid down into the chair resting his head on its back. In her room he could see Edith, wrapped in an oversized sweater trying to sleep in a large reclining chair, occasionally stirring uncomfortably. Steve closed his eyes and tried to ease the tension out of his tired body. He felt old.

He thought about Anne and Johnnie. Poor bewildered Johnnie, who had been so terrified in the car and ran so bravely when told to. Steve tried not to think about what could have happened to his little John, so young and trusting, in shock from these events and now without his dad.

Steve pushed down his anger. He needed to rest. He settled into the chair and relaxed his exhausted muscles. In moments, he drifted off.

A hand touched his arm, waking him. He opened his eyes to see Edith.

"Dr. James?" she said tentatively.

"Edith, not now, please."

"What are you doing here?" The gentleness and concern showed in her voice.

Steve dropped his tired feet to the floor and sat up in the chair, rubbing his burning eyes.

"Does it have something to do with the news I saw on TV last night?"

"Yeah."

"Is any of it true?" she asked.

"Huh?"

"The lawsuit, the suicide attempt with your boy."

"Oh." Steve shook his head. "No. It's all made up." Steve sighed, not wanting to discuss his troubles, but the look of concern on Edith's face made him continue. "Somebody tried to run me off the road. Last night, they burned my house down. I just put my wife and son on a plane to get them out of town. For their safety." He fought down a flood of self-pity, "I'm not feeling too good about things right now."

Edith leaned over and placed her hand on his arm again. "Well, for whatever it's worth, I know you're a fine doctor."

Steve nodded absently, wishing he were elsewhere. Maybe he should have gone to a hotel after all.

"No, I mean it. You really care. Whatever people are saying about you, I know it's not true."

Her earnestness made Steve smile "Thanks. That's nice of you. But then I see Shirley . . ."

"I know." She self-consciously pulled a stray lock of graying hair behind her ear, averting her eyes. "To tell you the truth, when you told me it might be Eden, I was really upset at you for giving it to her."

She paused, pursing her lips, "But not anymore. Let me tell you why."

Steve at that moment was not remotely curious. He wanted to slide back into the chair and rest. It had felt so good.

"I was reading her diary and came across something."

"Her diary?" Steve knotted his forehead wondering how this could have the remotest bearing on the conversation.

"Yes. She kept one until about a year ago. I was looking for things at the house to bring in that would make her feel at home when I ran across it. I'd like to read it to you."

She reached into a pocket of her sweater and pulled out a bound, blue faux-leather book with gold edging on its leaves. There was a locking strap across the covers, which Edith unsnapped and turned to a page marked with a piece of scrap paper.

She began reading. "I'm entering a weight loss study tomorrow. I think it will be the best chance yet for me to lose weight. You know, I've tried about everything. I met Dr. James today. He is so nice. He explained everything to me and gave me confidence in myself and what I'm doing. If this works I'm going to be so happy."

Edith dabbed her eyes with a tissue. "Sorry, I've done a lot of that lately." She picked up the diary and resumed reading, "I'll wear the clothes I always wanted to. Guys will ask me out. People will see me as me and not that fat girl. I can't wait."

She lowered the diary and said with a stronger voice, "So you see, because of you, she had hope. Dr. James, I lost my husband in a car crash. We'd been married only two years and I loved Harry with my whole heart. When he died, I . . . I hurt so much. But little Shirley gave me a reason to keep going. She was just a baby." She wept, "I'm going to miss her so much."

Steve held her hand gently, feeling renewed anger at what Eden had done to her daughter.

"I'm sorry." Edith wiped her red eyes. "I just don't know what I'm going to do without her. I'm so alone." She paused, gathering herself. "That's why I was so upset with you. Then I read her diary and remembered that you were trying to help and—and really you did. When she got on Eden, she had so much more fun. She was still my little Shirley, but happier. It changed her life. You didn't know that this would happen."

From the back of the diary, Edith pulled out a wallet-sized picture and handed it to Steve. It was a photograph of Shirley, smiling in that carefree way only young people can.

"She sounds like a wonderful daughter. I wish I had known her better."

With an intensity that caught Steve by surprise, Edith leaned forward and clutched his arm, "Dr. James, there are other daughters out there who may be getting this terrible drug. They have hopes and dreams just like my Shirley did, and their families will suffer like me. I can't do anything about this, but you can. At least I think you can."

Steve, already overwhelmed, did not know where he would find either the time or the strength to do anything, even if he could. How could he possibly continue his pursuit of Eden's disease?

Steve's eyes returned to the picture, again feeling the warmth of Shirley's bright smile.

How could he not?

There was a familiar stirring of energy somewhere inside. There were nearly a hundred pictures just like Shirley's all around the country. "I'll do what I can." He handed the picture back to Edith as he found a new resolve taking the place of his gloom and self-pity. "You don't know how much your faith means to me."

CHAPTER 66

It had been a long night, Mallis thought as he let himself back into his hotel room. He had wanted to personally kill James and his family, but with the neighbor's interference, Mallis had to be satisfied with their dying in the explosion. The explosion had been gratifyingly loud with the house consumed in flames as they drove off.

Afterwards, Joe and Doug split off to connect taps to the phone lines at Sheridan's house and office while Mallis had made clean-up trips to James's hospital and office. Masquerading as an on-call doctor, he had found Shirley's hospital chart. Looking through the progress notes, he identified several references to prions in Shirley's records. He had surreptitiously pulled those pages. Inspection of James's office revealed a stack of printed journal articles about prions which he dropped into a Safeway dumpster as he drove away.

Although tired, Mallis's sexual arousal after his operation drove him from the hospital to Van Buren and its streetwalkers. At that early hour, he was lucky to find one. She was young and street-wise, but not looking for a John when he pulled up beside her and called her over to the car.

He took her hard with his hand over her mouth to stifle her screams. With no small satisfaction, he saw that she had bled, although not as much as he expected. He paid her well for his pleasure before he left her.

And now, back in the comfortable Ritz Carlton, he turned the TV to the first news show he could find. He needed closure, confirmation of his success. Watching his crimes reported on TV or in the paper was like reading the reviews of a triumphal Broadway opening. The news reports of his killing were tributes to him and his skill.

He flipped the TV to Channel 3 and its local Good Morning Arizona news show. It would do. He slipped out of his clothes and into the hotel's thick terry cloth bathrobe in anticipation of a hot shower.

Ahh, there it was, the report of the famous, then infamous and now dead Dr. James. As he expected there were copious pictures of Dr. James's flattened and burning house. Then Mallis stared in abject disbelief. *It wasn't possible.*

The footage had been taped earlier that morning while the house still burned. And there was Dr. James, wrapped in a blanket and with his arms around his wife and kid, getting into a patrol car. An officer shut the door and they were whisked away.

For a moment, Mallis refused to believe what he had just seen. It was like seeing his own dead father. *It wasn't possible.* James was dead—he had heard the explosion moments after he left. He couldn't possibly have gotten out in time. The scene should have shown the corpses in body bags. But it didn't.

Mallis finally had to admit what his eyes told him.

Dr. James was still alive.

CHAPTER 67

Third Avenue near the Maricopa County Courthouse in downtown Phoenix was lined with seedy, shopworn buildings and storefronts that housed bail bondsmen and criminal lawyers. Steve looked at the back of detective Harmon's card with the scribbled address on it and then at the off-yellow 1950s brick building with the matching address. Its soiled patina and dirty windows spoke of an absentee landlord who never had to look at his property.

The elevator doors opened onto the fourth floor hallway with an old, slack, rust-colored carpet. Steve found the suite he was looking for and pushed through a glass door that read in hand-painted letters, ANTHONY VALENTI, PRIVATE INVESTIGATOR. Underneath, it said: *Surveillance, Photography, Insurance, Confidential.* Showered and now wearing hospital scrubs, he was early for the appointment he had set up that morning.

Steve walked in, his hand in his pocket, touching his cell phone, his only link to his family. They had called him when they landed in Las Vegas telling him they had made it fine and were on schedule for the Portland flight. Anne promised to call when she landed in Portland and her parents had picked her up.

Steve found himself in a small, surprisingly modern office with light wood furniture. There was a standard L-shaped reception desk with a computer screen turned on, but the receptionist was gone.

"Hello . . . Anyone here?" He heard a grunt from behind a partially closed door to the right of the receptionist's desk. He pushed the door open to see a sizable man in his late forties, feet propped on his desk, holding up a *People* magazine that obscured his face with only his dark wavy hair showing above. The maroon striped shirt had short sleeves revealing arms that were thick, but without apparent tone, an athlete gone to flab. Steve was not impressed.

"Mr. Valenti?"

"That's me."

A hell of a way to greet a prospective client. "We had a ten-thirty appointment . . .?"

"So we did."

"The secretary was gone so I looked around."

The magazine dropped a hair revealing two bored eyes with fleshy eyelids.

"You're . . .?"

"Dr. James. Steve James."

"Right. So what can I do for you?" The magazine hovered in place.

"Well, Detective Harmon told me you were a good private investigator. I could use someone with your experience. I need to find out who's framing me."

"Framing you." Valenti rolled his eyes.

That did sound incredibly lame, Steve thought. Until that moment, he had never actually said the word 'frame.' But that's what it was.

"You may have read in the papers—"

"Never touch them," interrupted Valenti. "Please, go on."

Getting more pissed by the minute, Steve walked towards a chair in front of Valenti's desk. He noticed a muted TV tuned to CNN and didn't see a turned up flap of the area rug. He tripped over it, but caught himself on the chair. He sat down.

"Well, since I have to drag you from the trash you're reading and inform you, here's what happened. For some reason I've been sued for sexual abuse, called up by the medical board to answer allegations of malpractice, had advertisements placed in the paper alleging malpractice, and had faked pictures sent to my wife supposedly showing me in bed with another woman."

"Was she beautiful? That's always the tip off that they're fake. Nobody has affairs with beautiful women."

"And someone tried to run me off the road to kill me—"

"Bad driving."

Steve tried to stare through the magazine. "—who followed me and shot at me." Steve finished sure that would provoke a reaction.

"Bullet? Too dangerous. Not interested."

Valenti raised the magazine back up.

"But somebody's behind all this. I need to find out who and why."

Valenti lowered the magazine showing his eyeballs again.

"Can't you figure it out?" he said, as if he were lecturing a child. "You poked someone's wife. Her husband found out about it and is very mad. He filed the complaints and placed the advertisements. He's so mad, he's gone to chasing you and couldn't push you off the road, so he takes a potshot at you. You want me to come in to make it look like you've been wronged and to help make up with your wife, who I suspect left you and took the children with her. No thanks. Go see your priest and ask for forgiveness." The magazine went back up.

Steve opened his mouth to protest when he looked at the magazine cover, actually seeing it for the first time. It was a *People* magazine headlining the "World's Richest Bachelors." The cover photo featured Vicktor Morloch, Chairman of Trident Pharmaceuticals. Under his name, it listed his personal worth at eight billion dollars. Steve stared at it for a moment and then leaned over the desk to snatch it from Valenti's grasp, a thought forming in his mind.

"Hey!"

Steve paced as he stared at the cover, trying to pull it all together. It had all started after his call to Trident. Morloch was worth billions all on the basis of Eden, Trident's only drug . . . and in a rush, all the pieces tumbled into place.

That's it. It's got to be. His realization at once illuminated and terrified him. He sat back down in the chair in front of Valenti's desk. "Oh my God. I've made one of the richest men in the world a personal enemy."

Valenti, arms folded across his chest, wore a puzzled look. "What on earth are you talking about?"

Steve sat motionless in the brown vinyl covered chair, critically evaluating his own conclusion. This was totally foreign to him. Was he even rational? So many things had happened so fast. Could it really be that Vicktor Morloch would even notice him at all, much less send hired killers to eliminate him? Had his overwrought brain invented an enormous conspiracy? Steve couldn't tell for sure. He needed a reality check, a sane person to talk him out of his psychotic notion.

He eyed Valenti, still waiting expectantly for his magazine, although he did have a curious expression. Steve tossed it back and Valenti caught it against his chest. "Well, must have been a good article," Valenti quipped. "Keep it. I'll get another one."

Steve looked at the bemused PI. Why was he treating a prospective client in so cavalier a manner? Whatever Harmon saw in him wasn't at all apparent but . . . "Thanks, but I'd rather tell you a story instead. Care to make a short trip?"

Valenti stuck out his bottom lip as if in thought. "Well, I'm a very busy man . . ."

"Of course you are." Steve appraised Valenti's double chin and sizeable gut. "I'll buy lunch . . ."

Valenti squinted at Steve for a long moment. "OK, deal."

CHAPTER 68

"Proteins 101," Amos Sheridan began.

Steve and Valenti sat in Amos's hopelessly cluttered office, a striking contrast to his pin-neat laboratory. The animated Sheridan loved teaching and waved his arms as he explained the science to Valenti. Even on short notice, he was happy to talk about his research.

"Proteins are made up of chains of amino acids." Holding up a set of plastic snap beads in a clear bag, he reached inside and pulled out a fistful, popping a series of them together as he talked.

"You eat protein in the form of a chicken leg or a hamburger. The stomach breaks it down into its constituent amino acids, like these beads, and absorbs them into the bloodstream. The cells take up the amino acids and re-assemble them into the proteins it needs. Voila." He held up the strand of beads.

"Well, just remember, I flunked high school chemistry," Valenti warned. "Go too fast and my brain hurts."

"Don't go to sleep and you'll pass." Sheridan's eyes twinkled. "Now, proteins, once made, fold up into a three dimensional shape that makes them work. If they do not fold up in the right configuration, they do not work. Uhh—" He looked around his desk and seized a paperclip. "Like this." He showed it to Valenti. "It holds papers together by virtue of its shape. If it is mis-folded . . ." He mangled the paperclip into a twisted piece of wire, ". . . it can't hold papers together. It is a defective protein."

"Proteins are found everywhere in the cell, as enzymes and as parts of the cell membrane. If a critical protein does not fold up right, it doesn't work right and you get something like muscular dystrophy or sickle cell anemia. Okay so far?"

"Okay. So I need to eat protein to live and they need to fold up right."

"Good enough," Steve replied. "Now, change gears for a moment. Bacteria and viruses cause most infectious diseases. But there are newly identified infectious diseases caused by a mis-folded protein. It's called a prion."

"A prion." Valenti rolled it around in his mouth. "So?"

Sheridan cut in, "A prion is a mis-folded evil twin of a normal protein that all of us have in our bodies, including our brains. It has the same amino acids in the same order—it's the same protein, really, but it folds up differently. In its normal state, it's called the prion precursor protein."

"Evil twin," Valenti said, "The scientific term?"

Steve ignored him. "We don't actually know what this precursor protein does in our bodies, but we know it's almost everywhere in the body. Now, here's the juicy part. When the bad protein, the prion, touches its normal precursor counterpart, the normal protein re-folds into a prion. Then the new prion touches and transforms more precursor proteins, which converts even more. Like a nuclear chain reaction, prions trigger sequential conversions until there are few normal ones left."

"So if it touches another one like it," Valenti said, "it corrupts it into a bad character. Catholics into Baptists." He grinned. "Or like . . . a vampire protein."

"That's it!" Sheridan exclaimed. "Vampire proteins. Only there's no wooden stake."

"Huh? You lost me."

"The prions are really, really bad. They kill nerves and brains."

"Well, how come I've never heard of them?"

"Ever hear of mad cow disease?" Steve asked.

"Sure. You mean that's caused by these vampire prions? Don't you get it by eating bad beef?"

"Or people," Sheridan grinned. "Prions were first discovered in cannibalistic New Guinea tribes, killing thousands of them. It spread because they ate infected dead people, particularly their brains."

Valenti paled a bit. "Well, of course. That's why I don't eat dead people."

Sheridan continued, "All known human versions, except one, are caused by transmission of the actual prion into the next victim, like a virus or bacteria. It acts like an infectious disease, so if you get infected growth hormone or had brain surgery with contaminated instruments you can get it. Until now, that is."

"This is gonna get worse, I can just feel it." Valenti absently picked up a red plastic reagent squeeze bottle and started toying with it until Sheridan gently pulled it out of his hands.

"I wouldn't. Pure potassium chloride. Eats your skin right off."

Valenti recoiled, "Friends shouldn't let friends play with that stuff."

"Now follow me." Sheridan went to a large refrigerator-like insulated cabinet and opened its door. He pulled out a flat glass tissue culture block and placed it under a binocular microscope. "This is a healthy nerve cell culture. Look."

Valenti looked into the microscope. "It's full of cells or something all jumbled up like rush hour at the amoeba convention."

"Right. Those are nerve cells, nice, plump and healthy." He put that plate back and after donning gloves, pulled another out of a second insulated cabinet. Placing it under the microscope he motioned Valenti to look. "Now, this one started out like the last one, but has been overrun by prions."

Valenti looked through the microscope. "It's like a ghost town."

"Right, now look again, only this time I'm using a black light to show up the fluorescent labeled prions." Sheridan picked up a small black plastic box with a bluish light bulb exposed on one side. He plugged it in and aimed the light at the plate.

Valenti stared down the microscope. "Prions? Holy Jesus. There must be millions."

"But here's the point." Sheridan leaned forward, eyes gleaming. "We never put a single prion into the nerve culture. All the prions, you see, came from the normal precursor proteins that all cells have."

"How'd you do that?"

Steve answered. "Something science has never seen before. We introduced a catalyst. A short chain of amino acids called a poly-peptide."

"A catalyst?"

"Yeah," Steve said, "a catalyst that hundreds of millions of people are taking every day. In fact, it's the most widely prescribed drug in the world."

"Huh? A drug?" Then he caught on. "Eden? Eden? Oh, my sainted aunt." He muttered something under his breath that Steve couldn't hear.

"What?" Steve asked.

"The apple—the apple of the garden of Eden."

"Of course," Steve understood immediately. "Paradise lost."

Valenti motioned to the cell culture. "And Eden did all this?"

"Yep, and Eden is the sole reason Mr. Vicktor Morloch, Chairman and principal stockholder of Trident and magazine cover playboy is worth over eight billion dollars."

"Hells bells, I'd kill to protect eight really big ones. Well, maybe not. But tell me, are people really dying from this?"

"Follow me," Steve beckoned with a motion of his head. "I've one other place to take you."

"Why do I feel like I'm following the Ghost of Christmas Future?"

CHAPTER 69

Shirley's glass ICU door was tightly closed to mute her screams. Edith and Shirley's nurse each held one of Shirley's hands and spoke in calming voices, trying to settle her down, their faces reflecting their strain and fatigue.

Valenti followed Steve into the nurses' station where Steve put a copy of Shirley's most recent MRI scan up on the X-ray view box.

"Here's Shirley's brain. See the white streaks starting here . . ." he traced the abnormal pathways with his finger, " . . . and radiating here and here."

"Looks bad," Valenti said.

"It goes in your nose. That's how it enters the brain."

"That's right, it's a nose spray, isn't it?"

"It's normally absorbed through the nasal membranes into the blood, but the small nerve endings that pick up smells also absorb a little bit of Eden. They then transport it back into the rest of the brain." Steve smiled slyly. "Ever get a whiff of that perfume a long lost flame used to wear?"

"Who says she's long lost?" Valenti shrugged. "Well, sure, I remember."

"Did you instantly remember her and picture exactly where you were? Wasn't it vivid, like it just happened?"

"Yeah, now that you mention it. Every time I smell this one perfume, Chloe, Valerie, from high school, pops into my head. That's funny. I never thought about it before."

"The sense of smell is very old in our evolutionary development. It was so important to survival that it went directly to the memory and emotional centers of the brain. It's literally the most direct and strongest path from the outside world to our memory—and our emotions. Chloe's smell travels down a broadband connection to your memories and feelings for Valerie. The strong emotional events associated with smell, like a perfume, are forever linked. The fragrance pulls your memories right back."

"Ahh, so that's why I can never forget Valerie. Why so important here?"

"The damage from the prions caused by Eden initially occurs where the olfactory nerves take them—the memory and emotional centers and that means the symptoms will occur there first."

"Like what?"

"Initially, loss of taste and smell. Then your memory and reasoning decline along with your judgment and emotional control. Later, you begin to get delusions and nightmares; mostly old memories you thought had long been forgotten. Then muscular twitching."

"I don't like the sound of that; especially the old memories. There are some things I'd rather forget."

"All three cases I know about have all shown the same pattern. The Captain of the jet that almost crashed in Washington had Vietnam flashbacks. Another re-lived being attacked by wasps when she was a young girl."

"Why only bad memories? Why not recall all the good things that happened?"

"How many good dreams do you remember compared to how many nightmares?"

Valenti thought a minute. "You're right. I mostly remember the bad ones."

"Again it's because of the way the brain is organized. Danger is key to our survival and it is over-represented in the memory so that we can survive. It's the same with diseases that disturb the memories. It's never pleasant."

"And is this contagious or are these just isolated cases?"

"We have the three patients I mentioned, but we think there are at least a hundred more."

"Really! How do you know that?"

"We sent out an E-mail survey with MRI pictures. A bunch of radiologists responded positively and most of the cases were known to have taken Eden."

"That's really scary. How come no one has heard of this before? A hundred of anything is an epidemic."

"I think it's because the cases are all isolated. I probably see one puzzling and undiagnosed illness every three years or so. I ask for my colleagues to look in on it, but typically we decide it is due to a viral encephalitis or an auto-immune disease and that's it."

"And you don't report them to some central CDC like place?"

"If I think it is isolated, I don't usually bother. That's why this thing has stayed under the radar for so long. By itself, it is very unusual, but if you only see one, you chalk it up to the mysteries of medicine. If you see more, like I did, you look for the common thread. In this case, it's Eden."

"But someone must have found cases like you did. You know, at the teaching hospitals."

"I would imagine so," Steve agreed. "Now, I'm wondering if they met the same fate I was supposed to."

Valenti whistled. "I see what you're thinking, Doc. So they all die, you know, the patients? There's no cure?"

"That's it. Prion diseases are the deadliest in the world. No cure and no remission. It literally turns your brain into a spongy mush like you saw in the cell cultures." Steve sat down into a chair. "I know it sounds like science fiction, but it happened to England with Mad Cow."

"I wondered why everyone was so worked up about it."

"You should have known her before this happened. Nice normal girl. Now, she's got prions all over her brain and there's nothing I can do for her."

"Who?"

Steve turned around and nodded at Shirley who was still screaming.

Valenti stared at her for a long moment. "My God," he said quietly. "So this is Christmas future."

Even now, seeing Shirley like that got to Steve. He recalled Edith's words of this morning. *Dr. James, there are other daughters out there who may be getting this terrible illness. They have hopes and dreams just like my Shirley did, and their families will suffer like me.*

Steve's anger and resolve now had direction and focus. *I can't do anything about this, but you can. At least I think you can.*

"So Eden kills people," Valenti thought aloud still staring at Shirley, "and you think Vicktor Morloch kills doctors to protect his ass and his money?"

Steve watched Valenti closely. For him, the stakes couldn't be higher.

"Maybe you're onto something, Doc."

Steve let out his breath. Valenti had just—almost—validated his theory, but still, the way Valenti had initially treated him grated. In the end, however, it came down to Detective Harmon's endorsement and the fact that Steve desperately needed help. "Then, will you take the case?"

Valenti looked at Steve with some surprise and then at the ground for a long time. "I'll regret this, I'm sure." He shook his head in disbelief. "Yeah, I'm on it."

"Well, then, I owe you lunch." Steve said, relieved to have made the decision and happy to have an ally. He hoped Valenti would be a good one.

"Why, yes you do," Valenti agreed, "but you've completely ruined my appetite." He eyed Steve thoughtfully. "Right now, though, you need to perform a magical disappearing act."

"A what?"

CHAPTER 70

Presidential aides scurried around the Oval Office attending to last minute details before the meeting. Bell and Resnick flanked the President as they walked through the parting staffers and official White House photographers to his desk. He sat on its edge with his arms crossed and faced Resnick and Bell.

"Okay, Mr. President," Resnick said, "we've got two minutes before President Quin comes. I want you to remember one thing. We cannot back Taiwan's bid for independence."

"Yes, yes, of course. Stop lecturing me." His clothes and hair were immaculate and his shoulders square. Resnick thought he looked good, sturdy and clear-headed.

"Mr. President," Bell added, "if you feel the need to take a break, just signal and we'll get you out of here."

"Take a break? I don't need your mothering. I'm fully capable of handling this without your—" The President's right cheek jerked several times like it was connected to a marionette string. With a look of confusion, Dixon's hand flew up to his face.

"What was that?" Resnick asked.

A door to the Oval Office opened and an aide announced, "Mr. President, I present the honorable Mr. Quin Shi Lai, President of Taiwan."

A handsome, erect man strode in followed by his aides. President Dixon put on his best welcoming smile and formally shook hands with President Quin amid the flashing camera strobes.

"I am honored by your visit," Dixon said graciously, dipping his head in a shallow bow.

President Quin bowed deeply and replied. "I am equally honored by your hospitality and comforted by your country's commitment to freedom and self-determination."

And so it starts, thought Resnick.

CHAPTER 71

"Hiding from anyone, especially someone with the resources and capabilities of your perps, requires leaving absolutely no trace of your location." Valenti lectured Steve who sat slumped low in the passenger seat of Valenti's Grand Cherokee. As instructed, he held his hand up against his forehead to shield his face from casual identification.

"It's the cardinal law of disappearing. Anyone in the witness protection program knows it. No visiting any of your old hangouts, never calling family, an acquaintance, no one."

Valenti gestured with his hands and looked at Steve while he drove, making Steve nervous. Steve, in turn, watched the road like a hawk.

"We always took them out of their home town, and usually out of the state, if not the region." Valenti flashed a grin, "You'd be surprised how many Chicagoans and New Yorkers we relocated to Phoenix."

Once Valenti agreed to take on the case, he had immediately begun making arrangements. This included draining all of Steve's bank accounts and contacting his broker with instructions to liquidate a substantial sum of money for Steve and Valenti to use. Valenti had also confiscated Steve's wallet and emptied it of all his identification and credit cards.

"Cash is the gas that powers our search and your survival. Get all you need now," Valenti explained. "The minute you need more, you start leaving a trail for someone to follow."

Valenti arranged with Steve's new attorney to handle Steve's financial arrangements and the insurance claims for his house and cars. She would mail Valenti a power of attorney form for Steve to sign. As a precaution, Valenti made arrangements for a daily bug sweep of the attorney's office and home.

Valenti pulled into a service station and up to a pay phone. "Call Sheridan. Have him make copies of all his data and mail them to me, his attorney, your attorney, and a copy for his safe deposit box. That's damning evidence against Eden and I'll wager Trident knows about it."

"How?" Steve asked, amazed that anyone would know that kind of detail. Steve's cell phone, the one Anne had somehow saved from the burning bathroom, began buzzing, "Just a sec." He pulled it out of his pocket and answered it. "Dr. James."

A familiar voice spoke in his ear. "Hi, baby, we just got to the house."

"Anne!" Steve's heart leaped. "Are you okay?"

Valenti's face went white and he snatched the phone from Steve and hit the end button.

"Hey, that was my wife!" Steve shouted.

Valenti shook the phone at Steve. "Do you know what this is?"

"A cell phone. Of course I know."

"It's a radio. A radio! Do you know what that means?"

Steve made the connection. "Anybody can listen."

"No shit, Sherlock. And I'd bet big money Trident's listening to every word you say on this thing."

"I thought only the government could do that."

Valenti rolled his eyes. "Look, Doc. I won't practice neurosurgery—"

"Neurology."

"Okay, whatever. I won't practice neurology if you don't try and second-guess me in my specialty. Understood?"

Steve gritted his teeth with frustration. Anne's voice had sounded so good. But it also answered a nagging question that had lingered in his mind. How had the truck been able to find him on the dark side street? They must have been listening to his cell phone instructions to the operator. *Damn!*

"You want them to trace where your wife is?" Valenti pressed.

"I get it now. You're right." Steve said irritably.

The phone rang again as Valenti held it. Steve stared at the phone knowing his anxious wife was wondering what had happened to him. "Can't I talk to her on a different phone?"

"Not now." Valenti was unyielding. "I've seen too many people killed because they did the predictable thing. Remember what I told you about not calling family and friends."

"But—"

"It's called survival, Doc. Otherwise you're wasting my time and yours. Just get out here and play on the freeway. You're going to get yourself killed anyway and that way I don't get caught in the crossfire."

Steve stared at Valenti's stony face. The phone still rang in Valenti's hand and Steve's deep desire to talk to his wife nearly made him grab it back—but it would put them in danger.

Steve nodded. "Okay. Your rules."

Valenti relaxed a little and let a sympathetic look cross his face. "You're a good man, Charlie Brown."

Steve slid lower in his seat, missing his Anne and Johnnie. But the reason they were in Oregon came back to him and the energizing anger seeped back into his bones. He would do whatever it took to get those assholes. Valenti was right. His stupid sentimentality could fuck up everything.

"Right. I'll call Sheridan and tell him to protect his ass."

"Correct. And tell him to take a long vacation without telling anyone where he's going. Impress on the 'not tell anyone' part, even his travel agent—and tell him to pay in cash."

"He needs a vacation." Steve smiled without humor. "This is just the thing to get him to go."

Valenti stopped at a service station pay phone and Steve opened the door to get out of the car. "You're one paranoid bastard."

"I'm still alive." Valenti shot him a humorless grin.

Steve made his call.

CHAPTER 72

President Quin and President Dixon sat by the Oval Office fireplace. Quin's English was workable and he made his initial presentations without his interpreter, whom he waved off.

"President Dixon—Robert," Quin began, leaning over towards Dixon. "I want to make a special gift before we talk about more substantive issues. As you know, my wife died last year of leukemia."

The President looked surprised and confused. "I'm sorry, I did not know."

Resnick did not react visibly, but clearly remembered that Quin's wife's death was in the President's briefing package. *Damn, didn't he read his materials?* Vice President Sullivan had attended the funeral. But, Resnick tried to remember, was it leukemia? And where was this going?

Quin continued, "Your mother died two years ago of leukemia. Both of us suffered a terrible loss that can eventually be prevented."

Dixon, recovered his composure and said, "Our scientists are working on cancer research. I am advised there are some promising new developments."

Quin smiled. "We have read many of the same reports. My country recognizes your scientists as the best in the world. But can they not always use more funding? My small country has elected to support your country's outstanding leukemia research with a donation of one billion dollars. I have with me the first annual installment of one hundred million U.S. Dollars."

He motioned to an aide who produced an envelope and handed it to President Quin who, in turn, handed it to the U.S. President. Dixon looked stunned. His right mouth and cheek twitched several times Resnick noted with alarm. She had never seen that before today.

Quin continued, "My people give this gift to our good friends knowing you will use it well to eliminate the terrible disease of leukemia. With this gesture, my people and I wish to play a small role in the effort to stamp out leukemia in our lifetimes." He paused to consult a note card in his hand. "May we soon stop the deaths of our mothers and fathers, of our wives and husbands and, most importantly, may we stop the deaths of our children."

Quin looked at the President whose eyes had begun to mist over, surprising Resnick who could not recall when Dixon had ever shed tears in public.

"I . . . I . . ." Dixon began.

The Taiwanese President grasped the President's hand and leaned over whispering so only the closest aides could hear. "This, Robert, is a genuine token between our two great nations. Use it in the noble fight against a disease that knows no borders and spares no race, religion, or political orientation."

This was way too thick, thought Resnick, but the President seemed completely under Quin's spell.

"Mr. President," Dixon said softly, almost hesitantly. "I'm not sure what to say." He wiped his cheek with his hand. "This means a lot to me. I can tell you, we will put it to good use. Then we will have you visit and meet the doctors who are working on the cure."

He grabbed President Quin's hand and shook it firmly. "Thank you. On behalf of the American medical community, and in the interest of the people of the world who stand to benefit from your generous gift, I thank you and God thanks you."

CHAPTER 73

They walked into Steve's newly rented room at the Residence Inn. It had felt strange to hear the receptionist call him Mr. Jones. He had scrawled his new name on the registration slip as nonchalantly as he could, sure the attendant was about to yell "Imposter!"

Earlier, they had made a stop at a south Phoenix shoe store with a non-descript sign in the window that read *Passport Photos*. Inside, Valenti had arranged for Steve to get a new driver's license, credit card, and a prepaid cell phone—a new identity.

Valenti had grabbed the key card from the desk clerk. "Let's go, Jason." Steve was slow to respond.

Valenti tapped his shoulder. "C'mon. You'll get used to it. I did."

Inside the room, Valenti turned on the TV, tuned it to CNN, and then muted it just like he had done in his office. A true news junkie, thought Steve.

"This is your new home," Valenti announced. "I recommend leaving it as little as possible." He sat down in a brown Naugahyde upholstered chair. "In fact, you're not to leave it without me. Ever."

Steve walked around the bed and looked out the window to the court-yard with the pool and the token plats of grass surrounded by gravel desert landscaping. He looked at the room's décor with brown plaid upholstery and the kitchenette, complete with refrigerator, range, and coffeemaker.

"I know why you're doing this, but I feel like a prisoner." He held up his hand. "I know, it's the only way to keep my sorry ass alive, as you so delicately put it and, believe me, I appreciate what you're doing."

"I hope you value it as much as your wife does and you don't do anything brave or foolish, which, in my book, are the same thing."

Steve must not have looked convinced because Valenti continued. "I'm not kidding. If I were on the other side of this and I had Trident's resources behind me, I'd have you located in about a day even if you had left town."

"Okay, just to play along, how come so many felons escape?"

Valenti made an exasperated motion with his hands. "They don't. Ninety-five percent get caught from stupid mistakes. They go see a friend or stay with a family member, use a credit card, go to a spot where people can recognize them, fail to leave town, call family and friends, and a hundred other things that anyone with half a brain would know could get them caught.

"Right now, I bet every phone line at your hospital and office is or was tapped. There are computers that pick your voice out of a thousand, or pick out thousands of key phrases, all monitored by one bored technician in an office deep in Cincinnati."

"Okay, I can't communicate with anybody, how do I work with the police and my lawyer?"

"Through me." Valenti made Steve feel like a child getting a lecture. "Listen, Doc—"

"Steve."

Valenti looked at him for a moment. "Okay, Steve." He seemed to like that. "We're going to get to know each other pretty well until this is over. I hope it breaks soon so you can get on with your life, but there is a chance it might not. I want you to know that."

Steve sighed and rubbed his eyes. "I guess I knew that." He walked into the bathroom and took the paper cap off a glass and filled it with water from the faucet. He drank the contents and filled it again. He drank that one too, and filled the glass a third time. He returned to the sitting area somewhat more settled. "Well, let's get started. How do we nail the bastards?"

"We work with the police and keep tabs on their progress. In the meantime, I find out where the print ad came from and who the plaintiff in the lawsuit is. You bone up on Trident and Eden."

"Valenti," Steve said, as an idea struck him. "Let's go to the press and tell them the whole story, you know, Eden, the attempts on my life, everything."

Valenti looked amused, to Steve's irritation. "Sure, Doc. How does this sound? 'Mr. Reporter, I've been accused of malpractice, my wife's left me because I screwed another woman, oh, yes, I'm being sued for sexual abuse, and I tried to commit suicide with my son in the car, and, oh, by the way, we've found a previously unsuspected problem with the blockbuster drug, Eden.' Headline stuff, that."

"You don't think they'll believe me?"

"It's exactly what our friends planned. You've lost your credibility, pal. Look at it this way, Steve. You're a reporter and you see some doctor, who makes four times your income, come to you with a wild story. The world's biggest selling drug is causing people to go nuts. But the doctor who's telling you this is getting sued by a woman who claims he dropped his drawers in front of her and maybe did more. And worse, his allegations have no shred of proof."

Steve saw Valenti's point. Going to the press was a two-edged sword. It cut both ways and he had no control of it. The words of Secretary Jacob Castell came back to him. *They love you today; hate you tomorrow. Keep them at arm's length.*

"So," Steve thought aloud, "we're stuck with no plan except to try and find clues that may lead nowhere."

"Welcome to real life."

"Fuck!" Steve flopped onto the bed. "Well, don't let me stew. I need to get busy on this. Make me useful. Let's tie all this up with Trident. Where do you want me to begin?"

"Let's figure this out together." Valenti's fingers drummed on the arm of his chair. "You work on finding a link between Trident and this prion thing. While we can prove it's Eden, Trident will deny any prior knowledge. If no one can pin any fraud or conspiracy on them, they walk. If we think they covered this prion thing up, and we do, we've got to prove they knew about it and covered it up. And you know how unforgiving the public is about a cover-up."

"I'm ready. Lets get going."

"But," Valenti held up a finger, "Remember, your staying alive is job one. Even if we can't pin a cover-up on them, it'll piss Trident off."

A strange movement on the TV caught Steve's eye. He turned and saw President Dixon standing in front of the blue curtains of the White House pressroom. Steve watched, but nothing seemed out of the ordinary. Then it happened again—the movement—the President's face was twitching.

"Valenti, turn it up."

"What?"

"The TV."

Valenti looked blankly at Steve. "Huh, why?"

"Oh, hell." Steve grabbed the remote and un-muted the volume. President Dixon's voice filled the room.

"—a really generous gift from our friends in Taiwan of a billion dollars to fight leukemia through research."

"Political bullshit." Valenti reached over and pulled the remote from Steve's hand.

"Wait, wait. Just watch."

Valenti's fat finger paused on the remote. The TV had moved in for a close up of Dixon, his shoulders and face filling the TV screen. The President's right eyelid and corner of his mouth twitched. Just once, but it was there. Valenti frowned for a moment before realization dawned on him. "Say, aren't those like—"

"Yes, they are—like Shirley's."

They listened with new intensity to the President's words.

"We've seen the sharp end of China's bayonet in the Hong Kong massacre," Dixon said speaking in his measured political voice, "with their violent and bloody suppression of peaceful demonstrators. Their promises to leave a reunited Hong Kong alone were lies and treachery. Our good ally, the Taiwanese, in contemplating the reunification of their island with Mainland China, cannot risk the same fate that befell Hong Kong and the militarization of their peaceful island."

He paused. "And so, in defense of our good friend, in support of freedom and in defiance of tyranny, I have committed the support of the United States of America to defend the freedom-loving, island-nation of Taiwan in its declaration of independence from China."

The reporters murmured audibly, but the President raised his voice. "This includes the commitment of the full force and might of the U.S. military. I have already ordered the Seventh Fleet to the Taiwan Straits to assist our ally, the newest nation in the world, the Republic of Taiwan."

CHAPTER 74

"Independent Taiwan?" Valenti exploded at the TV, "Jesus! That's the most stupid-ass thing I've ever heard."

"Oh, crap," Steve muttered. "Not him."

Valenti muted the TV and turned to face Steve puzzled. "What? You think he's got the big bad vampire bug? Aren't you seeing things? You're so screwed up, everything is looking like your brain thing."

Steve smiled patiently, ready to join the debate. "Maybe. But you saw it."

Valenti narrowed his eyes dubiously. "I saw a twitch, so what?"

"Well," Steve laid out his first strategic question. "What was he saying about recognizing Taiwan's independence? I thought that was a no, no."

"Right. A stupid move."

"Why so stupid? Convince me."

"OK, I'll play your game here. China. They'll fight over Taiwan."

"You think so? Really?"

"Well, what would the President do if Hawaii seceded from the Union?"

"Well, ok." Steve cocked his head at the TV. "So, this supporting Taiwan's independence, how bad is it, really?"

"Bad. It's one thing for us to say we'll defend them in the event of an attack from China, but Taiwan declaring itself independent would be like the South seceding. It means war. China has no choice unless they want to relinquish all current and future claims on the island."

"No choice?"

"Well, I suppose Lincoln had a choice in fighting the South, but from what China's always said, if Taiwan declares independence, it will go to war. The U.S. joining in only means it'll be our boys shedding their blood, too." Valenti went over to the refrigerator, looked in and closed it in disgust. It was empty. "He didn't even leave himself any wriggle room. He just came right out and said it. Stupid."

"Could that be a loss of judgment?"

Valenti looked sharply at Steve and whistled. "Touché." Valenti scratched his ear thoughtfully. "Then, how can we narrow it down?"

"Well, if he's taking Eden and gets intermittent delusions, it's almost certain, I'd say."

"Maybe he already does, you know, have the delusional thing."

"Right, but we can't tell from here, besides, I can't imagine anyone letting it go that far . . ." Steve held his fist to his lips in thought. "Of course, they don't really know even if they are seeing some of the early symptoms. Maybe we—"

"Oh, no you don't. Not 'we.' That isn't our problem."

Steve raised his eyebrows.

"No way." Valenti protested. "Besides, I got out of Washington with my hide intact, well, sort of, and I'm not showing it around there again."

Steve shrugged with a slight smile. "Okay, if you don't want to . . ."

"What about your problems here?" Valenti crossed his arms.

"Who else knows about Eden's disease?"

"Sheridan. Trident."

"Right. Any of those goons around the President know?"

"Probably not."

"And who's going to tell them?"

Valenti stared at Steve a long time. "Fuck. Fuck you."

Steve smiled to himself and walked into the kitchenette and put his glass into the sink. "How the hell do we tell him?"

Valenti fell back on the couch and put his hands under his head. "Well, easy. You march in to the President and say, 'Mr. President, you are dying of an incurable brain-eating disease and I'm relieving you of office.' Simple."

"And don't start a war with China," Steve added, walking back from the kitchen.

"Yeah, and please overlook that tax thing last year, I didn't really mean it."

Steve frowned. "So, who do we call?"

"Ghostbusters? Jeez, Louise, I haven't a clue. Who's your congressman?"

"Mine? Hell if I know. Who's yours?" Steve scratched his chin. He had not shaved since yesterday morning and his whiskers itched.

"Won't work," Valenti continued, "too political, with a congressman wanting an investigation of the president. Who do you know who has connections in the administration? Like an appointee from this state or something? I don't hobnob with the blue-bloods like you doctor people."

That stopped Steve. Who did he know? "Nobody I can think of . . ." his voice trailed off. "Wait, I know," Steve said. "What was his name—he was on the airplane. The Secretary of HHS. Crap. What's his name?"

"Castell?" Valenti offered? I remember his interview after your plane crash.

"Yeah, that's him. We met. I think he'd remember me."

"Well, he damn sure owes you. Still, politics is a very fickle mistress. He might get clued in on your problems and bail."

"Well, we should at least try."

"Are you going to call and tell him you think the President's gone Loony Tunes, or whatever technical term you docs use for those things?"

"Yeah, that's exactly how we talk." Steve rolled his eyes. "Say super sleuth, can you find his number?"

"Sure, it's a semi-public record, being that it's a civilian agency and all. Just a minute." He punched a number on his cell phone. "Dianne," he said after a moment. "Can you get me the number of the Secretary of Health? . . . Yeah, in Washington . . . Right. Call me back."

To pass the time, they watched the TV pundits analyzing the President's announcement. They were as nonplussed as Valenti had been.

After a while, Valenti's phone rang. He jotted a number down on a piece of hotel scratch paper. "Okay, thanks, Dianne." Valenti handed it Steve. "Here. Actually, it's his cell phone number. That Dianne, she amazes me."

Steve looked at the number beginning with area code 202—Washington, D.C.—and pulled his cell phone out of his pocket. Valenti plucked it out of his hand.

"Wait. Not that. It's only for emergencies. It can be traced and then you can be located." Steve looked up irritated at Valenti's paranoia.

"We'll use a pay phone. Someplace far away from here."

"Damn it, that's too much trouble. For nothing."

"Get used to it or I'll have a dead client and no way to collect my fee. He pointed his forefinger at Steve like a gun. "Remember, the life you save is my retirement."

Forty minutes later, under a cloudless, deep blue Arizona dusk, Steve picked up the receiver of a pay telephone on the outskirts of Phoenix. A minute later he hung up, and pocketing the newly purchased phone card, he got back into the Cherokee. "Got it. In five days. Some place called the Mansion Club."

"I know the joint," Valenti said. "A swanky hang-out of the famous and wannabes. It's the kind of place that puts crushed ice in the men's urinals."

"You used to live there?"

"Eight years in the Bureau."

"FBI, right? Officer Harmon told me."

"Yeah. Sore subject. End of discussion."

ELLIOTT buzzed with a notification of an "event." The soft buzzing continued until a technician reluctantly put down his Kindle and rolled his chair over to the monitor. It was marked with a red "Priority" flashing at the top of the screen. He clicked the mouse and the buzzing ceased.

The screen read, "Jacob Castell, Mobile." This guy Castell had dozens of conversations with people all day, the technician mused. Why did this one pop up? He punched a few keys and ELLIOTT told him: the sentinel word that triggered the alarm was 'Dr. Steve James.'

Donning a pair of Koss headphones, he listened to the recorded conversation. It was actually with Dr. James. Castell apparently owed this Dr. James something and agreed to meet him.

The technician quickly downloaded the conversation and stored it on the server. He tapped out an automated phone notification to the client who, in this case, was Vicktor Morloch. The tech attached the compressed audio file to the message, marked it for priority delivery and hit the 'send' button. Automatically encrypted so only Morloch's private cell phone could unscramble it, the message disappeared from his screen.

The technician next sent Mallis a text. According to SOP, Mallis listened to every priority message over his secure phone. The technician wondered idly if his boss used the information for insider stock trading, but figured it was probably to sell the client more services.

His job done, the technician went back to his novel.

CHAPTER 75

"Long fucking day," Linda said, flopping down in a deep chair in Bell's office. She kicked off her shoes and rubbed her feet into the pile carpet. She had not remembered feeling this drained for a long time. The press had eaten her up when she tried to support the President's precipitous decision to support Taiwan. She, of course, agreed with them that it was a dumb move, but the President's position was clear.

"Drink?" Bell asked, walking to his bar.

"Scotch rocks."

Bell poured the drinks. "I know the Chinese are supposed to be inscrutable, but did you see the look on Quin's face? He looked like the cat that just ate the bird. Dammit, Linda, we got taken but good."

A knock on the door preceded Vice President Sullivan's entry. "May I join you?"

"Come on in, John." Bell waved his hand to an empty leather chair. "Drink?"

Sullivan held up a glass. "I'm set, thanks." He slid deep into the overstuffed chair. Sipping his drink, he watched Bell hand Linda her drink and sit down. "So what happened? I don't think there were two people alive who had any idea he would support Taiwan."

"Quin played him like a violin," Resnick said. "Masterful performance. But, get this, Lai's wife never died of leukemia, she died from breast cancer. Our latest bosom buddy lied to us. The President never saw it coming. And," she sipped her scotch, "neither did we."

"So what's your take on the one billion dollars?" Sullivan asked.

"It's bullshit, that's what," Bell said.

"But that's a lot of money," Sullivan responded, swirling the amber liquid in his squat glass.

"Look at it like this," Bell said. "He gives us a down payment of one hundred big ones. We go to war. If he loses, no more payments. China takes over and doesn't look back. If he wins, he's got a new country for a measly billion over ten years."

Resnick leaned forward. "John, he just bought the entire U.S. military for the price of five fighter jets and I can't talk the President out of it. He's temperamentally inclined to fight for the oppressed underdog and he's stubborn as a bull once he's made up his mind." She made a rueful face. "Plus, it spits in China's face and he loves that part."

Sullivan looked hard at her. "There's something else . . ."

"What?"

"He's changed."

Linda hesitated, not sure she wanted to talk about her own thoughts on the matter. "He's not the same."

"And his judgment . . .?" Sullivan pressed.

"We've all seen it," Bell sighed. "I've tried to discuss it with him, his bolting the White House and that prayer thing—thank God it blew over without a major stink—but this stress thing has gotten to him in a way I've never seen."

"And what are those twitchy movements?" Resnick asked, drawn in despite her initial caution.

Sullivan and Bell shrugged. Bell answered, "It's got to be the stress."

Sullivan swung his gaze from Bell to Resnick. "I'm worried about him. I think he needs to see a doctor. Jeff, do you think you can talk him into it?"

Jeff shook his head. "He knows unplanned visits to a doctor get a President in trouble and he's got his eyes firmly set on the next election."

"So, what do we do?" Resnick asked.

"Let's all think about it," Sullivan said quietly. "Reconvene in two days?"

CHAPTER 76

Piers Morgan leaned across his desk, facing the camera, and spoke as soon as the red light came on. "We're back and if you've been watching, you know we've been speaking with Vicktor Morloch, the enormously successful Chairman and CEO of Trident Pharmaceuticals, makers of Eden, the miraculous weight reduction drug, and he's on the cover of People Magazine, which named him among the world's richest bachelors."

Piers straightened up and looked at Morloch sitting across his desk as a different camera light came on. "Tell me Vicktor, you've sold the most successful drug in history—an incredible story—but what's your encore?"

Morloch was dressed in a navy suit with an open necked white shirt. "We have a new medicine called Paradise, which all our research says works just as well as Eden, and—" He held up a finger to help drive home his point, "—is better absorbed with less nose irritation. We look forward to hearing from the FDA soon, so that we can make Paradise available."

Piers laughed. "Paradise. Great name. I hope the FDA agrees with you, which is a segue to our next guest. She's Donna Windsong, president of the advocacy group, Families Against Drugging America. Donna's joining us from Tallahassee, Florida. How are you, Donna?"

Donna's face appeared on a television monitor positioned where Morloch could easily see it. Donna was attractive in an earth-mother kind of way, wearing a simple white dress with a navy jacket. "I'm great, Piers," she smiled. "Thank you for having me on your show."

"Donna, you have a bone to pick about prescription drugs. Here's your chance to express some of your concerns to one of the most visible representatives in the industry."

"I do, Piers, several bones." Windsong's voice took on the cadence of reciting previously memorized information. "My organization is worried about the insidious and pervasive infiltration into society of a pill mentality—that all your problems can be solved by a pill. This expectation has been fed and exploited by the powerful and rich pharmaceutical companies who make billions off sick and helpless people. As a result, prescription drugs are unnecessarily poisoning the people of America. Just look at the statistics, Piers, thousands of deaths a year are caused by drugs, either overdosing or drug interactions. Deaths due to prescription drugs are higher in Florida than cocaine and heroin combined. Piers, what's worse is the systematic drugging of our school-age children with ADHD drugs, weight loss drugs, anti-depressants, anti-anxiety drugs, and other mind-altering drugs. And—"

"Vicktor," Piers interrupted, "Donna says you make too much money and that there are too many drugs. What do you say?"

Morloch laughed pleasantly. "Well, Piers, I'm a bit unprepared for this, but I'll take a stab at her comments. First, Ms. Windsong, I absolutely agree with you that the physician should carefully consider every prescription before it is written. The patient needs education on the proper use and potential problems of the drug before taking it. Strict safeguards are needed, and are in place, to ensure that only safe and well tolerated drugs ever make it to market—"

"But," Windsong said, "don't you agree that drugs are prescribed way too much in this country?"

Morloch forced another smile as he looked at a very pleased Piers Morgan. "I am familiar with the articles, but I'm not a doctor and I cannot pass judgment on each conversation a doctor has with his or her patient, nor his or her individual judgment to prescribe a medication."

"But the drug companies are at fault for making all the drugs poisoning us."

"How are they at fault?" Piers asked.

"Because they flood the market with drugs like Eden and Viagra and Prozac that we don't need. I'm fine with blood pressure medications and antibiotics—at least some of them—but there are several hundred drugs that we simply don't need. And they're not safe."

Piers turned to Morloch. "Vicktor? She says your drug isn't needed and that it's not safe."

"Piers, Ms. Windsong is making the mistake of confusing the issue of availability with improper use. I don't think Ms. Windsong would advocate giving up swimming pools, yet hundreds of kids die each year in pool accidents."

"Donna?" Piers cut Morloch off.

"Well, I would have to look at the statistics . . ."

"Ms. Windsong," Morloch looked at her image on the monitor and wondered if she could see him as well. "I operate in a tightly regulated industry with the FDA looking over my shoulder at every juncture of a drug's development. I make a highly effective, and I might add, an extremely safe drug, and it is perfectly legal. If the FDA determines a drug is not safe, then it never gets on the market. I think you can be assured that the drugs in this country are the safest in the world."

"And you make billions of dollars from your marketing monopoly." Ms. Windsong interrupted.

"Since my picture and income are on the cover of People magazine," Morloch chuckled, "you know how much I am worth. What you don't know is the hundreds of compounds, very promising compounds, that don't make it, with billions spent on their research and development. If you were to cut the profit out of our industry, we wouldn't have the money to research and develop innovative new drugs, like Eden, that we all depend on."

"That bastard knew what he was doing bringing that new-age cunt on the show with me," Morloch snarled into his cell phone. He strode out of the CNN building and climbed into his limousine.

"I think you handled her beautifully," Oscar Perera said on the other end of the call. "You looked calm and poised as you countered her point for point."

"Yeah, but she wins points as a nobody just being on the show with me. Any reaction? Any news on this?"

"None on CNN. I've been watching. I'll give our PR guys a call and see if they have monitored anything, but I don't think there's any significant downside. She came off as shrill. You know, a fringe type."

A click in his ear told him he had another call. "Okay, Oscar. Later." He looked at the caller ID display. The call was from Mallis and Associates with a voice mail message. He punched the green button and heard the familiar scrambler clicks before a pleasant female computer voice announcement. 'This is a priority ELLIOTT message from Mallis and Associates . . . monitored person was . . . Jacob Castell.'

Morloch listened to the recorded conversation between Jacob Castell and Dr. James.

CHAPTER 77

"Sir, this just in. The Pentagon wanted you to see it right away."
The lieutenant in his starched dress blues handed the Secretary of
Defense a sealed manila envelope marked 'Priority' and 'Eyes Only.' The
White House usher, who had located a white-tuxedoed Mark Painter on
the ballroom floor and guided him to the side room, melted away.

"This better be good," Painter grumbled as he tore open the seal and
pulled out the contents of the envelope; he had left his wife standing on
the dance floor to see this message. The evening's event was a full-dress
occasion in honor of Taiwan's President. Painter's wife detested formal
affairs and hated being left alone during them even more. He would do
penance for this diversion.

Scanning the document, he frowned and then sat down in a heavy
leather chair to read the contents more carefully. It was a briefing from
General Samuel Taylor—on China.

According to the document, China had officially lowered their state
of alert from their DEFCON equivalent 3 to a more relaxed level 4.
However, their level of military activity had markedly increased. Painter
re-read the document carefully, feeling that he had missed a point somewhere. The analyst who wrote the briefing had not drawn any conclusions about China's activities, only that they were worrisome given the
context of the Taiwanese president's visit.

A frustrated Secretary of Defense stared at the pages, wondering what
exactly he was missing. Usually the pattern of activity gave U.S. analysts

an idea about the objective, but not this time. Instead, it described the observed military activity: troop movements without direction; redeployment of naval vessels to differing locations, but without any concentration; and supply trucks entering and leaving military bases above their usual numbers.

Painter frowned; there was something big afoot, but what was not clear. This level of military activity signaled an operation of considerable size, either large-scale war games or something more serious.

But why the DEFCON relaxation claim? It was counter to the military activity, which would signal an escalation of DEFCON in other circumstances. Maybe to flag the U.S. that it was all internal. Well, that made some sense in light of the Falun massacre. Maybe they were still stifling internal dissent.

He needed to talk to Bingham. He was here at the ball, too, unless he had left already. And Martha was still waiting for him. *Damn.* He hesitated, trying to decide who he should see first.

CHAPTER 78

Mallis sat cross-legged in an easy chair, his notebook computer sitting on his lap. He typed in eleven numbers in four groups, separated by three periods: an Internet address known to a very restricted number of authorized individuals. He pressed 'Enter' and after a moment he was greeted with a screen that said, 'Welcome to Verifone. Enter username and password.'

Verifone's card authorization was the lucrative service that authorized Visa, MasterCard, and American Express card purchases all over the world. Their databases were also a gold mine to law enforcement. Using special links, authorized law enforcement individuals could search the databases to track any card number they wanted. All that was necessary was a special software code and a unique hardwired-circuit plugged into the USB port, a type of electronic key identifying the request as coming from an authorized source. Mallis had both.

He tapped in Dr. James's business Visa card number and the expiration date. In a moment he saw a complete list of all transactions for the past thirty days. Mallis studied the list, and then frowned. There was nothing from the last two days: no hotels, no gas, and no restaurants or grocery stores.

A buzzing from the desk across the room distracted him. He looked up to see that it was his android phone in vibrate mode, signaling the arrival of a text message. He ignored it and turned back to the computer.

Mallis typed in another number, this one Dr. James's gold Amex card. The results flashed down his screen. Mallis scowled again—nothing from the last two days. No clothes purchases, no airplane tickets, no apartment rental.

He typed in the US Air Visa card that James held jointly with his wife.

Bingo. Mallis sat back in satisfaction. He found two airline tickets to Portland Oregon. But he scowled in thought. Why two? His son would have to have a seat, too. There was only one explanation. James had stayed behind and sent his wife and son to Oregon.

He clicked on the USB thumb drive that Doug had made of James's home computer files. He opened the contact database and clicked the find key. He typed in Oregon and hit enter. Three names popped up. He looked at each one in turn before he smiled. Jack and Joan Pritchard. It must be Steve's wife's—what was her name, Anne? It must be her parents' house. They lived in Eugene, Oregon, on 345 Douglas Fir Road. Good, thought Mallis. He cut and pasted the information into his Word file on James. Their phone number would be monitored as well.

But where was Dr. James? His phone buzzed again—a short one to remind him of the waiting message. Mallis had one more card number he wanted to try. It was James's Discover card. He typed a few more keys when his cell phone rang.

Mallis crawled out of the chair and snatched up the device. "Mallis," he growled, but only heard the encryption clicks at the other end.

Morloch shouted in Mallis's ear. "Mallis, what the hell's going on out there?"

"We didn't get James, yet."

"I know that, you idiot! Why the hell not? Are you jacking off up there? Sun tanning by the pool? Goddamn it, what the fuck have you been doing?"

"It's under control," Mallis said smoothly, but inside he struggled to control his temper. He knew Morloch was right—he had never had a subject escape once, much less twice. But how did Morloch know?

"He just got lucky," Mallis continued, "It's just a matter of time—"

"I don't have fucking time." Morloch hissed. "You're supposed to shut these things up. How could you let this fucking doctor connect me to this thing?"

"Now, *I* don't know what you're talking about," Mallis said. "How do you know he's connected you with Eden?"

Morloch's voice raised a pitch. "What do you mean you don't know? He's called Castell to set up a meeting. Jacob Castell, of the goddamn Health and Human Services. The FDA's under him. James is going to the top."

"How did you know—?"

"From you, you idiot! I got one of your priority e-mails!"

Shit! The text message. That must have been about James's call to Castell.

Morloch heard Mallis's silence. "Mallis!" he thundered. "Do I have to tell you every goddamn thing?"

Mallis's face stung. "No. I have not listened to that message yet," he replied. I've been working on locating Dr. James."

Now Morloch sounded incredulous. "Locating him? What kind of cluster fuck's going on?"

"He's dropped out of sight." Mallis measured his voice. "He hasn't been to his house or office all day and we don't know where he's staying. But," Mallis hastened to say, "as I said, it's just a matter of time before we pick him up. He'll make a mistake. They always do."

"You mean to tell me that a doctor with a wife, a kid, a mortgage, a medical practice and a fucking dog just dropped out of sight?"

"For the time being, but we'll find him." Mallis didn't tell Morloch they had killed the dog.

"Well, he's going on the offensive, Mallis. Despite your goddamn high-priced antics, you've deterred him, not one fucking iota. You better find him before he spills his guts to Castell. And no fucking loose ends, understood?"

"Yes, sir."

Mallis hung up the phone embarrassed and furious. *Goddamn James!* Mallis slammed his fist into the wall, punching a hole through the expensive Ritz Carlton sheet-rock.

Mallis called in to listen to the phone conversation with Castell. Morloch had been right. James was planning a meeting. Well, now he knew exactly where and when Dr. James would be available. He had five days to locate James before the meeting, or he would be at that Washington meeting himself. *I'll fuck James but good.*

CHAPTER 79

Steve woke up abruptly and sat bolt upright in bed. His aching muscles protested the sudden move. The light filtering around the heavy motel curtains told him it was morning and time to get started. The night had been a bad one, with the achiness not completely controlled by the ibuprofen and when he was awake, he obsessed on how to get out of his bind.

One conclusion, even if the police caught whoever was responsible for trying to kill him, Morloch would send someone else. He rubbed his burning eyes with the knuckles of both hands. So they had to get Morloch.

Steve grimaced as he climbed painfully out of bed. His scalp ached where the stitches closed the bullet wound and his neck throbbed with each movement and swallow. He felt like Mike Tyson had used him as a punching bag.

He made his way into the bathroom and splashed cold water on his face. It felt good. He splashed his face several more times, letting the liquid cool his skin. He examined himself in the mirror. The hazel eyes that looked back at him saw an older, grayer, thinner man than he knew. His hair was a tangled mess and the half-inch thick line that ran across his throat was crimson red, except for some dark blue splotches in the center. Probing it gently, it responded with sharp bolts of pain. He wet his hair and combed it with his fingers into a semblance of order, avoiding the stitches in his scalp. He had no energy for a shower.

Wanting some noise, he turned on the television. Ignoring the program, a morning news and chat show, he walked into the kitchenette and opened the refrigerator. Valenti had brought him some groceries, but the sight of milk, eggs and hot dogs turned his stomach. He closed the refrigerator door and sat on the bed.

The phone sitting next to the bed alongside the clock radio caught his eye, tempting him. Who would know? Just a short call. 'Anne,' he would say, 'I'm fine. How are you?' He imagined hearing her voice filled with love and concern. He smiled thinking of how good it would be to just—

A knock on the door made him jump. Suddenly alert, his heart began racing. *Who was it?* Probably housekeeping. *Calm down.* He got up and looked through the fisheye peephole. Pulling the chain off, he turned the deadbolt and opened the door.

Valenti stepped in and closed the door. He carried a plastic shopping bag full of something soft and light. "Jesus, Doc, you look like you got beat up by a horde of angry women at a mud wrestling match."

"Good morning to you, too." Steve turned around and sat down at the small oak dining table.

Valenti dropped the bag onto the table. "I brought you some clothes. I think I got your size right. I always had an eye for those things." He opened the refrigerator, pulled out the gallon jug of milk and opened it.

"Except shoes. I always had trouble estimating shoe size. I'm pretty good with men, but women—now that's an estimating nightmare for you." Pulling a short, fat glass out of the cupboard, he poured himself some milk. "I got slapped once estimating a woman's shoe size incorrectly. You wouldn't think they'd be so sensitive about those things, but they are. By the way she reacted, you would have thought I had guessed her weight at twenty pounds over or something."

He downed half the glass of milk. "But men's clothes, I'm usually within an inch of their height and suit size. Anyway," he pointed with the hand holding the glass. "See if you fit into those duds. They're pretty nondescript."

Steve had pulled out the bundle of clothes and was looking at them. There were two long-sleeved white dress shirts and a pair of Wrangler jeans. He checked the sizes and shook his head in amazement. The sizes were pretty much spot on, Pants inseam 36 and shirt sleeve length also

36. Valenti had purchased his exact sizes except for the waist, which was one size too big at 34 but it would do.

Next were several pairs of white athletic socks, an XL hooded sweatshirt and a package of Haynes briefs, size thirty-four and a package of three white t-shirts. At the bottom of the bag was a brown leather belt curled up around a pair of tennis shoes.

"Nice job," Steve said. "Did you go in and tell the sales lady that he's about your size?"

"Go now, and leave the sarcasm to me."

Soon he had showered and dressed in his new clothes making Steve feel considerably refreshed. He was still sore, but perversely, welcomed the physical discomfort; it was more tangible and transient than his other worries.

When he walked out of the bathroom, Valenti had apparently made another trip out, this time to Taco Bell. He was elbow deep in burrito wrappers and towering soft drinks.

"Come eat," Valenti said between bites of his Taco Supreme. "You like Mexican, don't you?"

Steve discovered an appetite and sat down. The brand new cotton smell of his shirt reminded him that things were different. At home, he would have washed it first. He was conscious of the wrinkles and fold lines in the shirt, pulled straight from the package, and its stiffness chafed his neck. All the more reason to get cracking.

"At home, Maria makes me eat right, you know, green stuff and broiled chicken and fish. But out on assignment, I'm the master of my own fate."

"At least your diet," Steve said, eyeing the three paper bags bulging with food. He pulled out a crispy taco and unwrapped it. "Did you buy one of everything on the menu?"

"At least. Food will make you a whole man."

"And this food will make me a whole lot of man."

"Ahhh, sense of humor's back."

"Mmm. So what's on the agenda?"

"I went to your house this morning with Detective Harmon."

"Anything left?" Steve recalled watching the last parts of his house collapse in flames, including Johnnie's bedroom. He already knew what to expect. But still, hearing it would make it more definite and final.

"Anything that's recognizable is being taken to a storage warehouse for such time that you or your wife care to look through the items. It's pretty much all gone, though, I'm afraid."

"Photo albums?"

"Probably not." Valenti concentrated on his burrito.

Steve was ready to choke the man who was responsible for this.

Valenti glanced up. "Good. Mad is good. You'll need that energy." Looking back down, he added in an offhand tone, "By the way, your house was bugged."

"What?"

"Yeah."

"They could hear everything?" Steve's voice rose.

"Probably." Valenti took another bite.

"Jesus, isn't that—" he stopped. The rules didn't apply. He kept thinking things were supposed to be normal. They weren't. Not anymore. "Fucking assholes."

"Eat. Keep your strength up. My mom's not here to nag you, so I'll have to."

Steve looked at the taco in his hand and the salsa he had just squirted onto it. If eating were an act of defiance, he was going to eat. He bit off the end and chewed.

"If you're feeling stressed, it's fine dining we suggest. Besides, this is my dietary swan song. I'm done with greasy fast food and back on the training circuit." Valenti shoved in another bite before he had swallowed his previous one. If eating were an act of defiance, then Valenti was giving his assailants the middle finger. The thought lightened Steve's mood, if only a little.

Really, he thought, things were no better or worse then they had been 24 hours ago. Except now he knew more and was better prepared for what he needed to do. Plus he had an ally. He was suddenly glad Valenti was on his side.

"Yesterday," Valenti said after taking a long draught from his huge soda cup, "I was pretty sure these guys were pros, but after I found the Jenny—"

"What's a Jenny?"

"A bugging device. After I found the Jenny, I knew these guys were professional."

"And?"

"Well, for one, pros are expensive. Someone's willing to pay a lot of cash to scratch you. They want containment."

"Containment?"

"They want this thing shut up tight. That means anybody attached to you professionally is in real danger. It would be relatively easy to just plug you and make it look like a random thing, but they went to the time, expense, and risk to bug your house. If they go to that kind of trouble," he continued, "they want to know who knows what. If they have that information, they can contain the leak."

"Great. My friends are all potential victims because I'm trying to do the right thing."

"No good deed goes unpunished. But we now know something about the fucks after you. They're scary."

"Yeah, I know."

"Amateurs make mistakes. These guys didn't. They're smart and experienced. They have lots of money to play with and they have ways to find out more about you than your wife knows. Probably the most dangerous thing about them is their detachment from the outcome. They're hired assassins with a mission . . . in some ways like plumbers. You're just another clogged toilet for them."

"Great, I'm a shit hole."

"Well, you've become a little more than just a shit hole. You're currently stinking up the whole house and they can't find you. But the point is—" Valenti took another drink, "—they're good. We just have to be better."

"Are you that good?" Steve watched Valenti closely.

Valenti carefully wiped his mouth with a paper napkin before he answered. "Used to be."

"You used to be in the FBI."

"Bad subject."

"But you used to, right?"

"Right. You get to ask one more question, then drop it."

Steve thought a minute. "Nah. It's your life. Tell me when you want to."

"When the Cubbies win the Series. And one more thing. You can't go to the medical board hearing. Too obvious."

"I already figured that out."

"Good thinking, Doc. Your lawyer's going to try and postpone it, since you're not practicing anyway, but she's not sure it'll work. She says they smell blood and a chance to grandstand about how they're protecting the public from charlatans, snake oil salesmen, and the like. Sorry."

"Like I said, I'm already past that. I was thinking, even if we catch the hit man, Morloch will only send another."

"Not if we catch him alive. Men at this level don't work in a knowledge vacuum. They are far and away more effective as partners in the operation."

"So they're not just hit men hired in a smoky club on Van Buren."

Valenti laughed. "Maybe they go there, but it's for a piece of ass."

"So we catch them and they talk."

"Maybe. Probably."

"Well, what's the first thing?"

Valenti leaned over and fished inside a leather athletic bag on the floor. He slid three things across the table to Steve, a pair of dark sunglasses, a fake moustache and an Arizona Diamondbacks baseball cap.

"You're going incognito, my man."

CHAPTER 80

HHS Secretary Castell had one thing on his mind as he walked into the White House for an early morning appointment with the President. The housing bill, the one that Castell had personally supported, was now in House committee and not faring well. He wanted to talk the President into lobbying for it. So far, President Dixon had shown only tepid support, mindful of his congressional budget compromise. Castell, convinced of the political benefits it could buy the President, wanted the bill. Besides, Castell had friends depending on its passage.

Castell grew up in moneyed Boston where he attended Tufts Medical School and finished his residency in internal medicine at Northwestern University. He joined the Food and Drug Agency where he rose to prominence, not in science, but in management, becoming the Assistant Director of the Food and Drug Administration. It was then that he began moving in Washington circles. His ability to interact effectively with the influential elite assured him the director's role once the position opened.

As director, most observers judged Castell a capable administrator, successfully pushing key drugs for approval while keeping costs in line. He also promoted the director's position relentlessly; making it clear to Congress and the nation that he was on the side of reduced bureaucracy in government, and had a no-nonsense approach to approving needed medications. A year after Dixon had won the White House, in a surprise move, he had asked Castell to head the Department of Health and Human Services following the scandal and resignation of his predecessor.

Following Joan Pascal, he passed chief White House aide, Wesley Rojas, who was just leaving the Oval Office. Castell nodded in passing. "Morning, Wesley."

Rojas dipped his head. "Good morning, Mr. Secretary,"

"Jake, welcome," Dixon said, putting a white pharmacy sack into his top desk drawer. He took Castell's outstretched hand. "Come in. Sit, sit."

"Thank you, sir." Castell sat in one of the chairs opposite the mahogany desk. To Castell's relief, the President seemed to be in a good mood.

"I'm sorry I had to keep postponing our meeting, Jake, but this damn China thing, you know." Dixon looked at a printed schedule on his desk and looked back up at Castell. "So my party needs help with the housing bill, does it?"

"Yes, sir. The provision for continuing the discount on mortgage rates and mortgage insurance for under-employed people is making some members of Congress nervous. The cost, you know. But it would be a tremendous boost to you and some of your key—"

"Right, right, I remember." Dixon seemed uncharacteristically distracted and kept rubbing his temples. "We can afford it?"

It was a softball question that gave Castell plenty of room. "Of course, sir." He leaned forward to press his carefully rehearsed points. "And with the election season on us, we need this bill. In fact—"

"Sure, sure." Dixon waved his hands abstractly, interrupting the speech Castell had started. "Whatever you think."

Castell peered carefully at Dixon. While it was going better than he expected, something wasn't right.

"Jake, are you a religious man?"

Castell blinked at the President. "Uh, yes, sir."

"Then let's pray for the right answer. I find it makes things more clear."

"Certainly, sir." He hesitated, but Dixon was already kneeling, holding the desk for support. He looked at Castell raising his eyebrows, making the secretary distinctly uneasy. "Uhh, I'll pray at my office, sir."

"Come join me, Jake. Please."

"I'm a little uncomfortable with this, sir."

Dixon shrugged and closed his eyes. Castell looked at the secret service agent—D'Agostino was it?—for a clue as to how to behave, but saw only an impassive face. Dixon stood up and seemed refreshed with a new alertness.

"Well, Jake, I think we need to push for the insurance provision if you think that'll help the bill." He nodded thoughtfully. "Let them know I support it."

"Can we have some of the leadership over for a lunch, sir?" Castell remembered almost belatedly the instructions of his strategist.

"I'll see. China, you know." The President's face twitched visibly.

There it is! He had been warned to expect it. Although a physician, he could not tell what it was. It was not a simple tic, nor was it a tremor. Neurology had been his least favorite rotation during medical school and he had stayed away from it since.

The President smiled and sat down. The meeting was over and Castell had to be satisfied. As he left through the east entrance, he couldn't remember a time when the President had prayed during a meeting like that. But then, the President had given him much more latitude than he had expected. Castell's step picked up. He had calls to make.

CHAPTER 81

"Tell me about Eden, how it works, and how it got approved," Valenti asked. They had just visited another of Valenti's underground specialists, this time on the west side. The product they had ordered would be ready in time for their trip to Washington in three more days. They drove east on Olive Avenue, back towards Steve's motel near the Phoenix airport.

Valenti had just finished a sliced turkey sandwich for lunch and sucked on the straw that led to his bottle of water. It wasn't enough to hold body and soul together, he had bemoaned, but was determined to mend his overeating ways. Steve, slumped low in the seat, stuffed Valenti's wadded up trash back into the paper sack and tossed it onto the floorboards at his feet. Steve had already finished his tuna sandwich, eating in the swift, methodical way doctors learn to do, after long experience with interrupted meals.

As he thought about the answer, he watched the passing streetlights silhouetted against the brilliant azure of the afternoon sky, contrasted only by wispy white jet contrails crossing high overhead.

"Actually, prion stuff aside, Eden is the miracle drug of the new millennium."

"You sound like an ad."

"Well, yeah." He shifted, feeling his tailbone grind uncomfortably against the front edge of the bucket seat. "A really effective drug for weight loss was the holy grail of drug research for decades and Eden is it."

"I know it's good, but it's that good?"

"Better than you could hope for. Everybody who takes it gets to their ideal lean body weight without going on a diet. In fact, they can eat pretty much whatever they damn well please. Trident hit a home run on their baby and no one else has anything close, either now or on the horizon."

"Until the patent runs out. So how does it work?"

"By a primitive hormonal system little known until Trident pounced on it. The system helped our anthropological ancestors to regulate their body weight and heat production."

"Huh?"

"Okay. Suppose you are a Cro-Magnon man."

"My best feature according to Maria." He glanced at Steve. "My wife, by the way."

"Okay, Cro-Magnon man, your diet consists mostly of fruits, nuts, and plants with a little meat thrown in for good measure."

"You mean salads." Valenti's face showed his disapproval. "No pasta?"

"Actually I'm getting to that. Now the Cro-Magnon diet isn't high in calories, so the body trained itself to store every scrap of excess energy it could to see us through periods of famine. Now when we eat our pasta, refined sugars, and Big Macs, the body, acting on its age-old habits, stores every excess calorie as fat."

"So wives get big hips and we get pot bellies, storing up for a famine? The calorie savings and loan plan."

"Mostly savings, but that's half of the story," Steve explained. "The other half is the body's capability to burn calories at will. Exercise physiologists—"

"Who?" Valenti asked.

"Exercise physiologists. They study the body when it exercises."

"I'd be a black hole to them."

"Most likely." Steve smiled, despite himself. "Anyway, they've known for some time that elite athletes burn energy much more efficiently than you or me. In addition, people who live in very cold climates also burn energy efficiently. For a long time, it was assumed that variations in the circulation were responsible."

"You mean their hearts delivered blood better than regular people?"

"Something like that, yes," Steve agreed. "What Dr. Blumenthal, the original founder of Trident, found was that the basic cellular process that converts food into energy could be manipulated at its most fundamental level. Athletes more effectively utilize energy, turning it into muscle output. People in cold climates literally burn energy at rest like a stove to keep the body at a constant warm temperature, a burn rate much higher than we thought."

"So our bodies can adapt to their special conditions."

"Right. What science just recently realized was that these two systems are linked and are under the control of the same hormone system, which in turn, is controlled by low-level brain operations. While it takes us months of training or living in a cold climate to change our energy usage, our Cro-Magnon ancestors probably adapted in a single week.

"But then, we discovered agriculture with rice and wheat, delivering a high carbohydrate diet. It overwhelmed the system with excess calories and it shut down. Except in extreme circumstances, like intense training and living in a cold climate, it's dormant."

"I think that's really something, but I'm not sure what you just told me."

"Fair enough. It means, through the administration of a hormone like Eden, we can tell the body to burn off excess calories until we reach our highly-trained body weight."

"Without a diet or exercise?"

"Correct. Although there are good reasons to exercise, weight loss doesn't have to be one of them. But there's more."

"More?"

"When a person reaches his or her lean body weight, they have several unanticipated benefits. For one, it reduces or eliminates the requirement for insulin or diabetes drugs in adult onset diabetics. It normalizes cholesterol and thereby reduces stroke and heart attacks. It may also reduce certain types of cancer, if another study we did for Trident was positive."

"This sounds good. Everyone would want to take it."

"Well, there's more."

"More? You've just summarized four years of Cosmo articles on this stuff."

Steve raised his eyebrows.

"My wife buys them at the supermarket." Valenti shifted uncomfortably. "She leaves them by the toilet. So what?"

CHAPTER 82

Morloch lounged in his favorite media room chair with Vivaldi playing in the background. A steaming cup of English Breakfast Tea sat next to him on the occasional table and three untouched newspapers lay in a pile on the floor. The manila folder resting in his lap contained the background material he had requested on Dr. James. It was pedantic, speculative, and too often laudatory, but Morloch found reading about Dr. James a reasonably interesting, if necessary, homework assignment.

Dr. James had become the biggest burr under his saddle and he wanted to know everything he could about this adversary. Trident's PR firm had compiled a sizeable stack of newspaper articles and broadcast transcripts with or about Dr. James. Morloch had budgeted an extra hour this morning to read it all in a single sitting.

First, there were a few local Phoenix newspaper articles about his research in Alzheimer's and obesity. Dr. James was reasonably articulate, Morloch concluded, to the extent one could tell from the few quotations and statements, but he gleaned little else. He had been, in his interviews about his Eden research, an effective advocate of the drug.

Saving the airliner from crashing brought Dr. James widespread press, national as well as local. Reading through that coverage took more time, but after a few interviews and reports, it became repetitive. Amazing, Morloch thought, how little imagination reporters have when writing a print or broadcast story. Dr. James had portrayed himself as lucky and in the right place, with a lot of the 'aw shucks' modesty Morloch despised.

It was a remarkable characterization, especially when Morloch knew that it was no accident James was able to pull the plane out of its dive. He had a clear head when it mattered.

Morloch sat up when reading Jacob Castell's eyewitness reports. He had forgotten Castell had been aboard the aircraft, personally witnessing James saving it. That's why, Morloch realized, James had called Castell to meet him and why Castell had acceded to the request.

The most recent articles were the result of Mallis's handiwork. 'Dr. James crashes and burns,' one headline announced and another proclaimed, '747 hero flames out.' The articles described Dr. James's multiple unexplained troubles, including a sexual abuse suit, malpractice allegations—with the Arizona Medical Board scheduling an urgent hearing on his license—followed by allegations of Dr. James trying to commit suicide with his son in the car, and speculations that he had set his own house on fire with his family inside. Although there were the usual disclaimers of the unconfirmed nature of the reports from unnamed sources, Morloch saw that Mallis had done his job of discrediting the esteemed Dr. James quite thoroughly.

Judging from the pictures of the damaged freeway ramp and the rubble of his house, Dr. James should be dead—twice. There were even some mentions of Dr. James's troubles on some national news outlets, but surprisingly, and to his credit, Dr. James had never allowed an interview. Apparently, following the house explosion, he had not been recognized publicly. He had indeed vanished.

Morloch put the folder on the table and picked up his now lukewarm tea. He was sure that Dr. James was now planning to tell Castell about Eden. That would have serious ramifications. Castell, as Secretary of Health and Human Services, could order the FDA to investigate Eden. As much as he trusted Perera to keep quiet, with enough pressure from prosecutors and offers of immunity, he probably would talk. While Morloch was certain that nothing could be connected to him personally, it would tank his company and his billions of stock, Paradise or no Paradise.

And with Dr. James in hiding, Morloch had no expectation that Mallis would find him before the scheduled Castell meeting. Since Mallis and his team knew the time and place of the meeting, they had an opportunity to get James either before or afterwards. The timing could be critical to the suppression of Dr. James's story and Morloch needed to carefully think everything through.

Apprehending Dr. James just before the meeting seemed to be Mallis's plan, but the more Morloch thought about it, the less he liked it. The wild card, and the factor he couldn't eliminate, was the possibility that James had already sent Castell information and data about his Eden allegations. Killing James right before the meeting, would give his allegations credence. But killing him afterwards would give James the chance to make his case in person. There had to be a third and better option.

CHAPTER 83

Secretary Resnick sat down at the polished elm wood table in Defense Secretary Mark Painter's office and nodded at the other attendees at this early morning meeting, CIA head, George Bingham; the National Security Advisor, August Crusoe, and Secretary Painter. Resnick covered a deep yawn, tired and stiff from a night that had stretched into the early hours. Called by Painter last evening for this six o'clock meeting, she hadn't gone home, choosing to catch a couple of hours on her office couch. Vice President Sullivan knocked softly on the door before letting himself in.

"The seventh fleet is on their way to Taiwan," Painter began. "The Eisenhower and the Stennis battle groups are converging and will get there in three days, but I can tell you, my chiefs are giving me hell about the mission. It's like Afghanistan all over again, only the stakes are higher." He leaned forward and forcefully tapped his index finger on the table to emphasize his point. "We have to limit the commitment, narrow the nature of our involvement, or even abandon the commitment altogether. Otherwise, we might have a disaster on our hands."

Crusoe asked, "You really think China would attack? We all know they can't invade Taiwan."

"If we are behind Taiwan and out of the Straits, I think we would be fine—but interposed," Painter shook his head, "we're in full range of China's missiles, not to mention their navy and air force. They could cause major damage." Painter shook his head. "Admiral Havelind's extremely unhappy at his deployment. It's a no win for us."

Sullivan spoke. "Did anyone see Dick Samuels on *Meet the Press?*" They all nodded except Resnick. "I think the Speaker coming out as strongly against this as he did indicates the sense of his party. Last night, I got my ear chewed off by my staff and more of the same today by members of the congressional leadership. The President's staff is in a tizzy about how to sell this."

He looked around the table. "Congress can give us a lot of trouble, both financially and politically. We must make a case for the defense of Taiwan or this issue will sink the President in the next election," he paused as he looked at the group, "which may give him a reason to significantly moderate his position on this."

Crusoe leaned forward resting his elbows on the conference table. "I thought the President was clear. And unless I miss my read, he's fully committed. I believe we should act in accordance with his wishes unless and until we're instructed otherwise. Our current deployment is the right one and a significant deterrent to the Chinese. Our intimidation is much stronger in the forward position."

Sullivan looked at Secretary Painter. "Do you agree?"

Painter pursed his lips. "They can inflict significant damage, but can't defeat our forces combined with Taiwan's. Conventional analysis says their problem is their lack of a navy of sufficient size to punch through Taiwan's costal defenses and ferry enough troops across to capture the island. But, and it's a big one, their air and missile capability can hurt us a great deal, even sink some ships. For example, they can numerically overwhelm us by air simply because of the close range in the Taiwan Straits."

Crusoe nodded. "I agree as far as that goes, but you haven't addressed the psychology. China is much more likely to be intimidated by the show in their own front yard, in their face, as it were. That will pressure them to capitulate much faster than with a carrier fleet in some obscure location on the other side of Taiwan. If you do that you are looking at an unlimited open-ended commitment that pins down your resources indefinitely." He looked at Painter. "Do you want that?"

"You're convinced they won't attack?"

"Quite sure. It's the strategy that will most likely bring about a rapid conclusion and China's recognition of Taiwan. Besides, they're too tied up economically with Taiwan to want to take her militarily. The faster we sew up the agreements, the faster we can get on with something else. It's the logical thing for them to do."

"It depends on how logical they are thinking right now." Resnick said. "I believe the hard liners to be in ascendance, which makes aggression much more likely."

Crusoe smiled and tapped his pipe in his hand. "I guess we agree to disagree."

"Look, all this military activity has me nervous." Painter thumped the stapled report on his coffee table. "It says that their apparently random activity continues unabated. It's disorganized—moving supplies by truck and train to all corners of the map. There's a net flow of materiél away from the bases, it says, but it's not concentrating, particularly not near the coast. There are massive troop movements, but in no particular direction. It goes on . . ." He threw up his hands in frustration. "It's like they're shuffling the deck."

"Lots of effort and energy, but for what?" Crusoe asked. "The pattern should tell us something, which it doesn't."

"But the military's on the move in a big way and we don't know the objective. Why not Taiwan?"

"Can't," Crusoe replied. "There's no massing of military power across from Taiwan, plus they cannot invade for reasons we've already discussed."

Bingham added, "We have a list of possible objectives, Mark. Hong Kong, Taiwan, Russia, India, and so on, but there is insufficient information to—"

"Look, George, Augie," Painter said, "If they invade Russia or India, I don't give a rat's ass. We don't have a defense pact with them. But we do with Taiwan. And Taiwan has to be their target, given the stalled negotiations. They started their movements within hours of the President's announcement of support, as though we turned on a switch."

"It's still no," Crusoe said. "Especially with the fracture at the top, they can't possibly mount a major offensive. Besides, the Seventh Fleet and Taiwan's coastal defenses stand in their way. That's a formidable barrier. That's why Taiwan cannot be their objective. It's unrealistic."

"Why is it so formidable?" Painter challenged. He had learned this lesson during a sharp lecture from his Joint Chiefs.

"Because it has tremendous offensive power," Crusoe shrugged, as if it were obvious.

"Which we can't use because we are not at war," Painter rejoined.

"However, it can prevent ships from invading Taiwan. But," Crusoe added, pulling his pipe from his sweater, "you're right, its best use is in projecting force at a distance."

"Which we don't have," Painter said, like the professor he once was.

"Which? Force or distance?"

"Neither. The Taiwan Straits is about a hundred and fifty miles wide. We're in range of China's coastal defenses and their missiles. We need more than a two-hundred mile radius in open sea for optimal security and flexibility."

"Hmm, possibly," Crusoe allowed.

"Even pulling back close to Taiwan, we have at most a hundred miles open sea to China, a point that has been made crystal clear to me by the Secretary of the Navy, who's also getting an earful. That's my problem. If we stay out of the Straits, we have room to operate, but the President wants the force interposed, which gives the Chinese a huge juicy target. We're sitting ducks out there."

Crusoe shook his head in disagreement, sticking his unlit pipe into his mouth. "It's the right deployment, Mark. China cannot launch any invasion force with our battle group out there. It's a *force majure*. They can't."

Painter thought a moment before responding. "I have the feeling they have some confidence in their plans for reasons we don't understand. This is another peacekeeping mission with our men in the crosshairs of someone who wants us to get the hell out of Dodge. I will apprise the President of my concerns."

After the meeting broke up, Painter sat on his couch a long time reflecting on their conversation. If China was preparing for an invasion of Taiwan, how would they organize it? All the military movements looked disorganized. *Maybe we're supposed to think it's disorganized.*

On inspiration, Painter got up and walked over to his bookshelf. He had to hunt a minute, but there it was, a slim, red paperbound book, almost invisible between two larger volumes. He pulled it out and walked over to his desk.

The Art of War, by Sun Tzu. He had not read it since his undergraduate years, nearly forty years ago. If Chinese generals were reading it, he should too. It still had corners turned down on the pages of immutable truths he had wanted to remember, but had long forgotten. Why it had traveled with him through all the years and countless moves, he could not say. Looking at it flooded him with old memories.

Irene, his girlfriend at Columbia, the one with the dazzling smile and cheerleader energy. He had proposed to her one night when he was drunk and horny, and she had wisely ignored it. Ultimately, they broke up. Painter shook off the melancholic spell and opened the book to the first dog-eared page and read the underlined words:

"War is a matter of vital importance to the state; a matter of life or death, the road either to survival or to ruin. Hence, it is imperative that it be studied thoroughly."

Right, war is hell, thought Painter. He turned to the next marked page.

"All warfare is based on deception. Hence, when able to attack, we must seem unable; when using our forces, we must seem inactive; when we are near, we must make the enemy believe we are far away; when far away, we must make him believe we are near. Hold out baits to entice the enemy. Feign disorder and crush him."

Painter caught his breath. *Feign disorder,* he thought about all that randomness the Chinese were showing them. Painter stared at the page. If China didn't act now to invade Taiwan, they would pretty much forfeit all future claims. But how does all this disorder come together? Painter closed the book and leaned back on the couch. How?

It all pivoted on China's ability to land their huge army. If they managed to do that, Taiwan would be lost. It all came back to knowing China's tactics and strategy, which they had, so far, successfully managed to hide.

CHAPTER 84

Valenti showed up at Steve's room late the next day to greet an impatient and stir-crazy client. He waved an envelope at Steve. "Special delivery from your wife and offspring."

Snatching it out of Valenti's hand, Steve sat on the unmade bed and tore it open. By prior arrangement, it was a printed email sent to one of Anne's Phoenix friends for Valenti to pick up. He had dropped off a message from Steve to send back to Anne. His message was, by necessity, positive, but also neutral, avoiding specifics and bad news; there was plenty of time for that later. The important thing was that they knew he was fine.

Reading and re-reading the printout, Steve absorbed the words on the page. They were generic, meant for semi-public consumption, but it was still a link. There was even a section from Johnnie asking when they could come home. A lump rose in Steve's throat. He didn't want to put it down and break the connection.

"I also got you a laptop," Valenti said, handing Steve a box with HP written all over it. "That'll keep you amused while I'm not here. I pre-loaded it with anonymous surfing software, an industrial strength version, so you can visit all sorts of porn sites and nobody will be the wiser. You don't even have to tell me."

"As if." Steve needed the computer for all the research he wanted to do.

"Let me catch you up on the latest gossip," Valenti began, sitting down at the small dining table and pulling out a white legal pad with the bottom edges curled and bent.

Steve reluctantly put the email in the drawer of the bedside table and scratched at his unshaven whiskers.

"First, the ad. The Republic took camera-ready copy from an agency in California, paid in advance. I called the agency's number and got a fax machine squeal. Reverse look-up showed it to belong to a Subway sandwich shop in Irvine."

"Dead end?" Steve stood up to walk near the window and looked out at the swimming pool through the sheer curtains.

"Pretty much. I talked the woman at the newspaper into giving me a copy of the paid bill. It was paid by a credit card: a Gold American Express."

"That should be easy to trace."

"It was," Valenti said. "It was yours."

Steve stared at him. "They paid for this thing with my credit card?"

"Yep. Makes it look like you're setting yourself up as a falsely injured party. The newspaper wants to interview you about it and about a hundred other things."

"I bet they do."

"They're slick, I have to give them that. Now then . . ." He consulted his notes, turning a page on the legal pad. "The letters sent to the Arizona Medical Board are deemed privileged and cannot be released except with a subpoena. We won't be able to investigate them, not yet anyway. They took a dim view to my suggesting they were forgeries."

"Figures."

"And I checked with your attorney about your house. The insurance company declared it a total loss, including your wife's car in the garage."

"I expected that."

"The investigators found the valve that piped the gas into your house."

"Valve . . .?"

"A piggy-back jobbie screwed onto your hot water heater gas line."

"And?"

"Arson."

"Right," Steve said, "we knew it was arson. So?"

Valenti glanced at Steve and then back down at his paper. "Insurance doesn't pay for arson. At least when it's suspicious."

Steve stared at Valenti, not comprehending. "Even when it's a criminal act?"

Valenti shook his head. "According to them, *you* might have set it."

Steve couldn't believe what he was hearing. "Bullshit! Someone tried to kill me and my family—I can't believe they would be so stupid."

He stopped. Of course they would think that—too many funny things had happened to him, a pattern of unusual events, with no one else to identify as the cause. *Damn, damn, damn.* He would lose the total value of his house. How could they recover financially from that?

"Cheer up, it's a preliminary finding. They might change their mind or something."

It rang hollow. Steve could see Valenti didn't believe it. The insurance company would make a case for Steve setting his own house on fire. Except for Rich next door, nobody had seen any arsonist and Rich could be a false witness. As far as the insurance company was concerned, it was a set-up by a desperate man who needed sympathy and money. They wouldn't pay. Not unless they had a confession or a conviction of someone else. They might even bring charges against him.

Steve took a deep breath. It was a chess game and he had missed the rule changes and given them the first three moves. He stood at the window and looked out at two fully clothed women lounging by the pool in the cool afternoon December sunshine, not a care in the world.

"They hold all the cards don't they?" His stomach churned with frustration and anger. He wanted to hit something, anything. The killers were probably sitting back laughing at him right now.

Kirk Mallis slammed his fist on the table. "Goddamn you, James!"

Mallis and Joe sat in the Soma café, not far from where Dr. James had lived. His credit card charges indicated it was a frequent haunt and they had parked themselves here in the hope he would come in. Mallis had just checked VeriFone's web page on his notebook computer and had done so every three hours, at least, to see if James had any new credit card activity—only to come up blank. He did find that James's bank and investment accounts had been drained, giving him almost two hundred thousand in cash. He could hole up for a long time with that kind of money.

"Still nothing, huh?" Joe said, looking up from his *Men's Journal* magazine.

"Not a goddamn thing."

He tried to think of something he had overlooked, a place to locate James or someone's phone to monitor, but James hadn't made any amateur mistakes—even calling his wife at her parent's home. Mallis doubted James would attend the medical board hearing in the morning, although he still planned to watch the building. He wasn't even sure if James was still in town. Mallis, to his utter frustration, had reached a dead end. Unless they got a break, they would have to wait the three more days for the meeting with Secretary Castell.

"Should we pay his attorney a visit?" Joe asked. "She might know where he is."

"I'd like to, but no." Mallis shook his head. "James's vanishing has fucked up everything. With the police watching Sheridan's house and lab, they're probably monitoring his attorney, too."

"So, we'll clean-up later?"

Mallis's eyes narrowed. "Maybe not . . . I've got an idea. It depends on if they give tours."

CHAPTER 85

Valenti watched Steve pace restlessly around the room digesting all his bad news. He changed the subject. "If Eden is so bad for people, how did it get past the FDA and onto the market?"

Steve took some time before answering, his anger and frustration balled up like a lump of dry bread caught in his throat that wouldn't swallow. He allowed himself the self-pity only a short while before he shifted his mind back into problem solving mode. Doctors were good at that. He was still learning the rules, and had just learned another one, but he now had a little time to plan their next move.

"They had to know. The pre-clinical package is quite extensive with multiple laboratory, cell-based and lab animal testing. Unless Eden's disease is species specific."

Valenti didn't say anything for a full minute. Then he announced, "I know you used English and I actually understood your words, so speaking slowly won't help. But to save my sinning soul, I didn't understand a damn thing you said. Can you please explain all that in plain English?"

"Okay, umm. It begins when a new compound is made in the lab. Testing begins in test tubes, followed, if it looks promising, by testing in cell culture for specific toxicities, which is then followed by lab animal testing. They test for everything you can think of, including cancer, reproduction problems, organ toxicity, heart conduction, and stuff like that. They get an idea how it's absorbed and metabolized and what doses have some effect and what doses are lethal."

"Basically, you're telling me I never want to come back as a lab rat."

"Probably not."

"What then? Say it passes all the guinea pig stuff. People?"

"Right. You file with the FDA and then you start phase one. That's the first time in man. You are looking at safety and tolerability of the drug. You give a tiny dose to a group of normal people, usually poor college students who get paid for it, and see how they react. If they do okay and their EKGs and blood tests are all normal, you increase the dose and see what happens."

"Do you keep going up and up?"

"Until they reach maximum tolerated dose." Steve grinned. "That's when they puke their guts out."

"Sounds fun. Where do I sign up?"

"Drop by our office."

Valenti made a face. "Maybe not."

"Phase two and three are where they pretty much prove the drug works the way it is supposed to and that it's safe."

"Why didn't anyone get this Eden's rot during the trials?"

"Long latency."

"What's that?"

"The disease might take a year or more to show up after first exposure. Remember the New Guinea natives who got a prion disease by eating humans?"

"I'm trying to forget it."

"A Dr. Carlton Gajdusek figured it all out after spending years living among the affected tribes there. He taught them to stop their cannibalism. Even so, the last woman didn't show the disease until over forty years after her last human meal."

Valenti whistled. "If I understand you, people who take Eden may not show any signs for a long time, years even."

"If it follows previously known prion latency patterns, yes. So far as I've seen, the range is about eighteen months for Captain Palmer and four years for Shirley. I did not find out how long the third woman took it before she got sick, but my guess it took at least a year."

"And Trident could have finished its testing, gotten FDA approval and never seen a case."

"It's possible." Steve remembered Sheridan's cell culture results. Some cell lines converted, but most did not. Probably there were differential susceptibilities in people and different time lines for each person.

"Don't they follow their research patients long enough to see those things?" Valenti asked.

"It sounds really short," Steve said, "but it's only thirty days after their last visit unless someone becomes pregnant during a study."

"Thirty days? That's all?"

Steve shrugged. "That's what the regulations say. They have to do some long term studies, but as I recall in Trident's case, it only lasted a year, no longer."

"Well then, maybe Trident doesn't know? You know, about the disease, because no one has made a connection there."

Steve had already considered this. No, too many things pointed at Trident. Like the timing of the events following his reporting of Eden to Trident's Safety Officer, what was his name? Then there was the likelihood that Eden had been tested in nerve cell cultures and other lab animals. "I don't think so," Steve said. "Too many coincidences."

"I think you're right. In my field, there are no such things as coincidences." Valenti grinned. "But then, I believe in all sorts of conspiracies. You know, X-files and stuff."

"This latency thing is important," Steve said. "If three hundred million people are taking Eden and it has a latency of, say, one to five years, we could be looking at the beginning of something huge."

"How do you figure?" Valenti asked.

"Take a disease, say avian flu or an outbreak of plague, which still occasionally crops up."

"Here you go again, spoiling my appetite."

Steve grinned, enjoying the teaching and Valenti's discomfort. "Plague starts within days after exposure. As soon as people know it's out there, they go on a rat eradication campaign and quarantine all cases. The exposure stops and the outbreak runs its course fairly rapidly. There is a bell shaped curve from the first case to the peak incidence and back down to the last case, all in a matter of weeks."

"Okay, I now know not to be a rat and not to associate with rats."

"You clearly have a stunning intellect. With a long latency, lots more people get the disease before they show symptoms. Only then can you look for the cause and stop the exposure, but for lots of people, that's too late. In this case, the bell curve is much wider and more protracted."

Valenti whistled. "So we have three hundred million blissfully ignorant people taking Eden every day."

"And that scares the crap out of me. We may just be on the early part of the bell curve. It could get much worse."

"All three hundred million?"

"Probably not, but—"

"Why wouldn't everybody get it?"

Steve thought about the question before answering. "All sorts of things. Even with the plague, not everybody who was exposed died. Natural resistance, genetic factors, duration of exposure, size of each dose and so on all play parts in triggering the disease. Only a few of Sheridan's cell lines converted, so there is something that make some people more susceptible or resistant than others."

"How do you find out?"

"More research. Like Sheridan was going to do."

"But not if Trident keeps whacking them." Valenti shifted the subject. "Tell me about Trident and Eden."

"Trident had to test Eden in animals before they got to humans, including cell cultures."

"Nerve cell cultures?"

"I think so, yes."

So they would have seen the prions like Sheridan did."

"Right."

"Can you check on that?"

"Sure. I think so."

"And what about animals?"

"Here, I'm less certain. One prion disease called Scrapie infects only sheep. You can't catch it even if you eat the meat. That's why when cattle came down with Mad Cow Disease, people didn't believe you could get it by eating it. But this time they were wrong. It jumped species from cow to human."

"Is it important if Eden can't cause the disease in animals?"

"Not really. We have evidence that it causes conversion in human brain cells and in humans. It would be nice to see it in animals, but it would not change the evidence we already have."

"Trident will claim no knowledge of this whole thing," Valenti mused. "They'll tell the world that they had no way of knowing. Plausible deniability."

Steve thought back to his conversation with Trident's safety officer. Valenti was right. It would be hard to pin prior knowledge on Trident. "If they destroyed their offending records, then it would be nearly impossible."

"We need to find a live witness, someone who can name names and make it stick." Valenti said. "Something else bothers me, though. If they have over a hundred patients with this Eden's thing, and you stumbled onto it, others have also figured it out or will. What's Trident's end game?"

"What do you mean?"

"Trident can't go around killing every doctor who thinks Eden is a problem. There's got to be more to it than that. Or something we don't know."

"What do you think?" Steve asked.

"I was going to ask you. Is there something about who gets this or do only selected people get it? How can Trident figure there is any long-term future if their drug kills off its customers? Do they have a replacement drug in the works?"

That last comment made Steve sit up. "That may be exactly it. My last studies for Trident tested a new version, a shorter chain of amino acids that they said would have the same effect, but better absorption." Unconsciously rubbing his chin, he tried to remember the details of the new formulation. "I wonder," he said after a minute, "if they think this new version won't cause the same damage." If only Sheridan wasn't out of commission, Steve thought, he could test some of this new medication in nerve cell cultures. He sat back stunned by the implications of a possible cover-up.

"Trident knows that its multi-billion dollar drug is a problem." Steve said. "I bet they're keeping it under wraps by hook or by crook until the new formulation gets approved. Then they do a switch for the new, improved version and, voila, problem solved. Ordinarily a company would wait for their previous drug's patent to wear off before finalizing its replacement."

"Makes sense to me," Valenti said. "In the meantime, they knock you guys off until their replacement drug is up and running." He grinned. "You're pretty good at conspiracy theories, Doc. What happens if their new formulation doesn't work?"

"They lose. Somebody will figure Eden out and make it stick."

CHAPTER 86

Dixon woke up in a panic, drenched in sweat, his body racked with shivers. "Elise?" He reached over to the other side of the king size bed and touched her shoulder. "Elise," he said louder.

Elise rolled over and peered at her husband in the dim light. "What is it, Honey? What's wrong?" Her hand sought out his.

"Another nightmare," he said, almost embarrassed now. But his heart was still pumping hard in his chest like he had been on one of his runs. It was that dream again.

Elise slid over in the bed towards her husband. "Want to talk about it?"

Dixon felt her warm arms encircle him. It was exactly what he needed; then as his mind recalled the dream, he stiffened up again.

"What is it?" Her soft soothing Virginia accent encouraged him. "Tell me, Honey."

"A trip to hell," he started to say and then stopped as it came flooding back again. Instead of getting more fuzzy and indistinct like most dreams did after waking, it stayed vivid.

Elise rubbed his back as if trying to pull the tension out of him. "Go on. It'll help if you tell me."

"It was nothing—literally nothing. A small, empty room, nothing else." He tried to find the words to describe the feeling. "No people, forever, understand? Not you, nobody, and I knew it would be like that . . . forever." His arm twitched again and it all flooded back. "I must pray," he said, overwhelmed by the image and desperate for reassurance. "Only God can save me."

"It's okay," Elise said calmly. "It's just a dream. You're not going to hell, Honey, you're too good a man. I know that for a fact. You're just too good. You listen to me, Mr. Robert C. Dixon. God's going to bring you home when He's ready. Just not yet. I want more time with you first."

Dixon had immediately known the source of his horror since his first flashback—but only now confronted it. He was back in that laundry room. As an asthmatic child, his parents had sent him to Utah for a summer to live with his Aunt Bonnie in the dry desert air. Without any children of her own and, while well meaning, she had never seemed to know the right thing to say or do with eight year old Robert. Instead of taking him with her to the store or shopping, she would lock him in the laundry room, sometimes for hours at a time. Once, she had left Robert inside throughout a long, terrifying night, later professing forgetfulness.

That room was small with just enough space to stand in front of the washer and dryer, or in his case, to curl up on the warped, speckled-green linoleum floor. He could still smell the laundry detergent and the Clorox, the Pine-O-Pine and the Borateem soap, sitting on the bare wooden shelf over the appliances. The gas hot water heater in the corner and the shelves of Del Monte canned beans and peas and the jars of pickles and peanut butter, were all burned into his memory from hours staring at them.

Without a window, the bare light bulb determined whether he could see or not. When immersed in darkness he would panic, his mind filled with frightening visions of monsters and wild animals, or scorpions and spiders creeping in to get him.

Robert became fearful of being alone for any length of time even back at home. He had consciously arranged his life to always be with people, running for school president, joining social clubs and fraternities, having roommates all through college—and eventually running for public office. And now, the images he saw in his dreams were of that feared room in Utah, images he had blocked out of his conscious mind for decades, had for some reason reared up again.

Looking back, he recalled that his only avenue of salvation after his aunt shoved him, screaming and crying, into the laundry room was praying to God for his rescue. He would pray fervently for hours and each time his aunt let him out, he came to feel personally delivered by the hand of God. To Robert, that laundry room was hell with all the isolation, loneliness, claustrophobia, and separation from human companionship that hell represented.

But why was all this coming back now and after he had successfully buried the memory for so many years? Dixon took a deep breath feeling the conviction of his wife's words settling him down. He had not told her that the vision recurred more and more frequently now, even when he was awake, and that he saw glimpses of it nearly every time he twitched. His fear drove him to pray—as his only hope of deliverance. But Elise was right; it was only a dream. He became aware of Elise gently stroking his chest as she pressed her cheek against his shoulder. He brought her hand to his mouth and kissed it.

CHAPTER 87

With the morning breakfast crew assembled, President Dixon walked in, forcing a smile. "Good morning," he said, shaking hands all around. He settled comfortably in his chair. "I read the PDB," he began. "Lots of activity. What's China up to, Augie?"

"Two options," said the National Security Advisor. "One is they are working on some internal issue, possibly more suppression of religious groups or something similar. Option two is they are getting ready for an external military objective."

"So which is it?" Dixon asked.

Crusoe chewed on his cold pipe a minute before replying. "We don't know."

"George?"

"I have already ordered new deployments for our ground assets, but it'll take time. People there are not so mobile, particularly not in the countryside where most of this is happening."

"Make it fast, okay George?" It was an order delivered as only Dixon could.

Sullivan spoke. "Mr. President, I am hearing concerns from military, political, and commercial interests that your support for Taiwan will have grave consequences."

"And?"

"I think there are things you can do to mitigate our commitment."

"I don't want to mitigate my commitment," Dixon said. "I want us to move ahead with all the arrangements as soon as possible. Our friends are counting on us and I made a promise."

Linda knew Dixon would use that reasoning. He had always been a man of his word. His commitment was not always easy to secure, but once given, he was steadfast. Or pigheaded.

Dixon's right arm twitched. "Besides, I prayed about it all last night and it's the right thing to do."

"Politically, it's going to be a disaster," Sullivan added.

"Don't you think I've thought of that?" Dixon seemed to sink into his chair somewhat, but his eyes burned their conviction. This wasn't going well at all, thought Linda.

"I have some very worried Chiefs of Staff," Painter said. "And a very pissed off admiral who is heading to Taiwan. We need to keep our battle groups away from China's land-based defenses, behind Taiwan."

Dixon seemed to consider a moment. "I think it would be important to stand with our Taiwanese allies between China and their homeland like Augie advises."

Painter let out a long breath from between his teeth. "Sir, all symbolism aside, we have a duty to protect our men and women on those ships. While I don't think China can take Taiwan, to deliberately put our ships in harm's way . . ."

Linda thought she saw a moment of confusion cross the President's features.

"I've made up my mind," Dixon said finally. He stood up. "I leave the rest of the implementation in your capable hands. Good day." With that, he rose and walked out.

Linda Resnick walked into Bell's office and closed the door. Inside Jeff Bell and John Sullivan waited for her.

"That didn't go well," Sullivan said.

"I'll say so," she replied, taking a seat. "And it's heating up. I just got a call from Forest Garrison at the UN. The Chinese are lambasting our recognition of Taiwan and at the seventh fleet heading for the Straits."

"We figured that, of course," Sullivan said.

"Right. Taiwan's Ambassador Gao was apparently cordial, but clearly enjoyed himself as he told the Chinese there was absolutely no room for negotiating anything short of a complete abdication of Taiwan as a province of China."

"I bet Ambassador Gong was pretty unhappy."

"It was, as I said, cordial, but the feelings were apparent. China made it equally clear they had no intention of relinquishing any claim of the Island."

"I suspect not, but what are their options?"

"Actually quite a few. If they shut off trade with Taiwan, then the Taiwanese economy all but collapses. China gets stung, but it'll tank Taiwan."

"I suppose we get stuck with the bailout," Bell said.

Resnick stood up and walked to Bell's bar refrigerator and pulled out a Diet Coke. "Would we support Taiwan indefinitely? "

"Can you get me one, too?" Sullivan asked. "In answer to your question, I don't know, but I'm alarmed at the potential for a quagmire. I don't want Taiwan to become the American Cuba."

"Exactly my thoughts." She handed the cold can to the Vice President. "I don't like how this is playing out with American interests so intimately tied to the issue."

"What about the President?" Bell asked. "He's doing more of those tic things. Worse, he doesn't seem to remember details like he used to."

"I see it, too," Resnick said.

"I've been thinking about that," Sullivan said leaning forward. "It depends on Dr. Green's willingness to cooperate."

CHAPTER 88

"Over here are the walk-in freezers where we store our brain specimens." The young man, who had introduced himself as Dr. Pfeiffer, stopped in front of two large doors with heavy handles. "Over the years, we have accumulated over two thousand brains from people with various neurological diseases all banked here for study."

Joe Branson stood to the back of the twenty or so people in the weekly tour of Sheridan Laboratories. He actually found it interesting, but looked forward to seeing the actual laboratory space. So far, they had seen only offices and electron microscopes.

"These work like an airlock," The man wearing a long lab coat continued. "These outer doors open into a zero degree freezer. There, the outer doors are closed and any water from the air is frozen and removed by filtration in a procedure that takes about thirty seconds. Then the second door is opened and then you can walk through into the minus seventy degree space."

Joe looked around restlessly. After a few questions from the mostly senior citizen audience they moved on. Following Pfeiffer, they walked through two swinging doors into a laboratory that matched what he had expected to see.

The room was well lit from a long bank of windows along one wall. It felt bright and airy, not like the dark and smelly basement labs of his freshman chemistry class at Nebraska. Fortunately, the lab was entirely empty, as Joe had hoped it would be on a Friday afternoon.

The workspace consisted of about fifteen rows of long black stone countertops above white laminate drawers and cabinets. Each counter had, at intervals, three pointed valves clearly marked *air*, *vacuum*, and *gas*. Above each were glass-fronted cabinets containing various bottled chemicals. Most counters had tabletop lab equipment, including centrifuges and racks of automated pipettes and on several counter-tops were stands of crowded metal glassware racks. Some things never change, thought Joe. It was exactly what he was looking for.

As Dr. Pfeiffer worked through the lab pointing out the electronic scales, the refrigerated centrifuge and the warm boxes full of cell cultures, Joe hung back. Eventually they walked out the other side of the lab and out of view. Joe knelt in front of a counter and opened the cabinet doors. In front of him were stacks of filter paper and plastic funnels. Behind those were the three metal tubes leading up to the valves on the countertop.

Pulling a self-tapping valve out of his coat pocket, he kissed it, and quickly screwed it to the pipe marked *gas*. To the valve's spigot, he attached a timed valve pre-set to open at midnight. Onto that he attached a sparking device timed to go off at one thirty-seven AM. He opened the self-tapping valve with the gas flow halted by the timed valve. Satisfied, he closed the doors and stood up.

Turning, he saw Dr. Pfeiffer entering the room. "Please," he said, "you must stay with the group."

Joe held up his cell phone and grinned. "Sorry, my wife wanted me to pick some things up at the store on the way home."

Dr. Pfeiffer smiled. "Come on, we're almost done. At least you didn't get lost."

"Thanks for coming to look for me. I sure might have."

Outside, Joe's last act was to drop a leather work glove from a plastic bag onto the pavement adjacent to his car before he started it up and drove away.

It was one taken from Steve's garage.

CHAPTER 89

"Okay, Mr. Morloch, we've just completed the revisions."

"Fine, let's see, Ken."

Morloch sat in a folding chair in the cavernous ballroom of Philadelphia's Four Seasons Hotel and watched as the first of his slides jumped up onto the huge dual projection screens. The lowered lights made the images on the screens bright and dramatic. From habit, Morloch glanced at his script as the slides flashed by in sequence, but he already knew it cold.

Morloch was preparing his presentation to Trident's principal stockholders and analysts for his annual stockholders' meeting, a media and analyst feeding frenzy now that Trident was the brightest star in the pharmaceutical heavens. And because of his company's legendary secrecy, most everything was fresh and new.

Karen, his administrative assistant, walked up and whispered in his ear.

"Not now," he said.

She whispered in his ear again.

"Okay, okay." He stood up and began walking to the back of the ballroom. "Ken, hold it for a minute, will you? I've got to take a phone call."

"Right, Mr. Morloch."

Outside in the lobby, Karen, a tall blonde with green eyes handed him a cell phone.

Morloch walked outside to the courtyard before he spoke. "Well?"

"He's still scarce," Kirk Mallis's voice informed him.

"I see," Morloch responded, watching the low waterfall cascade into a pool.

"I'm going to fly in and head him off at the pass."

"I expected this," Morloch said. "And I think we should allow this meeting to take place as scheduled."

"Why?"

"I think I shall have a little social chit-chat with the Secretary first. Then, after the meeting, he's all yours."

Mallis chuckled as he realized what Morloch had in mind. "We'll be ready."

Morloch walked back into the ballroom lobby where Karen patiently waited. He handed her the phone on his way into the ballroom. "Confirm Castell's attendance at the meeting tomorrow."

CHAPTER 90

Steve pulled on a rowing machine, chasing a video opponent that, after he had raised the level to maximum, always seemed a just a bit ahead. Valenti had been right. The exertion had him sweating buckets and more grounded than he had felt in days. He had been shut away like a plant in the dark in frustrating inaction and investigative dead-ends for far too long. He looked forward to the meeting with Castell in two more days, and the prospect of getting out and moving again.

Next to him, Valenti jogged on a treadmill, six-pound weights in both hands. He had converted his garage into a plush, carpeted and sky-lit home exercise room with a multi-station weight machine, in addition to the treadmill and rower. Valenti had dragged a restive but eager Steve over to the house for a little R&R.

Valenti was in better shape than Steve had guessed. Despite a potbelly, Valenti was well muscled and had decent endurance. He was exercising like a madman—even on his second fifteen minute run at six and a half miles per hour. Steve would not have been able to easily outpace him— at least not this week. He longed for his mountain bike and a steep and rocky trail in front of him, his definition of a relaxing day.

"Ever fight a man?" Valenti huffed, stepping off his treadmill and wiping his reddened wet face on a towel.

"Yeah, in high school," Steve said between pulls of the rower. "It was over in one punch." He pulled again. "I got a split lip, he got a bloody hand." Another pull. "Fairly even, I'd say."

"Very Rambo," Valenti said, amused.

"Thanks."

"Pistols? Firearms?"

"I had one, but it disappeared from my closet when I needed it that night."

"Disappeared?"

"Yeah, it wasn't where I kept it." He puffed. "It was supposed to be in the closet, but wasn't there."

"I wonder if our friends have it."

"I sure as shit didn't have anything to point at them." Steve felt his anger growing again and pulled extra hard on the next several rowing cycles. "Those fuckers."

"Yep, but," Valenti hung the towel around his neck. "It's our turn, now."

"How?"

"I've yet to see a company do systematic illegal activity without leaving a trail. Remember Enron? Watergate? Madoff? It always reaches a point when just too many people know about it to keep it under wraps."

Steve pondered for three pulls. "Okay, Morloch had to make himself the center of all the information in order to control it."

"Right. What else?"

"Well, at the time, Trident was a much smaller company and it's a lot easier keeping a secret in a small one than a large one."

"Right. So, they had to limit the information to just a few people in order to pull this off. Can that be done in a biotech company?"

"Sure, if it's small enough."

"Then, as I see it, Morloch controls the information and applies the external pressure."

"What do you mean?" Steve asked in between deep breaths as he tried to catch the video competitor who had steadily increased his lead.

"To keep a deep secret requires threats of consequences or promise of great reward. The only other thing is intense personal loyalty to a person or cause. I doubt Eden is such a cause or Morloch such a person, so I return to the first two. Reward and or threat."

Steve crossed the video finish line a sad second to his electronic opponent and let go of the handle. "The reward part is easy. Stock options."

"Right, but I'm a cynical bastard. When you have human lives at stake, the stick probably needs to be employed."

"Okay, so we figure out who had access to the critical information." Steve ran his towel through his wet hair.

"It's may be a little more complicated than that," Valenti said. "You can have any number of people in on part of the secret as long as they don't have the whole story. A technician may have access to an abnormal finding, but isn't in on the secret because he doesn't have the larger context."

"So we target the higher-ups."

"Both. If we can identify who may have had partial information, we can draw the conclusions ourselves." Valenti screwed the top off a water bottle and took a long draught.

Steve reflected on that. "Morloch would have a close group of executives and it shouldn't be too hard to figure out who. One might talk. We could also find out who worked in the lab when they were doing the early work on Eden."

Valenti grinned. "You're pretty smart for a Doc. That's our initial strategy. Begin with public sources to identify likely candidates—you'll need to help with that—and then we make personal visits and ask lots of questions."

"Doesn't sound too hard."

"Trident's big game, Doc." Valenti pointed the water bottle at Steve. "Wound it and you get trampled. It's got to be a kill shot."

In the guest bathroom, Steve pulled three items from a bag that Valenti had left for him. He laid them out on the counter and examined a bottle of black hair color, a disposable razor and a new electric hair clipper.

He started with the hair clipper. He placed the small trash basket on the counter and, leaning over it, started cutting his wavy brown hair with the clippers, watching without emotion as clumps fell into the basket. He had chosen the largest snap-on attachment, which would leave him with about half an inch of hair all around. He cleaned up the hair clippings that sprinkled the counter and then read the instructions for the hair dye. He thoroughly rubbed in the hair color and let it sit the prescribed time.

He then took a long hot shower, where he rinsed off his hair. Emerging, he dried off, and, with the towel wrapped around his waist, he used the razor to shave, leaving a growing outline of a Van Dyke. Once done, he appraised the minor transformation in the mirror. His new short black hair and the emerging beard did not look like him; not a lot different but still different. There was no liking or disliking it; it was his disguise, another edge over the adversary.

Finally, he dressed and emerged from the bathroom to wonderful cooking smells. Finding his way to the kitchen, he discovered several pots steaming over the stove tended by a petite dark-haired woman. She looked up when he walked in.

"Hi, I'm Steve."

A wide smile crossed her face revealing two rows of perfect teeth. "Hi, Steve. I'm Maria, Tony's wife. Come on in." Maria's dark hair cascaded to her shoulders in abundance and she wore a colorful apron over her jeans and white blouse. She gestured with her hand to the maple kitchen table, "Have a seat."

A slender girl of about eleven sat at the table in front of a textbook watching him. She was dressed in a sweatshirt and a stone-washed denim miniskirt. "That's our daughter, Elissa. Elissa, Dr. James."

Steve sat down in one of the cushioned wooden chairs that surrounded the kitchen table. "Hi, Elissa."

"Hi, Dr. James."

"What are you reading?"

Elissa made a face. "Social Studies."

"One of my favorite courses," Steve lied. "What are you learning?"

"How money changes hands and how it's printed and stuff like that."

Just then, another girl, about nine or ten, ran through the kitchen without stopping, ear buds sticking out of her head and singing something Steve did not recognize.

"Natalie," Elissa said with sibling distain. "The next child star."

Maria put a tall glass of ice water in front of Steve. "Here you go. Dinner's on in about ten."

"It smells good. What is it?"

Valenti walked in. "Pasta for energy and Lentil soup for your soul. Maria's the best cook in the world." He leaned over and gave his wife a kiss. "But she never cooks enough pasta."

"You don't look like you're starving to me." Maria could easily hold her own with her husband.

"I see you met my number one daughter. She's bound for college and wants to bankrupt dad by going to Notre Dame." He grinned. "We're holding out for scholarships."

"USC, Dad," Elissa objected. "And why not scholarships? My grades are good enough."

"That's what I said, isn't it?"

Steve chuckled. "My man, you're totally surrounded and out-maneuvered."

"Don't I know it." Valenti's happy look said that life just couldn't get any better.

CHAPTER 91

"Jeff, what in the hell's going on over there?" Dick Samuels barked through the phone at the President's Chief of Staff. "I thought we were on track for the budget reconciliation bill."

"We are," Bell said calmly while trying to figure what had gotten the House Speaker's dander up this time. The representative from Vermont, known in the White House as the Varmint Man, called Bell's staffers regularly to berate them about something or other.

"I'm not so fucking sure. I'm hearing from Castell that the President is strongly supporting the Housing bill. I thought we had put that to rest."

"We did. Where did you hear this?" Bell said. His kept his tone level, but underneath he was trying to figure out if Castell had gone off on his own.

"If it's been put to rest, you need to reign in your hotshot Secretary. He's arranging lunches with all the committee moderates and trading votes to get his bill through." Samuels lowered his voice. "Look, you know we can't support another drag on the budget. We'll work with the President on that, but not if he blindsides us by sending out Castell to lobby for budget busting bills."

"Right, Dick. I'll check on it."

"Like yesterday, Jeff. We've got the damn budget in committee."

"I know. Like I said, I'll check and I'll get back to you."

"Do that," Samuels growled.

Bell hung up. He had a sinking feeling he knew what the answer would be.

CHAPTER 92

It was dark in Sheridan's labs except for a glow of light from Cindy Eckhardt's lab bench. She debated with herself whether or not she should stay and set up the experiment for the next day and get a jump on the work for tomorrow. A yawn decided the issue. She threw away the last of her cold pizza and turned out the lights. Locking the doors at eleven-forty six, she walked past the guard at the front entrance.

"Night, Juan," she said.

"Hi, Cindy. Let me walk you to your car." Juan Vargas got up from behind his desk and walked with her out to her car in the well-lit parking area. She got in, waved bye, and drove off. Juan looked over at the police squad car that had been parked in the lot since five o'clock. It was a regular feature every night since Professor Sheridan had gone on vacation. He waved although he couldn't see anyone as he went back inside.

Upstairs in the main laboratory, precisely at midnight, the timed valve opened and a strong stream of gas poured out from beneath the counter, uninterrupted, for an hour and a half. Long enough for the gas, which was heavier than air, to fill the laboratory space and settle its way to the first floor, pooling in the stairwells and the elevator shaft.

The heat pump heater sucked in the gas and distributed it to all parts of the building, including the offices and lab spaces. Had the lab used a gas furnace, the flame would have ignited the gas much earlier. This would have caused a large fire and extensive damage. With the flameless heat pump, however, the building gradually filled with an enormous quantity of gas making it a huge two-story time bomb.

On the first floor, Vargas put down his Clive Cussler novel and looked at his watch. It was one thirty-four and past time for his rounds. As he stood up, he smelled an unusual odor. *Gas!* Where was it coming from? He walked around the lobby trying to locate the odor's origin. After a couple of minutes, he decided it came from the air conditioning vents. He opened the stairwell door and a powerful gas odor washed over him. *Shit, the whole building was full—*

Vargas never finished his thought as the automatic sparker ignited the gas precisely at one thirty seven. The laboratory walls and glass erupted like paper around a firecracker from the explosion that rocked the neighborhood and engulfed the entire building in flames.

CHAPTER 93

"This way, Dr. Green," Joan said, opening the door to the Oval Office. Although Green had been to a number of dinners at the White House, he had never actually been in the Oval Office. It looked just like the pictures, although the colors were richer than he had expected.

Robert Dixon looked up from his desk, his head outlined by the rose garden seen through the windows, brightly lit by the early morning sun. Seeing him, Dixon jumped up and rushed over. "Tom, how are you? I didn't see your name on my schedule. How did you slip in, you old trickster?"

"Great to see you, Robert. How are things?" Tom appraised his old friend, looking him over carefully. Tom did not actually think of him as the President, he had known him too long as Robert.

"Shitty. It's this China thing, you know. I can't seem to let it go. All those innocent people, you know."

"Terrible," Tom agreed.

Dixon turned back to his desk and looked at his schedule. "I've got about 20 minutes. You timed your visit perfectly. What do you want to drink?"

"Just water, thank you," Tom said feeling a little guilty. Jeff Bell had carefully planned his perfectly timed visit in advance—a visit initiated by a call from Vice President John Sullivan. Dr. Green remembered yesterday's call clearly, as much for its disturbing portent as for the office of the caller.

The President pressed a button. "Joan, can you bring in water for the good doctor and a cranberry juice for me?" He grinned with delight. "So what brings you here? You've never lobbied me before for anything. It must be important to drag you away from your precious viruses."

"Uhh," Tom was never good at lying, particularly to a friend who trusted him over nearly anybody else in Washington. "Valerie and I wanted to invite you and Elise to dinner Saturday night."

The President looked genuinely puzzled for a moment, then he laughed. "Tom, you had me there. You know I have no control over my life. Either Jeff or Joan completely manage my schedule, at least the part Elise lets them have. I haven't made plans for a night's engagement myself in almost eight years."

Joan walked in with the drinks on a silver tray and put them down on the desk. Dixon handed Dr. Green his water and took his own juice.

Tom took a drink. "I did check with Joan and she said you were free."

"And Elise? She would love to see Grace again, but she probably has plans this late in the week."

"Joan checked with her, too. You are free, my man. I hope you accept."

"I don't know. Uh—" Dixon looked puzzled again and sat down.

Then Tom saw it. The right side of Dixon's face twitched several times. *What was it?*

Dixon's eyes looked confused and then brightened. "Sure, I just seemed to get lost there for a minute. Gee, that was a tough decision. Not that I had any difficulty visiting with you, Tom, just—" His arm twitched this time. No rhythm, just an irregular shoulder jerk.

"What was that, Robert?"

"What? Oh, that. Just something that's come on over the past few days."

"Does it bother you?"

"No."

"Can you tell when it is about to happen?"

"No."

"How many times a day do you have them?"

"Tom, this is a social visit, remember. Not an office visit."

"I'm sorry. You're right." Tom tried to sound reassuring. "Why don't you come over to my office and let me take a look at you." He held his breath.

"Nah. I just saw you. Remember? You gave me a clean bill of health."

"But," Tom tried to keep the urgency out of his voice. "Perhaps you should drop over and let me poke at you a few minutes. I'll have Jeff arrange it."

"Tom, in case you haven't realized it, I'm the President of the United States. I can't just drop over anywhere, especially in this town. Can't you see the headlines now? President makes unexpected trip over to his doctor's office. Before I get back, the rumors would be all over about the treatment for cancer you discovered on my last visit."

"Well, since I'm here, can I ask you a few more questions?"

The President narrowed his eyes. "Why exactly did you come in here? Not to ask me to dinner. No one drops in on the President. What is it?"

Tom wanted to disappear. This was not going the way he had discussed with Bell and Sullivan. "I did just come by. I was in the area after lunch and thought a personal invitation would be nice." It sounded completely inadequate and Green knew Dixon wouldn't fall for it.

"Thanks," Dixon said sarcastically. "Always the considerate friend. But something's fishy about your just popping in and then asking me all sorts of questions, pushing doctor visits and—"

"Don't get so bent out of shape, Robert. It's me, Tom, your old chemistry buddy."

Dixon eyed him suspiciously. "You wouldn't lie to me would you? No one put you up to this? Everyone wants something in this town. You learn to smell it, like a sixth sense. Come clean, my friend."

Tom cringed inside, but the words of Sullivan came back to him. 'He cannot know I put you to this task. If he does, it will completely undermine all our efforts to get him help. I must tell you in the strongest terms how serious it is not to let him know.'

Tom had spent the night trying to think how Sullivan might be playing him against Dixon. But Sullivan refused to tell him even what he suspected, insisting Tom make up his own mind.

In the end, Jeff Bell tipped the scales in favor of the ploy. Jeff had known Robert for at least twelve years and Robert trusted him as a brother. Jeff, too, said it was important for Tom to make his assessment, saying only that Robert had changed.

Well, he had changed. His friend was more paranoid, more confused, less decisive and with those twitches, there might be something medically wrong. But what? He needed more information and the key to that information was to get Robert to cooperate.

"Robert, don't even think like that. We've been through too much together. But from what I've seen of those twitches, I definitely think we need to get some more information."

"What information? I have a foreign policy crisis with China and an election coming up. I can't fuck that up with rumors of a lingering illness. I can't."

Tom thought of a compromise. "Look, Robert, I can do most of what I need to at my home. I can do a physical and take some blood. If I come up with anything we can discuss it at my house."

"I don't know. I don't know. Tom what do you think?" A momentary look of helplessness crossed Dixon's face.

"I definitely think you should come over to dinner." Tom set down his water glass.

Dixon's face began twitching again. "Do you think praying would help?'

"I'm sure it would. But—"

"Okay, I'll pray."

"Robert," Dr. Green interrupted. The President looked up. "I'll tell Joan we're on for Saturday night. That's three days from tonight."

"Okay, sure."

Tom offered his hand to his friend. "I'll see you then, Robert."

The handshake was limp.

CHAPTER 94

"Jacob, Dick Samuels says you're pushing for your housing bill." Bell had finally reached Castell on his cell phone.

"Of course I am. The President himself says he wants it."

Bell didn't doubt Castell, but there was more to the story here. Politics being what they were, he would never find the truth, nor would it change what he needed to say.

"Jacob, I don't know what he told you, but we've got to deep six the housing bill or we lose the budget agreement."

"Too late, Jeff. I've been lining up the votes. I've got about six committee members on board and three on the fence."

Bell knew what he was about to ask, but the budget had been a hard fought compromise giving Dixon money for his key priorities in a tight budget year and the housing bill wasn't a priority. "Jacob, I'm telling you we cannot support your housing bill."

Castell's voice took on an edge. "What are you telling me? Did you trash my bill to him?"

"I didn't need to. It was DOA. And you should have known it. You were fully briefed on the legislative strategy."

"You can't do this. You cut my legs out from under this and my effectiveness is shot." Castell's voice rose. "The President doesn't want that."

"Mr. Secretary," Bell felt like he was lecturing. "You just can't push this. Not this year."

"I want to hear that from the President."

"You just did." Bell hung up frustrated. He didn't mind the hardball, but he hated wasting it on internal politics.

But a much larger issue remained. Why was Robert Dixon screwing up like this?

CHAPTER 95

The Philadelphia Four Seasons Hotel ballroom was filled to capacity with the expensively dressed representatives of the principal stockholders and analysts, the less expensively dressed reporters and the blue jean and plaid shirt clad cameramen and Internet broadcast technicians, all bumping elbows in an egalitarian porridge.

The lights dimmed, hushing the audience. Gidget Daws, head of Trident's PR department, stepped to the microphone to master the ceremonies. She would build suspense for Vicktor Morloch's sudden appearance on stage—he insisted on entering only as he was announced. Gidget swiftly worked through the preliminaries, announcing the retirement of Chief Scientist and Trident founder Dr. Samuel Blumenthal. Better news followed, including the near completion of a new manufacturing facility in Puerto Rico to keep pace with increasing demand. "And, she said, "the new facility will also make Trident's new drug, Paradise, once it gets approved by the FDA."

Generous applause marked her comments as she spoke, but everyone knew the real news would be from Morloch. The ballroom lights dimmed further until Gidget's face and dazzling smile shone in a solitary spotlight.

"And now, ladies and gentlemen—" Before she could even announce Morloch's name, the applause began. Gidget raised her voice. "I have the pleasure and privilege to introduce Vicktor Morloch, Chairman and CEO of Trident Pharmaceuticals."

From behind one of the giant projection screens, out stepped Morloch. The spotlight caught him as he emerged, smiling and nodding to the audience. The two screens each showed videos of him in action: in the Trident board room, striding through the Trident research laboratories and talking to workers in the production plant with his necktie loosened, all just like a major political candidate.

Morloch walked around the stage pointing at people in the audience and waving, fully at ease. He wore his trademark crisply pressed navy suit, with subtle pinstripes cut to accentuate his lean body and his patrician good looks. The applause was an unabashed tribute to the man who had made them a lot of money.

Once the ovation finally died down, Morloch stepped to the lectern. As he prepared to speak, Morloch smiled to himself. On paper, he was worth almost nine billion dollars. After today's announcements and the expected stock jump tomorrow, he could well be worth over ten. Not bad for a day's work.

"Eden has FDA approval for nine conditions, a feat never matched by any other prescription medication, and covering more lives than any drug in history."

"In short, if you are overweight, have diabetes, elevated cholesterol, or have had a heart attack or are at increased risk for a stroke, you need our drug." Then like a candidate on the stump, he punched the next sentence, "The rest of you, *what are you waiting for?*" At the enthusiastic applause, Morloch allowed a smile to show.

FDA rules forbade Morloch's mention of Eden's widespread off-label use; nevertheless, he was fully aware that up to a third of Eden prescriptions were used by people who did not fit into any of the FDA authorized categories—including slightly overweight people who did not reach the official guidelines for obesity and a burgeoning reputation for lifestyle enhancement. Like Prozac in its heyday, segments of the population used Eden for all sorts of reasons, including depression and athletic enhancement. Tales of Eden increasing sexual performance, recited by popular magazines and TV talk shows, added to its mythos—and propelled still more sales.

"And—" Morloch motioned with his hands for silence. "And, in discussions just concluded in secret, now approved by the boards of both companies and pending regulatory approval, Trident is purchasing Bristol Myers Squibb Pharmaceuticals."

A stunned silence followed. Morloch smiled; he had really surprised them.

Then the jaded investors and advisors leapt to their feet cheering.

Following his remarks and the question and answer session afterwards, Karen, standing in the dark shadow behind a large screen grabbed Morloch's arm as he walked off the stage. His eyes, accustomed to the spotlight, relied on her to guide him out of the dark ballroom and into the food service access corridor.

The question and answer period had gone swiftly and reinforced the magnitude of his announcements. He always planted the audience with pre-planned questions to drive home his best points and today's session was a winner.

"Have you located Castell?"

Karen nodded, "He's here. In the third row, on the right."

"I can't see anybody with those damned lights in my face. Just find him during the reception and get him to me. Watch your timing. I need to have a private conversation."

"No problem," she said, squeezing Morloch's arm.

CHAPTER 96

At the knock on his door, Tyrone Grune shouted, "Come in." The press secretary looked up as Jeff Bell walked into his office. It was neat by White House standards with a compulsively clean desk. A bank of family pictures clustered on the credenza, including one of his grandparents that had been taken at his family's ancestral home of Fussen in the German Alps.

At the sight of Bell, Grune's perpetually anxious face furrowed anew. "Now what?"

"Samuels had the honor of calling me to tell me Jacob was promising the President's backing."

"Oh hell. That screws the budget compromise," Grune shook his head. "Did the President actually green light him?"

Bell shrugged. "Don't know. When I asked him, he vaguely remembered giving Jacob approval to move on a housing bill. When I told him it would tank the budget agreement, he threw up his hands and said, 'Can't I get anything right?'"

"The President said that?"

Bell sat down in one of the heavy wooden chairs facing Grune's desk. "I had a little talk with Jacob and told him to pull this thing back in. He's pissed and rightly so. It'll screw his credibility with Congress."

"That's an understatement," Grune said, "but you can't put it on the President."

"Ty, he knew the housing bill would tank the budget compromise, yet he went straight to the President. I don't know what he was thinking."

"But you didn't come in here to muse your legislative agenda with the press secretary."

"Right. Umm . . ." Bell pursed his lips, choosing his words. "I'm bugged that the President didn't toss Jacob's modest little proposal out on its butt."

"I think I get your drift," Grune said chewing the end of his BIC pen.

"Then you understand why I want you to keep the President under wraps. No public appearances, no live TV or radio, no press conferences, nothing that we can't script."

"Damage control."

"Right. Until this stress thing blows over."

"What'll I tell the press?"

"You'll figure something out. Just run it by me before you go with it. I'll also tell the rest of the crew."

"And the President?"

Bell produced a smile. "He gets a break."

CHAPTER 97

Larry Calhoun sat hunched over his desk reading raw intelligence reports of China's puzzling military activity. His knees jiggled back and forth in concentration. He briefly thought of Ernie Whiteside's request for political asylum for CNN's Hong Kong station crew. He had not heard anything about their progress and wondered what had happened to them. Maybe, when he got a moment, he would call Ernie to ask.

Focusing back on the reports in front of him, Calhoun tried to piece together why the analysts could not detect China's net movement of materiél. Something big was going on, but what? He read the CIA speculation that it related to internal issues, dissident suppressions, or training exercises. *Bullshit.* The Chinese weren't stupid. But Calhoun knew he was too far removed from the imaging data to evaluate it. He needed to get his hands on the actual satellite imagery.

He buzzed Harold Wright. "Harry, what are you working on?"

"Well, hello, Mr. Calhoun," his technical analyst answered. "Top of the day to you, too."

Calhoun smiled. "Thanks. Look, I need your help on the China thing."

"What's up?"

"Seen the troop movement reports?"

"Nope, I'm not on the guest list."

"Okay, I'll get you a copy. In a nutshell, China's military is moving trucks and trains all over the map, confusing the analysts. I want you to get me access to the actual photos so we can go over them together. Can you do that?"

"I figure I can. Take me until tomorrow unless this is hot."

"Tomorrow's fine. Say around . . ." Calhoun looked at his desk calendar, mentally rearranging the day to accommodate Harry. "Eleven?"

"Eleven it is. See you then."

Calhoun looked back down at the report in front of him. "I'll nail down your plan, assholes."

CHAPTER 98

Following Morloch's surprise acquisition announcement, the lights came on and white-gloved ushers directed the excitedly chattering attendees through suddenly opened side doors into the adjacent reception room. As everyone gravitated towards the food and beverage stations, waiters wandered through the throng with wine, champagne, and canapés balanced on trays. A three-piece string ensemble played soft Baroque music.

Morloch appeared and soon faced a line of happy stockholders and analysts who filed past him, each shaking his hand and congratulating him on Trident's success and the pending merger. He chatted casually with the last several people in line until he felt a light touch on his shoulder. Turning, he saw Karen holding the arm of Castell. Morloch beamed as if surprised. "Jacob, how are you?" He shook Castell's hand "I was hoping you'd be here. After all, you're responsible for all this."

Castell coughed self-consciously, "Sure, Vicktor."

"Do you have a minute? I'd like to catch up." Morloch smoothly steered Castell away from the bulk of the reception and into the massive foyer outside the ballroom. Morloch stopped in front of the floor to ceiling windows looking out onto the formal garden.

"I only have a few minutes before the press gets a chance at me."

"Well, you're the man of the hour and deservedly so."

"How's June?"

"She's great. She's involved in the Junior League and all that stuff. She really loves the social side of things."

"I'm glad. She has the energy of three of us."

"That she does," Castell smiled.

"Jacob," Morloch lowered his voice. "I was surprised when our new Paradise submission didn't get expedited review."

Castell cocked his head at the statement and looked at his friend. "I'm afraid you've caught me off guard."

"Our new compound, Paradise. I think we need expedited review."

"We got you expedited review on your initial application—"

"For which I am grateful." Morloch did not have to mention the one hundred thousand shares of Trident stock sitting in a private Cayman bank account, controlled by Castell, in return for the favor.

"Why do you need it?" Castell asked cautiously. "Certainly it's not to increase sales."

"Of course not. This is not about money. It's because the new formulation reduces nose irritation and is more rapidly absorbed. It's for increased benefit for our patients."

"Oh." Castell paused, as if considering. After a moment he said, "Let me think about it."

"My previous offer applies here as well." Morloch said softly, with a bland smile on his face for the casual onlookers.

Castell met Morloch's gaze briefly and looked away, nodding slightly.

Morloch moved to his next agenda item, wondering if he had pushed the Secretary too hard. "I understand you had a near calamity on that flight in from London."

"Yeah." Castell brightened. "That was one hell of a scary ride."

"So, did the doctor, what was his name? James? Did he do everything the papers said he did? That was quite a story."

Castell nodded. "Yeah, he did. He's the reason I'm here at all."

Morloch wore a blank look. "Very interesting . . ." He let it hang.

Castell peered at Morloch. "What?"

"Oh, nothing." He feigned an offhand tone. "How's work?"

"No, no. What about him?"

"Well, Dr. James . . ." Morloch waved his hand like he was searching for words.

"You know him?" Castell sounded surprised

"No, not really . . ." Morloch shook his head. "It's just I can't square the Dr. James who saved a planeload of people with the Dr. James who used to work on my studies."

"He's the same Dr. James?"

Morloch nodded.

"And you have a hard time believing what?"

"Well, he's, um . . . irresponsible."

"Really?"

"It seems he's had some troubles. Perhaps you were unaware."

"Like what?"

"Well, if I recall correctly, his license is up for possible suspension, he's been sued for sexual abuse and, no surprise, his wife has left him."

Castell looked surprised. "Really?"

"I had a hard time believing it, too."

"He seemed so . . ."

"Ordinarily I don't care about that kind of personal crap, but in this case," Morloch's expression turned dark. "Dr. James has been spreading some very disturbing lies about Eden. He was one of our most active investigators, having worked on a number of our studies. When this surfaced, I instructed our QA people to look into his performance.

"His data quality was spotty at best even though he was a prolific enroller. In all fairness, we should have caught it long ago, but we, I am told, were beguiled by the numbers of patients he put into our studies." He gazed out the windows like he was more sad than angry.

Castell said, "I had no idea. Maybe he's, I don't know . . . manic-depressive or something. That's so strange. He seemed perfectly normal when I saw him in the emergency room." His face clouded over. "Vicktor, you should know, he's requested to meet me tomorrow evening."

Morloch feigned surprised. "You? Really? What for?"

"He called me. Something I needed to know, but vague. He wouldn't say."

Morloch turned squarely towards Castell. "Anything at all you can tell me?"

Castell shook his head. "He didn't tell me anything specific."

"I'm speculating," Morloch continued, "but based on what he's said to individuals in my company, I'm concerned he's trying to hurt Trident by saying unsupported things about Eden. If you ask me, he's going to the top and using you to do his dirty work."

Morloch ran his fingers through his wavy salt and pepper hair. "See, we pulled all our remaining studies from his clinic. We had to, based on the data quality we were seeing. It could get us in trouble with the Agency, you know. Ever since, he's been calling our staff and causing a lot of internal heartburn."

Castell said, "Then I should cancel the meeting."

Morloch looked as if he were considering it. "Jacob, we go back a long way. You know Eden very well. Cancel if you think it's best. On the other hand, it might prove useful to hear him out to see what rumors he's spreading. And," he added, "it would help us immensely."

Castell nodded. "Well, if it will help, I can make that meeting. Sure, Vicktor."

"My company's reputation and integrity are at stake. It would be of enormous help to us in countering his allegations. It is important to me that the truth triumphs here."

"Right, right. Of course."

Morloch held out his hand. "You'll call me after the meeting?"

"As soon as it's over." Castell shook Morloch's outstretched hand.

Castell sat in his limousine on the way back to the Philadelphia airport deep in thought. Since he had become Secretary, he had kept his nose clean. He knew that cabinet members came under closer scrutiny than lower federal officers and he did not want to get caught taking bribes. Besides, he was pretty well set from the Trident stock he had earned by getting the original Eden fast tracked for approval.

He had felt justified in his actions because Eden probably would have been approved anyway, so why not get a little retirement money to put away? It was not as if he had orchestrated a drug approval that wouldn't have happened otherwise. Castell knew the time advantage by getting swift FDA approval of a blockbuster drug was worth hundreds of millions to a pharmaceutical company. Lipitor earned Pfizer up to ten billion per year at its peak and now Eden was scooping in fourteen to fifteen billion and still rising. But why would Vicktor need the follow-on compound so quickly? Castell could not figure how Trident stood to gain a financial advantage from its rapid approval. The new drug would just cannibalize sales from Eden. Maybe, as Vicktor said, it wasn't about money after all.

Morloch had promised another allocation of Trident's stock if he got the new version fast tracked—the same offer for Eden. But, tempting though it was, Castell did not truly need the money. The Trident stock he already had made him wealthy. Plus, he had lots of favors coming his way when he stepped down in a few years—if he stayed that long.

Suddenly, the rage and frustration at Bell's phone call this morning returned. Already the Congressional offices he had lined up behind his housing bill were calling to back off their support. Worse, it was the secretaries and aides calling, not the Congressmen. He was fast becoming irrelevant on the hill, he knew, and it was because Bell had cut him off. He might as well resign for all the political future he had.

He realized just then how tempting it would be to take Morloch up on his offer. Then he would resign and leave them scrambling to cover his position. Bell's move would always be a stick in his craw, but with the extra Trident stock, he would have more than enough fuck you money to retire in style.

CHAPTER 99

Robert Dixon prayed as he brushed his teeth in preparation for bed. It was becoming a ritual for him; every task undertaken with a brief prayer for salvation or grace. The lit candle caught his eye. Elise had insisted on trying something called aromatherapy to calm his nerves and she had set out a fragrant candle in a glass jar. It burned with an orange-vanilla scent or it was supposed to, based on the label on the box. It was lost on him, he thought as he pulled out a length of dental floss and said another prayer. It smelled like any ordinary candle.

His stomach growled. Over dinner, Elise had pressed him to try and eat some food, and he had tried, managing half of his linguini. It simply didn't taste good. No, that wasn't quite right. It didn't taste like much of anything, just salty paste that wouldn't go down. He seemed to have lost his taste for just about everything. That, and his headaches were worse. He actually looked forward to seeing Tom Green. Perhaps he would know what to do that would help him feel better, maybe some pill or other.

As he wrapped the floss around his fingers, his right hand jerked several times and his mind briefly flooded with his desolate vision of hell. Another prayer tripped from Dixon's lips. His jerks occurred more frequently, now. Sitting on his hands partially suppressed the arm jerks, but it didn't prevent him from seeing hell each time and it took several seconds for him to shake the vivid image and remember where he left off. Why was the China thing causing him this much stress?

Elise had also said something about another aromatherapy treatment: lavender linen mist on the pillow so he could smell it all night. Just what he needed, Dixon thought with some amusement, to go to work smelling like flowers. What would the team say? Next, Elise would have him burning sandalwood incense in the Oval Office.

Dixon leaned over and picked up the candle to carry it in to the bedroom where Elise was reading a book. She was so worried about him. He wanted to make her think it was working. "Hi, sweetie."

Elise looked up from the book and smiled when she saw the candle in his hand. A sudden twitch flung it onto the floor, the liquid candle wax running into the deep pile carpet. He half noticed, awash in his vision. He sunk to his knees in prayer pleading for salvation.

"Honey!" Elise exclaimed, jumping out of bed and running over to her husband and the now extinguished candle. "Honey," she said, "It's okay, it didn't burn anything." She saw her husband kneeling in prayer, his arms and shoulders twitching in the worst spell she had seen. Kneeling next to him, she clasped her arms around his head. "Robbie, it's okay. It's going to be okay."

CHAPTER 100

Steve boarded the late afternoon US Airways flight to Dulles Airport. Unable to resist, he stood at the door to the cockpit and stared at the captain longer than a casual passenger would.

"Please keep moving, sir," a flight attendant said, giving Steve a searching look.

Bulging athletic bag in hand and sweatshirt hood pulled low over his head, Steve walked back to the coach section and identified his seat on the aisle next to Valenti. As he shoved his bag into the overhead bin, he thought about his family.

On the way to the airport, Valenti had handed Steve another message from Anne and Johnnie. They were both well, but missed him greatly. Steve wondered what Anne and Johnnie were doing and he palpably longed for them. That was the good news.

As Steve sat down the hole in his stomach reminded him of the bad news. It had been in the paper this morning—Sheridan Labs, burned up in a gas explosion. Investigators speculated to reporters that arson was under consideration. After reading that it had been caused by a massive natural gas explosion, Steve had no doubt about who was responsible. It triggered a flood of vivid recollections of his house exploding and his trying to get Anne and Johnnie out safely.

The report noted that the night guard was missing, making him either dead or a suspect, probably dead, Steve guessed, buried somewhere inside the lab's wreckage—Eden's latest victim. He wished he had never dragged Sheridan into this whole mess. Doing so had put his friend's life at risk and now his precious lab, built with scarce money cobbled together from private donations, had gone up in flames. The loss would devastate Amos, he knew. Valenti, however, had been prescient. They had Sheridan's Eden data on a compact disk with a duplicate stored in a bank safe deposit box. And Sheridan was off in parts unknown, hopefully watching his backside.

The other bad news had come from yesterday's medical board hearing. It had gone as expected. Steve's attorney had been unable to get a postponement and without Steve's being present to defend himself, the board said it had no choice other than to suspend the license. The attorney said they would appeal the decision when he was out of danger, but as of now, he was branded as an unfit physician. Apparently the Republic thought he was still newsworthy. They had slotted his suspension on the front page next to the lab explosion article.

Steve pushed his ruminations out of his mind and pulled out the printed articles on Trident and Morloch that he had downloaded from Trident's website and other news articles he had found on the Internet. In addition, he had compiled a list of Trident's board of directors and senior officers. For all its billions in sales, Trident was still a small, one product pharmaceutical company. He was thankful he wasn't facing a Lilly or a Merck with its hundreds of people in senior management positions.

Steve's thoughts turned once again to his disagreeable conversation with Trident's safety officer. "Hey, I think I know how they finger the problem doctors."

"How?" Valenti looked up from his own stack of articles.

Steve looked a little sheepish. "Well, I can't remember his name, but it's the safety officer, the one I talked to when I reported Eden. I must have spilled my guts to him, naming Sheridan and Walker." Steve chastised himself. "How stupid."

"How the hell would you know he'd send the hit squad after you? But if you could think of that guy's name, it would make my job a little bit easier."

"I just remember he was arrogant." The plane began accelerating for take-off.

"And no doubt he told you there was nothing to your rampant speculations."

"Of course."

"And every doctor would call that person asking about problems with Eden?"

Steve thought a minute. "Yeah. That's got to be how they know who's made the Eden connection."

The airplane gave a sudden lurch and Steve grabbed the armrests.

"I saw you check out the pilot," Valenti chuckled. "So the safety officer's a prime suspect."

"I would guess. Anyway," Steve added, "I thought of something else; how they kept the info partitioned. Back then, Trident was a small biotech company and biotechs outsource lots of their early work, you know, rats and things. If something came up suspicious or abnormal, Trident would pay the vendor and tear up the results. Then they would farm out the same test to a different contractor. This time they'd substitute another compound for Eden or dilute the concentration and the new contractor would then give Trident a clean report, which goes to the FDA."

Valenti nodded. "Sounds plausible. Here's what I want you to do tomorrow at the Library of Congress. Find out as much as you can on Trident's early days, focusing on the senior staff. Look for people, officers really, who quit the company and who may have a piece of the puzzle, plus anything else you can dig up. Also more on Morloch. I'll also ID the safety guy you spoke to."

"Okay, but it's a big place. I'm not sure I can find my way around."

"I've arranged for someone to help you. Now," he said, pointing at the articles Steve had given him. "From what I've read, the big hurdle is getting the FDA to approve a drug. And Eden got fast-tracked. Is that unusual, or common with this situation?"

Steve frowned. "The fast-track status may be unusual considering it fundamentally alters the chemistry of the body."

"But, fast-tracking a drug means more money for the drug company, right?"

"Sure. It would mean a difference of hundreds of millions for the drug company. So, even though it was a needed class of drug, it still seems a little precipitous, particularly with all the bad press weight loss drugs have received."

"You mean like Fen-Phen?"

Steve nodded.

"Look, Doc, it all comes down to people. We find the right one and the whole stack of cards comes tumbling down. That's when we get the whole story.

"But why would Morloch do all of this?"

Valenti cocked his head as if the question was obvious. "Money."

"Just money?"

Valenti laughed. "That's ninety percent of what we did at the FBI. We chased perps who wanted more of that folding green and weren't too particular what they did to get it."

Steve shook his head. "I just don't understand."

Valenti playfully punched Steve's shoulder. "That's why I like you so much, Doc. You don't think like most people. There's something charming about that. Really charming."

CHAPTER 101

Valenti walked into Café Mocha, in Washington's Georgetown district, and spotted her sitting at the back table. She wore a dark red suit with a white ruffled blouse that was unbuttoned enough to reveal a double strand pearl necklace. Pulling out a padded wooden chair, he sat opposite her at the small round table. Valenti couldn't keep from grinning. It had been so long since they had last spoken. "Hello, Victoria."

"Hello, Tony," Victoria Hogue replied with a broad smile.

"You look great." And indeed she had retained the slender face and high cheekbones he remembered. Valenti looked down at his robust size. "But I've gone to pot, I'm afraid."

"It's good to see you again," Victoria said in her throaty voice thickened by too many cigarettes. "How long has it been?"

"Thirteen years." Valenti had already counted. "I'm married now and have two wonderful kids. You?"

Victoria shook her brunette hair, cut in a short, professional look. "Still playing around. I'm married to work. You remember."

"Only too well." Victoria's first love had been politics and her outlet was reporting for the Washington Post. "I read your columns regularly. It even has your picture. I could pick you out of a crowd. Oh, and congratulations on landing the White House beat."

Victoria's mouth curled up at his acknowledgement. "So what drags your carcass back into the cesspool?"

"Work."

Her eyebrows shot up. "Anything I can have? I want an exclusive if it's good."

"If it's ever news, you've got it. But maybe you can help. I need some info."

"What do you want?"

"How's the President?" He tossed out the question with feigned nonchalance, his face expressionless.

"Why?" she asked, her voice guarded, but her face betrayed her surprise.

There *was* something going on with the President. He shrugged. "Sorry, it's privileged."

Her eyebrows shot up. There was no faster way to get a reporter's attention than to withhold information. "Tell me later?" she countered. She needed something, too.

"If I can," Valenti said.

"And I thought this was for old times." Her hazel eyes flashed. Glancing around the coffee shop, she leaned forward and spoke in a lowered voice. "Okay, here it is. Dixon's not right. It's a source of rampant speculation in the corps. Rumor has it, he's completely consumed with this China massacre thing. He's moody, short-tempered, obstinate, and he's got some sort of constant headache. Worse, he's making bush league political mistakes and driving his staff crazy covering for him. This is all unconfirmed, of course, too insubstantial to run with it, but we smell something afoot. Get this," Victoria continued, "he prayed in a public school, but his office squelched it, denied it to the rafters. Now that isn't the Dixon we all know."

Valenti, despite his confidence in Steve, felt a perverse sense of relief. Everything Victoria said sounded like that Eden crap. "And his backing Taiwan?"

"That's the stupidest thing I've ever heard from him. Mind you, I like the guy, or did before all this. But something's rotten in the state politic. He hasn't given a press conference since the one recognizing Taiwan. I don't expect one every day, you know, but he's deployed the Pacific fleet to the Taiwan Straits and Congress is screaming for a better explanation, but the big guy only issues press releases and sends his minions out to joust. China's livid and I don't blame them. Look," she said, her hushed voice strident, "Dixon and Taiwan have left no room for compromise. It's balls to the walls."

"Jesus." Valenti couldn't help himself. "And his twitches?"

"Everybody's seen them. You saw them on national TV. It's from stress, they say."

"And you say?"

She shook her head. "I think he's losing it. Nothing I can publish, not yet, but we're watching him very closely. He fell asleep in the National Cathedral, no big deal, right? But he was confused or something when he woke up. We downplayed it, but the question remains, what's going on?"

"Is he sick or something?"

Victoria locked her eyes on Valenti's. "What do you know?"

Valenti shrugged, holding her gaze. "Nothing—right now."

"Not fucking fair," she complained. "I still want that exclusive." Her expression softened. "I've missed you, Tony, but I never could figure you out."

Valenti smiled. "We're even, then."

CHAPTER 102

"Larry, I took the liberty of reviewing the Chinese sat-pics before we met," Harold Wright said, settling in at the State situation room conference table for their eleven o'clock meeting. "I think there are a few things worth looking at that weren't mentioned in the reports."

"Okay, show me what you've found."

Wright plugged a monitor cable into his laptop and tapped on his keyboard. Within a moment, images popped up on the wall-mounted screens. "These are from the real-time birds, the KA-48s and 52s in low orbit. Good resolution for our purposes. We'll be seeing infrared night imaging."

"Because they only move at night."

"Correct." Wright pulled his laser pointer from his shirt pocket and aimed it at the first image. "Here's a group of eighteen trucks pulling out of Fuqua Ti Air Base. As you can see, all are covered with an opaque tarp. Probably dark military green, but of little matter for our purposes.

He turned to the second image. Here, they break up on different roads into three groups of six. Now look here." Harry manipulated his mouse and the image zoomed in on one group of trucks. "They're passing a street light right here. Now see that shadow?" He pointed a red laser over the back part of one tarp-covered truck.

"Yeah, but I don't know what it means."

"It's the tail of a jet. The configuration matches their J-8, a fighter, and the length is compatible with the fighter's fuselage."

Calhoun sat up. "You're saying that China is moving fighter jets around on trucks?"

"I looked at several other convoys from this air base and the answer is yes. What I didn't show you is that each group of trucks is loaded in warehouses away from our sky eyes, so we can't know for sure what's in them. But look at the two other six-truck convoys." He brought up two more images and pointed to another truck shadow. "It took awhile to find a light that hit each convoy at the right angle—there aren't many street lights in rural China—but there it is right here . . ." The pointer jumped to the next image. " . . . And here."

Now that he knew what he was looking for, Calhoun saw it immediately.

"Now, what do you need if you have a fighter fuselage?" Wright asked.

"Wings, parts, fuel, ammo, missiles."

"And here's what we found. This," he pointed to another image, "is a fuel truck. Pointing to another, he said, "This payload seems a bit wider than the rest, which is probably the wings, and the others are standard trucks that can hold anything, including parts and munitions.

"So, they're moving planes? Where?"

"That's what's giving the analysts fits. Look, if the tarps are stretched over a metal frame, they will look full even if they are empty and it's nearly impossible for us to tell which. Worse, when they arrive at a destination, they pull into covered structures so we cannot see any loading or offloading."

"But if they're all covered by the tarps, we can't know which direction things are moving."

"Can't or don't?" A sly smile curled the corners of Wright's mouth.

"So, what have you got up your sleeve?" Calhoun said.

"Travel time comparison."

Calhoun figured it out. "You time trucks going the same route, or a segment of a route, loaded or empty. Loaded trucks are slower. Since you can easily measure travel time, you can now tell when the trucks are heavy or empty."

"Perfect." Wright beamed, pleased with himself. "Now, it's tedious, but it won't take long to detect a pattern. I just haven't had time to personally map every round-trip route, much less measure the time for representative segments, but NSA with their computers can in a hurry."

Calhoun sat back trying to put all his bits and pieces into a picture that made sense. He imagined trucks and trains moving stuff around, full in one direction and empty on the return leg. With this pattern, China could accumulate a massive amount of military materiél somewhere without the US knowing where.

The random convoys crossing the countryside reminded Calhoun of his high school marching band. His bandleader devised a march routine in which the whole band, playing the school fight song, broke up into multiple groups of six students. Each group marched seemingly at random and looking completely disorganized until on the last refrain they all fit, suddenly and neatly together in a giant letter "P," the initial of the school. Out of apparent chaos, order suddenly emerged—and, importantly, the audience had no clue what was planned until the final moment.

In a real sense, this was a massive Chinese marching drill, and out of the chaos a complete military formation would suddenly emerge. His pulse quickened. It had to be Taiwan; there was no other answer—but there was still a huge piece missing. Even with a massive build -up along the coast facing Taiwan, China didn't have a large enough Navy to invade Taiwan. Exasperated, he mentally threw up his hands. What *was* the goddamn Chinese strategy?

"Harry, how long would it take you and your team to give me a quick and dirty estimation of the net flow of cargo? I want you to concentrate on the Chinese coastline closest to Taiwan."

Harry looked up at the ceiling for a moment. "About six hours if I put everyone on it."

"Can you do that for me?"

"On my way." Wright folded up his laptop and hurried out.

CHAPTER 103

Steve climbed out of the taxi on 23rd street and looked up at the new George Washington University Hospital. Walking through the glass front entrance doors, he was fulfilling a promise he had made to himself the moment he knew he was coming to Washington. He was going to visit Captain Palmer.

He had spent the morning at the Library of Congress, and by lunchtime he had reached a good stopping place. Valenti had arranged for Heather, a research librarian, to help him and she had assisted in amassing a pile of articles about Trident enabling Steve to find key bits of information, including hire and departure dates for most of the top employees, especially the early ones. One departure in particular had stood out, a press release announcing that the founder of the company and its chief scientist, Samuel Blumenthal, MD, had just retired to his suburban Baltimore home.

Overall, the picture that emerged was what Steve had expected. At the outset, Trident, originally named Medici Biopharma, had performed their discovery and initial animal research in-house. They then floundered for lack of money, thus setting the stage for Morloch's company-saving investment. In what looked to Steve like a *coup d'état*, Morloch renamed the company Trident, made himself Chairman and CEO, and demoted Dr. Blumenthal to Chief Scientist. Then, as Steve had predicted, Trident had begun to outsource its work. As he read, the pieces fell into place. He knew it was all circumstantial evidence at best constructing a necessary, but not sufficient chain of events pointing to Trident's culpability. Someone would have to talk on the record to implicate Morloch and Trident.

On a hunch, he had requested Trident's 10-Q filings for the last six years. The 10-Q's would describe all material changes in the financial or operational condition of a publicly traded company. Rummaging through them, he discovered a chunk of Morloch's personal stock had been transferred to an offshore account in the Cayman Islands. He had noted the date and parked that information away for later reflection.

Just before he had left for the hospital, Heather had walked in with a surprise. She had managed to obtain a copy of the Summary Basis of Approval for Eden. It was the FDA's report of its review of Eden and its reasons for approving it for human use. He had thumbed through the table of contents and the signature page listing all the officials involved before getting to the synopsis. He only had time to skim it, jotting down a couple of thoughts before snapping his pen closed—time to go see Captain Palmer.

The ICU was state-of-the-art with glass-walled rooms and mounted electronic monitors over each bed. He found the room he was looking for and walked in, pulling off his sweatshirt hood.

Dimly lit, the small room was nearly filled by the bed, IV pumps, monitors, and emergency equipment. On the far side of the bed, facing its head, was a large vinyl blue chair. On the other side, nearest to Steve, stood a young woman, probably in her late twenties, wearing blue jeans and a cable knit sweater. She looked up when Steve walked in, but otherwise registered no surprise. There was no such thing as privacy in ICUs.

"Hello, I'm Doctor Steve James. And you are?"

"Mia, his daughter." She slid out of the way to let Steve near the bed.

Ready as he was, Captain Palmer's condition still shocked him. The previously tanned and vigorous looking pilot was now pale and his face had aged. His eyes were closed, perhaps in sleep. Steve noticed a fiftyish woman sitting in the blue chair with bright, but tired eyes.

"Steve James," he repeated.

"I'm Yvonne, his wife."

"A pleasure to meet you."

"What kind of doctor are you?" she asked. There was no hope in her voice.

"I'm sorry, I'm just here on a social visit."

Recognition registered on Yvonne's face. "You're the doctor from the airplane." Seeing Steve nod, she began to weep quietly. "Your beard. I didn't recognize . . ."

"Of course," Steve said.

"Thank you for what you did and . . ." She wiped her cheeks with a Kleenex. "Thank you for coming. Dr. Walker said you were very helpful to him."

Hearing Dr. Walker's name saddened Steve. He wished Marty were here to greet him with his massive handshake and hearty voice. He could see how the family would have liked and trusted him. "I only knew him a short time, but I had a great respect for him."

"We miss him, too," Mia said. "His replacement seems competent enough, but not very friendly."

"How is the Captain?"

Yvonne stood up and held the bed rail. Looking down at her husband, she replied resignedly, "Not good. He's getting worse. He's rarely lucid and his flashbacks are almost continuous when he's not sleeping." She pulled her husband's hand from under the sheet and held it. It was blue and bruised from multiple I.V.s. "He doesn't recognize us much anymore. That's the worst part." Her lips tightened as she struggled to hold her emotions in check. She took a deep breath and looked at Steve. "It's only a matter of time now."

Captain Palmer jerked once and opened his eyes. They were full of fear. "I'm hit! Fire!" He flailed the air with his hands clutching at something only he could see. Mia and Yvonne each grabbed an arm and held it tightly. Mia bent over and whispered softly in his ear. "It's okay now, Daddy. It's all okay. You're safe with us."

Steve spent the next several hours sitting at the bedside of Captain Palmer, with his family. They looked at pictures in a photo album showing them all together smiling as Mia narrated. Yvonne told stories of their life and travels together. They were a very close family, reminding Steve poignantly of his own. All too soon, his four o'clock rendezvous with Valenti approached.

Standing up, he announced, "I need to go now. Thank you for letting me spend time with you." He hugged Yvonne and Mia and left with an ache inside. It all was so sad. And so fucking wrong.

Back at the library, Steve hurriedly packed his work and articles away into a rented locker and, in the bathroom, changed his clothes into the recently purchased suit he would wear for this evening's meeting with Secretary Castell. He examined himself in the mirror and shrugged. Not pretty, but he decided it was as good as he was going to get under the circumstances. Per Valenti's strict orders, he wore the sweatshirt with the hood pulled up and carried his suit jacket.

His watch indicated he still had a few minutes left before four. Too wound up to sit, he walked out through the main entrance and looked down past the wide stone steps onto 1st Street. The air was cool and it felt good after the stuffy air in the library. He stood next to the massive foyer entrance and watched the cars drive by on the mist-wet road, thinking about the visit with Captain Palmer and his family. Revisiting the hospital where he had first met Marty Walker caused Steve to miss him even more. Marty would have been charged up for the fight with Trident and full of ideas about how to tackle the company. He smiled remembering the king-sized physician.

A large pickup truck with shot mufflers drove past, loud even where he stood, reminding him of the pickup truck that had tried to push him off the overpass. Suddenly, he doubled over like he had been punched in the solar plexus. It was so goddamn obvious. Why hadn't he seen it before?

Marty had been murdered.

Steve fell against the stone wall, his stomach in tumult. According to Marty's secretary, he had run off an overpass and died, but Steve now realized it had been no accident. Marty had been knocked off the overpass. Steve closed his eyes in frustration and anger.

CHAPTER 104

Linda Resnick, accompanied by Larry Calhoun, strode into the State situation room, late for a hastily scheduled National Security Committee meeting, but without the President. That would come afterwards. Joining them by invitation was General Valenzuela, the Chairman of the Joint Chiefs of Staff.

Calhoun walked around the table passing out a stapled report. As she took her seat, Resnick began. "I am very sorry for my tardiness. In front of you is a transcript of a visit from Ernie Whiteside, senior Washington producer at CNN who just passed on some critical information from China. I have brought with me my INR head, Larry Calhoun. I want him to summarize the information, plus other new intelligence, which has special bearing on our position on China."

Sitting down at the conference table to Resnick's right, Calhoun first described Wright's satellite imagery findings that detailed the covert military movements, including the fighter jets, as well as Wright's strategy for estimating the net direction of the materiél. He then read a note Wright had handed him as he walked to this meeting. "The early estimates of laden versus unladen trucks show a net movement of materiél towards the Chinese coast nearest Taiwan."

There was a stir in the group. Crusoe cleared his throat. "This doesn't indicate intentions or actual plans on the part of China."

Calhoun shrugged. "Perhaps not, although in my world, capability projects intentions. In any event, Ernie Whiteside's information is critical to this equation. His Hong Kong station manager Herb Wong felt that his freedom was at risk because of CNN's broadcast of the massacre. Wong and his staff had to covertly escape Hong Kong. Figuring Hong Kong's airports and common carriers would be monitored and therefore dangerous, he and his close staff members slipped into Mainland China, traveling overland. They moved north along the coast planning to take a private boat across the Straits to Taiwan. Of course, they had no idea Taiwan would declare independence."

"They are now holed up in a small town called Shantou waiting for an opportunity to leave, but during their travels, they made some interesting observations and passed them to Whiteside. First, they saw frequent convoys of army trucks traveling at night. Of importance to us is that they appeared to be full when moving towards the coast and, on at least one occasion, they observed a broken-down truck convoy headed away from the coast that was empty. The tarps we see from our satellites cover a welded-metal frame."

"That's enough for me," Painter said. He had skimmed the rest of Whiteside's transcript in his hands.

Calhoun continued. "They also discovered China is billeting some unknown, but large numbers of army troops in the coastal cities they traveled through, with the locals complaining about the imposition. Most importantly, China has commandeered their heavy commercial fishing boats and loaded their holds with tanks and materiel."

"How?" Crusoe demanded.

"They modified the front of the hulls and drove the tanks right in—all done at night. Realize, these are steel-hulled vessels that range from one hundred to three hundred feet. Those CNN reporters were clearly in the right place at the right time. Now, I did some quick research," Calhoun continued, "and based on satellite estimates of China's fishing fleet, our analysts tell me the Chinese can land a two battalion-size invasion force, with the combined civilian and military flotilla. And they can return to the mainland and be back on the island within nine hours, increasing their forces rapidly. We estimate China can land, even with naval losses from submarines, coastal batteries, and missiles over five battalions in just over thirty six hours."

"Shit," Painter said. "Taiwan only has three active battalions and two more in reserves. I can't see how they can repulse the invasion."

Crusoe looked dubious. "But their Navy can't compare to ours. We'll blast them out of the water."

Calhoun replied, "There are over a thousand fishing vessels along the coast of China within easy distance of Taiwan capable of carrying substantial men and equipment. They would be hard to find and shoot under optimal circumstances, even if we could get away with systematically shooting civilian vessels. But I believe that's the second part of a two-pronged attack. First, I think they plan a massive air strike against the battle groups."

"How?" Crusoe demanded.

"Recall our belief that China is moving jet fighters by truck. Based on our spot review of satellite imagery, we think they have moved many of them, perhaps hundreds. Since they traveled on these trucks, we haven't been able to track all their locations. The ones we have tracked seem to be making a circuitous route to the coast, putting them within quick striking distance of the Straits. I'm guessing now, but I think each one is based in a remote place where it has a short strip of road for take-off. If I'm right, they could take us completely by surprise with overwhelming numbers."

"But their air force can't touch ours," Crusoe said, crossing his arms.

Bingham asked, "Mark, how capable are you against three or four hundred fighters and bombers all at once?"

Painter shook his head. "Not good. We've got less than half that. I don't have the assets to shoot all of them down, thrown at us at once."

Speaking smoothly like a cross-examiner in a courtroom, Bingham continued, "And what about the secondary wave of planes that would follow within the hour? Can you refuel and re-arm in time?"

"That first wave would pretty well deplete our resources—and that would only be the first attack. China has over four thousand military aircraft. Even if we see only eight hundred of them, they would be able to cripple us and damage or sink much of the battle group."

"And land-based surface to surface missiles?" Bingham prodded.

The Joint Chief's Chairman, Valenzuela spoke up. "You've made your point. We can't handle the landing flotilla."

"China has had decades to prepare their strategy," Calhoun observed. "They're executing a well-honed plan."

Crusoe sighed. "This is worse than any of us imagined."

"It's perfect Sun Tzu," Painter whispered.

"What was that?" Sullivan asked.

"Sun Tzu," Painter repeated. "We're getting a tutorial in ancient Chinese warfare."

Sullivan, his face ashen, summarized. "So, at the very best, we take huge losses and, at the probable worst, lose much of our fleet and Taiwan."

They all looked at Calhoun who nodded.

"Does Taiwan know this?" Sullivan asked.

"They must," Bingham answered. "They've got better ground intelligence than we do. I think they've been withholding intel."

"Then," Sullivan said, "we need to speak to our Taiwanese colleagues and see if they are interested in a compromise position with regards to their independence bid. After all, their prime motivation was to avoid heavy-handed treatment on the part of China. We must find a way to return to the previous agreement in a way that protects Taiwan's interests while staving off the Chinese invasion."

Resnick spread her hands in frustration. "But even if we did, who in China can we negotiate with? Premier Chow is scarce and we can't officially call General Yao. So, even if the President does back off his promise to defend Taiwan, he might not have anyone to discuss the issue with.

"And remember," she added soberly, "It may hinge on Taiwan's agreement to modify their independence demand. If they don't, the President may not unilaterally modify his stance, in which case, we've effectively relinquished control of the United State's Chinese foreign policy to Taiwan."

CHAPTER 105

Sullivan looked at the three people sitting around Resnick's office coffee table. "I am becoming increasingly concerned about President Dixon's mental state." Painter and Treasury secretary Norris sat on the couch. Sullivan and Resnick sat in chairs opposite. It was an impromptu meeting Sullivan had requested as the Security Council meeting broke up. That they were all cabinet members told Resnick the nature of the meeting.

Resnick said, "It's apparent something's not right."

Sullivan sighed. "I've known Robert for ten years. He's earned my respect for his many strengths, but he is not the man that took office." He spoke softly and chose his words slowly. "Under ordinary circumstances, this would be of concern, but after the meeting we just held, a crisis is imminent and we need the best mind in that office."

"I asked Dr. Green to drop in on the President unannounced," he continued. "I only told him that I wanted him to visit with the President and form his own opinion about how his old friend was doing. Dr. Green called me afterwards and told me he thought something was wrong, but did not know what it was without a real examination and tests."

"Did he have any idea?" Painter asked.

"No and he was very adamant about not wanting to speculate. He did say it could be stress related, but the body movements worried him. President Dixon is understandably reluctant to visit Dr. Green's office with the press scrutiny so, Dr. Green arranged for dinner tomorrow night at his house. He hopes to get blood samples and do a more thorough examination. Maybe we'll have more information after that."

"I hope so." Resnick hated going around behind the President's back.

Sullivan nodded slowly. "For his part, Dr. Green is worried enough to pursue a diagnosis."

"If he does find something, what then?" Helen Norris asked.

"Depends," Sullivan said. "Dr. Green will need to make a determination about how serious it is and an estimation of whether or not it is treatable in the short run. Depending on his findings, he will order a second opinion. If the second physician concurs that a significant disability exists, they will report to the Vice President and Cabinet. Then, if the VP and a majority of the cabinet members agree with the physician's findings, they will go before the President pro tempore and the Speaker and ask that the President be replaced."

"The twenty-fifth amendment," Painter said. "I didn't realize the part about the two doctors, though."

"That's the approach Congress took to get a handle on the most difficult aspect of determining presidential disability." Sullivan said. "It's not when a President gets shot or has a stroke; it's the insidious loss of competence, like an FDR or a Ronald Reagan."

Sullivan paused and looked around at the group, his voice dropping slightly. "At what point does a president lose the capacity to govern and what criteria should be applied? A secret congressional finding determined that two concurring doctors would be helpful in instructing the Cabinet about presidential competence. That's the law, but," he shrugged, "it's never been implemented."

CHAPTER 106

"Valenti," Steve exclaimed as soon as he got into the taxi, "I think my friend Dr. Walker was murdered by the same guys that tried to get me." Steve slammed the door shut and pulled the hood off his head.

"Hold on, Doc. You sprung a leak there." Valenti leaned forward and spoke to the driver. "Mansion Club, please." Turning back to Steve, he inquired, "Now what's got your engine racing?"

Steve told him his suspicions about Marty Walker's death.

"Might have something there." Valenti mused. He took a sip from a bottle of water. "I could get a look at the police report."

"Valenti," Steve began, "I think other doctors may have died unexpectedly after calling Trident. Can we find out?"

"You mean, can we find other doctors who have been killed and link them to recent calls to Trident?"

"Exactly. It's circumstantial but it could prove pivotal."

Valenti turned the thought over in his mind before speaking. "Possibly. Certainly if we got a DA to start looking into this thing, they could pull the resources together for something like that. We can't possibly do it ourselves. Do you know how many calls Trident gets in a day?"

"Hundreds. Easily. But not all to the safety officer. I'm sure they have a policy of all like questions getting funneled to his office."

"Right. Records access and the right computer nerd could make for some for interesting hunting."

"But let's get what we can about Marty's death. I bet it was their guys."

"I'm not taking that bet. Timing and mode were too coincidental, like Sheridan's lab going up in smoke. Which reminds me." Valenti shifted in his seat in a manner that Steve was beginning to recognize as a forerunner to bad news.

"What?"

Valenti took a long drink, draining the rest of his water bottle. He wiped his mouth. "I got a call from Detective Harmon about their investigation into Sheridan's lab explosion."

"Arson?"

"Yes, but that's not why he called. They found a work glove at the scene. It matched your DNA."

Steve stared at Valenti. "They can't suspect me, can they?"

"They're not sure. Since it happened at night around midnight, you theoretically could have left your hotel and done the nefarious deed."

"OK," Steve replied, analyzing the ramifications. "What motive?"

"I told Harmon you were set up and he seemed to believe me, especially since they had a squad car on the scene watching the place. They're not issuing any warrants, but when we hit town, they're going to want to question you."

"Well," Steve said sarcastically, "We'll just look forward to that, won't we."

"Saw an old friend," Valenti said, changing the subject. "Reporter type, tuned into White House goings on."

"And . . .?"

"She tells me the head man's off his rocker."

"Like how? What'd she say?"

Valenti waved a hand. "Like he's not himself: mistakes, impatient, headaches, and some strange twitching. Rumor has it, his staff is scrambling to keep him out of the public eye. He did not make his weekly radio address last week."

"Well, that fits. I wonder what his doctor is doing about it?"

"If I were him, I'd want to keep it under wraps. It would be explosive." Valenti's eyes lit up as he spoke, warming up to his favorite subject. "Seems unnamed sources also tell my reporter friend that China's really pissed at the Taiwan thing. She understands that the U.S. and Taiwan have left no room for negotiation on the independence thing, which backs China into a corner. This is hot."

"Not good, I presume."

"Stupid, stupid." Valenti waved his hands again. "And China's military activity is up to a fever pitch. I think China's gearing up for an attempt to take Taiwan by force."

"Really?"

"Well, that's the fun part. Conventional wisdom says they can't."

"Can they?"

"Well, I'm told that's what the National Security Advisor thinks and the President apparently agrees with him. It's right, all right, as in dead right, but it just makes China get creative. Look, what if Alaska declared independence with Russia's backing? You're the President and you just got told you could not win it back by force. What would you do?"

Steve thought about it a moment. "Play a surprise game."

"And if you were Russia, would you feel complacent?"

"No way. I'd be trying to cover my ass."

"Basically, it's a no win for the U.S. We have nothing to gain and much to lose."

Steve thought for a minute, digesting what Valenti had just said. "And you think the President is complacent."

"Complacent or arrogant or both—or demented from your Eden brain rot. I just hope somebody talks him out of it."

"Maybe we'll find out something tonight when we speak to Castell," Steve said, not feeling hopeful.

Valenti leaned forward and spoke to the driver. "Let us out here."

The driver double-parked in front of a Starbucks coffee shop. Steve paid the taxi driver and slid out.

Valenti followed Steve out of the taxi and guided Steve into the Starbucks. "I've been here the last two hours snooping around for any sign of a problem."

"And?" Steve asked.

"It's been clear. Just keep your sweatshirt and hood on until we get inside the club. He handed Steve a thin nylon sack holding a bulky item. "Here, I brought you something."

Steve took the bag, unzipped it and looked inside. He already knew what it was. "Oh, you shouldn't have."

"Button up and put it on, then get a cup of coffee and sit tight," Valenti ordered. He cocked his head to the building across the street and Steve read the sign, *The Mansion Club*. I'm going to go over and again case the joint."

"Case the joint?" Steve mocked.

"Look wise-ass, you expect me to talk like that. It's part of the show."

CHAPTER 107

Resnick sat at her desk, her phone cradled against her ear, drumming her fingers while the Taiwan ambassador's assistant went to get him. Suddenly, a man's voice spoke in accented English. "Yes?" It was Zhou Lishin.

"Ambassador Zhou, this is Linda Resnick."

"Yes, Linda," he said pleasantly, "What can I do for you?"

"I have some disturbing news about China's military capabilities. Recent developments point to the likelihood of China's success in an invasion of your country."

"No, it is not possible." He sounded genuinely surprised.

"New intelligence, Mr. Ambassador. It is probable that we will be unable to stop it."

"Is this true? Tell me how you know this."

Resnick outlined the facts surrounding their new assessments. She concluded by saying, "I'll send you a report of our findings."

Resnick knew Taiwan had a very capable intelligence presence in China and should be able to corroborate many of the facts in the report. Their conclusions, however, might be different.

"Ambassador Zhou, after you communicate this information to your government, will you please let me know their response, especially if there are any new options your government would like to explore."

Zhou took a long time responding. "What does your President say?"

The Taiwanese ambassador knew that the majority of President Dixon's cabinet opposed the new arrangement with Taiwan. Dixon's position would be a key gauge for any Taiwanese decision. Resnick wanted Dixon's opinion left as vague as possible to let them fear the worst. Possibly they would consider backing off their bid for independence with the prospect of a successful invasion.

"I have not apprised him of the situation yet. I wanted to notify you of this change in situation as soon as possible."

"I see." Zhou paused before continuing. "Of course, I will take it to my government, but I would like to know your President's recommendations first, if that is at all possible."

"I understand your request, although he may best judge if he first has a sense of your government's position given the new developments." Resnick had a great reluctance to have President Dixon personally involved in negotiations.

"Am I to conclude that your support is one of convenience and varies depending on the chance of success or failure?"

"Not in the least," Resnick said smoothly understanding his ploy. "But if your goal of no Chinese domination over your island is to be realized, other strategies may be more productive."

"Dear Madame Secretary," Zhou said. "I hear your wish to revoke your commitment. As I recall, your President pledged to defend freedom, democracy, and self-determination. Is it only a firm commitment if no American blood is lost?"

Resnick knew the ambassador was under intense pressure to maintain the American support. "I understand your interest was to avoid the arbitrary and violent treatment Hong Kong suffered at the hands of the People's Republic. While the previous arrangement seemed suitable enough, now your declaration of independence may provoke the very reaction you sought to avoid."

"I ask you this question," Zhou replied. "Was your freedom worth a fight to the last man?"

Resnick wondered at that moment if she had misjudged Taiwan's motivation for independence. Was it for security from Chinese maltreatment as she had assumed or was it the genuine desire for freedom that drove them? "That is a question we have answered. I think that decision is now yours."

"It seems you have a predisposition regarding our decision." Ambassador Zhou couldn't keep the bitterness out of his voice. "Of course, I will communicate with Taipei and we will speak more tomorrow. I should be available at ten. Good day."

CHAPTER 108

The Starbucks overlooked the street diagonally across from the Mansion Club. Steve sat at a counter by the window, nursing a coffee while Valenti walked along the wet street on both sides of the Mansion Club before he entered. It looked expensive, judging by its fancy façade of Southern antebellum décor with white columns supporting the *port cochere* entryway, where uniformed doormen helped the clientele, dressed in pricey designer clothes, out of their fancy cars. It was not his kind of place.

"Can I sit here?" A woman indicated the stool next to him where he had laid his coat. The coffee shop was crowded and seats were scarce.

"I'm sorry, but I'm expecting a friend to join me."

"Oh," she said, and looked around for another seat. Steve caught a man staring at him. He had high cheekbones and strikingly clear blue eyes. When Steve looked at him, he averted his eyes, leaving Steve feeling unsettled.

After a moment, Steve glanced back and saw the man watching him, this time with what appeared to him as a sly smile. *Does he know who I am?* Steve averted his gaze. Who was he? He racked his brain to remember the face.

The man paid for his coffee and started walking towards Steve, looking steadily at him before he bent over to pick up a free newspaper from a stand. He turned away, making Steve breathe a little easier. Then the man turned back towards Steve. He puckered up in an air kiss, and blew it at Steve. He then walked out of the coffee shop and past the window in front of Steve, smiling.

Steve felt a cold sweat break out, angry with himself for getting so upset. The man was just playing with him. He took a deep swallow of the hot coffee to settle his nerves.

Across the street, Valenti walked out of the restaurant and nodded at him before heading into a pub next door, which, in an imitation of the Cheer's bar, required his walking down a half flight of stairs to the entrance. Steve saw its name on a vine-framed sign bolted to the railing above the semi-basement entrance: *The Sticky Fingers Bar*. Probably a pick-up place, Steve figured. A few moments later, Valenti emerged in the gathering dusk and crossed the street and within moments slid onto the stool next to Steve.

"Looks clear. We have a reservation at the Mansion Club under the name of Thorpe."

"Why not Jones?"

"Why advertise? Say, you don't look like your usual self. Something happen?"

"No. Somebody just looked funny at me. That's all."

Valenti frowned. "What happened?"

Steve described the man in as much detail as he remembered.

Valenti sighed. "I can't leave you anywhere. So tell me about your library adventure."

"Here's my Reader's Digest version. Between Morloch's stock and vested stock options, he owns a little over ten percent of the company. At one time he owned almost forty-eight percent, but his share is still enough to maintain control. I looked up today's stock prices and he's worth almost ten billion."

Valenti stuck out his lower lip. "That's some cool cash."

"The stock has at least doubled every year since it opened, counting splits." Steve recited from memory. "Compared to most other pharma companies, it's overpriced with a p-e ratio of nearly forty-two. The current share price is one hundred eighty-seven dollars. The company has a market valuation over ninety-five billion, higher than Lilly. I looked up the comps."

"Jesus, that's serious money, all from fat people," Valenti marveled.

Steve continued, "The analysts are convinced Trident has a lock on this thing. Their patent doesn't run out for another seven years and the manufacturing patents run for another ten after that. It's a difficult molecule to package and formulate. That alone may keep them exclusive for seventeen years, although the money involved creates a huge incentive for another company to make a run at it."

"Anything about the prions in the reports?"

"Nothing. I even got a copy of the FDA's report approving Eden for marketing. There's nothing."

"What about the officers of the old company?"

"I have a complete list back at the library," Steve said, "but I ran across one thing that I think is interesting."

"What's that?"

"The company founder, Dr. Samuel Blumenthal, subsequently demoted to Chief Scientist, retired last week."

Valenti sat up. "Really? What else?"

"It was a press release. None of the papers picked it up except for a one-paragraph blurb in the Philadelphia Inquirer. Anyway, the press release said he had moved back to his old home in Baltimore and wanted to re-join the faculty at Johns Hopkins."

"Not too far from here, either . . ." Valenti's voice trailed off and they sat in silence looking through the darkness and the rain sprinkled pavement toward the Mansion Club. "Yep," he said, "You've vanished into thin air and Trident hasn't a clue where you are, which is pissing them off to no end. We're on the offensive now, Doc." Valenti rubbed his palms together. "They've got to be throwing a conniption."

Steve smiled at Valenti's enthusiasm. Why had he left the FBI for a pedestrian life as a private investigator? He clearly loved the cloak and dagger. The occasional allusions to Valenti's unhappy experiences with the FBI and Washington, DC had Steve guessing, but it hadn't been the work that had driven Valenti away. He was much too animated and excited. It must have been something else that led him to Phoenix and a different life.

"Steve? Are you in dream world?" Valenti nudged his arm.

"Huh?"

"I said, 'let's go.'"

Steve checked his watch. It read six fifty-five. "Right." He stood up and pulled off his sweatshirt and slipped on his navy wool suit jacket. Wearing a dark suit in Washington was almost like camouflage.

As he followed Valenti out of the coffee shop and into the cold drizzle, he wondered how he should address the Secretary? Secretary Castell, probably. Saying it that way rang a bell. Steve frowned. *Jacob Castell.* He had seen it recently at the library, but among all the articles and briefs he had read, he couldn't remember where. He pondered it while they waited for a break in the traffic before walking across the wet street and into the bright entrance of the Mansion Club.

From a sedan down the street, Kirk Mallis watched the pair walk out of the Starbucks and cross the street. He lowered the pair of night-vision binoculars, his blue eyes sparkling. "Fanelli, you fucking asshole," he exclaimed with undisguised glee. "I finally found you."

CHAPTER 109

Linda hung up the phone, her stomach roiling. How could it have happened so fast? She had just gotten home to catch a rare meal with her husband when Chinese Ambassador Gung had called with Beijing's ultimatum. *My God.* They weren't ready for this; it was inconceivable. Her hands shaking, she dialed Jeff Bell.

"Bell."

"Jeff. Call the morning crew for a meeting with the President."

"Now?"

"It's China. I just spoke with Ambassador Gung. They launch in twelve hours."

"How in the hell—?" She heard Bell take a long breath. "Okay, right. I'll get on it. Meet in half an hour?"

Resnick squinted at her microwave clock. "Okay, that's seven-thirty."

Hanging up, her mind whirled as she tried to prioritize her next actions. First, she would call Ambassador Zhou. She had to do what she could to avoid the conflict. She would inform him of the ultimatum and China's offer of a last minute compromise. If the Taiwanese didn't change their stance, she knew President Dixon would not alter his support for Taiwan.

Even if Taiwan agreed to a compromise, she wasn't sure President Dixon would agree to negotiate. She felt as if a noose were tightening around her neck.

CHAPTER 110

Steve and Valenti slid into a posh booth with a good view of the bar and entrance.

The Mansion Club continued the Deep South motif inside, complete with dark wood floors, a large fireplace with a white painted wood mantelpiece and white marble countertops. Candelabras on the walls and oil lamps on the tables lit up the room with a soft glow, enhanced by the dimmed overhead halogen lighting.

A waiter dressed in a starched white cotton jacket took their drink orders. Steve tried to relax, hoping that Castell had not forgotten the meeting. He and Valenti passed the minutes quietly looking at the people mingling at the bar.

A movement across the room caught Steve's eye. He stared, not believing what he saw.

"Valenti, look," Steve pointed at a beautiful woman at the bar engaged in conversation with a handsome, slickly dressed man.

"Nice," Valenti said appreciatively. "I thought you were lonely for your wife."

"Shut up, you letch. Look again."

Valenti looked back at the woman whose face suddenly jerked several times in succession like a flurry of tics. Her hands hurried to cover the twitching and her look of embarrassment. Valenti's smile vanished. "Wow. Do you think she has . . .?"

"I'd bet on it. I'm going to go talk to her." Steve started to get up.

"Stop," Valenti grabbed his arm. "Are you stupid? First, her date's likely to punch your lights out. Two, you are in deep hiding and you can blow it right here. Third, and most important, she'd laugh at you. You like being laughed at by a woman?"

"But she's got to know."

"Look, Doc, even if you're right, what can you do about it? Think."

"But . . ." Steve protested, even as he realized the truth in Valenti words. What would he say to her? Anything he told her would either sound like lunacy or seriously frighten her. How would he feel if a stranger came up and told him he had a terminal disease?

Castell slid in next to Valenti, across from Steve. "Nice view, gentlemen?" He nodded at the woman they had been watching. Valenti looked chagrinned at having missed Castell's arrival and quickly surveyed the area.

"Sorry I'm late," Castell said, helping himself to the bowl of honey-roasted cashews sitting in the center of the table. "Phone rings and I'm stuck on another important call." He popped a nut into his mouth. "How are you, Dr. James? You look different. I almost didn't recognize you." He shook Steve's hand, then to Valenti, "Jacob Castell."

"Tony Valenti." They briefly shook hands.

Turning back to Steve, Castell asked. "So, what is on your mind, Dr. James?" He reached for another handful of cashews.

"You remember the Captain?"

"Of course. I'll never forget it. You saved all our lives."

"I know what's wrong with him. He has a prion disease like Mad Cow."

"What? Do we have human Mad Cow disease in the United States? Are you sure?"

"Not Mad Cow, Mr. Secretary, but like it. It's caused by a drug."

"Really? What drug?"

"Eden."

CHAPTER 111

President Dixon, followed by Bell, strolled into the Oval Office. John Sullivan, Linda Resnick, Mark Painter, August Crusoe, Treasury Secretary Helen Norris, and Joint Chiefs Chairman General Valenzuela all stood as he entered. Each had been briefed before the meeting about the call from Ambassador Gung. The President, wearing rumpled clothing, took his place in the seat by the fireplace.

"Why all the long faces?" he asked.

Resnick spoke. "I called this meeting because I have bad news. The Chinese Ambassador just called and because of our refusal to negotiate on a compromise over Taiwan's independence, the Chinese have issued an ultimatum. We have twelve hours before they launch their so-called liberation attack, unless we roll back our position to substantially the way it was before Taiwan's independence bid."

"No way—" the President began.

"In addition," Resnick continued, "they are initiating a total embargo of any exchange of people, money, or goods between China and Taiwan and the U.S., in essence, creating financial and human hostages."

Painter leaned forward on the couch, his elbows on his knees. "Mr. President, they've planned this for a long time and have been executing their strategy for the past two weeks. We just figured it out and we're going to get creamed. Not only that, but China's plans include an invasion of Taiwan. We strongly believe they will be successful."

The President frowned at him. "Bullshit. They cannot hold a candle to us. You all have said so many times."

The Secretary of Defense shifted uncomfortably. "That was our belief at the time. We have had to revise our estimations based on new intelligence. We believe they can defeat our carrier fleet where it sits in the Taiwan Straits. We're in their backyard, sir, within range of their coastal missiles and a determined attack by air. The fleet is a sitting duck. Not only that, their invasion strategy is likely to succeed. So we lose the fleet and the Island."

Turning to Resnick, the clearly irritated President questioned, "What's Taiwan's position on all this?"

"Even though they have not changed their position, I believe they underestimate the magnitude of the threat arrayed against them. I think they have an unjustified belief of our carrier fleet's capabilities."

Dixon listened carefully to Resnick, causing her to believe that she had made some impression. "The Taiwanese are still committed?"

"Yes, but—"

"Augie?" Dixon turned to look at his National Security Advisor.

Crusoe nodded. "I'm in agreement with the rest."

"Well, the answer's no. We're not going to change our plans. I have a hard time believing the peril is as great as you say. And the US does not abandon its friends, not on my watch."

"But the Strait's a no-man's land, sir," Valenzuela urged. "At least pull them back behind Taiwan. If we move now, they can be in a more defensible position in twelve hours."

The President shook his head. "No. I'm not going to discuss this again. The people of Taiwan are not going to be shields for the United States Navy. Besides, how can we interdict an invasion force if we're on the wrong side of the Island?"

Linda listened to Valenzuela and Painter. If she were convinced by the information, why wasn't the President? With a sinking feeling, she realized there would be no negotiated settlement to this crisis.

Treasury Secretary Helen Norris spoke. "Even if the military predictions don't come true, our economy is too tightly linked with China's. We'd have another recession on our hands, not to mention the devastation of Taiwan's whole—"

President Dixon had a spasm of twitches in his face and arms. It was worse than anything Resnick had seen before. Everybody stared. After a moment they stopped and Dixon, clearly embarrassed, looked around the room. "I'm sorry," he mumbled. "I think we're done here." He started to stand, but stopped when Sullivan held up his hand.

"Mr. President, Congress is deeply split on your decision, but the vast majority are against it. They are calling for a cutoff of funds for the fleet. This would be political suicide and the end of any possible second term."

The President stared at his Vice President a moment and then answered softly. "This is too important to deviate."

Painter said, "Sir, I have concerns that this may go nuclear. We may face options we don't want."

"Nuclear?" The President's face twitched lightly several times as he spoke. "Really, now. We'd rain so many on them they would never need birth control again. The fleet is armed with tactical nukes? I authorize their use."

Sullivan face paled. "Sir? It would be far better to help Taiwan negotiate a favorable deal now while China thinks we may go to the mat for them. I believe if we tell China we'll return to our support of the previous arrangement, Taiwan maintains their security with our non-invasion guarantee and China has no need to invade."

"Enough," Dixon barked sharply. "I'm done here. I suggest you make sure we are prepared for whatever the Chinese throw at us. I'll be interested in your reports." He stood up and walked out.

Bell looked around the room at the shocked faces. He got up and followed the President out the door.

In the adjoining restroom, he found Dixon washing his face over the marble basin. Bell hesitated, composing his words. "Bob, I have some concern that you are not feeling as well as you should."

"Nonsense, I feel great, never better." Dixon said in a hearty voice. "My last doctor's appointment, as you know, was flawless."

"I'm aware of that, but your concentration is not what it used to be and, uh, you've had these twitches."

Dixon dried his face deliberately before looking at his Chief of Staff. "And you question my judgment."

Bell felt the frustration of the last several weeks begin to bubble up. "You don't seem right to me and frankly Bob, we're all worried about you. What about your sudden spontaneous car rides without the Secret Service?"

Dixon folded the hand towel and replaced it on the bar with care. "Just keeping them on their toes. If they can't keep up with a fifty-nine year old man, then fuck them. I need the space sometimes. I need time away to think without meddling." He dropped his voice. "Time to pray . . ."

Bell struggled with his failure to reach the man with whom he had done so much. Reason and logic, Dixon's strengths, weren't working. What else could he say?

The President raised his voice. "Leave me alone."

"Bob," Bell pleaded, "I'm your friend. Talk to me. Tell me why you won't bend?" But, by then, the President had turned his back. Bell stared at him for a long minute. "You're abandoning your men in uniform to slaughter at the hands of the Chinese. You're their Commander in Chief. By God, act like one and get them out of there. Take the advice of your entire Security Council and make the right decision."

Dixon did not move. "I have made a commitment to Taiwan. As the voice of the United States, that damn well ought to mean something."

"You have a commitment to the people of the United States and to the carrier fleet. China's got a good plan. It won't help your Taiwanese buddies overwhelmed by waves of Chinese troops pouring onto their island after they trample our Navy on the way in. Then what?"

The President, twitching, held onto the sink for support. He still did not turn around and face his friend. "I have made my decision. Please go."

"With all respect, sir, are you still capable of making the right decisions? There's a lot at stake here."

"The honor and commitment of a promise made by the United States is at issue." Dixon's voice was a whisper, barely audible. "My decision stands."

CHAPTER 112

Steve stared at Jacob Castell for a long moment. The Secretary didn't seem to be surprised. It should have knocked him over.

"Eden?" Castell repeated, a bit too smoothly. "Of course not, Dr. James, surely you are mistaken." He sounded like he was trying to convince Steve.

Steve couldn't believe his ears. "I've got proof."

Castell frowned. "That's impossible."

"It's not. We have people dying from a prion infection in their brain and they were all taking Eden. You need to understand that there is a deadly disease out there and the public hasn't a clue that their medicine may be killing them."

"Good God. This is too much." It was more an expression of exasperation than concern.

"It's a lot to swallow, sir, but Dr. Amos Sheridan of Sheridan Labs did the testing. It's here in these reports." Steve slid over a data CD to Castell.

Castell picked up the disk in its sleeve and examined it as if it would speak to him. "I'll have my scientists look into this. I just don't—"

"Dr. Sheridan put Eden in nerve cell cultures and they got prions. Eden acts like a catalyst for the conversion."

"Really." Castell looked plainly unconvinced.

This was going far worse than Steve had hoped. But he had no other course. "There's more, Mr. Secretary. This Eden's disease," Steve paused making sure he had Castell's full attention. "I believe the President has it, too."

This time, the Secretary's eyes widened. "The President?"

"Look, Mr. Secretary, all the cases start out with twitches and impaired judgment. I saw President Dixon on TV. His twitches are the same as the pilot's. You've seen them. And you know about his failing judgment with Taiwan, his policy errors, and the efforts to keep him away from public appearances. You know something's wrong with him. I think it's a prion disease."

Castell started to speak, but Steve continued.

"No, listen. He's going to get worse. It's incurable—all prion diseases are. Mr. Secretary, we are moving towards a possible fight with China with a President who is losing his ability to lead."

Castell didn't respond.

"Get him to his doctor. There's a test that can diagnose him. An MRI or a lumbar puncture. The NIH has a test on CSF for prions. That's all I ask."

Castell's color deepened. "This is too much science fiction. Really, now. The President has an undetected brain disease?" He spoke too evenly, his voice too controlled. "There's no way I'll go barging into the White House and tell the President a doctor saw him on TV and thinks he has a fatal neurological disease. You have no idea what you are asking." Castell held up the disk. "Dr. James, I'll have my top men look at this carefully before I do anything."

Steve's face was flushed. "Not doing something would be worse."

Castell thought a moment before speaking. "Dr. James. I don't have anything else to say about your allegations until my people look at this." Castell took another handful of cashews and palmed them. "But, if there is anything, how do I contact you?"

Steve wrote on a napkin and slid it across to Castell. "Here is my cell phone number. There's not much time, sir. The President's a sick man just like our airplane pilot was. You've got to get him to take that medical test."

Castell stood up and scowled at the arriving waiter who beat a hasty retreat. Pointing at Steve, he admonished, "Dr. James, you keep this crap to yourself. Do not go around spreading this fairy tale." He then wheeled abruptly and strode off.

Steve sank, defeated, into the deep cushions. "Dammit, Valenti. What just happened?"

"Nothing," Valenti spat. "Not a goddamn thing. I saw his eyes. He's a fucking, do-nothing, suck-up Washington bureaucrat. The head on his dick is bigger than the head on his shoulders."

Steve almost chuckled at Valenti and then shifted uncomfortably. "Let's get out of here. This thing is hot."

Steve and Valenti walked out of the Mansion Club and along the damp sidewalk. The drizzle had lifted, but the air was a good bit colder. It felt good after the stuffiness of the bar. Valenti turned his coat collar up and buttoned his overcoat. "Who else can we talk to?"

"Someone who understands medical issues." Steve said. "It's got to be someone who gets it."

"You'd think dickhead who's an MD would . . . Wait." Valenti snapped his fingers. "He's got a doctor, doesn't he?"

"Of course. That's a great idea." Steve paused. "But who is it?"

Down the street, a dark blue Ford Explorer pulled away from the curb and merged with traffic.

Valenti's eyes reflexively tracked the vehicle. He saw the passenger window roll down and a man aiming a pistol. "Down!" Valenti grabbed Steve's arm. Multiple automatic weapon shots erupted from the pistol and Steve jerked as the bullets slammed into his chest.

"Doc!" Valenti shouted. He pulled Steve to the ground and rolled on top.

CHAPTER 113

Steve doubled up in agony. "Damn that hurt. What the hell was that?"

"A machine pistol. Get up, let's go." Valenti pulled a groaning Steve to his feet. The Mansion Club's uniformed doormen had dived for cover when the shooting started. A few pedestrians stared at them from a safe distance.

Valenti tugged Steve back towards the Mansion Club. "C'mon, Doc, we gotta move it."

A Camry jumped the curb aiming right at them.

Valenti shoved Steve out of the way, the car struck Valenti sending him sprawling over the hood. He slid off the passenger's side and rolled to his feet pulling out his pistol. He grabbed Steve who was staggering to his feet and turned to run down the clear sidewalk past parked cars lined up against the curb.

As the Camry skidded to a stop, Mallis jumped out, pistol in hand. Valenti looked back and saw Mallis. He froze. Mallis grinned as he aimed at Valenti.

Steve grabbed Valenti's arm and yanked him down between two parked cars just as Mallis fired.

"What the fuck are you doing?" Steve yelled.

"Jerking off," Valenti mumbled as he looked under the car and saw the cautiously approaching feet of Mallis. He looked around quickly and pointed at the Sticky Fingers Pub fence with its basement landing across the sidewalk from where they hid.

"On three," Valenti whispered, "jump over that railing and run into the pub. One, two three." Valenti shot at Mallis through the windows of the car making him duck. Steve jumped over the fence followed by Valenti. Once on the landing, they scrambled through the door.

The Sticky Fingers Bar was smoky and packed. Massive, blown-up pictures of the Rolling Stones hung on the dark wood-paneled walls. Steve followed Valenti as he shoved and elbowed his way towards the back. One huge rugby type blocked their path. "What's your hurry, mates?" His foul beer breath washed over them.

Valenti looked at the ceiling and pointed up. "Look up there." The man, despite himself, looked up. Valenti punched him in the throat, crumpling him. "Aww, you missed it." They stepped over him as the crowd parted.

Over his shoulder, Steve saw a man enter and push towards them. It was the same man he had seen in the Starbucks! That man had known who he was the entire time. The thought made Steve's skin crawl.

He fled after Valenti through the restaurant kitchen and out the back door. They found themselves in a blind alley facing two other doors, the rear entrances to other stores. Valenti closed the pub door and slid a wooden pallet under the doorknob to hold it closed. They ran towards the open end of the alley, but another man, dressed in a blue denim shirt, came running around the corner holding a pistol.

Valenti fired first, but aimed poorly. It was enough to cause the man to dive behind a dumpster.

Steve heard a sound behind the pub door and it partially opened, cracking the pallet. It would not hold long. Valenti fired at the man peering out from behind the dumpster, and then fired twice at the lock on the nearest door across the alley. He yanked it open and shoved Steve in.

Inside, the room was dark. A small trickle of light through a doorway just ahead drew them towards it. Steve took a quick look around and saw they were in a dusty back room filled with cardboard boxes.

They followed the dim night-light down a narrow hallway and entered a showroom floor. As they sprinted towards the front entrance, they passed faintly lit mannequins dressed in S&M leather. Valenti marveled, "Your buddy Castell sure hangs out in classy neighborhoods. This is top quality stuff."

Crashing noises came from the back. Valenti grabbed a mannequin off a display case and heaved it back at the storeroom door. Someone stitched it with a spray of bullets.

The front door was firmly dead-bolted shut. Steve seized a heavy leather chair and heaved it through the front window, shattering it. Alarms screamed. As Valenti fired several covering shots behind them, Steve dove through the broken window and onto the sidewalk. Valenti leaped through, tripping on one of the display mannequins, landing heavily. Gunfire from inside the shop followed him.

"Run!" Valenti huffed, rolling to his feet and they sprinted down the street.

"What now?" Steve shouted running after him.

A black Capital taxi turned the corner and headed down the street towards them.

"Follow me." Valenti jumped in front of the taxi, a beat-up Crown Victoria, forcing it to slam on its brakes. Steve piled into the back seat and Valenti, brandishing his gun, pulled the driver out of his seat. "Sorry bud. Hop out." Valenti jumped in as Mallis and Joe leaped through the shop window.

A shot shattered the taxi windshield forcing Steve and Valenti to duck. Valenti jammed on the accelerator, the wheels spun on the wet pavement before grabbing traction, when they did, the taxi roared off, fishtailing down the street.

CHAPTER 114

Castell sat in the back seat of his black Lincoln limousine and dialed his cell phone.

"Morloch."

"Hello, Vicktor."

"Jacob, how did it go?"

"You're right; he's a nut case. Totally out there, babbling something about Eden causing prion diseases."

"That's him all right. I hope we can get him to back off soon. If he gets the ear of the press, well, we'll just have to deal with it."

"He seemed so convinced," Castell added.

"Those are the most dangerous kind; absolutely the worst. Anything else?"

Castell knitted his brows. "He told me the President has this prion disease from Eden. He actually gave me a CD with so called proof of his allegations."

Castell did not hear any response from Morloch. He looked at his cell phone display to see if he had lost the connection. "Vicktor?"

"I'm here. Uh, why don't I send someone over to your place tonight to pick up the disk? I'd like my guys to have a look at what he's saying about our favorite product."

"Fine with me. I'll be home in about twenty minutes," Castell answered, thinking that would give him time to copy the disk before handing it over.

"Great, Jacob. I'm glad you called."

"Oh, I almost forgot. He gave me his cell phone number."

"He did?" Morloch sounded surprised. "What is it?"

Castell read him a string of numbers from the napkin. "By the way, I made a few calls and I think I have everything lined up for you. You know, the matter we discussed yesterday."

"Right, right. That's great. When will you know?"

"In a couple of days, but it's really only a formality at this point."

"Excellent. That's really good news."

A taxi screamed past Castell's limo, cutting them off. The limousine driver slammed on his brakes, throwing Castell to the floor. "What the fuck?"

A moment later, a dark blue Explorer sped past Castell's limousine on the wrong side of the street and turned after the taxi. Castell climbed back into the seat, and felt for his cell phone on the dark carpeted floor. "Goddamn idiots."

CHAPTER 115

Valenti weaved through traffic, honking his horn. Oncoming cars swerved to avoid the black Capital Taxi.

"Where are we going?" Steve yelled through the Plexiglas barrier between the seats.

"Somewhere they ain't." Valenti saw Mallis's SUV behind him and turned a fishtailing corner. "Damn, I think he saw us."

Valenti suddenly confronted a knot of cars stopped at a traffic light blocking his path. He looked back through the rear view mirror. "Shit!"

The blue SUV had turned the corner and narrowed the distance. Gunshots shattered the taxi's rear window. Steve dived to the floor. Valenti hit reverse and backed, tires spinning, straight towards the front of the SUV. The massive Crown Vic's rear-end slammed the front of Mallis's SUV, demolition-derby style, shoving it into a parked car.

"Yee ha!" Valenti shouted, shifting back into forward and spinning his tires.

Steve stayed hunkered down, stiff with fright, as he heard more shots, his world reduced to ticking seconds and the dirty black vinyl flooring beneath his face.

Valenti jumped a curb and sped down a sidewalk, scattering newspaper machines and pedestrians. The SUV freed itself from the smashed car and raced down the sidewalk in pursuit.

At the corner, Valenti turned right on 10th Street and floored it.

Steve cautiously sat up and looked out. Ahead, on Pennsylvania Avenue, he saw a large Washington Metrobus crossing their path, making a slow, wide left turn into their lane. Valenti leaned on his horn, but didn't slow down.

The bus driver registered an astonished look as the honking taxi bore down on him. He swerved out of their lane and overshot, hitting a parked Volkswagen Beetle. The front wheel rolled up and over it, flipping the bus onto its side—dead ahead of the speeding taxi.

Valenti swerved into the oncoming lane to avoid hitting the bus and saw another oncoming Metrobus directly ahead. "Shit!" Valenti slammed on the brakes and skidded on the wet pavement. Steve watched helplessly. *There was no room!*

The second bus driver, eyes wide, swerved abruptly to his right, shoving cars off the road. A tiny space opened up between the buses and slowly widened. Valenti, trying to control the fishtailing taxi, aimed for it.

The space slowly open up, but it wasn't wide enough! With a horrendous screeching of metal, the taxi scraped between the two busses, crumpling both sides of the car and showering them with broken glass from the shattered side windows. Then they were through and accelerating.

"Ha!" Valenti hooted in triumph.

Mallis's SUV easily slipped between the two buses, gaining on the taxi. Gunshots punctured the Plexiglas divider behind Valenti. He turned and aimed his pistol wildly out the back.

"Gimme that gun," Steve yelled. "You drive." He grabbed the pistol and aimed at the SUV through the shattered back window and fired. The recoiling gun ripped a piece of skin off his thumb. He howled and shook his hand, sucking the wound. The Explorer raced in so close, he could see the three men inside. He fired again shattering the windshield and the SUV quickly backed off. Mallis leaned out the side window aiming his pistol. Steve ducked as several slugs slapped the car with tortured screeches of metal. Steve rose up to shoot again, but in horror saw a trail of burning gasoline spewing from their gas tank. The Explorer fell back into traffic.

"Valenti!"

Valenti looked over his shoulder and saw the fire. "Time to bail." They hurtled across Constitution Avenue and into the parking lot beside the Smithsonian Museum of Natural History. He skidded into a handi-capped sign as the rear of the taxi burst into flames.

Steve tumbled through his door rolling onto the pavement. Jumping up, he chased Valenti to an aluminum-framed glass door on the side of the building.

"Gimme the gun." Valenti shot the door lock twice and pulled it open, setting off deafening alarms. Steve and Valenti flew through the door and ran down the dark hallway. Valenti huffed as he sprinted. "Security will pour in here in about two minutes and get Mallis and his buds out of our hair."

Steve, with his longer legs, reached the door at the end of the hall first and threw it open, revealing a long workroom with only a couple of the low hanging fluorescent fixtures left on to illuminate the vast area. Rows of sturdy wooden specimen tables covered with bones and tools filled the space, with the walls lined with metal shelves holding chemical bottles and books.

"That door," Valenti pointed. "Let's go." They ran for the opposite side towards the only other door to the workroom when the door behind them burst open. Hearing that, Valenti yanked Steve down behind a wooden specimen table, only twenty feet from their destination. Peering over the table, they saw the group of three pursuers split up and head towards them.

Several security guards burst through the door behind Mallis and his men yelling, "Freeze! Security! Drop your weapons!"

Mallis and his men immediately held up badges, shouting, "FBI! FBI! Clear out. We're in control here. Clear out." They turned back, ignoring the security officers.

The guards, with puzzled looks, huddled.

Mallis yelled over his shoulder, "Clear out." The three guards looked at each other and hesitantly withdrew.

Valenti, who had been watching over the table, sat down. "So much for the cavalry." He checked his gun clip and snapped it back in. "Empty. Figures. We need a diversion." Valenti felt around on the worktable next to him and clutched a long petrified bone and hurled it at a shadowy moving figure. The noise prompted a burst of gunfire and then the room fell silent again.

Steve examined the chemical bottles arrayed on the shelf next to him. They contained a number of familiar chemicals, including glacial acetic acid, acetone, and concentrated potassium chloride in a red plastic squeeze bottle. He spied a liter-sized clear glass bottle labeled 'Ethanol, reagent grade U.S.P' and seized it. *Pure alcohol.* Steve unscrewed the cap and the sharp odor of the ethanol hit his nose. Pulling some paper towels out of a trashcan, he twisted one into the mouth of the bottle. Perfect, he thought, a Molotov cocktail.

Steve leaned over and whispered, "Match?" Valenti shook his head.

Shit! No way to light the damn thing! Steve heard approaching footsteps. The gunmen were right on top of them!

CHAPTER 116

Suddenly, all the overhead lights came on. Steve hurled the alcohol bottle at the light fixture over the closest man's head, shattering the fluorescent bulb and the alcohol bottle. The sparking element ignited the alcohol with a brilliant flash and rained burning liquid down on the gunman.

Mallis screamed as his clothes caught fire and he rolled on the floor. Doug rushed over to help him, slapping at the flames.

"Come on," Valenti whispered, grabbing a pointed rock hammer and dashing for the nearby doorway. Steve, without thinking, snatched the red squeeze bottle and ran hunched over, following Valenti, sliding the thin flask-shaped container into the breast pocket of his suit coat.

Steve and Valenti ran down a short, narrow hallway and through another, smaller door. They sprinted up a narrow flight of stairs and out through a low wooden door, entering the museum itself. A T-Rex skeleton suddenly loomed large in front of them. They were in the dinosaur room.

"Jesus," Steve said, startled.

Valenti shut the door behind them and pointed up the ramp to the second floor balcony. "No time for sight-seeing. Let's bug."

Steve hustled to keep up with Valenti. "Where are we going?"

"Just follow me."

The door behind them opened with a bang followed by running footsteps. Steve's neck tingled with fear, but he didn't dare turn to look.

Several bullets slammed into his back before he heard the gun burst. Knocked off his feet, he sprawled headlong onto the balcony landing, writhing in agony from the impacts on his Kevlar vest. He looked up to see the muzzle of a heavy pistol aimed at his face held by the blue-shirted man from the alley.

"Freeze, FBI. Get up slowly. Keep your hands up."

Despite the burning hot impact sites on his back, Steve held his hands carefully away from his body as he sat up. *Where was Valenti?* Steve stared at the thick, heavy pistol as he awkwardly got to his feet.

The man moved carefully around so that he stood facing the second floor, his back to the balcony railing. He wore a sheer nylon stocking over his face, which blurred his features, but Steve saw that the man's eyes swept the room behind Steve, obviously looking for Valenti. Steve didn't dare look back over his shoulder to see where Valenti might have gone. He just couldn't believe he would vanish like this, but really, what could he do anyway? He had run out of bullets. Why wouldn't he run?

"I've got James. His bodyguard got away," the man said out loud.

Who was he talking to? Steve then saw a coiled plastic tube under the stocking curling up to the man's ear. It was a radio. He must be talking to the men in the specimen room.

"Roger." The man said apparently in response to something he heard.

Steve fought down a wave of helplessness as he stared at the gun. Valenti was gone. He was on his own. What could he do? The man was stout, obviously strong and conditioned. Steve could see no way out. His back screamed like a hundred hornet stings. The sudden reversal of events from Valenti's confident proclamation that they were on the offensive had come to this.

Steve forced himself to think. Surveillance cameras! There must be surveillance cameras. He began to shout. "He's not FBI, he's trying to kill—"

The man's machine pistol slammed Steve's left temple, splitting open his scalp. Steve doubled over clutching his head in pain as blood oozed down his face and hands. He couldn't breathe. Something cold touched his nose and only gradually did he perceive the steel of the pistol barrel pushing his head up. The pressure increased and Steve, still holding his head, raised back up to stare into the man's grinning face.

"There's no sound on the monitors, you dumb neurosurgeon." His voice was patronizing, sarcastic.

Steve, in a flash of anger, spoke very clearly. "It's neurologist, stupid."

"Have it your way, then." The man pressed the gun against Steve's forehead, his eyes intent and focused. "Goodbye, neurologist asshole."

The man's eyes suddenly darted towards something behind Steve. The gun swung away just before a hurtling rock hammer flew past Steve's head and buried its pointed end deep into the skull above the man's left eye. Screaming, the man grabbed at the hammer and staggered backwards. Steve leapt at him, slamming the man against and over the balcony rail.

Steve looked over the rail and watched the man fall hard into the tail of the large T-Rex skeleton. The man frantically grabbed for a handhold, but slipped off and fell to the display base. He landed hard on his face, the hammer still imbedded in his brain, collapsing the wood display platform around him.

The force of the impact unbalanced the tall skeleton and it tilted sideways in slow motion before coming to a precarious halt. The man, cradled in the broken plywood, lay motionless.

Valenti joined him on the balcony and looked down at the tilted skeleton. "It looks like it's grinning," he said. "I bet ol' T-Rex was pretty hungry for a kill after all these years." Valenti picked up the dropped machine pistol and checked it.

Steve leaned on the railing awash with relief. "I thought you'd left me."

Valenti looked at Steve, surprised. "Let's go." Valenti trotted off. "Come on, we can see the Hope diamond on our way."

Steve followed, grimacing with discomfort. "Where are we going?"

"This place will be swarming with police in about three minutes. Time to bug out."

"How?"

A few minutes later, Steve followed Valenti up a concrete ramp adjacent to the National Aquarium and onto the grassy mall near the Ellipse. The cool moist air smelled sweet after the dank, stagnant smell of the underground maintenance tunnel.

Through the trees and the rising mists, Steve could see the brightly lit White House, beautiful in its alabaster luminescence. It seemed so close to him now, closer than it had ever felt, even when, as a schoolboy, he had once stood at the bars and looked at it from across the north lawn. But as close as it seemed to him now, it was still beyond his reach.

The sounds of sirens drawing near quickened Steve's feet. He caught up with Valenti who was moving at a brisk pace across the mall. There they would find a taxi and become invisible again.

CHAPTER 117

Steve sat across from Valenti in a booth at an all night pancake house. He held a wad of damp paper towels to his lacerated left temple. It matched the bullet wound on his right temple. Much to his chagrin, he had begun to shiver uncontrollably.

The white-aproned waitress glided by setting two steaming brown coffee mugs on the table without slowing down.

Valenti slid one across to Steve. "Here. A cup of joe will help."

"What the hell am I doing, anyway? I'm a fucking neurologist. The most boring, nerdiest, fucking doctor there is. What the fuck am I doing, going up against these guys?"

Steve stared out the window. His whole body ached and throbbed. "I want my life back. Great life. Great family. Anne watches out for me. She'd be horrified. 'Steve, what do you think you're doing? Are you out of your mind?'" He slid his free hand under his thigh to stop its shaking. Valenti looked amused, irritating Steve.

"What would your son say?" Valenti asked.

Steve thought about that a moment, enjoying the thought of his family. "Way to go, Dad." Steve's mouth turned up in a flicker of a smile. "Kick some butt. He actually said that."

"Good son. I like him already." Valenti sipped at his coffee, making a face. He tore away the paper covering from a little plastic creamer tub. Pouring it into his coffee he stirred it with a cheap metal spoon.

"I used to get the shakes, too," he said conversationally. "After a tense operation like this, it used to hit me just like you, but I got over it." He poured in a large quantity of sugar from a glass dispenser and stirred it again.

Tasting his coffee, he looked satisfied and took another, longer sip. "Creepy about that woman in the bar, knowing she's going to die and all. And not a damn thing we can do either. What a total waste of a life."

A steaming carafe of coffee appeared and the waitress, balancing three plates in her other hand, topped off Valenti's cup. Steve picked up his mug with both hands and felt its warmth. He gingerly sipped at the strong black liquid, which burned as it went down. "Why did that guy make you freeze up back there?"

Valenti looked disgusted. "Kirk Mallis. Blast from the past."

"You *know* him?" Steve was incredulous.

"Knew him, yeah, at the Bureau. We were both stationed in the district office here and occasionally worked together. So, I guess I knew him." Valenti sipped his freshened coffee and waved his hand as if dismissing the whole affair. To Steve, his casualness seemed forced.

"I heard he started a private agency, you know, with top drawer clients who want stuff and don't really care about how it happens. Valuable, if you know what I mean. Trident's gotta be in tight with him."

"So what happened between you two?"

Valenti's eyes grew distant, guarded. "Nothing to tell."

"Why else would a competent professional ditch his career, move to Phoenix, and take up chasing philanderers? The dots don't connect."

"The dots don't connect?" Valenti's mouth turned up slightly. "You've been watching too many bad detective movies."

As Valenti stared into space, Steve could only imagine the memories he must be dredging up. What possibly could have happened to make a man want to shoot a former associate?

"It's been over almost thirteen years now that I got out."

"Why?"

"What I am about to tell you is confidential. Even Maria doesn't know this." He leaned back and stared off toward the ceiling. "I was born Anthony Fanelli in Rochester, New York. I became an FBI agent, my lifelong dream, you know, apple pie and everything. Saw too many bad detective movies, I guess, but there I was, full of myself, all proud and everything."

"Then reality butted in. We had a shithead for a station chief, too interested in looking pretty and doing everything for political reasons. The whole section hated him. Don't get me started, but morale sucked. He singlehandedly dashed my all-American illusions of saving the world."

"After awhile, I fell off the straight and narrow, you know, taking drug money in exchange for protection. It was easy money and since we were damn well not likely to close down the drug trade, I didn't see much harm in it. We all did it; it was that bad. I struck a deal with some suppliers that kept them somewhat in bounds and they kept me in Calvin Klein's." Valenti looked out the coffee shop window and took a long drink from his coffee.

"Here's where it gets nasty," he said, putting his cup down. "Mallis was an agent in my section. He confronted me about my little deal and wanted a part of it. He threatened me with exposure so I cut him in. In fact, he had cut himself into lots of deals, really, extorting his fellow agents and we all hated him for it, almost as much as we hated ourselves.

"Well, it was just peachy for a while until he began mixing sex with the money, taking turns with the addicts. Not just ordinary sex, mind you, he likes it rough and bloody. I warned him not to mess with that stuff, but he wouldn't listen. Then he ended up killing a woman who pissed him off for some reason. He called wanting my help to dump the body; some slut, he said, who had it coming to her. What got me," Valenti continued, "was her two-year old. The little girl kept trying to wake up her dead mommy."

Valenti stared out the large window again. Steve watched him, enthralled and sickened at the same time. He never would have guessed a story like this. But, Steve realized, it would take something really dark to cause someone like Valenti to walk away from his past.

"That was it," Valenti said, "I couldn't rationalize my bullshit any longer."

"What did you do?" Steve asked.

"I arrested all the dealers and closed down our cushy ride. We got investigated, of course, after a number of them claimed that we had been on the take. While the charges didn't stick, Mallis and I got booted. We had quite a scene, we two, with all sorts of threats that I took literally. So, I left town and changed my name."

"And Mallis has a grudge."

"That he does." Valenti smiled wryly. "I guess I figured we'd run into each other someday. Funny how the world works."

"Is that why you were so reluctant to take my case?"

"You noticed? Well, not the Mallis part, I couldn't have known it would be him; I—" Valenti studied his coffee. "I was rusty and you were high profile." He stopped a long minute before continuing. "Too many years gone by. Harmon called after you two spoke. He said you might call, but I wasn't sure I wanted the case."

"What convinced you?"

Valenti picked up his mug and held it in his two large hands, elbows propped on the table. "The girl, you know, with the Eden thing. Something about her reminded me about that murdered woman. It made me think."

Steve reflected on Valenti's story and the all the melancholy held inside. "You just stopped one life and started all over? Jesus, Valenti or . . . Fanelli?"

Valenti set his mug down carefully, his eyes sad. "Fanelli's gone; he no longer exists. Maria's never even heard the name."

Steve recalled Valenti's explicit instructions on how to disappear and had a pang of guilt for the resentment he had felt towards Valenti in the first few days. Valenti knew what it took—in spades—having not only disappeared himself, but also with no chance of reclaiming his past life. He had been exactly the right person to guide Steve into his hiding. What had happened to his family? His parents or siblings?

Valenti's words broke Steve's thoughts. "But now that Mallis knows I'm in this, well, I'm worried about her and my girls."

"Oh, shit." Steve clapped his hand over his mouth. "I'm so sorry—"

"Stop," Valenti interrupted. "Don't. Look, Doc, I talked with Maria last night. She told me Elisa—you met her at the house that day—"

"Sure, beautiful girl."

Maria just found out she'd been taking a friend's Eden prescription."

"Oh, no—"

Valenti held up his hand "I told Maria to have her stop. I don't know how long she's been doing it, but whatever, this has gotten real personal." Valenti looked at Steve pointedly. "So, *Dad*, we've got some ass-kicking to do."

CHAPTER 118

Anne sat on the overstuffed couch in her parent's den with Johnnie resting his tired head in her lap. She stroked his hair as she reread the printed email message from Steve that had arrived earlier that day.

"Dear Anne and Johnnie, I am fine and well. I miss you both dearly. I think of you constantly and want only to be with you and hold you both for a long, long time. We're making progress, but nothing I can tell you. Be safe and happy. Love, your husband and dad."

Anne tried to imagine what Steve was doing and how he was managing to make progress. He was such a fish out of water with all this. And he probably was not eating or sleeping with all he must be going through.

If only . . . she forced herself to stop thinking like that. It didn't help and it made her crazy. She hated being shunted away, not able to help. If anything, her instincts were to fight for her family, not run away. She was going nuts cooped up at her parent's house, but she had to take care of Johnnie. If it had not been for him, she never would have left Phoenix. What a decision to make, between the two men she loved most.

She wondered if she had made the right one.

CHAPTER 119

Morloch sat in his limousine staring distractedly out the window. He was in a pensive mood that the sultry model, Sandra, sitting next to him couldn't lift. He should be happy about Castell's decision to get him fast-track status, but Mallis hadn't called him about Dr. James. He sipped his champagne automatically without thirst or enjoyment.

"Honey," the woman said in her thin soprano, "lets go to Rocket's and stretch our legs." To make her point, she leaned over pressing her breasts against Morloch's arm. "Please?"

"Not now." He wanted closure on the James.

"But you said we could go." She stuck her bottom lip out unhappily.

"Why don't we go back to my place and I'll call up a massage for you by the Jacuzzi?" That would give him some quiet time.

She seemed to like the idea. "And what about you? I don't want you to be lonely."

He smiled at her and slid his hand up her thigh. "I'm happy if you're happy."

She got a far away look on her face as she pulled his hand even higher under her skirt. "I'd love a massage. Can you get Andrea? She's the best."

"I'll see if I can get her." He flipped the limo intercom switch. "I want to go home."

"All right, sir."

"And call in for a massage. See if Andrea can make it."

"Right away, sir."

Morloch's cell phone buzzed in his pocket. He slid it out and flipped it open. "Morloch," he said before the scrambler clicks had stopped. That would make it Mallis. "Morloch," he repeated.

"Vicktor, he got away. He had a vest on. We gave chase, but he has a—"

"How in the hell did that happen?" Morloch snapped, his tone incredulous.

"I was just telling you. He has a bodyguard, ex-bureau. We shot James, but he wore Kevlar. We chased him, but he got lucky."

Morloch's mouth worked in amazement. "Goddamn it! How did you fuck this up so thoroughly? Why can't you fucking kill him? He's just a goddamn doctor."

"Vicktor," Mallis's voice had an edge that made Morloch stop. "We lost one of ours."

"You did?" Morloch struggled to believe how his professional team could have failed so thoroughly. He forced himself to calm down and think clearly. "What are you going to do?" He had completely forgotten about Sandra sitting next to him.

"I'll need a break. I think he's still in Washington, but I don't know for how long."

"Perhaps I can help." Morloch fished a piece of paper out of his pocket. "I have James's cell phone number."

"Give it to me," Mallis said immediately.

After he hung up, Morloch turned to Sandra and saw her frightened expression. *Damn.* He forced a smile. "Sorry, Honey. Just business." He reached for her, but she shrunk away from him.

"Take me home, please."

"Sure, baby. No problem."

CHAPTER 120

"Linda," Pierre Justice said over the secure phone, "My assistant trade attaché just walked in and handed me a bombshell."

Justice's call from Beijing caught Resnick in her office between a flurry of frustrating calls to the Pacific Rim allies. She had an old cup of coffee in her hand and a bitter expression on her face. "What now, Pierre?"

"Actually it might be a bit of good news."

"We can use something good around here."

"Well, she had lunch at a restaurant with high-backed booths here in downtown Beijing and overheard two men talking at the next table. They were in the military, colonels my attaché thinks, and clearly should not have been discussing the subject she overheard. Maybe they were drunk. Apparently one was bragging about his role in the shut down of the Hong Kong press before the massacre. His friend called him Ye. We did some research and we think he is a Colonel Tanggu Ye of the PLA. Tanggu kept referring to 'The General' so a little more checking and we found he is attached to General Yao Wenfu."

"General Yao! Can you be sure?"

"Well, it gets a little more interesting. He kept referring to someone as the little turtle's egg, a Chinese insult by the way, which puzzled my trade attaché until the name Chow came out. She thinks it was Premier Chow."

"If the General is indeed Yao, that would make sense."

"We thought so, too," Justice chuckled. "Here's the best part. He also said that the turtle's egg didn't have the balls to stand up to the General. Since they were still talking about the Hong Kong affair, I think that Chow was powerless to stop the invasion. I know I am reading a bit into this, but it hangs together with what I know of the two players."

"I'll be damned," Resnick said. "So our guesses were reasonably correct about Yao in ascendancy and Chow as a figurehead."

"I agree, but just today I had a little chat with a highly placed source who said Yao's really twisting a lot of arms to pull off this invasion so quickly without giving diplomacy more time to work."

Resnick shrugged. "I'm not sure how, but I'll keep it tucked away. The bit about Yao behind the massacre is very useful, however. How do we know it wasn't a set up?"

"We thought of that and I think it is unlikely. The restaurant was not one she frequents and the officers were there when she arrived."

"Pierre, can you send me your full report?"

"It's on its way," Justice said. "Otherwise, nothing's changed."

"Thanks, Pierre." She hung up wondering what use Pierre's information might have. Justice's e-mail arrived on her computer and she carefully read it.

"Ursula," she buzzed her assistant, "can you bring in a fresh cup of coffee?"

When Ursula walked in, her boss was staring out the window deep in thought. She hardly noticed Ursula replacing the old cup of coffee. Turning back to her desk she picked up the mug and sipped it as she made up her mind. She then dialed Larry Calhoun in the State situation room. "Larry, I need the number of Ernie Whiteside."

"Huh? Sure. Wait a sec." He paused and then read it to her. "You going to tell me what this is for?"

"Maybe. We'll see."

Hanging up, she dialed the number Calhoun had given her.

CHAPTER 121

"Valenti, I got the President's doctor—it's Dr. Thomas Green." Steve sat at a terminal in the Cyberstop Cafe reading about the President's latest physical in the online archives of the Washington Post. "So how do we get his number?"

"Look it up in the phone book," Valenti mumbled, intent on his own monitor.

"It's unlisted. Doctors do that, you know."

"Maybe not, you never know. Say," Valenti looked up with a sly grin, "you want to drop in on Dr. Blumenthal?"

"Huh?"

"If anybody knows the scoop, he will."

"Think he'll tell us?"

"Maybe."

"Okay . . ." Steve said uncertainly. "How?"

"He lives in Baltimore, near his old Alma Mater, remember? It's only an hour's cab ride away. I even got directions from Map Quest."

Steve caught Valenti's meaning. "Tonight?"

"Why not?" Valenti's expression turned evil. "We'll get there at about one-twenty in the morning. I think a man with a heavy conscience would be awake at that hour."

"Sure, let's do it, but I want Dr. Green's number first."

Valenti typed at the keyboard a moment. Then he smiled. "Yep, my old patented PI tricks came through again."

That pricked Steve's ears. "You got Dr. Green's number? How?"

"Top secret. I start giving away my techniques and I'm out of a job." He jotted the number down.

Steve looked over at Valenti's terminal and then at a smug Valenti.

"I Googled it." Valenti grinned. "Come on, let's ride."

Later, sitting opposite Valenti in the back of a D.C. Radio Flyer Taxi and bound for Baltimore, Steve asked, "How the hell did Mallis know? Where did we go wrong?"

"I've been thinking about that." Valenti shifted uncomfortably on the bench seat. "There is no way they could have traced the call to us. It must have been on Castell's end."

"How would he have known to tell Trident? I didn't mention Eden or the reason for my visit. For all he knew, I was calling to ask him to raise Medicare rates."

"I don't know." Valenti stared out the window as they passed the Maryland City exit. Except for the occasional road sign and passing car on the Washington-Baltimore Parkway, there was nothing to look at. "Unless Trident had tagged him for observation. I wonder if they had him under surveillance or bugged."

"Why him? They can't bug everybody."

"I don't know. What does the Secretary of Health and Human Services do?"

That triggered Steve's previous recollection about seeing Castell's name, but he still couldn't place where. "He's in charge of all Medicare, housing and stuff. Maybe they were scared he would hear about Eden and act on his own."

"Maybe." Valenti didn't look convinced. "There's got to be a relationship or connection we don't know about."

"Can't we go to the police and tell them Mallis is after me?"

"We don't have anything like proof."

"Surveillance tapes from the museum?"

"Good point. You may have noticed they were wearing sheer masks over their faces. It was enough to blur their features and keep them from being positively recognized."

"The SUV they were driving?"

"Stolen and they wore gloves—no prints."

"What about the dead man?"

They probably hauled him off through the same tunnel we left through. It's common knowledge at the bureau."

"DNA from the blood?"

"They have to have someone to match it to."

Steve considered awhile. "Well, at any rate, we now know who's after me."

Valenti's laugh was hollow. "Great, I use my client as bait to flush his assassin. Think of my reputation after this gets out."

"It bugs you, doesn't it?"

"Hell yes. You almost got killed back there."

"The point is," Steve said, "you didn't drop me like a hot one."

"So you'll respect me in the morning?"

Steve considered. "We'll see. The night's not over."

CHAPTER 122

Steve climbed out of the taxi and looked up at a large, upscale house constructed of vintage brick in a pseudo-Tudor style. It was set well back from the street on a manicured lawn lined with rose bushes. No lights shone in the windows, Steve saw. So much for a bad conscience.

Valenti strode up the sidewalk to the front door and rang the bell. "Let's see what happens." He rubbed his hands together in anticipation. They waited. Impatiently, Valenti rang the doorbell again.

Steve backed up and looked at the dark windows. "I hope he's not on vacation somewhere." Then a light came on inside followed by the sound of footsteps. The porch light flicked on and the peephole went dark as someone looked through it.

"What do you want?" a man's voice yelled at them through the door.

Valenti briefly held up his unfolded wallet and yelled, "former FBI, open up." He mumbled the 'former' part. It worked. Steve heard the deadbolt snap. "Oldest trick in the book," Valenti said under his breath.

The opened door framed a bathrobe-clad man with a grandfatherly face, peering at them anxiously through horn-rimmed glasses.

"I'm Anthony Valenti and this is Dr. Steve James, my associate." Valenti walked in as if he had been invited. "Dr. Blumenthal, I presume?"

"Why are you here in the middle of the night?"

"Just wanted to ask you some questions. But first, Dr. James wants to tell you a little story. May we sit down?" It was a practiced delivery.

Steve and Valenti sat on a cloth-covered couch in a spacious, but cluttered den. Large format books lay everywhere, mixed with newspapers and scientific journals. Blumenthal stood beside a large overstuffed chair as if this would be a brief visit.

Steve began. "Dr. Blumenthal, I have evidence that Eden causes prion conversion in human nerve cells."

Blumenthal's face remained impassive. "Is that right?" he said evenly.

"I have also personally examined two patients who are dying of a prion disease and know of a third who died with identical symptoms. They were all taking Eden."

"That correlation doesn't constitute proof." Blumenthal pointed out, crossing his arms.

"In addition," Steve continued, "I have evidence of possibly a hundred more cases scattered across the globe with characteristic clinical findings of this disease." Steve leaned forward. "With virtually all the patients taking Eden. That classifies it as an epidemic."

"Jesus." Blumenthal wilted, sagging into the large chair. "Jesus," he whispered again. It seemed Blumenthal did have a conscience. "I was afraid of this," he finally said. "I prayed it would never happen."

"Tell us what you know."

"I don't know where to begin. A hundred . . . my God." Blumenthal closed his eyes for a long time. "It started," he began, "when Vicktor Morloch invested a large sum of venture capital into my startup company before it became Trident . . ."

A soft buzzer disturbed a Mallis and Associates technician from his magazine. Rolling his chair over to the monitor, he saw a priority message flashing on his screen. "Morloch" was the key word. He clicked his mouse and Blumenthal's voice came through his headphones.

". . . we needed the cash. Morloch insisted on control and I stupidly let him. I was desperate, you know. We were ready to liquidate, but he could rescue the company and keep all its patents intact. It was too good to pass up, but once he took over, my word, everything changed. He fired most of our in-house research staff and hired a couple of his own. They farmed out all our studies to outside vendors. What did he know about drug research? But we were finally making progress and I thought things were going okay. I signed reports and the stock price did okay. Then the mouse brains came back with prions. I never actually saw that report, only the ones that Morloch actually showed me but I knew just the same. All those reports he had represented it to me as valid, I believed them and I signed off. But a—"

The technician picked up a phone and tapped a number.

"Mallis."

"Priority, Mr. Mallis. From mister, uh, Doctor Blumenthal's house. I'm patching you in." The technician clicked another button and hung up, the transfer complete.

Mallis sat at his office desk and listened to the message, the handset pressed to his ear by his shoulder. He was stripped to his underwear with Silvadine burn cream smeared on the bright red and blistered areas on his face, torso, and arms. As he listened, his eyes narrowed. "It's James and Fanelli," he said to Doug, who had been cleaning up the medical supplies. "Blumenthal's squealing like a pig. Let's move."

". . . I was not in Morloch's inner circle, see, and I only learned about the prions from a slip-up by Dr. Tobias, one of his hires. By then, I didn't know much of what was happening in the company I founded—everything went through Morloch, everything, you know? When I found out, I confronted him with it. Look, in other companies, this sort of result would have triggered many more studies in tissue culture and in other animal species to understand the nature of the problem. It probably would have killed the drug. I mean, he had a potentially lethal problem here."

Steve and Valenti listened intently to Blumenthal as he paced in front of the brick mantelpiece fireplace.

"You know what he said? 'Fuck off, Blumenthal,' I couldn't believe it. I was Chief Scientist and founder and he just—" Blumenthal shook his head.

"Why didn't you tell someone?" Steve asked.

Blumenthal sighed. "This is where the nightmare really began. Morloch warned me that I could go to jail since I had signed the forged federal reports. This sounds so asinine now in retrospect. I was so stupid and scared."

"Is that what really kept you from going to the police?" Valenti asked.

Blumenthal stared at Valenti, then looked away. He stood up and walked over to the fireplace where some hot embers still smoked slightly. Blumenthal picked up his poker and pushed it into the ashes stirring them to renewed brightness. Ever so quietly, he answered. "In my heart, I thought it would work. I wanted my baby to succeed. I had invented it and I wanted it to make a difference. It was going to change the world, you know? Maybe even a Nobel. Maybe the pre-clin results wouldn't affect humans—like Scrapie only affects sheep, right?"

He turned and looked almost pleadingly at Steve and Valenti. "It was all built-up lies and rationalizations, but I had a lifelong dream that was teetering on disaster. It's hard to let go of something like that." He slumped into a chair. "Eventually, I would have told someone. It started getting to me, the possibility people would get prions and die. I guess Morloch knew that and had this scary guy show up."

He stared up at the ceiling. "I still remember that day like it was yesterday. He told me what would happen if I said anything. Real quiet like, you know, confident and rock certain that I would die if I told anyone. I didn't dare talk after that. No way. But, a hundred . . ."

Steve was struck by the agony of this brilliant scientist whose past was unraveling in front of him. "What is the real reason for the new formulation we are doing trials on now?"

"I'm not in on it; not really. But the official word is that it's an improved version that works the same way as Eden. It's supposed to work faster and is better absorbed." He shrugged. "The company line."

"Is it to avoid prion conversion?" Steve prodded.

"Probably, but I don't officially know. I ran a couple of tests on my own on it, in secret of course, and it didn't kill the cultures, but I couldn't tell for sure without an electron microscope or special reagents, which I didn't have and didn't dare request, so it was inconclusive."

"Do you have any proof that Morloch did all this?" Valenti circled for the score.

Blumenthal took his time answering as he stood up and jabbed again at the embers making the fading coals spark and snap. "I wish I'd never taken any of Morloch's goddamn money."

CHAPTER 123

Mallis and Doug, dressed in black body suits, trotted silently up to Blumenthal's house. Doug picked the lock and they slipped in, latex gloves on and pistols drawn. They found Blumenthal sitting at the kitchen table, his back to them, sipping from a coffee mug, apparently lost in thought. He hadn't heard them come in. Doug moved on to search the rest of the house.

After checking around the kitchen, Mallis grinned. "Samuel, old boy, how are you?"

Blumenthal whirled around, his face quickly drained of color. "Jesus! What are you doing here?"

"You've been a bad boy, Samuel. Where are they?"

Blumenthal stood up to face him. "Who?" His voice shook.

Mallis kicked Blumenthal in the groin. Blumenthal grunted and fell to the floor, doubled up with pain.

"Where are they?"

"They're gone," he gasped. "You're too late."

"Goddamn it. What did you tell them?"

Hatred narrowed Blumenthal's eyes. "Everything, you bastard, the whole story. They're going to hang you. I gave them all the evidence. All the stuff I'd accumulated on Vicktor's and your bullshit over the years. They're going straight to the FBI with it."

Mallis paled and then kicked Blumenthal in the ribs. "Fucking bullshit. I've been over this place a dozen times. There's nothing here."

"No sign of them," Doug trotted back to report.

Mallis held out his hand. "Dr. James's gun, please."

Doug handed Mallis a plastic Ziploc bag containing the pistol. As Mallis pulled the gun out, Blumenthal's bravado evaporated. He crawled backwards until he backed into a wall and could go no further.

CHAPTER 124

"Blumenthal has a story and his speculations, but no evidence." Valenti sighed. He and Steve sat in the back of the taxi heading back to Washington, DC. "Nothing we can pin on Morloch. I hate to leave empty handed."

"Me, too. At least we got some validation."

"Yeah, that." Valenti yawned. "Right now, I need some nourishment. We haven't eaten since lunch."

They fell silent, fatigue creeping in. Steve leaned his head back on the blue vinyl seat and closed his eyes. Something Blumenthal said about filing the reports with the FDA nagged him. Suddenly his eyes flew open. *Castell*. He was head of the FDA when Eden was approved. Castell's name had been on the signature page of the Summary Basis of Approval and he had completely forgotten it. He could have influenced Eden's passage somehow.

The car radio broke Steve's thoughts. "We interrupt this program to bring you a special news bulletin." The driver turned it up. ". . . Earlier this evening, the White House announced that China's ultimatum for their attack on the U.S. Pacific carrier fleet expires at seven o'clock this morning. The administration reports the USS Eisenhower and USS Stennis carrier battle groups, stationed in the Taiwan Straits, are ready for any assault from China."

Steve and Valenti stared at each other.

"Shit," Valenti said as they both checked their watches. It was three forty-six.

"...our ABC news consultant, retired Rear Admiral John Buckingham, says there is no maneuvering room for the U.S. fleet or their fighters and with an all-out point-blank assault from Mainland China, there are likely to be heavy casualties. Admiral Buckingham says the destruction could be the largest Navy loss since Pearl Harbor."

"Meanwhile, at the White House, the President still stands firm in defiance of China's ultimatum. The President maintains that the freedom loving people of Taiwan should not be subject to China's oppressive rule. There is no word of last minute negotiations with the Chinese to avert the conflict.

"U.S. government sources tell us that China appears to be readying its forces. Chinese Ambassador Gung has told ABC news that they desire to settle this conflict through diplomacy and peaceful means and he places blame squarely on President Dixon for provoking this conflict by his refusal to negotiate."

"Dammit," Valenti said. "We've got to get to Dr. Green."

Steve's throat tightened as he contemplated the deadline. "How could they have done this so fast? Doesn't it take months to prepare for this kind of assault?"

"Normally, but remember, when you're the underdog, you do the unexpected. China may be about to pull off a huge tactical victory and we learn the goddamn lesson."

"Wait," Steve said. "Listen."

"... Bizarre break-in and gunfight in the Smithsonian Museum of Natural History between the FBI and two armed men. One FBI agent was killed during the gun battle..."

Anne, wearing one of her mother's nightgowns, stared out the second-story bedroom window into the back yard. A cold front was blowing in fresh snow, creating swirling patterns in the glow of the rear porch light. It wouldn't last past noon at their altitude, she knew, but the mountains would get a fresh layer. She looked forward to seeing it in the morning. She sighed as her thoughts returned to Steve.

Anne got up nightly at this time in a routine she both hated and appreciated for the solitude. Her parents did their best, but they couldn't bring Steve home.

How was he doing? His last message said he was well and making progress but that was all. It was unsatisfactory, like getting a birthday card with only a signature inside.

The clock radio was tuned to the news, her habit now. Music isolated her and she needed to feel connected. Tonight, however, she almost turned it off with the monotonously repetitive reports about the pending attack on the U.S. carriers. Still, she listened with half an ear.

Then something else caught her attention, something new. ". . . with notable destruction of precious artifacts during the confrontation, including the large Tyrannosaurus Rex skeleton for which the Smithsonian Museum is famous. Amazingly the two suspects are still at large. They have been identified as Dr. Steven James of Phoenix and—"

She whirled around and gasped. "Steve!"

Steve and Valenti looked at each other in alarm.

". . . Anthony Fanelli also known as Anthony Valenti also of Phoenix. Police are actively searching for them."

"Dr. Green's number—now," Steve said.

"All right, all right." Valenti fished in his shirt pocket. "I just wanted to savor the moment."

He read off the numbers as Steve punched them into his cell phone. The phone rang until a coarse voice growled into the earpiece, "Yeah?"

"I'm Dr. Steven James. The President's sick and I know what's wrong with him."

"What?" The voice changed to surprise. "Who the hell are you?"

"Steve James, a neurologist. I think I know what's causing the President's myoclonus and failing cognition. You're Dr. Green, right?"

"Yeah. Now tell me what you think you know."

A computer monitor beeped in Mallis and Associates computer room. In response, the technician donned a set of headphones and tapped on the keyboard, muttering at the computer. He heard a voice say, ". . . Do you know anything about prion diseases?"

Another voice replied. "Shit. Do you think that's what he's got?"

"Yes, but it's a new variant that—"

The technician dropped his headphones back around his neck and picked up a telephone. Punching a speed dial number, he listened to the ring three times.

"Mallis."

"Another priority, Mr. Mallis. It's a Dr. James on his cell phone. It's from that number you gave me earlier. Busy night, sir."

"Just play the damn call," Mallis snapped.

"Certainly," the technician said pleasantly and punched a few buttons. "From the top."

Mallis lowered his cell phone thoughtfully. *The White House?* That raised the stakes tremendously. He itched at the prospect of killing Dr. James under the Feds' noses, especially in revenge for Joe. He stuck his head into Blumenthal's plush, wood paneled study. "We're done here." Doug looked up from Dr. Blumenthal's computer and nodded.

Back in the kitchen, Mallis checked Blumenthal's body one last time before they left. In five minutes the house would go up in a gas explosion that would consume any hidden evidence Blumenthal might have kept on Eden. Dr. James's gun was back in it's Zip-loc, but would be deposited in a dumpster or garbage can about a block away to be found if the police were doing their job. Doug joined him and they left through the front door. Getting into their Explorer, they drove off, back towards Washington and the White House.

CHAPTER 125

Dr. Green absently hung up the phone, reeling from Dr. James's fantastic story. The call initially had sounded like a crank, but the more Dr. James had explained the details of this strange disease, the more it made sense—and it pulled most of the pieces together. A prion disease, from Eden yet! He had never prescribed Eden for the President, nor would he. And Robert knew he would never prescribe it. That would be a key piece of evidence and a test of Dr. James's story. The clock radio dial glowed 4:01 and with the Chinese ultimatum due to expire at seven . . .

Dr. Green felt a chill run through him. An incapacitated man was possibly leading the country.

Wrapping himself in a bathrobe, he went to his study and looked up a number in his Rolodex. He dialed the White House Secret Service.

"Davenport."

"Aaron, it's me, Tom Green."

"Dr. Green, what's up at this time of the morning?"

"I need a piece of information and I believe you or Elise can tell me."

"What is it?" Davenport sounded cautious.

"I need to know if the President is taking a drug called Eden. I'm not prescribing it for him, but he might be getting it from someone else. I need to know this immediately, please."

"Hmm. I don't know, but one of his personal detail might."

"Can you find out right away?"

"I sure can. I'll get one on the horn now."

"Thanks." Dr. Green was placed on hold listening to a military band play lively, irritatingly upbeat marches. He mentally reviewed Robert's last office visit. It had been normal, excellent really, with the cholesterol back to normal. Then it hit him—the weight. Robert had lost almost thirty pounds. He remembered asking Robert about it. What was his answer? Oh, right. He said he was running for re-election. No answer at all. He had let it pass at the time but now . . . If Robert were on Eden and if his myoclonic twitching were the same as the others, then Dr. James was probably right. Robert might actually have a prion disease. Shit.

Dr. Green was startled by Davenport's voice. "I spoke to the detail. They don't really go through his personal effects, so they don't know."

"I've got to find out, Aaron."

"I figured. I sent a maid up to the First Lady's drawing room to get her on the phone. I presume you can't ask the boss himself."

Dr. Green felt like Benedict Arnold. "No, I can't."

"I think I understand."

"Have you noticed anything?"

"I can't really speak about that, Dr. Green. Sorry."

"Of course." He impatiently drummed his fingers on the desk while he waited.

"Dr. Green," Davenport presently announced, "Mrs. Dixon is on the line. I'll patch you in."

There were a couple of clicks and then Elise Dixon said, "Hello?"

"Elise, it's me, Tom Green."

"Tom, what's going on?"

"Elise, I'm so sorry to bother you at this time of the night, but do you know if Robert is using Eden?"

"Of course he is. Why wouldn't you know? Didn't you give it to him?"

Dr. Green's throat tightened. "No, I didn't. I wouldn't, not the President."

Elise didn't say anything for a minute. "Well, I don't know where he got it then. He told me you gave it to him."

"How long has he been taking it?"

"At least a year, possibly more. I really haven't paid much attention. Why is it so important?"

"He hasn't been himself, has he?"

"No," she said slowly, "he hasn't. I thought it was stress. Is it something else?" Her voice now worried. "What is it?"

"I'm not sure, but I think there is a possibility Eden is causing a problem. Has he been complaining of headaches?"

"Yes, bad ones."

"And his appetite? Taste?"

"Vanished. I thought it all was from stress."

"Has he been having delusions or nightmares? Is there anything he is particularly afraid of?"

Elise didn't say anything for a long moment. "Yes, and it's getting worse. What is it? Can you help him?"

He's got it, Dr. Green concluded. His old friend had all the symptoms Dr. James said he would. "I'm sorry, Elise. I just spoke with a doctor who has more experience with this than me. I want him to see Robert, tonight, you know, with this China thing."

Dr. Green next called two other hospitals, names he had gotten from Dr. James, and spoke to the nurses taking care of Captain Palmer and Shirley Rosenwell. The descriptions of their symptoms were exactly the same as Dr. James had described. The nurse taking care of Rosenwell also knew Dr. James personally and answered questions about him to Dr. Green's satisfaction. As a final check, he called a neurologist friend, an expert on Cruetzfeld-Jacob, and asked her a series of questions.

Finally assured that Dr. James was right, he picked up the phone and dialed Vice President Sullivan.

CHAPTER 126

The Secretary of State sat at the oversized mahogany conference table in the White House situation room. It was crowded with the Security Council members, the remaining cabinet members, and assorted VIPs. Their aides crowded the side-tables lining the walls, many with laptops glowing and fingers flying over keyboards. Dominating the room was a massive projection TV screen flanked by other flat screen monitors.

Joint Chief's Chairman, General Valenzuela was accompanied by a contingent of military experts and technicians, further crowding the space. He walked around introducing Captain Kroller, who had commanded the USS Eisenhower during its last tour. Kroller would explain the details of carrier operations to the Security Council and President. Others would help decipher the events on the projected displays of the theatre for the President and his advisors. President Dixon was not in attendance and Resnick did not know where he was. She had expected him to be here and felt a little miffed that he was not.

An intern walked over to Vice-President Sullivan and whispered in his ear. Sullivan stood up and walked out.

Resnick had personally appealed to Ambassador Gung for a delay in the attack. Gung had curtly informed her that if there were an immediate and substantive movement away from support of Taiwan's independence they might consider a change in their attack plans. In China, Pierre Justice was still unable to get an audience with Premier Chow, General Yao, the Minister of Foreign Affairs, or any senior Chinese official. Even the Swiss ambassador, who tried to make a last minute plea for restraint, could not make any headway.

The United Nations Security Council had met in an emergency session and the US ambassador had endured a blistering attack from China's UN ambassador for unacceptable meddling in the internal affairs of a sovereign nation. This was an internal civil matter, he had said, and called for the U.S. to withdraw its forces immediately. A certain veto from China stymied the Security Council from considering a resolution against initiation of hostilities. China had the momentum and was not going to squander it.

Taiwan's Ambassador Zhou had told Resnick that his country had been similarly informed and that internal discussions were underway. So far, Taiwan had not reacted to the new intelligence the U.S. had provided them regarding China's attack strategy and its likelihood of success. Taiwan must believe the U.S. would somehow triumph in the defense of their island—or that China was bluffing. Even so, and perhaps belying their own testaments, Taiwan's military was scrambling up to full readiness, marshalling their reserves, and mobilizing their own Civil Defense.

Following the ultimatum, Congress passed a resolution supporting the men in uniform, but in a blow to the President, they passed another resolution against the deployment and a warning that funding would be cut off in twenty days if the fleet were still in the straits. Congressmen from both sides of the aisle gave impassioned speeches against the President's actions, with only a few willing to publicly defend him.

Resnick's eyes were drawn to the large flat screen panels on the wall opposite her that displayed the position of each ship and aircraft in the theatre. It was a spectacle of the American technological capability but, ironically, the prominently exhibited US carrier fleet was in serious jeopardy from the less sophisticated Chinese.

Just before she had left her office for the White House, Ernie Whiteside had called to notify her of a pending story on CNN. She had quickly turned on her TV and watched an exclusive report about an intercepted conversation from a Colonel Tanggu Ye about General Yao. Citing unnamed sources, the report was faithful right down to the comment about Premier Chow not having the "male endowment" to stand up to General Yao. Resnick smiled. It was perfect. With luck, it would give some Chinese officials cover to bolt from Yao's camp and support Chow.

She wrote a quick analysis and arranged for it and a videotape of the story to go to each of the cabinet and National Security Council members.

The linchpin in the whole situation, however, was President Dixon. As long as he persisted in his support for Taiwan, there would be no stopping the attack.

Sullivan walked back in and caught her eye.

"Linda, let's get the Cabinet into Conference Room C immediately." He turned to Arthur Slywotsky the White House Counsel. "Art, I want you to come as well."

Within minutes, the Cabinet members assembled around the conference table behind a closed door. Sullivan cleared his throat. "I just got a call from Dr. Thomas Green, the President's physician. Art, I need you to review and advise us on Congressional Directive 112. Can you do that immediately?"

Resnick sucked in her breath. That was the directive that described the process by which two physicians evaluated the President for incompetency.

CHAPTER 127

Robert Dixon paced in an empty Oval Office, his stomach churning in indecision and anxiety. Ever since the Security Council's meeting, he had obsessed over their recommendation to change course on Taiwan. His face twitched and his dreaded vision crowded back in on him. *Wait*, what had he been thinking about? His continually wandering mind made it hard to concentrate. *Oh, yes*, should he back off supporting Taiwan's independence? If he did, it would screw his Taiwan friends who were counting on United States' support. But what if China actually invaded? Taiwan would lose everything. It was so hard to think clearly. He must pray.

As Dixon knelt, the curved walls played tricks on him, like they were closing in. Despite placing his trust in God, he felt his breathing getting shorter and his pulse rising in that panicked feeling he feared. He had to get some fresh air.

Outside in the colonnaded walkway overlooking the Rose Garden, Dixon felt the bracing coolness of the autumn air and his breathing slowed. He sat on the edge of a bench under the walkway and after another prayer, tried again to sort through his options.

Even with the new information about China, he had stayed with his earlier decision, relying on it because he had made it when his thoughts were clear. Dixon didn't trust his own judgment now. What had happened to him? He felt his own incapacity, caused somehow by that China massacre. It embarrassed and frightened him to think he was unable to lead his country through a crisis. His predecessors had all seemed to come through somehow. Why not him? He must pray again.

"Good morning, sir."

Startled, Dixon jerked in surprise. Turning around, he saw his personal White House aide, Wesley Rojas. "Oh, Wesley. I didn't see you."

"I'm sorry, sir." He held up a small, white, paper pharmacy bag. "I just came on duty and I brought you another inhaler. I was on my way to put it into your desk when I saw you sitting here."

"Oh, thanks. Sure, go ahead and put it in there."

"Certainly, sir." Rojas turned and walked into the Oval Office, leaving Dixon in the semi-darkness.

As Dixon sat, he became aware that the roof of the walkway overhead was closing in on him. He jumped to his feet, intending to walk out into the Rose Garden and get away from the building altogether. With the Chinese deadline looming, he had to think clearly now—there wasn't much time left. Wesley came out of the Oval Office and turned back to the main house. Seeing Rojas triggered a thought. Of course! It would make everything all clear. He struggled briefly with his promise to Elise, but decided he had to take the risk just this once.

He called out to his aide. "Wesley?"

Rojas turned back around. "Yes, sir. What can I do for you?"

Dixon walked towards his aide. "Did you drive your car here?"

CHAPTER 128

Threading their way past teams of TV camera crews, Steve and Valenti walked towards the brightly lit north White House guardhouse. A figure in a tailored tan suit emerged from the guardhouse and walked out to meet them.

"Dr. Green?" Steve said extending his hand to the large-framed black man.

"Good to meet you, Dr. James."

"Steve, please."

Dr. Green's face had laugh lines around his eyes, but tonight, in the harsh floodlights, his face was creased in worry. "I'm Tom."

"Tom, my associate, Mr. Anthony Valenti."

Dr. Green shook Valenti's hand. "I called ahead. Vice President Sullivan and the cabinet are expecting us. When I told them who you were, the Secret Service insisted you turn yourselves in for the break-in at the museum."

"They don't trust us?" Valenti deadpanned.

Steve smiled despite the tension. Valenti had told Steve to expect an arrest. "I understand. But is everything else as we discussed on the phone?"

"Exactly. We're both to examine the President. If he is mentally incompetent, the cabinet can decide to replace him with Vice President Sullivan."

"And that's why I'm here."

"I need your help with your knowledge of this Eden's disease." Dr. Green rubbed his forehead. "I've known Robert since college. I can't believe it's come to this." His shoulders drooped.

Steve watched the sadness wash over Dr. Green. "I didn't realize you were friends. I'm really sorry."

"The Vice President's waiting. They're in the situation room watching this thing unfold. I spoke with him in detail and he's readied the cabinet."

Steve looked at his watch. "We should go. We've got less than two hours."

"Right." Dr. Green led them to the guardhouse where a solid, square-shouldered man stepped out wearing the ubiquitous navy suit. A clear plastic tube coiled up the side of his neck.

"Agent Rhodes," Dr. Green said, "this is Dr. James, and Mr. Valenti."

"Gentlemen, I am with the Secret Service. You understand I must handcuff you before we enter." He shook his head as if apologizing. "This whole situation is highly unusual."

"You realize what's at stake here?" Steve asked.

"Yes, sir. I have a nephew on a destroyer out there." Rhodes cuffed Steve and Valenti, leaving their hands in front, and led them into the guardhouse to collect their visitor badges and then through and into the White House compound.

President Dixon walked rapidly alongside Wesley Rojas followed by an agitated Agent D'Agostino. "Come on, Wes," Dixon said, "I've only got about an hour before I have to be back." He was happy with his plan. He would only stay a few minutes and he would come back, but he had to hurry.

"Sir," D'Agostino pleaded, not believing the President was doing this again. "Please wait for the escort. They'll be here in just a few minutes."

The President ignored him and slid into the front passenger seat of Wesley's dark green Ford Taurus. D'Agostino scrambled into the back seat as the car started, noting, with some disgust, candy wrappers and children's grunge on the seats. He radioed the security base not noticing the car doors automatically lock as Rojas shifted into drive. Within moments they passed through the tunnel and the guard gate and drove out into the dark Washington morning.

President Dixon eased back in the seat and settled in for the ride. He cracked open the window and took a deep breath of the cold fresh air. Morning produce and newspaper delivery trucks broke the pre-dawn silence with their early rounds. A few early risers were commuting in to work, the wet streets reflecting their car lights.

D'Agostino radioed their position, although the transponder the President carried with him would give the security base an exact fix of the President's location. "Foxhound heading north on Connecticut Ave."

He could see the President whispering to himself. D'Agostino leaned forward to see better. Was the President—praying? That must be it. He had been doing that frequently the last couple of weeks, every time there was an important decision, it seemed. What had gotten to the President? D'Agostino reflected on his private discussions with Rhodes. The ordinarily crisp and decisive President had let this China thing eat him alive to the point that his dress and mannerisms had become unprofessional.

"Wes, turn left here," Dixon instructed.

"Sir," D'Agostino asked, "Where are we going?"

"You'll see in a few minutes."

The agent's eyes continually sweeping for threats called in another position report. "Foxhound just turned left onto Mass. Ave."

"Roger," base replied, "The escort just pulled out and should catch up with you in two minutes."

"Roger. I could use the help."

"Sorry, D. He caught us off guard this time. It's been over a week since he pulled this."

And this morning of all mornings, thought D'Agostino. Soon, the escort would guide Wes's car back to the White House and another nightmare would be over.

CHAPTER 129

Steve, Dr. Green, and Valenti walked into a side entrance of the White House and down a flight of stairs. Within moments they entered a bare, white-walled waiting room with linoleum floors. "This is the security office," Rhodes explained. "Wait here." He entered an adjacent room through a swinging door. The door did not close entirely and through the opening, Steve could see it was crowded with people, many in front of electronic displays and monitors. A salt and pepper-haired man with a military bearing greeted Rhodes, but Steve couldn't hear what they were saying. A moment later the man emerged and greeted them.

"Hello, gentlemen. I'm Aaron Davenport, Chief of the Presidential Security Detail. The President has temporarily left the White House."

"When will he be back?" Steve asked, puzzled. He had thought they would be shown right in to see the President.

Davenport smiled the smile of a man who dealt with uncertainties. "Soon."

D'Agostino scanned the tall ash and pine trees and the bushes and dense shrubbery of Rock Creek Park that lined both sides of the road looking for any suspicious activity. Sitting in the back seat restricted his field of view and exposed the President to sniper fire through the windshield. The overgrowth could easily harbor someone unseen until too late. The whole situation was at once ludicrous and aggravating.

Wesley slowed down almost to a stop behind a slow moving street sweeper. He drummed his fingers impatiently on the steering wheel.

"Can't you pass him?" the President asked.

"I can't see past him well enough, sir. Sorry." He did not see the series of twitches that began to shake the right side of the President's cheek. Neither did D'Agostino.

The President suddenly flung open his door and leaped out of the car, plunging into the dense vegetation of the park. D'Agostino, caught off guard, tried to open the car door, but it was locked. He slammed his shoulder painfully against it, but it still wouldn't open. Frantically, he pressed the door unlock button without any effect. Then he figured out why.

"Wesley! The child door lock! Unlock me!"

"Jesus!" Wes exclaimed, fumbling for the automatic door lock control.

"Wes!"

"Got it!"

D'Agostino burst from the car in a dead run towards the woods. "Mr. President!" he shouted, but the street cleaner's diesel engine and its brushes scraping the pavement made it almost impossible to hear anything. He neither saw nor heard any sign of the President. In mounting alarm, he scrambled through some brush and listened again. "Mr. President!" Where was he? He whirled around trying to penetrate the dark with his eyes. Still nothing.

He ran in the direction he thought the President had gone, pushing and shoving through the thick underbrush, making a tremendous racket. He stopped again to listen. Still, no sound of a person. D'Agostino tore through the vegetation onto a dark mown area, crisscrossed by sidewalks and gravel paths. There was no sign of the President, no footsteps, and no sound. Which way had he gone?

Oh my God, he thought as the reality crashed down on him. *I've lost the President.*

CHAPTER 130

"Base, Foxhound is ESO. Repeat, Foxhound is ESO." Steve could hear the sound of a radio through the door to the control room.

At that moment, the door opened as an agent walked out past Steve. Steve slid his foot against the door, preventing its closure.

"He ran into Rock Creek Park, and—" They could hear the voice on the radio more clearly now. "I've lost contact. Request RDF."

A stunned silence gripped the room. He heard Agent Rhodes mutter, "Jesus, D."

"Last known location," the voice continued, "is Rock Creek Park and Mass. Avenue, approximately 4200 block. Do you have a transponder signal?"

All eyes stared at the display for a long moment before the dispatcher replied. "It's on Mass Avenue, but it's not moving. It's in the car."

"Okay, Grant, Tolleson," Davenport shouted. "RDF, Rock Creek. Get going."

Steve pressed against the wall as two agents barreled past at a full run yelling into their radios. Rhodes looked like he wanted to leave with his fellow agents. Davenport turned to him. "You go too. And," he pointed at Steve, "take them with you."

Rhodes strode out, his face ashen.

Steve held up his handcuffs. "Can't you take these off?"

Rhodes pushed him toward the exit. "No time. Let's go." He led them at a trot into the White House foyer where several more dark suited men and women ran past. "Follow me," Rhodes said.

"ESO? RDF?" Steve asked, jogging behind Rhodes.

"Basically get everyone onto the scene ASAP."

A side door opened and two navy-suited men emerged, followed by a tired looking woman that Steve recognized as First Lady Elise Dixon. She spotted Dr. Green.

"Tom." They stopped and she embraced him.

Dr. Green clasped her hands. "Elise, I'm so sorry."

She wiped her tears with a tissue. "I wish there were some other way."

"He's not well, Elise."

"I know. I just hope you can do something for him." She hugged him again. "Go. You need to be out there when they find him." She cast a questioning glance at Steve and his handcuffs as she walked past.

CHAPTER 131

Mallis and Doug, their forged press badges around their necks, mingled with the news crowds outside the White House. They had their earpiece radios tuned to the assigned Secret Service frequency. The radio, an unauthorized version of the one the Service carried, decoded the scrambled communication signals for them. Listening, Mallis wore a puzzled frown. Many of the Secret Service abbreviations and acronyms were different from the FBI and were unfamiliar to him.

He scanned the guardhouse and the White House beyond with his night vision binoculars. They were a special, classified model restricted to the military and intelligence agencies. Through them, he saw a convoy of dark government sedans pour out of the White House driveway and scream into the overcast morning, the faces of the occupants visible through the binoculars.

What was going on?

As he watched, several more cars sped out through the gate. He heard a reporter next to him talking about the President having left the White House. Why was that such a big deal? Then more Secret Service calls came in. They were arriving at Rock Creek Park and doing something, again, unintelligible because of their acronyms. Doug, listening to the same radio chatter looked at Mallis. "They're looking for someone."

"Who?" Mallis asked. "Can you tell?"

"Someone called Foxhound."

"Foxhound?"

Doug's eyes blazed as he figured it out. "It's the President."

Mallis's mouth dropped. The President was missing in Rock Creek Park? Amazing.

Now where was Dr. James?

Another car pulled out of the White House driveway. Instinctively Mallis looked at it through his binoculars. *Yes!* Fanelli sat behind a driver, who, he guessed, was a Secret Service Agent. There were two unrecognizable people on the other side of the car. Probably, he concluded, Dr. James was one of them. "Gotcha, asshole."

CHAPTER 132

The USS Eisenhower Battle Force commander, Admiral Julius Havelind and his Chief of Staff, Captain Clint Longly, stood outside on the admiral's bridge and looked through their binoculars west towards China and the gathering dusk. It would be a clear evening, perfect for fighting.

"I don't know why I still use these things," Havelind muttered. "The Hawks will tell us long before we see anything." Havelind knew it was the calm before the storm and his heart was heavy. He knew lots of blood would be spilled tonight, much of it American, and the pride of the US Navy, two carrier battle groups, was likely to sustain heavy damage or sink.

He had not felt this pessimistic since his original tour in Vietnam flying F-4's. Then he had written his new wife every day certain the war would make her a widow. Since that time, he had trusted the government's promises not to engage in any more unwinnable wars, either by not committing sufficient power to prevail or by staying out of them altogether. In his estimation, Iraq had violated the first premise and this violated both.

Throughout his career, from naval pilot, test pilot, through nuclear school, and his first deep-water naval command to battle group commander, he had trusted those promises, but now he was commanding an overmatched force facing a huge committed foe in their home territory.

Havelind was fully cognizant of the consequences of underestimating an enemy. The Roman army, the most feared and capable fighting force in the world in its time, engaged the Parthians on their own turf. They were crushed through a combination of poor planning, poor execution, and arrogance. The surviving Roman Strategoi, their generals, lived the remainder of their lives as slaves to the victorious Parthians—a foe the Romans never defeated. This China conflict looked like it would be a repeat of the lopsided Roman loss.

Captain Longly, the Naval aviator advisor assigned to Admiral Havelind looked at his watch. "Every aircraft will be aloft in another twenty minutes." He paused. "We're sitting fucking ducks here."

"President's orders, damn it." Havelind raised his binoculars again. "Pray for a miraculous goddamn diplomatic breakthrough. That's about the only thing that could possibly save our ass right now."

CHAPTER 133

Massachusetts Avenue adjacent to Rock Creek Park was deep with police and Agency cars, their lights flashing as Rhodes pulled up. Helicopters hovered overhead with searchlights piercing the cold morning air. Steve got out of the car feeling as though he was on a movie set. They followed Rhodes, who ducked under police barrier tape and joined a knot of agents looking over a flashlight-illuminated map on the hood of a car.

Beyond the cars, teams of men combed the woods nearby, their flashlight beams moving side to side. As Steve's eyes adjusted, he saw that the area was full of searchers. A dark blue Ford van pulled up and two men opened the rear doors, releasing four bloodhounds. They, too, headed for the brush and undergrowth, with the dogs baying and pulling at their leashes.

"Holy shit, Valenti," Steve couldn't help remarking. "They really don't know where he is."

Valenti shook his head in disbelief. "In Washington, yet. Heads will roll."

"So what will the FBI do to find him?"

"They're here. Those dogs are part of the S and R squad."

"S and R?"

"Search and rescue. And some of those choppers are ours. They're equipped with infrared, but the area is crawling with men. They can't tell the goddamn President from anyone else. They'll be skirting around the periphery trying to pick up some hint of a signal."

Dr. Green looked forlorn. "I guess we stay put until they find him." He pulled his overcoat more tightly around him.

CHAPTER 134

"Secretary Resnick, call for you." An aide waved her hand to catch Resnick's eye. "Ambassador Zhou. Line eight."

Resnick picked up the phone, holding her finger in the other ear to hear over the busy din of the situation room. "Secretary Resnick."

"Madam Secretary, I am calling you back. I wish to convey the decision of our government." His voice sounded tight and his English more clipped and precise than normal.

"Yes, Mr. Ambassador." There was no doubt in her mind what their answer would be. In all her desires for Taiwan to retract its claim of independence, psychologically the Chinese could not. They would rather risk a military defeat than back down, particularly in the face of a hostile antagonist. She watched a Secret Service agent walk up and speak quietly to Sullivan.

"Our government and its intelligence service do not agree with your assessment of the danger of an invasion. Not as long as your commitment to defend us is in place. Certainly, without your support, it could very well succeed. It is my government's intention to pursue independence."

Resnick sighed inwardly. She wished the decision had been different. "I see, Mr. Ambassador." The Ambassador's reply was lost as John Sullivan held up his hands to quiet the room.

"The President is missing in Rock Creek Park."

CHAPTER 135

Rhodes walked over to Steve, Valenti, and Dr. Green. "No luck," Rhodes admitted. "He's just vanished. We've expanded the search perimeter, but frankly, we don't know where he's gone." Rhodes looked defeated. "We've got infrared, dogs, search lights, search teams . . ." He shrugged. "We know the President's not in Rock Creek Park or in any of the nearby streets. It's going to be house to house, now."

Steve glanced at the clearing sky. Dawn was fast approaching and time was running out.

"Mr. Rhodes," Tom asked, "was he wearing any warm clothing?"

Rhodes shook his head. "That's another thing. If he's out in this, he may be freezing. It's thirty-six degrees." Steve watched Rhodes swallow his chagrin and turn away.

"I guess we just wait," Dr. Green said, trying to bury his hands into his pockets even deeper. "There's nothing we can do."

Steve shivered, his cold body resisted thinking. He began to pace and the movement helped throw off some of the fatigue that had seeped into his cold bones. What would the President be thinking when he jumped out of the car? It had to be related to his delusions. Was he a war veteran? Maybe he had similar flashbacks to Captain Palmer. Maybe he had some childhood anxieties like nightmares or insects. Considering that each patient he knew had exhibited a consistent delusional pattern, Steve wondered if President Dixon harbored a similar pattern. "Tom, can you call Elise Dixon for me?"

"Huh?" Dr. Green asked, puzzled.

Steve rubbed his wrists where his handcuffs chafed. "I need to talk to the First Lady, Tom. Do you know how to arrange that? It's been over an hour since he disappeared. I think he must have known where he wanted to go."

Dr. Green looked at Steve with a quizzical expression.

"Look," Steve continued. "A sick man wandering around would have been picked up by now. I think he had a destination and bee-lined for it. I just don't know where."

Valenti grinned at Dr. Green. "Our boy has a theory. Perhaps we should humor him."

Dr. Green shrugged. "Can't do worse than us freezing our butts out here. Okay."

Dr. Green pulled out his cell phone and punched a couple of numbers. He briefly announced why he was calling and handed the phone to Steve. "It's the First Lady."

"Mrs. Dixon, this is Dr. Steve James. You saw us leave the White House with Dr. Green."

"Yes. What is it?" She sounded impatient and worried.

"I don't think your husband is still in the Park."

"Why not?"

"I think your husband had a specific destination in mind when he jumped out of the car."

"Why would you think that?"

"Each Eden patient that I know has experienced a consistent pattern of symptoms. They all had their own unique, but consistent, thought disorder or delusion. You understand?"

"Yes, sort of."

"One thought he was back in Vietnam, another had recurrence of her childhood nightmares. I'm guessing the President has something similar to that. If he does, perhaps his behaviors and comments over the last couple of weeks will give us a clue as to where he is."

"Well, if you think it will help . . ." She paused. "He's been praying all the time. He's always been a man of faith, Dr. James, but now he's . . . obsessed with it. He's convinced he's going to hell."

"Was it worse when he had his shakes?"

Elise Dixon's voice quavered. "Much worse. I could hardly get him to speak to me."

"I understand. Believe me."

"Dr. James, it's horrible. Do you know what he's got?"

I think so, Mrs. Dixon. I'd like to talk with you later after the President has been located and cared for. I can answer your questions then. Right now, I need to go."

"Please find him and bring him back to me, Dr. James."

Steve had his clue. He walked over to the huddled agents pouring over the Washington street map and leaned over to look. He studied it and after a minute, he walked over to the cluster of parked Agency vehicles.

"What did you find out?" Valenti asked, following Steve.

Steve found an empty sedan with the keys still in it and jumped in.

"Hey!" Valenti said. "Where are you going? Don't you need to be here when they find him?"

"But he's not here." Steve started the car and awkwardly backed out with his hands still cuffed. "I think he's at the National Cathedral. Just a hunch."

"I'm coming, too."

"I'll call you. Right now you're my link to the Secret Service."

"Wait!" Valenti yelled as Steve spun his tires. Valenti kicked the pavement in disgust. "How can I save your reckless butt if I'm here?"

Behind the police barricades, Mallis lowered his binoculars. Seeing Dr. James dash out in the car aroused Mallis's hunting instincts.

"Let's go."

CHAPTER 136

The cloud cover had blown over leaving a cold, clear sky. Steve barely noticed the lightening horizon as he pulled the car into the National Cathedral's north parking lot. He jumped out and ran to the north transept door and pulled the ornate handle. It was locked tight.

He ran around to the front doors, but they were also locked. *Could he have been wrong?* He ran around to the south transept entrance where he saw footprints on the sleet-covered grass leading to the south side. Steve flew up the six steps and with both cuffed hands, he grabbed the handle and pulled on the heavy wooden door. It swung open. Inside, it was dark and cold, like a cave. Steve took a breath and walked in, the door slowly closing behind him.

He did not see the Camry pull into the Cathedral parking lot.

Inside, the transept led to the vast arched nave. As his eyes adjusted to the dim light, he could see the massive stained glass windows and the beautiful Gothic ribbed pillars that vanished into the darkness above.

Laid out in the traditional cathedral cruciform floor plan, the nave formed the long part of a cross with the transepts its cross member. A tall, ornately carved stone pulpit dominated the junction of the nave and transept. Steve listened, but heard no sound. He walked down the south aisle of the nave, but didn't see anyone. He ran back up the center aisle, past the crossing of the transepts and through the wood-veneered Great Choir, to the alter—still no one. He whirled around, searching. There!

Sitting in the Children's Chapel, a small ornate room just off the south transept, sat a slumped figure.

He walked into the chapel and saw President Dixon shivering and with his head bowed in prayer. Struck by the vulnerability of the man, he sat down next to him on one of the small child-size chairs. "Mr. President?"

President Dixon jerked in surprise. "I didn't hear you come in."

"I'm Dr. James. I came to talk to you." In the growing daylight, he observed with a shock how haggard and exhausted the President's face had become.

"I figured someone would come to fetch me sooner or later."

"How are you feeling, Sir?"

"Been better." The President looked at him keenly. "You said you're a doctor? Do you know what I've got?"

"I think so."

"It's bad, isn't it?"

"Yes, Sir."

The President shook his head sadly at the news. Several spasms jerked his face and shoulders followed by a look of confusion. After a minute, he found his voice. "I tried to see this thing out. I wanted to do the right thing, but . . . I don't know anymore."

"You're human, Mr. President."

Kirk Mallis sat down next to Steve. "So sorry to break up this tête-à-tête, gentlemen."

Steve looked at him a moment before recognizing him. *Shit! How—?*

"Surprised, Dr. James?" He grinned. "We have unfinished business. See?" He pointed to his burned face.

"Friend of yours?" the President asked politely, somewhat puzzled.

Steve found his voice. "He's tried to—"

Mallis's fist slammed into Steve's mouth, knocking him to the cold limestone floor. Steve tasted blood from his split lip. He held up his handcuffs. "Hardly sporting is it?"

Mallis kicked him hard in the side making Steve crumple into a ball. He struggled to breathe.

"Hey, stop that." President Dixon stood up, but Mallis pushed him back, causing him to fall backwards over several chairs, spilling their hymnals.

Steve struggled to his feet, breathing in shallow gasps. He cursed the handcuffs as he tried to pick up a chair, but they were roped together. Realizing the futility, he backed away but failed to duck in time.

Mallis punched Steve again, slamming a fist into his nose. Steve dropped to the floor, tasting the blood that poured down his upper lip into his mouth. He felt strong hands grab his jacket and yank him to his feet. He quickly threw his hands in front of his face.

Mallis, instead, punched him in the solar plexus. Steve doubled over unable to breathe. A knee slammed into Steve's face and he collapsed in unbearable pain and fighting the darkness that crept in around him.

The assassin knelt behind Steve and pulled the handcuff chain hard against Steve's throat, cutting off his windpipe. In a massive effort, he twisted and tried to buck Mallis off his back. No use. Panic drove his last attempts to breathe as blackness closed in.

Dimly, he heard a thud somewhere behind him and the pressure on his neck released. Steve's lungs sucked in huge gulps of cool air. He raised his head. *What happened?*

Mallis was on his knees holding his head, blood flowing from his scalp. President Dixon was standing over him with a heavy candelabrum tightly gripped in his hand.

Mallis's thick arm snaked out and swept Dixon's ankles out from under, throwing the President to the floor. Grimacing, he pulled his pistol and pointed it at Dixon.

Steve snatched a hymnal off the floor and with both hands awkwardly threw it at Mallis hoping it would distract him from the president. He then jumped up and ran as fast as he could on his wobbly knees and turned a corner out of sight.

He had to find a place to hide—or a weapon. But where? Darting through the alderman pit, he spotted the pulpit. He dashed up the stairs and dropped to the floor. Crouching on his hands and knees, the solid stone balustrade hid him from view.

Within seconds, he heard footsteps directly below.

Steve's cell phone rang, a deafening noise in the stillness of the cathedral. *Damn it!* Looking down over the balustrade, he saw Mallis below turning his head trying to locate the sound of the phone. Steve quickly climbed onto the balustrade and dropped, landing his knees on Mallis's shoulders, driving him to the ground.

Steve searched the floor. *Where's the gun?*

Mallis groaned and started to rise. In desperation, Steve grabbed his short hair and tried to pound his face into the floor, but Mallis's neck was too strong. His solid, muscular body slowly got up on its hands and knees.

Steve reached around to gouge his eyes, but clawed only skin. Mallis bellowed and grabbed at Steve's hands. Steve jerked free and jumped to his feet. Mallis was like a goddamn bull. He was just too fucking strong. Steve kicked Mallis in the side as hard as he could. He kicked again, but Mallis rolled away and scooped up his gun where it had lain beneath him.

"Gotcha, asshole," Mallis said, breathing hard and pointing the gun at Steve.

Steve held up his hands. Mallis wiped his bloody face on his sleeve where Steve's fingernails had left red marks across his eyelids and cheeks. Motioning with his gun, he pointed back in the direction of the children's chapel. "Move."

When they turned the corner to the chapel, Steve gasped. The President was gone.

"Goddamn it," Mallis cursed, whirling around.

Steve heard a noise like a bench scraping on the floor. It came from above. Mallis heard it too and cocked his head. "Up there," he said, pointing with his gun. "Move."

Steve walked up the stone staircase leading to the choir loft above the south transept. They stepped onto a balcony overlooking the Church interior. There, on the balcony sat President Dixon on a wooden choir bench, once again in prayer, his shoulders and face intermittently twitching.

"Pitiful, isn't it?" Mallis snarled.

"It's your boss's drug that did this to him." Steve retorted.

"And you making it your business will cost you." Mallis poked Steve with his gun. "Sit down." Mallis wiped his face again. "We're going to erase any trace of your stupid theory about Eden."

"Eden?" President Dixon looked over at them, his jerks having abated. "Is that causing my problem?"

"Yes, Sir," Steve said. "Eden did this to you. Our friend here is killing everyone who knows about it."

"Is this true?" The President looked up at Mallis.

"Irrelevant," Mallis snapped.

"You can't kill everybody—" Steve snapped back.

"Of course we can." Mallis grinned, "For example, we located your lovely wife in Oregon."

"No!" Steve lunged at Mallis.

Mallis pistol-whipped Steve across the temple, knocking him backwards. He collapsed, landing face down.

CHAPTER 137

Rows of manned computer terminals filled the dimly lit Eisenhower flag bridge monitoring the battle theatre as it unfolded in real time.

"Target accretion is accelerating," Captain Clint Longly reported, watching the larger command screen, which displayed all friendly and hostile contacts in the area. He pointed to several groups of Chinese blips. "We got J-elevens and J-eights here and here, followed by some SU-thirties. CAG's planning to engage at fifty miles." CAG, the commander of the carrier air group, based on the Eisenhower, controlled the air battle.

Havelind watched the screen as more fighter and bomber contacts developed from multiple places along the southern coast of China. "They're coming from non-military locations just as the intel said they would." He felt the familiar tension building up in his chest that he got whenever he confronted an enemy. "And they have nukes. Let's hope they left them at home."

As Havelind and Longly watched the screen, more enemy blips appeared, categorized by the computers into identifiable shapes and colors.

"I'm seeing a pattern here," Longley reported. "They're starting with a combination of their more advanced fighters and their less capable ones in a first wave. I now count about four hundred contacts. A second wave, here," Longly pointed to several areas on the screen, "is developing from the established air bases farther away, a mixture, it looks of bombers and fighters."

Havelind had already pictured this scenario. It was exactly how he would have attacked given China's armaments and resources. It was effective and, in all likelihood, overwhelming. "CAG's response?"

"The vortex. They want to engage our surface vessels. From the mainland, they can only fly directly to us one way. While they will engage at different angles and altitudes, they're over there and we're here. Basically, to get to us they have to fly across the straits right at us."

"So your outermost units are the most widely deployed," Havelind summarized. "It's good, assuming they fly right into it. From what I've seen, they prefer diversion and subterfuge. Fall back options?"

"Scramble. There's no room for anything else. By then, it's one on one."

Havelind knew the American pilots and machinery easily outclassed their Chinese counterparts, but they were far outnumbered. Each fighter was carrying their maximum load, but once spent, they would have to land to re-arm. By that time, the Chinese would have penetrated the fighter perimeter to attack the surface vessels.

Havelind watched the growing Chinese formations with dismay. The Parthians were gathering to do battle.

CHAPTER 138

Not Anne!
  "We might spare your son, if you behave."
  Steve wasn't sure he had heard Mallis. "What?" As he lay on the floor, head throbbing, he became aware of something in his jacket's breast pocket pushing against his chest. "Save Johnnie?" His mind grasped at Mallis's offer.
  "Now, Dr. James," Mallis growled.
  Steve felt the cold pressure of Mallis's gun at the back of his neck. Steve got slowly to his feet, facing away from Mallis, his chest tingling. "My son? You would spare my son?"
  The chest tingling triggered a recognition.
  "I said, I might," Mallis continued, "but you have to earn it."
  Steve's mind, now crystal clear, began formulating a plan. "What do I have to do?" *Stall!* Just a few moments was all he needed.
  "You kill the President, then commit suicide. It's beautiful. You go down in history as the man who assassinated the President on the eve of war with China."
  "That'll spare my son?" He kept his back to Mallis. "Let me think." His right hand slipped into his suit coat's breast pocket where he pulled out and palmed the small red plastic bottle from the museum—what was it, only twelve hours before? He had completely forgotten about it until now. Steve unsnapped the plastic squirt cap.

"You must do exactly as I say." The triumphant tone in Mallis's voice was unmistakable.

"Okay," Steve said carefully, "what, exactly, do you want me to do?"

"Surely you're not going to shoot me?" President Dixon asked, showing fear for the first time.

"My son and my wife mean everything to me, but . . ." he jerked his head toward Mallis, "I think he's going to do the dirty work himself." *Timing—it's got to be just right.*

"Bravo, Doc. I'll kill you first, of course. Here's where you earn your son's life. Kneel down, neurosurgeon scumbag."

Steve knelt on one knee. His hand kept the plastic bottle in his hand turned away from Mallis who placed his gun against Steve's temple.

Steve twisted his face up at Mallis. "You know, asshole, your man at the museum was the last person who called me a neurosurgeon and he died with a piece of steel sticking out of his brain."

Anger seared Mallis's features. He lifted his gun to strike Steve.

Steve's hands shot up. He sprayed a stream of concentrated potassium chloride into Mallis's eyes and face. Mallis screamed, clutching his sizzling skin. Steve stood and swung both cuffed fists as hard as he could at Mallis, knocking him to the stone floor. Mallis swiped at his face with his shirtsleeves. Steve jumped on him and pounded him again and again, his handcuffed fists moving in determined unison. He then grabbed Mallis's head and slammed it repeatedly into the floor until Mallis lay still.

"I think he's done with, Dr. James," he heard President Dixon say.

Exhausted, he slid off Mallis and leaned up against the pew, breathing hard.

Distant sirens approached. Steve looked at his watch. Shit! Eighteen minutes left. "Mr. President, I came here with the intention of declaring you unfit for office. I'm sorry, but it—"

Dixon nodded. "I understand. And I agree. It's time."

"But it takes two doctors and we don't have time to do it. China's going to—"

President Dixon held up his hand. "I've been praying for an answer. May I suggest a simple expedient?"

CHAPTER 139

Sullivan wore a hole in the carpet next to his chair. He alternately looked at the monitors and his watch. An aide, a young woman, approached Sullivan and whispered, "It's the President."

"Dixon? Himself?" Sullivan's face registered his surprise. "Put him on speaker."

The President's voice came through clearly. "John? Are you there? Is the cabinet there?"

"Right here, Sir. We all are. How are you?"

"Could be better. No time for small talk." He took an audible breath. "John, I resign the office of The President of the United States, effective immediately. I have served with pride and to the best of my ability, but I am no longer capable of carrying out the duties of my office."

Sullivan's face registered his concern. "Who is with you, Mr. President?"

"A Dr. James."

Castell's face reflected his surprise. "Are you under duress to resign, Sir? As the only doctor present, I feel I must ask." Sullivan scowled at him.

"Castell?" President Dixon said. "Of course, I'm under duress, you ass. I'm sick and may die and I'm resigning from something I care deeply about. Here's the verification code: Scissors, DaVinci, Mountain. Now, President Sullivan, cut the crap and get on with it."

"Yes, sir," Sullivan said, and then added gently, "Goodbye, Bob."

Dixon's reply was husky. "Right. Goodbye."

The line clicked off. Sullivan looked at the assembled cabinet plus the Speaker of the House and the majority leader of the Senate. "Are we unanimous?" They all nodded although Castell looked nervous. Bingham, observing this, exchanged a puzzled glance with Resnick.

Sullivan looked at the White House counsel. "Art?"

Art shrugged and nodded. "It's highly irregular, but in view of the circumstances . . ."

"Then it's agreed. Get me Premier Chow. Judge Hersell, let's get the swearing in done."

"Mr. President, Premier Chow is on the line," an aide said.

"On speaker," Sullivan said. The aide clicked a button and nodded to the President.

"Premier Chow? This is President Sullivan. I have replaced President Dixon, who resigned moments ago." They could hear their Chinese interpreter repeating Sullivan's words in Mandarin. They heard a slight murmur of surprise from the Chinese.

The prompt reply was in Chinese, followed by the translation from the US interpreter, Cassie Avon. "Yes, President Sullivan."

Sullivan cleared his throat and spoke deliberately. "President Dixon is suffering from a neurological disease that has impaired his ability to think rationally. That irrationality has brought our two countries to the brink of armed conflict. I want to stop this conflict before it starts. I have instructed our armed services not to fire unless first fired upon. Premier Chow, I am making a move for peace. I hope you will act decisively and call back your forces."

He paused as the Chinese translator repeated his words. Sullivan looked at Avon, who nodded. She then translated Chow's reply. "I hear your proposal. If we do pull our forces back, what promises can you give us that negotiations will produce fruit?"

Sullivan spoke carefully. "I can assure you that the U.S. will withdraw its unilateral support for the independence of Taiwan. The previous President, due to his illness, erroneously changed our longstanding policy in regards to Taiwan. Because of this, which we will declare publicly, we will resume our previous 'One China' policy. This includes our recognition of China's legitimacy in its non-violent reunification with the province of Taiwan, but only with the consent of the people of Taiwan. It also continues our non-invasion protection for Taiwan.

"Mr. Chow, if you persist in your attack of Taiwan knowing our position, we will defend Taiwan to the fullest of our ability."

Chow carefully replied. "You understand that we have an overwhelming advantage and have every expectation of succeeding in our initiative to take the island by force."

"Yes, I do understand. I also know that China does not want to win an unwilling bride, nor make an enemy of the United States if there is a better way to obtain a satisfactory outcome."

"Let me confer. I will ask that you hold the line."

The line went dead. Sullivan looked at his watch. "Eight minutes to seven." Looking at Resnick, he asked, "Comments?"

"I thought you were fine. Frankly, I think Chow shouldn't have mentioned his forces' capabilities."

"Our chances?"

"Depends," Resnick said. "If he has any power."

"If your analysis of the CNN scoop is correct, he has more than he did." Sullivan looked at Crusoe. "Augie?"

"I agree with Linda. The wild card is General Yao, but I agree with Resnick's assessment. He must have lost considerable influence after Colonel Tanggu's reported statements."

"Premier Chow's back on the line," Cassie Avon said.

Everyone turned and looked at the speakerphone. "Yes, Mr. Premier."

"I believe we have just concluded perhaps the fastest negotiations ever between our two nations. I have instructed our armed forces to pull back. They have strict instructions not to engage your forces. I only hope we are in time to avoid any encounters."

Sullivan's face broke into a broad grin. "I am very happy to hear that, Premier Chow. You have taken an extraordinary step towards peace. I commend you. With this as a new starting point, I will want to meet you in person and discuss each of our countries' needs with respect to each other."

"I, too, agree a meeting would be useful. Goodbye, President Sullivan. I wish you luck in your new office. My country sends its best wishes to President Dixon. We are saddened to hear of his illness."

"Thank you, Mr. Premier. Goodbye."

Sullivan made a small victory fist. There was a round of applause from the cabinet. Then Bingham shouted in his native drawl, "Yee ha!" The place broke up in shouts and cheers.

Sullivan looked at the situation screen. "Any movement?"

Valenzuela answered before the Colonel. "Not yet. It'll take a little time for the orders to go through the various levels of command. Wait. Some have begun turning back. Yes, they're definitely turning."

"Good," Sullivan said, finally sitting down. "Damn good."

CHAPTER 140

"Sir," The Eisenhower radar operator announced, "The Chinese aircraft are turning around. It appears . . . yes, the hostiles are turning around."

Longly looked at Havelind "What the hell?"

"Sir," an aide said, handing Havelind a handset. "The President."

"The President?" Havelind put the handset to his ear. "Yes, sir. This is Rear Admiral Havelind."

As he listened, a look of amazement spread across his lined face.

"Yes Sir . . . Of course, Sir. I will tell them myself . . . You're welcome, Sir. And, may I add, congratulations. We are all very pleased at the turn of events."

Havelind put down the handset with a look of amazement. Turning to Longly, he said, "Well, first off, we now have a new President—President Sullivan. He's apparently negotiated the pull-back of the Chinese forces."

Longly glanced at him from the situation board. "They're still pulling back, nearly all of them. It looks like you got your goddamn diplomatic breakthrough."

"Not soon enough for my ulcers," Havelind snorted. "Anyway, President Sullivan says, 'good job' and to express his appreciation to everyone."

He stared at the screen and the blips getting farther apart wondering to himself, *just what in hell happened back in Washington to get us into this situation in the first place?*

CHAPTER 141

Dixon, sitting on a wooden choir bench, handed the phone back to Steve. "What have I got?"

"Something in your brain. I'm sorry, but it's pretty bad." The sirens were very close now.

"Eden?"

"Yes Sir."

"Damn vanity." Dixon sighed. "It isn't curable, is it?"

"If that's really what you've got, then no."

The sirens stopped and Steve heard muffled shouts outside. A series of sharp pops made him jump—gunshots!

Suddenly, the voices were much louder. "Mr. President, Mr. President!" It was Rhodes.

Steve stood up and shouted over the balcony rail, "Up here."

"Where?"

"In the choir loft."

"The President?" Rhodes yelled.

"He's fine." Looking back, Steve saw Dixon praying again, his shoulders and face twitching in an irregular myoclonic pattern. The stooped man hardly resembled the President he knew from television. "He's just fine."

Rhodes and a crowd of Secret Service agents pushed their way onto the balcony. Several agents spotted Mallis and surrounded him.

Dr. Green emerged at the top of the stairs and walked quickly over to Dixon. "Wait, let me look at him," he ordered the agents who surrounded Dixon. "I want to make sure he's OK."

Valenti, his hands now free of cuffs, ran over to Steve. Appraising Steve's bloody face with evident concern, he said pointing, "He missed a spot, right there. Lordy, what a mess." Nodding towards Mallis, he shook his head. "Not Rambo, huh? Looks like dad kicked some ass."

The day-breaking sun hit the Cathedral's stained glass windows, splashing a dazzling array of colors across the floors and walls. Steve gazed with amazement at the incandescent windows filled with the fresh morning light.

"Look at that," President Dixon exclaimed. He started to stand.

"Here, let me help you," Dr. Green said, grasping Dixon's arm.

"It's beautiful, isn't it?" Dixon made his way to the balcony rail. "One of my favorite sights."

Steve joined him, steadying himself at the rail, and they shared the view. The cathedral spread out before them in its immense grandeur, its piers sweeping up towards the vaulted roof while colored lights played across the worked stones and carvings.

Two agents pulled Kirk Mallis, groaning and clutching his face, to his feet. His foot stepped on something heavy. From between his fingers, with his one good eye, he looked down and saw his gun.

"Wait. I'm dizzy," he said, bending over.

Mallis suddenly pulled his left arm towards him and leaned towards his right. As the agent pulled back, the one holding his right arm instinctively loosened his grip. Mallis yanked his right arm free and pushed the agent still holding his arm off the balcony. In a fluid move, he swung around and delivered a hard palm thrust to the second agent's nose, fracturing the cartilage and snapping back his head. The agent sagged and Mallis slid behind using the agent as a shield. Mallis scooped up his pistol and grinning, stared straight at Steve.

Shouts filled the air as agents scrambled to aim their guns at Mallis without hitting their fellow agent. As Mallis raised his gun, Steve grabbed Dixon, pushing him to the floor.

As they fell, Steve stared at the sneering, disfigured face of Kirk Mallis. He wanted revenge. For thwarting his plans too many times, for injuring him, for persisting and ultimately prevailing, Mallis hated him and now Mallis would kill him. In the periphery, Steve was aware of agents in motion, but he knew they would be too late to prevent Mallis from firing at least one shot.

The steady black hole of the barrel found his head and followed him as he fell on top of the President. Mallis squinted in concentration, oblivious to everybody rushing towards him, like a quarterback back to pass, deep in the pocket with goal to go and time expired on the clock. He had one opportunity and wasn't going to miss.

As Mallis's finger tightened on the trigger, Steve braced himself for the bullet that would penetrate his flesh before he would hear the shot. He would feel nothing as it tore through him, and maybe nothing ever again, if the bullet shattered his skull and ripped through his brain. He did not flinch or blink, but instead stared straight into Mallis's one good eye. He had beaten Mallis and Mallis knew it.

CHAPTER 142

Resnick leaned back in her seat and closed her eyes, still worried that things might slip out of control. Who was to blame for this? Obviously General Yao, but the situation should never have gotten this far. Dixon, had he been normal, would not have recognized Taiwan's independence bid in the first place, she felt certain.

Whose responsibility was it to recognize Dixon's problem—or any president's—and intervene before poor judgment risked lives and the security of the country? In the days of monarchs and emperors, with the divine right to rule, unrestrained bad judgment cost many their state and empire, but in a modern democracy, that should not happen—yet it almost just did.

Had the presidency too absolute an authority, which, like a king, the framers of the constitution had tried to avoid? Past examples of blind obedience of a president's staff to his wishes had led to egregious errors of judgment and criminal behavior. Where was the check on the president's power, the means to keep the actions and decisions within bounds? How could they prevent a repeat of the cascade of bad decisions from an incompetent president?

Sullivan hung up the phone after speaking with Admiral Havilland. "They're still going home?"

Valenzuela nodded. "The advanced formations are all going back. Some of the ones farther back are just now starting to turn. I expect they took longer to get the orders. Damned efficient actually. And, if I might add, Sir, good job."

Sullivan nodded. "But it is really our fault that you were here in the first place. We politicians failed you. Not to paint with too broad a brush, but our system did not perform responsibly. I should thank you for performing despite the flawed civilian rule." He sighed. "Now, let's get President Lai on the phone."

"I don't envy you that call," Linda responded.

"Don't forget," Crusoe said, "we actually averted a bloody and potentially successful invasion of his island." He wore a lopsided smile. "For all that's worth."

"Just keep in mind," Linda replied, "that we also sided with a totalitarian regime against an autonomous, democratic ally in its quest for freedom and independence. This is not a bright day for American politics."

CHAPTER 143

Valenti slammed into Mallis the moment his gun flashed. They both tumbled to the floor.

A scalding pain tore through the side of Steve's head, surprising him at its intensity. Penetrating wounds, unless they hit nerves or splintered bone, didn't usually hurt immediately. Yet Steve felt a searing white-hot pain on the left side of his head. He landed hard on top of Dixon and heard him grunt with the impact.

Mallis sprang back up whereupon he was riddled with a volley of bullets from the secret service agents. Mallis fell against the balustrade and toppled backwards over the edge and fell to the floor below.

Rhodes pulled Steve up and then they helped President Dixon to the choir bench. He waved them off. "I'm fine."

As Dr. Green hurried over to look at Dixon, Steve reached up his handcuffed hands to his throbbing head and touched wetness.

"Doc," Valenti said, coming up behind him, "You're bleeding."

Steve looked at the blood on his fingers. "It seems every time I hang around you, I get shot. This makes the third time today."

"Let me see." Dr. Green came around to Steve's side to inspect it with Valenti.

Steve suddenly thought to thank Valenti. Turning he said, "You saved my life."

"Hold still," Valenti growled, "Let Dr. Green look at you."

Steve winced as Dr. Green's fingers probed.

"As best I can tell," Green concluded, "it looks like it tunneled through some skin and took off some ear cartilage," Dr. Green said. "You're bleeding pretty good. You'll need stitches and eventually a plastic surgeon. Beyond that, I think you're one lucky camper."

He pulled Steve's sleeved arms up and pushed one against the wound, made somewhat awkward from the handcuffs. "There," he said to Steve, "Hold pressure on it to stop the bleeding until I can get some gauze or something."

"We lost a witness, damn it," Valenti groused.

Steve turned around. "Dead?"

Valenti cocked an eyebrow. "Come see."

Steve, holding his forearm to his ear, stepped to the balcony edge and looked over. Mallis lay on his back, head twisted at a sharp angle with blood pooling around his torso. Two agents stood over his supine body and another sitting on the floor holding his leg that bent at an unnatural angle at the shin.

"He can't talk now," Valenti observed. "And we needed him as a witness."

A flood of emotions rushed through Steve. That cold voice that had vowed to kill him now lay silent. Steve had no sympathy or regret that Mallis was dead, the bastard had nearly killed his family, but there was no joy, either; just relief—lots of relief, and now, a glimmer of a future.

"Still, it was too damn close," Valenti muttered. "By the way, we found Mallis's associate outside. He gave us a little trouble, but he's still alive. He just might talk."

Rhodes joined them and looked down at Mallis. "We got lucky, damn lucky." Turning to Valenti he said, "Thanks for bringing us here."

Valenti shrugged. "Steve's idea."

"I just spoke with HQ," Rhodes said, removing Steve's handcuffs. "Apparently President Sullivan talked the Chinese into turning around. Your efforts paid off, Dr. James."

Steve rubbed his raw wrists as he looked down at Mallis. "Good. That's really good." He put his left arm back up against his bleeding scalp and put pressure on it.

"Sure he's not a hardened criminal?" Valenti nodded at the handcuffs. "One can't be too careful these days."

Rhodes chuckled. "We know where to find him and you, too, Fanelli."

Steve looked around and saw Dixon sitting on a stone bench talking to Dr. Green. He walked over and sat beside him. "Mr. President," he said, remembering the First Lady's concern. "I think your wife is expecting you back at the White House. Let's get you home."

Robert Dixon nodded. "I think that's a good idea." He accepted Steve's right hand and stood up looking around at the multicolored light dancing across the Cathedral. "So beautiful," he breathed. "Wait, wait." Dixon twitched. "Pray first. I need to pray." He knelt down again, knees on the hard floor, still holding Steve's hand in support. Steve knelt down next to him, his whole body throbbing, but he was in no hurry. He was content to wait.

CHAPTER 144

Secret Service Agent Rhodes escorted a sewn-up and bandaged, but achy Dr. James into the West Wing of the White House. Outside the Roosevelt Room, Rhodes introduced him to FBI Special Agent in Charge, H. Walter Fitzgerald, whose cynical eyes appraised Steve at some length. "Dr. James," he said in a gravelly voice, "you have a great deal of information that we would like to know. If you please, we would like to interview you at some length."

Steve, still operating on adrenaline, nodded his assent, not sure what was in store, but wanting to get it over with.

Rhodes grinned as he opened the door. "In the meantime, we'll keep the reporters at bay." He led Steve and Agent Fitzgerald into the room. "They're rabid out there."

Sitting down at the head of the long glossy table, Steve faced a conference table packed with official looking, but nameless men and women, each with a pad of paper. A court stenographer sat in the corner. Omnidirectional microphones had been placed at intervals on the table for recording the interview and a video camera sat on a tripod across the table facing him.

The interview took over three hours. Steve told his story about Eden, Captain Ralph Palmer, Shirley Rosenwell and Rhonda Fowler, and their symptoms, Dr. Walker and Dr. Sheridan's research, and how he had come to the conclusion that Eden was responsible for the prion conversions that caused the brain destruction. He described his call to Trident's

Safety Officer and the subsequent attempts on his life, his engagement of Valenti, and how he came to suspect President Dixon had the disease, followed by his meeting with Castell and the chase through the streets of Washington and into the Smithsonian, and their nocturnal visit with Dr. Blumenthal.

He shared a bottomless pot of coffee with the others around the table until his nerves jangled and his heart pounded. He relayed his initial conversation with Dr. Green about President Dixon's illness and his conversation with the First Lady that triggered his deduction of the President's location at the National Cathedral and his subsequent fight with Mallis. Finally, he reported Mallis's comments about killing him to keep the Eden problem hidden.

He watched their heads bob and their pens and pencils scribble as he talked. The court reporter looked like she was playing an organ, silently pressing keys singly and in combination. She occasionally asked him to spell a medical word or repeat something. Finally, Mr. Fitzgerald stood up.

"It's apparent that we have a lot to do in a very short period of time, Dr. James. Thank you for your help. We will need your assistance here in Washington for the next several days and probably for some time after that, but I think now you can freshen up and get some rest."

"One last thing, but it's sheer speculation," Steve offered. His jaw was exhausted and his words came more deliberately than at first. The adrenalin had worn off some time ago and the false energy from the caffeine bowed to the tiredness that had spread throughout his bones. "Morloch made some stock transfers to an offshore account shortly after Eden was approved. I wonder if Castell, who was head of the FDA at the time, may have helped get Eden fast-tracked. I'd check to see who owns that account."

Valenti messily slurped a huge mouthful of spaghetti. Steve looked at him with some amusement. Valenti loved his food, no mistake about that and he was not shy about showing his appreciation for it either. He had tucked his napkin into his shirt at the neck and was hunched over his plate.

Straightening up, he glanced at Steve sitting across the blonde-wood table. "I'm hungry."

"Really? I couldn't tell."

"I like this place. Passable pasta, for sure." He looked around the spotless White House kitchen, with painted eggshell white walls, black and white checkered linoleum floors, and immaculate stainless steel counters and appliances. They sat at a table in a nook off to the side that seemed designed for quick snacks for on-the-go White House staff.

After his interview with the FBI, Steve had expected to be taken back to his hotel room, but Rhodes said Mrs. Dixon had insisted he and Valenti be accommodated at the White House. He had been promptly ushered into the Lincoln bedroom where someone had laid out a fresh change of clothes. Did everybody know his size?

Ignoring Doctor Green's instructions, Steve had promptly peeled off his new bandages and took a long hot shower. It felt wonderful to be clean again. Steve took his time shaving, while wrapped in a plush White House bathrobe. He suspected that many guests had accidentally packed them in their suitcases after a night's stay at the White House. He finally dressed and upon emerging from the Lincoln bedroom, had been escorted to the kitchen where he joined Valenti, who had also showered and freshened after his interview with the FBI.

"Imagine, eating at the White House," Valenti enthused. "The only reason I'd ever want to be President is having a full-time restaurant at your beck and call 24 hours a day."

"You'd be the first president who died from a pasta overdose."

Valenti's head dipped down for another large mouthful. "Tut, tut. Keep the day job," he muttered.

"I don't have a day job." Steve looked down at his tuna fish sandwich without an appetite. He should be hungry, but something was still bothering him—*Something undone.*

"Bad news," Valenti said.

Steve, surprised, looked at his friend. "What now?" After all that had happened, this was as unwelcome as it was unexpected.

"Our buddy Blumenthal is no longer on this earth. Found in his burned house sometime after four this morning."

"Oh, no." Steve had decided he liked the doctor.

"I just hope he really did have something in writing like he said. We'll need it. We still can't link Morloch with this thing."

A tall, distinguished man walked up to them, smiling. He looked tired and Steve guessed that he had been up all night. Suddenly Steve recognized him as Vice President Sullivan. No—he corrected himself—it was President Sullivan. Steve scrambled to his feet.

President Sullivan held out his hand. "Dr. James, it's a pleasure to meet you."

Steve took his hand, "It's all mine, Mr. President."

Sullivan turned to Valenti, who had by then wiped his face and hid his napkin before he stood. "Mr. Anthony Valenti, or should I say, Mr. Fanelli."

Valenti smiled and took Sullivan's outstretched hand. "Either will work just fine, Mr. President."

"Please," Sullivan said, motioning with his hand. "Sit down. I don't want to disturb your meal."

Steve and Valenti sat down. Sullivan sat in a chair next to Valenti. Steve hoped he didn't look as nervous as Valenti, who sat rigidly, ignoring his spaghetti.

"I understand you two have done a tremendous service to your country," Sullivan began.

"This hasn't been an ordinary day for any of us," Steve replied.

Sullivan smiled. "True. It was touch and go there for a while, with you as well as in the Straits. I don't want to imagine what would have happened had you not found President Dixon."

Steve shrugged, feeling self-conscious.

"Dr. James, you've paid a terrible price. Is there anything we can do for you?"

Steve started to say no, but stopped. He was still struggling with that uneasy feeling inside. He figured that with Mallis's activities exposed, he would get his license back and he could begin to pull his life back together . . . but, no, there was something else. Then it hit him. Steve spoke even as the plan formed in his mind. "Mr. President, actually, there is."

CHAPTER 145

Anne's mother, Joan Pritchard turned on the TV in her oak-paneled family room and sat down in her easy chair next to her husband, Jack. "Let's see what's going on with China."

Retired, they enjoyed their morning routine together watching Good Morning America and reading the newspaper. They had been doing this for the last four years, ever since Jack sold his popular breakfast restaurant, the Morning Edition.

Jack, his attention focused on the Marketplace section of the Wall Street Journal, mumbled an unintelligible reply. Not taking his eyes off the paper, he sipped the hot coffee from his huge Trailblazers cup. Joan's gasp made him look up. "What is it?" he asked.

"President Dixon, he's resigned."

Jack had read the front page with the stories about the impending Chinese conflict, but nothing about President Dixon resigning. He put down his paper and stared at Diane Sawyer's tired face, startled to see a senior news anchor at this hour. It took a few minutes for him to catch up on the story.

There had been no massive Chinese battle; that much was clear. It took a little longer to figure out that Dixon had resigned and that Sullivan was now President and he had negotiated the halt to the Chinese invasion of Taiwan.

"Well, it doesn't pay to go to sleep during a crisis, does it?" Jack observed. "You might just wake up to find a new president."

"Shhh." Joan leaned forward in her overstuffed easy chair. "I can't believe Dixon resigned. I thought he was doing a pretty good job up until this China thing." A clink of dishes came from the kitchen. "Is that you dear?"

Anne, wearing one of her mother's bathrobes walked into the room. "I'm up, mom. I'm getting Johnnie some cereal." She disappeared back into the kitchen. Anne had stayed up for hours after hearing about Steve on the radio, but with no new news forthcoming, she had eventually fallen into a fitful sleep.

The TV station announced the upcoming story before they cut to a commercial. It was to be a segment on former President Dixon's illness and the doctor who diagnosed it. They showed a file clip of Steve, taken after he had saved the 747.

"Anne," Jack yelled. "Steve's on the news."

Anne rushed in, still holding a spoon, an anxious expression on her face. "Is it about the break-in?"

Jack looked puzzled. "No, something about diagnosing President Dixon's illness."

"What?"

Johnnie ran into the room, his Sketchers' untied and his double cowlicks sticking up. "Is daddy famous again?"

Anne hugged herself. "Is he okay?"

Joan came over and put her arm around her daughter. "Look's like Steve's done it again."

Johnnie jumped up swinging his fist in a giant arc. "Yesss! Daddy's a hero!"

Anne still felt anxious and unsettled with a million bad things that might have happened running through her head. *Steve, why haven't you called? Is it still not safe?*

CHAPTER 146

Two bodyguards ushered Steve into the Morloch's office. He looked around taking in the ornate inlaid-wood furniture and leather-upholstered chairs. Steve identified a wall of Matisse sketches and an original W. A. Turner oil. He strode in to the middle of the room.

The corner suite commanded a breathtaking panoramic vista from its floor to ceiling windows. At the window, with his back to them, stood Morloch, dressed in a navy pinstripe suit. He stared out at the Delaware River, which could be seen past an adjacent modern, silver-tinted glass building on which hung a window cleaning crew.

The bodyguard to Steve's right spoke. "He's clean, Mr. Morloch. We just found a couple of photos and a home-made CD on him." He placed the items on Morloch's desk.

Without turning around, Morloch spoke. "Well, Dr. James, you've made headlines again. This time spouting all sorts of unfounded allegations about my drug and my company." Morloch turned to face him, his face dark against the bright windows. "Drink, Dr. James?" he asked pleasantly.

"Water, please."

Morloch walked over to a wet bar and opened the under-counter refrigerator. He poured the water from a clear bottle and then poured a glass of Diet Coke for himself. He handed the water to Steve.

"Castell was quite insistent on my seeing you, but he wouldn't explain why. You are here only as a favor to my friend. Perhaps you can tell me why you came?"

"I think you know."

"I do not play games!" Morloch slammed his glass onto his desk, splashing liquid, which fizzed on the polished wood surface.

Steve did not flinch. He had looked forward to this meeting ever since his request of President Sullivan. The President had endorsed Steve's request to agent Fitzgerald, who had actually rubbed his hands gleefully at the plan. After a whirlwind of phone calls and preparations, he had flown with Valenti on a government jet to Philadelphia and was then escorted to Trident's downtown office on Market Street. Castell, after a friendly suggestion from Agent Fitzgerald, had been instrumental in setting up the meeting.

"Oh, I think you are all about playing games," Steve replied, "gambling with millions of peoples' lives. Do you actually believe your own bullshit? You can speak freely, your hired goons here did a very thorough search job."

Morloch glared at him and shifted his gaze to the two photos. One was a picture of Mallis's dead face taken at the Cathedral. The other showed a much younger Mallis stamped "FBI Archive, Kirk Erich Mallis."

"Who's this?" he asked casually.

"You ought to know him well enough. It's Kirk Mallis, hired by Trident Pharmaceuticals to destroy my reputation, my marriage, and then kill me." As he said it, he realized how ridiculous it sounded. He wasn't surprised when Morloch laughed.

"That's rich, Dr. James. Been taking some of your own drugs?" He laughed again. "You have no proof."

"I met with Dr. Samuel Blumenthal. You remember, your former Chief Scientist?"

"Of course. Recently retired. He was killed in a fire last night. Very tragic."

"Oh yes, but not before he told me a story about your fraudulent dealings with the FDA."

Morloch shrugged and dropped the photograph back on the desk. "You can't prove anything and you know it."

"Can't I?"

"Unfounded allegations, Dr. James. His word against mine. And now that he's dead, yours."

"How sure are you? What if Blumenthal copied or scanned everything onto a CD and gave it to me?"

Morloch picked up the compact disk, eyed it carefully, and then tossed it back onto the desktop. "Blumenthal couldn't figure out a computer to save his life."

"Your game's up, Morloch. Eden's going to be yanked and all the people who get Eden's disease will know that you're the man responsible for their brains turning into Swiss cheese."

"No such thing will happen," Morloch said calmly. "You have no proof that Eden causes problems. It has a perfect safety record. The FDA said it was one of the cleanest submission packages they had ever seen."

"Yeah, with forged data. Of course it was clean."

Morloch laughed again. It was the laugh of a privileged man. "Let me tell you a fairy tale, Dr. James. I chose the name Eden for a reason. People who take my drug regain paradise: beauty, health, happiness, everything a man and woman could want."

"I think, instead," Steve said evenly, "that you are the serpent. You gave us an apple. People bite your apple and get tossed out of paradise into hell."

"You think you're so clever, don't you? Let me finish. As a doctor, you know that two hundred thousand people die each year from smoking, over a million worldwide? Sounds criminal, doesn't it, Dr. James? Yet it's legal."

"So?"

"So, Dr. James, my little fairy tale ending is this. Eden saves lives. It cures diabetes, virtually stops heart attacks and strokes. This medicine makes fat people history. Paradise regained, Dr. James. Surely that trumps the few people you allege get sick from Eden."

Morloch walked around the desk to face Steve. "Eden is a miracle drug, the fountain of youth. It helps people." Morloch almost purred. "In contrast, the legal drug, tobacco, doesn't do a damn thing for anybody. What's more, everybody knows the risk, but they smoke anyway. It should be outlawed, shouldn't it?"

"Forty thousand people die each year in car crashes, half caused by alcohol. Would you stop driving? Return to prohibition? Of course not.

Compared to smoking and drinking, Eden is, shall we say, heaven sent—even if it killed hundreds each year."

"That's the problem, really." Steve turned and walked over to the window. "Even if it kills hundreds each year, you say. That's really quite a generous assumption. We already know that nearly a hundred already have it."

"Really?"

"Some of Dr. Walker's work before Mallis killed him." He turned back and looked at Morloch. "But here's the problem. We don't really know how many will eventually get it, now do we? With hundreds of millions of people using it every day and with an unknown latency that may incubate for years, we may be in for an epidemic like AIDS. You're good with millions dead from your brain rot?"

"Sheer speculation."

"And at this point that's enough to worry me. I think you have a disclosure problem here, Morloch."

Morloch walked over to Steve and leaned close. His breath was perfumed. "It's too late to pull it off the market, Dr. James. It's part of the social fabric. It'd be a new prohibition all over again. People crave this drug and they'll steal and kill to get it. You're playing God, Dr. James, if you think you can stop this. You like that role? You feel comfortable with that?"

"You're the one playing God, Morloch," Steve rejoined. "You lied to the world about the safety of your drug. People can't make a choice if they don't know the danger. Without the facts, we can't make an informed decision. You're gambling with human life."

Steve poked Morloch in the chest. "You think you know better than anyone else what's good for them."

"I do know what's better," Morloch roared. "What's more, over three hundred million people taking Eden agree with me. When I invested in Blumenthal's pitiful drug company, I knew the huge pent-up desire—no, insane lust—for this drug. You're so right, Dr. James. I do know what's best—better than the sanctimonious FDA dogs. I am God to three hundred million people. I gave them Eden and they worship me."

Steve stepped back, away from Morloch's cloying smugness. This wasn't going like he had expected. Morloch wasn't telling him anything.

He had to raise the ante. A bronze plaque on Morloch's desk caught his eye.

All great things must first wear horrifying and monstrous masks, in order to inscribe themselves on the hearts of humanity – F. Nietzsche.

"You believe your own shit, don't you?" Steve pointed at the desk plaque. "You misconstrue the words of a philosopher to justify your actions. How pitifully dangerous. This quote from Nietzsche is out of context. You don't even know, yet you presume to patronize millions of people who might die from your drug. You are delusional."

Morloch's eyes narrowed. "You are the one who is delusional if you think that anything you do will make a whit of difference to me or Eden's sales. It's here to stay. People will take my drug no matter what might happen to them."

"Yeah, well tell that to Shirley Rosenwell. Your Eden threw her into the pits of hell and stole her mother's only child. Tell that to her mother, you bastard."

Morloch laughed mockingly. "Collateral damage, Dr. James. A pimple."

Steve threw a hard punch into Morloch's face, knocking him back against a heavy leather chair before he slipped and fell to the floor. Massive hands pulled Steve's arms painfully back behind him. As Steve squirmed in the bodyguards' grasp, he saw with satisfaction that Morloch's nose was bleeding.

"You little shit. You hit me." Morloch screeched. He touched the blood on his nose and glowered at the redness on his fingers.

"That's for Shirley, asshole. And what your shit drug did to her. Don't give me a second chance at you."

"Mallis should have slit your throat long ago," Morloch hissed.

"He was a little too fucking inept."

"Throw him out!" Morloch yelled. "I'm going to have your ass so smothered with lawyers, you'll choke on every word you've ever said."

"But you're going to jail," Steve retorted, as the bodyguards roughly hauled him out the door.

When they left, Morloch grabbed his phone and punched a number. The phone answered on the first ring. "Perera."

"Oscar, destroy all your Eden files, all your tapes, and all your prion complaints."

"I can't." His voice sounded panicky.

"Why the hell not?"

"The FBI's here. They've sealed off the floor and they're confiscating everything."

"Goddamn it, why didn't you call?"

"I tried to, but they cut off all outgoing calls."

Morloch slammed down the phone. He snatched the CD off his desk and slid it into his computer. He anxiously watched the screen. Instead, Led Zeppelin's *Stairway to Heaven* blared from his speakers. In a rage, he smashed the computer monitor off the desk.

CHAPTER 147

The two bodyguards hustled Steve out of the building's front doors and shoved him. He tripped and landed hard on his hands and knees. Valenti and Fitzgerald ran up to him and pulled him to his feet.

"We got it," Valenti shouted. "Every last word. Great job. You even got a punch in."

"I had to. He was stonewalling. Where's the phone?"

"Over here." They walked to a van parked on a side street where Fitzgerald handed him a phone handset. "Here."

Steve took it, stretching the cord to a comfortable length and held it to his good ear, while another agent punched in some numbers. Fitzgerald and Valenti listened on separate handsets.

It rang only once. "Morloch." His voice had a raw edge.

"It's me, again." Steve said as smoothly as he could.

"How the hell did you get my direct line?"

"Castell."

"Castell! That son of a bitch."

"Listen to me, Morloch. Castell just happened to be the FDA Director when Eden was approved. He broke the rules pushing your damn drug through. Then, as one of President Dixon's major campaign donors, you got Castell a cabinet post to fulfill your half of the bargain. In addition, the FBI's investigating a large block of Trident shares transferred to an offshore bank just after Eden was approved. We think it went to one Jacob Castell."

"I have no idea what you are talking about."

"Castell was the only person who had my cell phone number. That's how Mallis listened to the call we made to Dr. Green, and knew how to intercept us. He gave it to you and you turned it over to Mallis. Bingo, Morloch's in deep. The time for bullshit is over. Castell has turned state's witness and is talking to the FBI. The Justice Department has frozen your assets and is executing search warrants on all of Trident's holdings."

"You're full of shit. They can't possibly have done all that in one morning."

"No, Morloch, you're wrong. When you poison the President of the United States, you piss off a lot of very capable people. They are swarming like hornets around everything you ever touched."

Morloch did not say anything.

"Save those fucking lawyers you promised me. You're going to need them. And, by the way, look out the window and wave to the friendly window cleaners. They're FBI agents who just recorded everything we said while I was in your office."

"Shit!"

"You just gotta love technology. So long, chump."

Steve hung up the phone and handed it back to an agent.

"Great job." Fitzgerald said. "We might have enough. While you were getting escorted out of the building, he called a Mr. Perera. You know him?"

Steve recognized the name. "Yeah, he's the one I spoke to when I reported my suspicions about Eden."

"Well, Morloch had a few choice things to say about destroying all the Eden files and tapes and prion complaints."

"That ought to nail him," Valenti said. "That, plus Castell's testimony, and that guy we captured outside the Cathedral. It's a damn shame Mallis wasted Blumenthal."

"Speaking of Blumenthal," Fitzgerald turned to Steve, "Do you own a thirty-eight Smith and Wesson?"

"I did, but I couldn't find it that night my house burned down."

"Well, it resurfaced."

"It did? Where?"

"Near Blumenthal's house in a trash can. It was used to shoot him, we think. Your prints were on it."

"Jesus, just like the glove at Sheridan's."

Fitzgerald continued. "Right. Mallis and company implicated you in a pattern of arson and homicide that by all rights should have landed you in prison."

Steve's anger roared back. "Those—" He stopped. It was over. It was really over.

"They were professional, Steve," Valenti said. "You don't know how lucky you are to still be alive."

Fitzgerald nodded. "It could have easily gone their way. And we'd still be in the dark about Trident and Eden—worse, minus a Navy fleet in the Pacific."

"Excuse me for a minute." Steve turned and walked down the street, towards the river. He needed the movement and the open air. Valenti caught up with him and walked silently at his side.

"It's over," Valenti finally said

"Yeah."

"We made a good team."

"We did."

"I'm going to miss the excitement, the adventure . . ."

Despite himself, Steve had to smile. "I thought you hated bullets and guns. You told me on your first day when we met."

"It snuck back into my system. I had forgotten how much I loved it."

"Well, it looks like you've been rehabbed by the Feds."

"Yeah, I guess so."

"So what do you think you'll do? Go back to Phoenix and stay a PI?"

Valenti looked thoughtful. "Don't know. Probably, for now."

"You'll be as famous as Magnum PI. Maybe your clientele will be well-heeled and pay you those big bucks you've deserved all these years. Who knows, maybe a book and the talk circuit."

Valenti kicked a stone that bounced down the asphalt. "Too soon to tell." Nevertheless, he sounded pleased at the prospect. Then he looked at Steve. "Say, you're not shivering."

Steve shrugged. The truth was, he felt pretty good. He was tired and he hurt—Lord, he hurt—but he had shed an enormous burden. He could get his life back. Steve thought about Anne and her smile—the smile that had caught his heart the first time he met her.

Valenti grabbed Steve's shoulders and shook him affectionately. "I'm proud of you, bud."

"Oww, that hurts."

"Now, here's the phone, go call your wife." Valenti handed Steve the cell phone. "I know how much you've missed her."

"No way. That's a radio." Steve fished in his new pants pocket. "Got any change?"

CHAPTER 148

Resnick hung up the phone and smiled at her INR head sitting on the edge of his chair across from her desk.

"What did he say?" Calhoun asked.

"Ambassador Justice just had a short audience with Premier Chow. Amazing story. Apparently Colonel Tanggu's public statements caused some already nervous Generals to defect from the Yao camp and back Chow. But with the ultimatum already issued and without movement on the Taiwan independence issue, Chow was committed to go forward with the invasion. Sullivan's call gave him the break he needed to call the invasion back. Mind you, Chow didn't say all this directly, but Pierre is pretty good at reading a subtext."

"And Yao?"

"Marginalized for now." She chuckled. "I doubt Tanggu's characterization of Chow's manhood helped any. But he may resurface sometime." She paused. "Although we'll be pressing hard for his prosecution for the Thanksgiving Day Massacre."

Larry shook his head. It's amazing how a single event, in this case the CNN broadcast, can tip the course of history. Without that and Dr. James . . . well, we got real lucky."

"Damn lucky."

"What happened when President Sullivan called President Lai?"

"They're furious with us."

"Then, why are you smiling?" Calhoun asked.

Resnick's smile broadened. "They're alive to be furious with us. And already we're hearing that they are privately relieved at the turn of events. Their official missives are probably just posturing, hoping we'll feel sorry and send them lots of money."

"I don't think so," Calhoun said.

"I don't either. But I do expect to see the rest of President Lai's billion dollars for medical research. By the way, Pierre was able to get a guarantee of safe passage out of China for our CNN crew. I'll let you tell Ernie the details."

"Speaking of Ernie, who was that highly placed State source that leaked the story about Tanggu?" Calhoun prodded with a sly smile.

Resnick shook her head and shrugged. "Your guess is as good as mine."

CHAPTER 149

The kitchen phone rang. Anne, watching the TV, jumped to her feet and ran to pick it up followed by Johnnie close at her heels. Anne barely beat him and snatched it up. It would probably be another one of her cousins or aunts calling to tell her that they had seen Steve's name on the television, but just in case . . .

"Hello?" she answered while Johnnie pulled on her belt.

"Honey? It's me." Steve's voice was thick with emotion.

"Steve! Are you okay?"

Johnnie began shouting and jumping up and down. "Daddy! Daddy!"

Joan and Jack walked in from the TV room, smiling.

Anne leaned against the tiled counter for support, tears spilling down her face. "I love you, too, Baby."

CHAPTER 150

EARLY FEBRUARY

It was another flawless Phoenix winter afternoon with only scattered cirrus clouds and fluffy white jet contrails streaking the cornflower sky. A gentle breeze floated over the cemetery, quiet except for the measured speech of the priest, saying the words intended to reassure and comfort the gathered family and friends.

Steve stood at the back of the small group holding Anne's hand. The graveside service for Shirley Rosenwell had put him into a reflective mood and he only half listened to the sermon. His thoughts returned to the hospital and Shirley's final days. Over the last couple of months, she had lost all awareness of her surroundings and had slipped into a coma. Edith's only sister had flown in from Tampa and stayed with her at the bedside. Steve had spent hours in Shirley's room with Edith, sometimes accompanied by Anne and, on occasion, Johnnie.

The end was peaceful, but they all felt something missing after she died. That night, Steve had described it to Anne as they held each other in bed. "It's as if someone left the room," he said. "It feels lonelier because, you know. . . they're gone."

It was Anne's first time to see someone die. She described it as a natural progression to another stage, not necessarily the end. He thought she had a better intuitive acceptance of those things than he, despite all his experience.

Steve thought about Captain Palmer's funeral three weeks before. It had been attended by a number of his fellow United pilots, some of Dr. Walker's NIH colleagues, members of the press, and even some Trident employees, stricken by the knowledge their drug had killed him. Shirley's funeral was much more modest, but Steve felt it apt, preferring its simplicity and directness. It was important to him that it be right.

Following Captain Palmer's funeral, he and Anne had visited President Dixon in his Virginia home. A staff of nurses and physicians provided round the clock medical care. As he expected, President Dixon was heavily medicated to reduce his disturbing delusions and hallucinations. Elise insisted Steve and Anne stay for tea, but the strain on her was evident. They left soon after with Agent Rhodes driving them to the airport.

Steve's attention shifted back to the funeral ceremony. He scratched his nose and glanced over at Valenti with Maria standing next to him. None of their lives were the same. Valenti, as Steve had predicted, had become famous with work pouring in from all over. He had quickly taken on a partner and began hiring as fast as he reasonably could. Most were former bureau agents who wanted to work for one of their own. Steve continued to exercise with Valenti at his house and Anne and Maria had formed a quick friendship, arranging family get-togethers on a regular basis.

Steve's life gradually assumed something of its former self with the medical board re-instating his license and the insurance company agreeing to pay for his house. Steve went back to his neurology practice, but he had been named to a blue ribbon commission spearheading the research into Eden's disease, officially classified as a new prion disease. One of the commission's responsibilities included global case monitoring to develop statistics on the incidence and prevalence of Eden's disease.

With the disease and its symptoms more generally known, numerous additional cases came in; many patients were already deceased and just now getting the correct diagnosis. To date, over eighteen hundred cases had been identified worldwide, with more being reported every day.

Eden had been pulled off the market by a quick FDA mandate and Steve hoped to see a leveling off of cases, possibly within six months; but without knowing the latency, official estimates ranged all over the map. Theoretically, anyone who took Eden was at risk, however small. The popular press quickly picked up on this.

Headlines predicting widespread deaths dominated the Star and National Enquirer covers, each trying to outdo the other in their escalating predictions—now as high as a hundred million. Of course, they also reported a massive cover-up by the United States government to prevent worldwide panic. The irony, Steve figured, was that many of the reporters and editors of those very magazines had to be scared for themselves, since they most likely had been early and heavy off-label users of Eden.

More sinister were the professional doomsayers and tele-evangelists predicting that Eden's disease would become another black plague, disrupting the economic and social fabric of industrialized nations and creating new Babylons of sin and evil. Since, unlike AIDS, it overwhelmingly affected affluent people in the industrialized first-world nations, some had even predicted all the best and brightest would die, leading to a new dark age.

Determined efforts to identify the susceptibility factors for Eden's disease and therefore pinpoint who might eventually get it occupied a worldwide consortium of laboratories. Amos Sheridan, working out of rented lab space, had a big chunk of the grant money and already had three expedited publications in print. Three pharmaceutical companies and the National Institutes of Health had announced crash programs to develop medicines to combat prion diseases, but estimated that it would take at least ten years before anything could reach the public.

The remaining management of Trident, those not under indictment, pulled the Paradise application from the FDA, pending further testing of the drug. The stock analysts predicted in print that the FDA would never grant a marketing application to any drug that had the potential to cause a prion disease, no matter how clean the research. Prions in the human population were too likely to spread.

Trident stock had fallen to under a dollar and had been de-listed from the New York Stock Exchange. On a whim, Steve had calculated Morloch's paper worth. Based on his last reported ownership percentage, he came up with a figure of seven million dollars. Not bad, actually. Steve could retire comfortably on that kind of cash.

The reality, Steve knew from talking to many former Eden users, was that no matter what the outcome of the investigations and reassurances, each day, they and three hundred million other former Eden users would look at themselves in the mirror and wonder when—or if—they would start twitching.

The world had already changed because of Eden, but in ways not easily foreseen. Eden's disease was mildly contagious, as are all prion diseases, chiefly by blood products and organ transplantation, much like HIV. All donated blood was now screened for prions using Dr. Breen's new method, and testing was a requirement for public office, marriage, airplane pilots, surgeons, commercial drivers, and for any contact sport.

Doctors had now confirmed that cases of Eden's disease had been sexually transmitted before the disease had any outward symptoms. As a result, governments worldwide had launched educational campaigns to convince their citizens that if either partner had ever used Eden, condoms should be used. The changes to the dating scene were immediate and pervasive. Personal ads now read "NUE" meaning 'Never Used Eden.'

Black market sales of illegally produced Eden in the United States alone were estimated at nearly three billion dollars. It became obvious that some people would do anything and risk everything—for what? Steve remembered President's Dixon's simple indictment, 'Damn vanity.' On the street, Eden commanded a higher price than cocaine.

And the cause of it all, Vicktor Morloch, had left the building without anyone knowing how and had not been seen since. Valenti had speculated Morloch had hidden in the trunk of his secretary's car, but by whatever means he had escaped, his liberty worried Steve.

Agent Fitzgerald kept in regular contact with Steve and what little he could say in the midst of an active investigation was bad enough. Morloch had cleared out his foreign accounts and vanished. Fitzgerald was convinced Morloch had holed up on some small island without an extradition treaty with the United States. Chillingly, he and Valenti both had warned Steve to watch his backside. While he tried not to think about it, all the same, he now took precautions he never would have before.

The case against Morloch had not been strong, even with his FBI recorded statements during and after Steve's visit. That all changed with Oscar Perera. In exchange for a plea bargain, he produced a documented narrative of the events leading up to and following Eden's approval by the FDA, information he had surreptitiously collected following Paul Tobias' death. Also, a former girlfriend of Morloch's had stepped forward with a bizarre tale of his ordering someone's death while they were in the backseat of his limousine. Doug Hudnell, Mallis's associate captured outside the National Cathedral refused to talk.

The priest finished the service with a prayer and made the sign of the cross, saying 'Amen.' As the mourners began to disperse, Steve and Anne slowly made their way over to Edith. They waited patiently until only she and her sister, June, were left. Edith came over and hugged Steve for a long time. Steve looked down at Shirley's coffin covered with a blanket of flowers. Morloch's drug had done this and he fought down his anger again.

Gazing up at Steve with her red, tear-streaked eyes, she asked, "Are you coming over? We have lots of food."

Steve nodded. "I wouldn't miss it."

Anne hugged Edith and rubbed her back affectionately. So many times in the last months, he had counted his blessings for his amazing second chance to live with his wife and son; he hoped it would be for a long time. Life was so precious.

Walking back to his car, holding hands with Anne, they found Valenti and Maria waiting. "I thought you'd bring up the rear," Valenti said. "I think we need to go get us some of those casseroles."

Steve smiled; nothing like an irreverent Valenti to cheer him up. Eying his trimmer friend, he remarked, "You eating again?"

"Yeah, sure," Valenti snorted.

Without looking, Steve knew Valenti had the bulge under his coat and why Valenti had stuck around waiting for him. He also knew about the frequent cop cars and unmarked sedans Valenti arranged to cruise by his house at all hours. Valenti hadn't felt like his job was quite done. It was a little unnerving, but still, Steve appreciated it.

"Well, I've got an appetite," Steve lied. "Let's roll."

ABOUT THE AUTHOR

As a board certified a neurologist, Dr. Louis Kirby specialized in neurodegenerative diseases including Alzheimer's disease and Parkinson's disease. Subsequently, he founded several companies including Pivotal Research Centers, which grew to become one of the largest free-standing private clinical research operations in the US. Dr. Kirby's extensive drug development experience and work with major pharma companies worldwide provides the foundation for his fast-paced medical and political thriller, *Shadow of Eden*.

Dr. Kirby is intrigued with science and medicine as a driver of culture, politics, behavior and religion. His next novel, about a scientific expedition to find the Garden of Eden, continues to explore these provocative themes.

In addition to writing his next book, Dr. Kirby is co-founder of ZettaScience, a company designed to accelerate scientific innovation worldwide. See more information at www.ZettaScience.com.

He lives with his wife and daughter in Arizona.

Read more about Louis Kirby at www.louiskirby.com or follow him on Facebook or Twitter.

Made in the USA
Charleston, SC
09 September 2013